RACHEL ABBOTT was born an

CONNECT WITH RACHEL ABBOTT ONLINE

Website: www.rachel-abbott.com
Blog: www.rachelabbottwriter.wordpress.com
Twitter: www.twitter.com/Rachel__Abbott
Facebook: www.facebook.com/RachelAbbott1Writer

STRANGER
CHILD
Rachel Abbott

black dot
publishing

Published in 2015 by Black Dot Publishing Ltd

Copyright © Rachel Abbott 2015
Cover image © Rachel Abbott 2015 courtesy of Rick Hall

The right of Rachel Abbott to be identified as the author of this work
has been asserted by her in accordance with the
Copyright, Designs and Patents Act 1988.

ISBN 978-0-9576522-4-8

British Library Cataloguing in Publication Data
A CIP catalogue record for this book is available from
the British Library

Printed in the UK by Berforts Information Press Ltd
on responsibly sourced paper

For Al
Twenty years too late –
but maybe better than a killer whale?

Prologue

Another ten minutes, and she would be safely home.

Caroline Joseph gave a shudder of relief that the long journey would soon be over. She never enjoyed driving at night and always felt slightly out of control. Each pair of approaching headlights seemed to draw her towards them, their white light illuminating the car's interior as she gripped the steering wheel, struggling to point the car straight ahead.

Not long now, though. She was looking forward to giving Natasha a warm bath, a mug of hot chocolate, and tucking her up in bed. Then she could devote the remnants of the evening to David. Something was troubling him, and Caroline thought that maybe if they settled in front of the fire with a glass of wine when Natasha was asleep, she might be able to coax the problem out of him. It had to be something to do with work.

She glanced in her rear-view mirror at her precious daughter. Tasha was six – or six and three-quarters, as she liked to boast – although her slight frame made her appear younger. Her pale blonde hair fell in soft waves to her shoulders, and her delicate features were bathed intermittently in yellow light as they passed each streetlamp. Her eyes were closed, and Caroline smiled at how peaceful she looked.

Today Tasha had been her usual sweet-natured self, playing happily with her young cousins while the adults scurried around doing Caroline's father's bidding. He had issued one of his edicts – this time declaring that Caroline, along with her siblings and their families, must come for a pre-Christmas dinner. As usual, everybody had obeyed. Everybody, that is, except David.

The turnoff to the lanes leading to their house was fast approaching, and Caroline took a final glance at Natasha. Once they were off the main road and away from the brightly lit shop windows and the amber glow of the tall streetlamps, the back of the car would be in dark shadow. She had slept for most of the journey, but was beginning to stir.

'You okay, Tasha?' Caroline asked. The child just murmured in response, not quite awake enough to answer as she rubbed her eyes with her knuckles. Caroline smiled. She braked slightly and changed gear to take the turning. All she had to do was get through the last couple of miles of this journey along the narrow, hedge-lined lanes, deep in darkness, then she could relax. She felt a flash of irritation towards David. He knew she hated driving at night, and he could have made the effort – for Natasha, if not for her. They had both missed him today.

A sudden movement to her left caught Caroline's eye, and her head spun towards it, her heart thumping in her chest. An owl swooped low over the hedgerows, its white breast catching the full beam of her headlights, bright against the black sky. She let out a breath.

There was no moon, and the black tarmac on the narrow lanes that led to their home was glinting with fragments of frost. Everything around her seemed perfectly still, as if the world had come to a stop, and now that the owl had fled she was the only thing still moving. Caroline knew that if she opened her window there would be no sound other than the quiet hum of her engine. There was no light at all ahead or behind, and for a moment her natural fear of the dark threatened to swamp her.

She leaned forwards and switched the radio on at a low volume, reassured by the jolliness of the predictable festive songs. She would be sick of the sound of them soon, but right now their cheery ordinariness relaxed her.

She smiled as the phone on the seat by her side started to ring. Certain that it would be David asking when she would be back, she barely glanced at the screen, but at the last moment she saw the call was from a blocked number. She prodded the screen and cancelled the call. Whoever it was could wait until she got home. She steered one-handed round a sharp bend as she placed the phone back on the seat, and the car slid a little on the frosty road. She felt a small jolt of fear. But the car held, and she breathed again.

Caroline took the next few bends cautiously, but her tense shoulders relaxed as she came to a brief stretch of straight road with tall hedgerows shielding deep ditches on either side. Caroline leaned closer to the windscreen, peering into the night. Her headlights were picking up a darker shadow – something in the lane ahead. She braked slightly and changed down a gear, slowing in anticipation.

She dropped down to second gear to approach the obstruction, finally recognising in horror that it was a car, slewed sideways across the road, its front wheels buried in the ditch on the right-hand side of the road. She thought she could see a shadow inside, as if somebody was slumped over the steering wheel.

As Caroline crawled slowly towards it, her heart suddenly thumping, she pushed the button to lower her window. It looked like somebody needed help.

The phone rang again.

Her first thought was to ignore it, but if there had been an accident she might need to summon assistance. She snatched the phone off the seat and answered the call, realising as she did so that her hand was shaking.

'Hello?'

'Caroline, are you home yet?'

It was a voice she vaguely recognised, but couldn't quite place. Her eyes did not leave the obstruction ahead as she drew to a halt and released her seatbelt.

'Not yet. Why? Who is this?'

'Just listen to me. Whatever you do, you must *not* stop the car. Whatever happens, do not under any circumstances stop the car.' The man was speaking low and fast. 'Go home. Go straight home. Are you listening to me?'

The panic in the voice on the phone reflected Caroline's own rising anxiety. She hesitated.

'But there's a car across the road, and it looks like somebody's in it. Maybe they're ill, or they've had an accident. Why can't I stop? What's going on?'

'Just do as I'm telling you, Caroline. Do *not* get out of the car. Put your foot down now and get past that car and don't stop again for anybody or anything. Just *do* it.'

The voice was tense, urgent. Caroline felt fear rise in her throat. *What was this?* She glanced in the rear-view mirror, and made her decision. She flung the mobile phone onto the seat beside her and grabbed the steering wheel with both hands. The stationary car was long and low, taking up most of the width of the road with its back wheels slightly off the ground as the bonnet angled down into the ditch. There wasn't much space to get round the boot of the car, but she could do it. She had to do it.

She rammed her foot hard to the floor. The tyres skidded on the frosty road, but they gripped, and she swung the car to the left. Her nearside wheels rose up on the bank below the hedge and the car hovered at a perilous angle. She pulled the steering wheel back round to the right and her car landed with a bump, facing the opposite side of the road. Caroline pulled the wheel back round to the left to straighten up, the engine roaring as she accelerated.

Suddenly she felt herself begin to slide. She spun the steering wheel madly in one direction and then the other, but whatever she did, the car took no notice. Black ice, and she was travelling too fast. She remembered being told to steer into a skid, but that didn't feel right.

A name flashed into her head. She suddenly realised who had called her. *But why him?* She called out his name, but she knew that by then there was nothing he could do. Her eyes were drawn to the mirror, to the shadowy rear of the car, where all she could see were the whites of Natasha's wide, terrified eyes.

She slammed her foot on the brakes, but nothing happened. The car slid sideways, hit the bank again, rose up at an angle and flipped, turning over and over, crashing through the hedge and into the ditch, Caroline's broken body coming to rest half in and half out of the open window.

❖

The policeman drove along the narrow lanes, enjoying a rare moment of peace in the run-up to Christmas. An anonymous caller had phoned to say there was a car off the road somewhere around here, but according to the dispatcher the caller hadn't been able to give any details. The policeman was hoping this would be nothing more than some idiot dumping his car because it had run out of juice or broken down. He had had enough of dealing with drunks in the current party season, and a nice little abandoned vehicle should keep him out of the way for a while – maybe even to the end of his shift.

The realisation that his optimism was unfounded crept up on him slowly. It was the lights that convinced him. Nobody dumped their car with the lights on, and yet up ahead he could see a stationary white light, shining brightly, illuminating the bare trees at the side of the road. As he got closer, the dazzling beams from the twin headlights blinded him. He shielded his eyes slightly with the back of his hand, approaching as cautiously as possible in case there was a body he couldn't see lying in the road. He pulled up about twenty metres from the car and switched off his engine.

He knew immediately that it was bad. The car was upside down, the front end resting up the bank at one side of the lane. But it was the noise that chilled him. Cutting through the silence of the surrounding countryside, the gentle purr of an expensive engine provided a subtle backing track to the unmistakable sound of Bing Crosby's 'White Christmas'. The mellow music was escaping into the frosty night air from an open window through which jutted a woman's head at such an implausible angle that the policeman didn't need to approach the car to know she was dead.

He moved slowly towards the upended car to turn off the engine, and with it the music. He was able to breathe again. Now it was just a single-vehicle road traffic accident, although a tragic one. He reached for his radio.

While he waited for the paramedics to arrive, knowing that there was nothing they could do other than confirm what he already knew, the policeman organised the closing of the road, called for the specialist team to investigate the crash and asked for a PNC check on the car to determine ownership. He grabbed a powerful torch from his boot and shone it around the lane, in the ditches, along the bank, searching for anybody who might have crawled out of the car and could be injured, or anything on the road that could have caused the car to swerve. There was nothing. The road was empty.

For the policeman, it was a relief when the silence was disturbed by the sound of sirens, growing ever nearer, and a few minutes later the ambulance pulled up, its lights picking out a lone cyclist who was approaching the scene hesitantly.

The man hopped off his bike and stood some distance away. The policeman walked towards him.

'I'm sorry, sir – you need to keep back.'

'Okay, officer. I'm just trying to get home.'

'I understand, but I can't let you along this stretch of road at the moment, sir. I'm sure you appreciate that.'

'Is anybody hurt? That looks like Caroline Joseph's car. Am I right?' the cyclist asked.

'I can't confirm that at the moment, sir.'

The man peered around the policeman to get a better look at the car.

'Is that her I can see? Oh my God. She's dead, isn't she?' He looked at the policeman, his mouth half open in shock. 'Poor David. That's her husband. He's going to be devastated.'

The policeman didn't comment. All he could do was keep the man as far away as possible until reinforcements arrived, but even from this distance the woman's head was all too visible.

'She didn't have Natasha with her, did she?' the cyclist asked, his voice shaking. 'Her little girl? Cutest kid.'

The policeman shook his head with some relief.

'No, sir. The child seat is in the back but thankfully it's empty. There was nobody else in the car.'

HUNT FOR MISSING GIRL SCALED DOWN

A police spokesperson has confirmed that, as of today, the search for missing Natasha Joseph has been scaled down.

Detective Inspector Philippa Stanley of the Greater Manchester Police gave the following statement.

'Teams of professionals and volunteers have been searching the local area for over two weeks. We believe that every inch of the countryside surrounding the site of the accident has been covered. In addition to the teams on the ground checking any and every place that a young child might have crawled into to keep warm, we have employed sniffer dogs and helicopters with infrared detectors. I'm sorry to say that we have found nothing.'

Natasha Joseph – known to her family as Tasha – went missing after her mother's car crashed on Littlebarn Lane as they returned from a family party. Caroline Joseph was driving, and no other cars were involved. When police arrived at the scene of the accident, there was no sign of the missing Natasha. Mrs Joseph was pronounced dead by the paramedics.

The police are now pursuing other lines of enquiry. In particular they are continuing to ask members of the public who were anywhere in the vicinity of the accident to come forward.

'Whether people believe they know anything or not, it is always surprising how the smallest piece of information – the sighting of a specific car or a person acting in a suspicious way – can help, particularly when coupled with other intelligence that we have gathered. We are accessing the ANPR (Automatic Number Plate Recognition) system where appropriate, and have also secured CCTV footage from petrol station forecourts and other cameras in the nearby town. But we would urge anybody

who was out that night in the surrounding area to come forward. Our trained interviewers will help you to piece together each moment of that evening, and we are hopeful that the one vital piece of information we need is out there.'

The police have confirmed that while the physical search of the local area has been reduced, the team of detectives working the case remains at the highest level.

David Joseph, husband of Caroline and father of Natasha, and a successful Manchester businessman, issued an emotional plea on television last week.

'Somebody must know where my little girl is. She has lost her mother, and poor Tasha must be heartbroken, confused and so very scared. Please help me to find her. I need my little girl. I have lost everything.'

To speak to somebody in confidence, please call 0800 6125736 or 0161 7913785.

1

Six years later

DCI Tom Douglas found himself humming a tune as he walked down the corridor to his office. He always enjoyed the first day back at work after a holiday, in much the same way as he had loved going back to school after the long summer break when he was a child. It was the sense of anticipation, the knowledge that the day would bring challenges that he was keen to face. He enjoyed the camaraderie of his team – not quite friends, but supportive allies who he knew had his back. It wasn't the easiest job in the world, but he wasn't often bored, and there was a lot to be said for that.

He pushed open the door to his office and reached his left foot out to manoeuvre his doorstopper into place. His foot met thin air. Looking down, there was no sign of the fat pig that he used to hold the door open. He hung his jacket on the coat stand and crouched down to look for it under the desk.

He heard a brief knock on the door and muttered, 'Come in.'

The door opened, and he heard a voice he recognised well, trying to control a degree of mirth.

'You okay down there?'

'I'm fine – but somebody's nicked my bloody pig.'

Tom stood up, brushing the knees of his suit trousers to get rid of the dust from an un-vacuumed floor. 'Honestly, you'd have thought at police headquarters you'd be reasonably confident of finding upright, law-abiding citizens, wouldn't you? I thought he might have been kicked under here, or something, but he's nowhere to be seen.'

'I think if anybody kicked your pig, you'd find them limping around with a broken toe. And nobody steals from a detective chief inspector unless they're very stupid – although on that basis I suppose we have a few candidates to consider. I'll ask around for you.'

Tom pulled out his chair and sat down, indicating that Becky should do the same. 'How've you been, Becky? Anything exciting happened while I've been away?'

'Run of the mill stuff, on the whole,' Becky replied, as she grabbed a chair. 'Except for a particularly violent rape, which we thought was stranger rape but wasn't.'

'Who was it, then?'

'Her bastard boyfriend. He'd worn a mask and everything and was waiting for her on her way back from work. He beat her to a pulp, raped her viciously and then left her.'

'What gave him away?'

'She did. To start with, when she came round in hospital she said she had no idea who it was, but we could see she was hiding something. Turns out she was terrified that if she named her boyfriend, he would kill her. Finally she caved and told us, but said she wasn't pressing charges because there was no evidence other than her word.'

Becky leaned back and folded her arms.

'But we got him. He'd been smart enough to wear a condom, but then stupidly chucked the used one in a bin, fifty metres down the road. Said his girlfriend had it coming to her because of the way she was flirting with other guys in the pub where she works.'

Becky's lip curled in disgust, and Tom had a quick mental image of the icy determination with which she would have interrogated this guy. For all her personal vulnerability, his inspector had an uncanny ability to get the truth out of people.

'Anyway, how was the holiday?' Becky asked.

'Good, thanks. Leo and I had a few days in Florence, then we went to my cottage in Cheshire. I had a pile of my brother's papers to sort out, and Leo had to study for an exam, so it was one of those easy weeks that seem to disappear and be gone in no time.'

On the whole, Tom tried to keep his personal life private and had only recently started to occasionally mention Leo to his colleagues. He had been vaguely amused to find that one or two of them hadn't realised that Leo was short for Leonora, and he'd seen the odd startled expression until Becky put them all straight.

Only a handful of people knew about the Cheshire home that Tom had bought when he left the Met. He rarely mentioned his brother Jack, either, although he knew Becky was aware of the tragic accident that had cut short his life a few years ago, just as she knew Jack had left Tom a fortune from the sale of his internet security business. She never raised the subject, though, unless Tom did.

Tom's phone interrupted any further discussion about holidays.

'Tom Douglas,' he answered. He listened as his boss, Detective Superintendent Philippa Stanley, gave him the kind of news that he hated more than any other. His cheery mood disappeared in a flash.

He hung up the phone. 'Grab your coat, Becky. We've got a body, and I'm sorry to say it's a young girl, barely in her teens by all accounts.'

2

For once, Tom had relinquished control and agreed that Becky could drive them to the scene, but he regretted that decision a few minutes into the journey. Becky's one-handed steering and apparent lack of regard for other motorists had been a bone of contention between them since they first met, and nothing had changed. He had tried to get her on to an advanced driving course, but she couldn't see the need. As she said, she had never had an accident, and Tom could only assume it was because everybody saw her coming and simply got out of her way.

Now, as they screeched to a halt on a long straight road behind several other police vehicles, he was glad to get out of the car.

The road was lined with well-established trees that shielded some large detached properties from view on the right-hand side. On the left, a dense area of woodland was separated from the pavement by a solid wall. About fifty metres ahead, a uniformed officer was standing guard at an old-fashioned kissing gate that opened onto a narrow dirt path leading into the wood. A thin strip of crime scene tape was already in place.

Without a word, they pulled on their protective clothing and then made their way towards the path.

After a brief word with the policeman to establish their identities, Tom and Becky walked in single file along the muddy path, overgrown brambles catching at the legs of their suits, until they reached an arched tunnel. Tom assumed that an old, disused railway line ran above, and he saw Becky wrinkle her nose as they entered the dark and gloomy space. Based on the smell and the rubbish lying on the ground, it would seem the tunnel was regularly used for less than salubrious activities, and as they picked their way over broken bottles and beer cans, keeping to the centre of the path to avoid some of the unpleasant detritus littering the area further out towards the walls, Tom looked around. If the girl had been murdered, why kill her out in the open and not in here, where there was less chance of being seen? The place had crime scene written all over it – and if not this crime, he was sure the tunnel had witnessed its fair share of depravity.

Beyond the tunnel, another officer was waiting to point them in the right direction, and ahead they could see two white tents, erected either side of an oak tree and taped together to enclose its thick trunk. Standing just outside the scene perimeter tape, Tom spotted the oversized figure of Jumoke Osoba, better known to Tom as Jumbo. He was glad to see that – for whatever reason – this girl had been allocated the best crime scene manager that Tom had ever met. For once, Jumbo's huge, infectious grin was missing. Tom nodded his head in acknowledgement.

'What do we know, Jumbo?'

'Young girl – at a guess I'd say she's about twelve, but could be a bit older. Luckily for us, a Home Office pathologist was already in the area, so we haven't had to wait. He's with her now, and he'll be able to tell you more. It's James Adams, by the way, and he knows what he's about, thank God. Before we got the tents up I could see the girl had been there a few days at least – so it's not a pretty sight.' He looked at Tom with understanding. 'You going in?'

Tom nodded, and as he lifted the perimeter tape to stoop under it, he turned to Becky.

'I don't think this needs both of us, Becky. You talk to Jumbo. He can fill you in on anything we've learned up to now.' There was no disguising the look of relief on Becky's face. She had seen her share of bodies, but kids were always different – especially ones who had been dead a while.

As Tom entered the tent, his eyes were dragged to the body in front of him. From where he was standing, he could see that putrefaction was advanced. Given that it was early March and cold for the time of year, that meant the girl had been here for a while, slumped against the oak tree, partially buried in rotting leaf litter, wearing nothing more than a thin white nightie. On her feet were a pair of trainers, grey with age and splitting around the sole. What looked like a blue anorak was bunched up a few feet from the body, and the neck of the nightdress was ripped.

Tom looked around, but there was nothing more that he could see. It would be down to Jumbo's team and James Adams to collect the evidence, and Tom's job to work out what had happened to her. He spoke briefly to the pathologist and left him to his work.

Stepping back outside the tent, Tom took a deep breath of cold, clean air, closing his eyes for a second as he thought about the girl's family. If she had been reported missing they would identify her soon enough.

He made his way back along the approach path, careful as always not to deviate from the stepping plates and contaminate the scene. He could tell from Becky's body language that she was eager to speak to him. Hopefully, the team back at base had been doing their work and had a name for this kid.

'What have you found, Becky?' he asked.

'Nothing. Absolutely big fat zero. I've just had a call to say that no girl in the age range ten to fourteen has been reported missing in the last two weeks. We've drawn a blank so far. We're going to have to go back through kids that have been missing for longer that fit the profile and extend the search to neighbouring forces.'

'She can't have been missing for long, because I don't think she's been living rough,' Tom said, shaking his head. 'She's wearing a white nightie, for God's sake. How many street kids put on a nightie to go to bed? What do you think, Jumbo?'

Jumbo had been standing quietly by, listening to the conversation.

'We've found no personal effects, but until we move the body we can't search the area immediately around her. There's no ID in her anorak pockets. But I'm with Tom. She's not a street kid.'

'Was the anorak on the ground, away from the body?' Tom asked.

'Just where you saw it,' Jumbo answered. 'It was all photographed, of course, but I put it back when I'd checked the pockets so you could see it in situ.'

Becky's radio beeped and she moved to one side to leave Tom and Jumbo to talk as she pulled out her notebook and answered the call.

'If she's left home in the last week or so, obviously nobody's bothered to let us know. It makes me sick to think of all the runaways that aren't even reported,' Tom said. 'The parents or carers are probably expecting her to come back after a few nights of sleeping rough.'

'Yeah, and most of these kids have no idea how many predators are out there, waiting for the opportunity their isolation presents.'

The two men stopped talking as they heard a rise in Becky's tone. She turned round and came towards them.

'Has her ethnicity been established? They did a trawl of *all* girls, and we have a few that have gone missing that might fit the bill. It's all down to the ethnicity.'

Tom looked at Jumbo.

'James was certain she was white – although quite how he could tell, I don't know. Is there somebody in mind?'

Becky spoke into her radio again and all three listened to the response.

'We've been looking through old cases – kids who have been missing for months or even years. We've come up with three possibles: Amy Davidson, Hailey Wilson and Natasha Joseph.'

3

Tom's post-holiday good spirits had totally evaporated by the time he and Becky returned to headquarters. The sight of the body bag being transported from the tent had hit him harder than he had expected. It was always traumatic when children were hurt, but the image of the child dressed in a white nightie propped up against a tree with her thin legs stretched out in front of her was particularly disturbing. Tom thought of his daughter Lucy and wondered what she was doing at that moment.

The pathologist, James Adams, had called with his initial report.

'She was a white girl aged around twelve I would say. No identification on her, and no clear distinguishing features that I could see. Naturally blonde hair, very slightly built but not malnourished. We bagged her hands at the scene but I think it will be difficult to get fingerprints. We'll get what fragments we can when I've done the post-mortem. My initial estimate is that she had been there for about a week, but we've had some very cold weather – particularly at night – so I may want to reassess that. At the moment, I'm not able to give you cause of death, but you'll be the first to know. I presume you'll be attending the PM?'

Tom agreed that he would be there and was ending the call as Becky nudged his door open with her hip, juggling two cups of much-needed coffee while trying not to drop a stack of files held tightly under one arm.

'Here you go, boss. I think we both need this,' she said, putting the cups down and pulling up a chair. 'The incident room is being set up as we speak, but I brought through some notes on the three missing girls.'

Tom reached for his coffee and took a sip, not caring that the scalding liquid was burning his tongue.

'Okay, let's take a look at them, but any number of kids could have done a runner in the last couple of weeks and not been reported,' Tom said, 'so let's not limit ourselves to considering these three. I still can't quite work out what's bothering me about the nightie. It's as if she was plucked from her bed. But how many girls of that age wear white nighties, buttoned to the neck? I don't like the fact that the neck had been ripped either. The buttons were fastened, so a hand must have been placed inside the neck and the fabric torn with some force. It will be interesting to see if James can find any evidence of sexual trauma, but I'm not liking how this feels.'

Becky nodded and referred to her notes.

'James also said there were no obvious signs of malnutrition. So she's either a recent runaway who has somehow got caught up in something – been picked up by one of the bastards who prey on unprotected kids – or she's one of the long-term missing who may have been through God knows what. We can rule one of them out, though. Hailey Wilson has dark hair. So that leaves Amy Davidson and Natasha Joseph. Amy Davidson was a child in care. She started going AWOL when she was about eight, just for a night at a time, but her nights away became more frequent and then she stopped coming back altogether when she was eleven, eighteen months ago. We don't have any DNA to compare, and I'm not sure what the parental history is – we'll have to look into that.'

Becky put one of the files on the floor by her chair and picked up the next one. 'Natasha Joseph – do you know anything about her? You were here in Manchester at the time, weren't you?'

Tom nodded. 'I remember her case, but I wasn't involved.' He decided not to share the fact that he had gone on compassionate leave a few days after the child went missing. 'Her mother was killed in a car accident, and Natasha should have been in the back of the car, but wasn't. They never found a trace of her, or a plausible reason for the accident either.'

'Jumbo remembers the case too,' Becky added. 'He was called out when they realised it was more than a collision, but he says there was nothing of interest to report. No sign that the child had been hurt in the accident – in fact no sign that she had been in the car at all. They've got some DNA on file but he says we need to treat it with caution. It was from a hairbrush and could easily have been contaminated with somebody else's hair – although the father was adamant that nobody else would have used it.'

'Why don't you track down the father and explain the situation to him, Becky? Get a DNA sample for comparison but make it clear that we just want to rule Natasha out. Same for Amy Davidson. Social services will need to be notified in her case, and her carers, but see if you can trace one of her parents to take a swab. And we should notify Hailey Wilson's family that we know it's not her so they don't panic when the news gets out. Speaking of which, I want it kept under wraps for now until everybody relevant has been informed. In reality we know nothing about this girl, and we can't risk compromising the investigation by following up a mass of hysterical reports if it's made public before we're ready.'

4

Day One

'Come on, Mr Grumpy. You're all clean and dressed again now, so let's have a smile.'

Emma tickled Ollie's little tummy and he started to giggle – her favourite sound in the world. He had always hated being dressed. As a baby he had cried, and Emma had worried that he had something wrong with him – one of those terrible illnesses where children can't be touched because their bones break easily. For weeks she had dreaded dressing him, until she realised that at all other times he was happy to have his limbs manoeuvred. It was putting clothes on that he hated. Now he sometimes offered physical resistance as Emma tried to push his legs into his cute dungarees, and he shouted his indignation as loudly as possible – a trick he had learned from one of the workmen who had come to fit their new kitchen. The foreman had shouted 'Ay' every time he wanted something. 'Ay, Bill – pass us that hammer,' or 'Ay, missus – any chance of a brew?' and Ollie had copied, adopting it as his favourite sound. He could do a bad-tempered 'Ay', as if to say 'stop doing that' but more often than not it was just to get attention. Emma hoped he would grow out of it as his vocabulary expanded from its current limitation of about ten words.

Lying next to him on the bed, propped up on one elbow, she used her other hand to creep her fingers up Ollie's body, singing, 'Incy wincy spider climbed up the water spout.' Ollie shouted, 'Dow, dow.' He knew what came next.

'What a clever boy, Ollie.' Emma blew a raspberry on his tummy. She felt a burst of happiness at the thought that this beautiful baby was hers. She had been thirty-seven when she had married Ollie's father and hadn't dared to hope for children in case she was disappointed.

'Come on, let Mummy put your socks on,' she said, smiling to herself. She had always sworn she would never refer to herself in the third person – it seemed such a bizarre thing to do. But she got it now.

Ten minutes later, Emma carried Ollie downstairs, stopping at the bottom – as she always did when she was alone in the house – to look at the portrait facing her at the end of the hallway.

Her husband's first wife had been beautiful. There was no doubting that at all. Her delicate features and pale, almost translucent skin had been captured to perfection in a painting commissioned by her father on her twenty-first birthday. Emma tried so hard not to make comparisons between this woman's fragile beauty and her own rather more prosaic, if not unattractive, features. But it was difficult. She could never ask to have the portrait removed, though.

Irritated by her inability to shake off the last vestiges of insecurity, she pushed open the door to her fabulous new kitchen. It had taken Emma some months to get her own way with the alterations to this part of the house. David had lived here for seven years before Emma moved in and said he loved it the way it was. But Emma had explained the practicalities of demolishing the back of the house and adding a full-width extension to create one large room – a kitchen, dining and living room combined.

Since the builders had left this had become her and Ollie's daytime world. There was plenty of space for her son to play on a floor mat in the living area, and the under-floor heating made it warm for him even in the depths of winter. In truth, she couldn't deny that she had also wanted to stamp some of her own personality on the house. She had had to stop feeling like a visitor. The new extension felt like *her* space.

'London Bridge is falling down, falling down, falling down,' she sang as she walked into the kitchen, flicking the light switch and turning towards the sink, where the lunch dishes were waiting for her. Ollie started bouncing in her arms, banging his hand on her shoulder.

'Ay, ay,' he shouted.

Emma laughed. 'Are you joining in, sweetheart?' She gently put him into his chair, but he wasn't looking at her. 'You're a funny little man, aren't you,' she said, dropping a kiss onto his sparse blond hair.

She glanced out at the dismal day. The black clouds heavy with rain were creating such gloom that the kitchen lights were a necessity even this early in the afternoon.

Her eyes settled on the garden, which was in desperate need of some attention. The workmen had paid little regard to the niceties of maintaining the lawn or the flowerbeds as they had tramped backwards and forwards in their heavy boots, but she didn't mind. She had visions of the spring days just around the corner, out in the sunshine with Ollie playing on the big waterproof mat. She was going to plan and design a real cottage garden with lots of roses. She had always loved roses.

For a moment, Emma was in a trance, staring at nothing because in her head she could see summer days when the garden was finished, the beds bursting with newly planted flowers. She could almost smell the lavender she would grow in the borders.

She wasn't sure of the moment that it happened. It wasn't an instant in time, it was more of a gradual awareness, but as she stared blindly at the black window, dreaming of the happy months ahead, something moved at the edge of her peripheral vision. Her eyes refocused from the garden to the surface of the glass, the bright lights of the kitchen against the dark sky beyond creating a perfect mirror.

Every nerve ending in her body prickled, and she gasped as her brain finally acknowledged what she was looking at.

It was a pair of eyes. A pair of eyes that were behind her, watching.

Close behind her.

In her kitchen.

5

A beam of sunlight burst through the black clouds, hitting the kitchen window and obliterating the reflection as if it had never been there. Emma's fingers gripped the edge of the sink. Had she imagined it? But as quickly as the sun had come out, it was chased away by the squally clouds and the mirror image returned.

Locking eyes with the ghostly reflection that ebbed and flowed as the light outside adjusted from black to grey, Emma groped along the draining board, searching with her fingers for a weapon. There was nothing more than a plastic bowl. Reaching up to the cutlery holder, she felt a sharp pain and a rush of liquid warmth as her fingers grasped the blade of a sharp boning knife, and she followed the steel down to grip the handle with damp, sticky fingers.

Scared of breaking the fragile eye contact for even a second in case the person moved – moved closer to her or to Ollie, moved out of her line of vision or into the hall, where she would be forced to follow – Emma took a deep breath and spun round, leaning heavily back on the sink for support as her legs suddenly weakened.

Her heart thumping and her throat too tight with tension to scream, she stared at the person in front of her as adrenaline pumped through her body, preparing it for fight or flight.

It was a girl, little more than a child.

She was slightly built with straggly blonde hair that settled on the shoulders of her scruffy dark-grey duffle coat, her hands thrust deep into the pockets. The eyes that Emma had seen reflected in the window were mesmerising. Large, oval and the deep grey-green of a stormy ocean, they flinched slightly as Emma brandished the knife. But the girl didn't move.

Emma lowered the knife onto the kitchen island, but kept hold of it. She had no idea what the girl wanted, but, young as she was, Emma didn't trust her.

'What are you doing in my kitchen?' she asked. 'Get out now, before I call the police.'

The girl didn't move. She just stared back, her eyes never leaving Emma's face. In them Emma thought she could read hostility, but perhaps it was confusion, or fear.

'Ay, ay,' shouted Ollie, not used to being ignored. Neither pair of eyes strayed to him even for a second.

'I'm not going to ask you again. Either go *now*, or tell me who you are and what the *hell* you are doing in my kitchen?' Emma repeated.

Silence.

The girl stood where she was and stared at Emma, but her eyes narrowed slightly, as if sizing her up. For a second, she gazed at the knife in Emma's hand.

'Are you frightened?' Emma asked. She couldn't imagine what had made this girl come into her house, out in the middle of nowhere, but it occurred to her that perhaps the child was scared of something or someone. Was she running away? Maybe if Emma relaxed, the girl might tell her why she was here.

Emma took some deep breaths and felt her heart rate slow. If the girl had planned to attack, surely she would have done it by now?

Reaching forwards, she pushed the knife further onto the island. She lifted her cut finger to her mouth and sucked it, then pulled a tissue from up her sleeve and wrapped it around the painful wound. But she never took her eyes off the girl.

'My name's Emma. Nobody's going to hurt you.' She didn't know why she said that, but despite the girl's impassive stare she was, after all, only a kid. Surely she couldn't mean them any harm?

The girl slowly drew her hands from her pockets and Emma could see they were balled into tight fists, her arms held stiff and straight. And she was wearing gloves. Emma's body tensed – perhaps the gloves meant that the girl didn't want to leave any trace that she had been here.

'Please – just tell me what you want.'

Everything Emma said was met with silence.

The girl stared at Emma for a moment longer, and then her eyes flicked around the room as if she was looking for something. Emma used the momentary respite from the hypnotic gaze of those cold eyes to look more carefully at the girl. She could see that her coat was at least two sizes too big – as if she had borrowed it from an older sister, or even a brother. It fell way below her knees, and the sleeves hung beyond the end of her arms. She wore dark-blue jeans, crumpled over a pair of dirty white trainers. But in spite of that, she had a fragile beauty that was at odds with the hostility of her stance.

'Look, I don't know who you are or why you're here, but unless you tell me I'm afraid I'm going to have to call the police. Somebody will be missing you, wondering where you are.'

The girl's head spun round towards Emma, and her eyes opened wide. She glanced towards the back door, and suddenly Emma was worried that she was going to run. Two minutes ago, she would have been relieved to see her go, but something must have happened to this child for her to turn up here. Perhaps there had been an accident and she had walked here? Perhaps she was lost.

'Why don't you sit down? Can you tell me your name? I'm Emma, and this,' she turned her head, smiling at her son to reassure him, 'is Ollie.'

The green eyes betrayed no hint of warmth as they focused on Ollie, who was looking curiously at the girl and banging his plastic spoon on the tray of his high chair.

Emma's mobile was upstairs in her handbag, and the girl was standing between her and the kitchen telephone. Although Emma had put the knife down, she still didn't want to be within striking distance of the girl in case she had misjudged her.

'Please – sit down.' Emma raised her arm and pointed to the dining table at the far end of room. The girl didn't move and Emma edged slowly around her without getting too close, hoping that she could reach the phone. She kept her voice calm and level.

'Okay, I'm going to call the police now. Nobody's going to hurt you, and I'm not calling them because I want you arrested for being in my house. I just want you to be safe and to get you back home. I don't even know if you understand what I'm saying.'

The girl flew towards the phone, ripped it from its base and threw it across the room. She swivelled on her heel and ran across the kitchen, grabbing the knife from the island where Emma had left it. She backed up against the wall, one hand balled into a fist at her side, the other grasping the knife, ready to strike.

Emma stifled a scream of fear. She mustn't frighten Ollie. She wiped her suddenly damp palms on the legs of her jeans and circled to the other side of the island, placing herself between the knife and her baby, her eyes locked on the girl's. All kind thoughts about this child's welfare fled from her mind as she realised she was trapped. She couldn't leave the kitchen to get her mobile. Even if she could get past her, she couldn't leave Ollie here.

'*Get out*! Get out of my house right now. You're scaring my baby,' ordered Emma with as much confidence as she could muster. This is just a child, she told herself. You are in control here.

Emma risked a glance at Ollie, who was indeed looking confused. His gaze shifted from his mummy to the girl, his deep blue eyes filling with tears as the tension in the room sizzled around him. Emma reached out a hand and stroked his face with the back of a finger.

'Shh. It's okay, sweetheart.' She didn't want to shout at the girl again, but she wanted her gone. Alert to the girl's slightest movement, she picked up Ollie's drinking cup from the worktop and passed it to him. The girl wasn't looking at Emma now. Her eyes were darting around the room, her brows knitted together slightly. Was she searching for an escape route?

Emma looked at Ollie, still sitting in his chair watching the girl, and she felt her anger grow as she took in his sparse blond curls and his plump cheeks, damp from his momentary tears. Nobody was going to hurt her baby. It struck her with force that if the girl came anywhere near Ollie, she would fight against that knife with her bare hands without a second's hesitation.

She had no idea what to do. David wouldn't be back for hours, but maybe the girl didn't need to know that.

'Look, I don't know why you're here and what you want, but my husband will be back any minute now. And I'm warning you…' Emma stopped. She didn't want to threaten her. She didn't know if this girl was mentally ill and could be inflamed by talk of violence. 'Please, *talk* to me.'

Emma's fraught mind replayed everything that had happened. If the girl had wanted to attack, she'd had plenty of opportunity before Emma realised she was in the room. She had been silent, her expression blank, until she thought Emma was going to contact the police. She seemed to want something from Emma, but Emma had no idea what it was.

'I know you don't want to speak to me, but if I give you a piece of paper and a pen, will you write your name down for me?' Emma asked with a sudden flash of inspiration. It occurred to her that maybe the girl *couldn't* speak.

Gently easing Ollie's chair back slightly, well out of the girl's reach, she took a notepad and a pen from a shelf above the worktop and pushed them across the kitchen island towards the girl.

'Please, write your name down for me. I don't know what to call you, and if I'm going to help you I need to know who you are.'

The girl stared back at Emma, ignoring the paper and pen that were in front of her.

Emma closed her eyes in frustration. Maybe David would have more luck, and if not it would be down to the police to sort it out.

As if thinking of her husband had conjured him from nowhere, the throb of a powerful engine invaded the oppressive silence as David's Range Rover pulled into the drive. Relieved as she was, she had no idea why he was home so early.

A few seconds later, the front door slammed, and Emma desperately wanted to rush out into the hall to greet him. But somehow she was scared that if she turned round the girl would have disappeared and nobody would believe she had ever been here.

Her relief was tempered by surprise as the girl threw the knife onto the worktop, pulled the notepad towards her and started to write. Just a few letters, and she turned the paper round to face Emma.

'Emma?' She heard David drop his keys in the bowl in the hall and heard his footsteps coming towards them. 'Emma? Something terrible has happened. Where are you?' he called. She could hear anxiety in his voice as he strode towards the kitchen.

She stared at the five letters as if they made no sense. But they did. A shiver ran through her body and goose bumps covered her arms.

I must warn David. But it was too late. He pushed open the door and his eyes went straight to Emma.

'Em. I've had some shocking...' he began. His eyes were suddenly drawn to the corner of the kitchen. He glanced at the girl, and his brow knitted into a frown. He looked back at Emma as he walked across the room, his head on one side as if asking her a silent question. She knew she should speak, but for a moment she couldn't find the words.

'Ay, Dada. Ay,' shouted Ollie.

But David didn't respond to his son. He turned back to the girl and stopped dead, his mouth slightly agape. He stared, speechless, at her, and his face drained of all colour.

The girl stared back, two bright red marks on her cheeks betraying some emotion that was absent from her eyes. The silence felt heavy, and Emma was suddenly certain that from this moment forwards her life was never going to be the same.

Finally, David spoke, his voice barely more than a whisper.

'Tasha,' he said.

6

As soon as David had uttered those two syllables, the silent spell was broken. A gasp burst from his throat as he crossed the room almost at a run. Emma looked on helplessly as her husband stood in front of his daughter, his open palms stroking her upper arms as he stared down at her face, his expression switching from puzzlement to joy. Tears spilled from his eyes and ran unchecked down his cheeks as he tried to pull Tasha's rigid body towards him.

Emma was sure he would be thinking of Caroline, of how things used to be when it was him, Caroline and Tasha all together. She could imagine the scene if both parents had been here to witness the return of their lost daughter; how they would have rejoiced together. She realised that tears were running down her face too, and she brushed them away quickly. How cruel that David and Tasha had lost each other for so long.

There had never been an explanation for Caroline's accident, and there hadn't been a trace of Natasha from that day to this. David had told Emma how the whole town had come out to march up and down the fields surrounding the accident site. Helicopters had buzzed overhead. Urgent appeals had been issued in the press and on television. But there was no sign that anybody else had ever been in that car. Only Caroline.

And now Natasha was here. In their kitchen.

David had blamed himself for refusing to go to the family party. Even though he knew Caroline wasn't a confident driver, especially in the dark, he had rejected her pleas and stayed at home, pretending that work was the issue. That wasn't true. It was simply because he didn't enjoy spending time with Caroline's father. It had taken all of Emma's love and patience to get him to begin to accept that he wasn't responsible for what had happened.

Now he was talking non-stop to his daughter, and Emma's eyes had moved to Natasha, who seemed completely unmoved by anything he said, her gaze blank, her eyes turned away from her father.

'Tasha. Oh darling.' David shook his head as if he had no idea what to say. 'This is incredible. I've missed you – far more than you'll ever know. You're so beautiful – you're so like your mother – do you know that?'

Trembling with emotion, he tried again to pull her into his arms, but as Emma watched she saw Natasha stiffen even more, her eyes narrowing. She could tell that the child's jaw was clenched.

Belatedly, Emma saw the likeness to Caroline – the curve of Natasha's cheek, her long dark eyelashes despite her blonde hair and the delicate pink of her lips. Caroline had been so dark, but it was a superficial difference. Under that sweep of chestnut hair in the portrait in the hall, her husband's first wife gazed out with the same impenetrable gaze as the one Tasha wore now.

David was still muttering words of love, trying to get Natasha to respond to him.

'David,' Emma said softly. She walked over and gently put her hand on his back. 'I know this must seem strange to you, but Tasha probably doesn't remember you very well. I think she's maybe a little frightened.'

David turned his head sharply to Emma. 'Of course she's not frightened. She knows I'm her dad. Why else would she be here?' She could see the pain of Tasha's rejection in David's grey eyes and she barely recognised him as the same relaxed, confident man who had left the house that morning. Now his body was taut with tension, his skin flushed with anxiety.

His face relaxed into a smile as he turned back to Tasha and lifted a hand to gently push her hair from her face, but she shook her head so the hair fell forwards again and continued to stare blankly at the table.

'Why don't we all sit down,' Emma said, 'and we can talk to Tasha, discover how she's found her way back to you and where she's been for all these years.'

'She's back. That's all that matters, where she's been can wait.'

Emma stared at her husband. *Of course* it couldn't wait. What if she had been held prisoner? What if she had been abused? Somebody out there was guilty of keeping this child, and they couldn't pretend the last six years had never happened.

David guided Tasha across to the dining table at the far end of the room and pulled out a chair for her to sit down. 'I wish your mum was here, Tasha. She never knew I'd lost you, of course, but she would be so happy for both of us today.'

Tasha still hadn't spoken, but Emma was shocked at the look the girl flashed at her father. Was that anger she saw?

'David, I'm sorry – but do you think we can have a word for a moment?' She smiled at Tasha, but got a stony stare in response.

The kitchen suddenly felt oppressive and dark, even with all the lights on. It had always seemed like a haven of warmth on even the coldest, dullest days, but the dark skies had finally given way to heavy rain, which was pounding on the glass skylights that ran the length of the room.

David turned his head and gave Emma a slightly puzzled look, but he knew her well enough to know that she wouldn't be asking to speak to him for no reason. He leaned across the table and stroked Natasha's upper arm.

'Back in a moment, sweetheart.'

As he made his way round the kitchen island to where Emma was standing, she thought about her next words.

'If Tasha's staying, we're going to have to think about some clothes for her and getting a room ready. I can sort all that. What do you think?' Emma felt a moment's shame at her desperate need to escape the stifling atmosphere of the kitchen, to get Ollie somewhere safe where they could relax and breathe more easily.

'What do you mean, *if* she's staying?'

'David, of course we want her to stay. But I don't know how these things work, and neither do you. We don't even know how she *got* here. I don't know what social services will say about it, that's all.'

'You've phoned *social services*?'

'No,' Emma swallowed her irritation. 'I haven't called *anybody*. I was going to call the police, but…'

'*Police*?' David turned to Emma, and she flinched slightly at his tone. 'Why were you going to call the police?'

Emma closed her eyes for a second.

'There was a girl in my kitchen. A girl I didn't know, who refused to speak to me. I assumed she was lost, or had been in an accident, but she wouldn't tell me anything. Of course I thought I should call the police, but Tasha took the phone, so I couldn't.'

'She did *what*?'

Emma couldn't bring herself to mention the knife, sitting harmlessly on the worktop. Had she overreacted?

'Never mind that now. But we do have to call them. She's thirteen – and only just. We don't know if any harm has been done to her. We don't how she got here today, where she's been living, or what happened to her on that dreadful night six years ago.'

David ran his fingers through his fair hair, pushing it back from his forehead – a classic sign of tension that Emma recognised only too well in her husband. 'I just need a bit of time with her, Em. Is that too much to ask?'

Emma didn't know what to think. Perhaps if Natasha had been her child she might have felt the way that David did. Maybe she *was* placing too much emphasis on understanding all that had happened, rather than celebrating Natasha's return, but she was still a missing person as far as the police were concerned.

'She's a child, darling, and the police need to know she's home. They'll help us to find out what happened to her, to understand what we need to do to help her.'

David reached out and pulled Emma close.

'I know you're right. I'm just scared they'll take her away again. But I won't let them. Will you make the call? I want to be with Tasha.'

'Of course I will.' She hugged her husband tightly and felt his body relax against hers. 'I'll do it now.'

Emma gently let go of David and turned round.

Tasha was leaning against the door to the hall with her arms folded.

'No police,' she said, her eyes like marbles – hard and shining.

7

'No police,' she said again. 'Call the police and I'm out of here.'

Those were the first words they had heard Natasha speak, and Emma could see the fear in David's eyes that she meant every word of it. It was ridiculous. They *had* to tell the police.

Since Tasha's pronouncement, Emma had managed to persuade her to sit back down at the table, but she had failed to persuade her to take her coat off, even though in the warm kitchen she must have been far too hot. It was as if she wasn't yet sure she was staying.

'I need to make Ollie's tea,' Emma said, leaning forwards to give her son a gentle kiss on his cheek. 'Come on, little man, I'll make you your favourite, shall I?' She nuzzled his neck with her nose, wanting to hear him giggle. He smiled, but it was a much more muted response than normal. Poor Ollie. He wasn't used to unrest in this house where calm usually reigned.

She walked across to the iPod on its speaker stand and switched it on. As the opening bars of 'Pop Goes the Weasel' filled the room, Ollie started bouncing around in his chair. David and Tasha could think what they liked. It was time to focus on what her son needed.

'Can you give me a hand with something, please, David?' Emma asked. She had to speak to him. They had to decide what to do.

She could tell from the way that David looked at her that he understood her ruse, but with the music playing and Tasha seated at the other end of the room, they should be able to speak in private. David walked over and dropped his arm around Emma's shoulders, giving her a brief hug.

'It'll get easier in a day or two, I promise.'

Emma smiled at the typical David response. Ignore things, and they'll go away.

'We have to tell the police right away, David.'

He nodded. 'It's actually worse than you think. That's why I was home so soon. There's something I need to tell you. But not here, Em. I don't want Tasha to hear.'

'Well I'm not leaving Ollie on his own with her.'

'For God's sake, Emma, what is the *matter* with you? What do you think she's going to do to him? He's her *brother*.'

Emma didn't know how to explain it to David, but it wasn't going to happen. She wasn't leaving Tasha with Ollie.

'Turn to face me, speak quietly, and Tasha won't hear you.'

David leaned back against the kitchen units and spoke in a voice so low that Emma could barely hear.

'I had a visit from the police. They found the body of a young girl earlier today, and they thought it might be Tasha. They took my DNA to check.'

Emma stared at him in disbelief.

'*What*? Oh darling, that must have been terrible for you.' She reached forwards and gave him a hug then leaned back, her hands still holding his waist. 'So it's even more important that we ring them – tell them that it can't be Tasha because she's sitting in our kitchen? Some other poor parents have just lost *their* daughter, and the police need to focus on who the girl really is, rather than wasting time on checking if it's Tasha.'

David closed his eyes briefly and nodded.

'Look, why don't you give Ollie his tea and I'll have another ten minutes with Tasha, then we'll tell her together why we need to call the police. Is that okay, Em?'

Her arms slipped behind his back again and she pulled him

close to her. She felt the warmth of his skin through his thin shirt, but his lean body seemed vulnerable, insubstantial, and she held him tighter.

8

The drive home from his office should have taken Tom about twenty minutes, but tonight it was a stop-start marathon. It was all about timing, and this evening he'd got it wrong. Some boy band was playing at the Manchester Arena and the streets were heaving with young girls, giddy with excitement, practically skipping towards the venue with tolerant parents trailing disconsolately in their wake. He looked at their laughing, happy faces, and an image of another young face, distorted by the ravages of death, forced itself to the forefront of his mind. Whatever had happened to the child they had found that morning, he was going to get the bastard that did it to her.

Becky had volunteered for the awful job of visiting the families of the two girls that fitted the age profile. David Joseph had been easy to find, and Becky had seen him at his company offices earlier that day. However, Amy Davidson had been in care since she was two, and nobody knew who her father was. Her mother was in Styal Prison, and she had shrugged when told that the police were checking if a child found dead in suspicious circumstances could be hers. She hadn't seen the child since she had been taken into care and had never shown the slightest interest in her daughter. Nevertheless, hers was the only DNA they would be able to use for identification.

David Joseph had been a different matter. He had begged to see the body – to check for himself if it was his daughter – but Becky had, of course, refused. They had promised to rush through the DNA comparison, but she had been at pains to explain to him that there was every chance that this was some other child. Still, the sooner they could put the man's mind at rest, the better.

If the child did turn out to be Natasha Joseph, though, it would send the investigation in a different direction entirely, because when she had disappeared aged six she was definitely not a runaway and he didn't like to contemplate what might have happened to her in the last few years.

While Becky was out, Tom had made a call. 'Jumbo, sorry to disturb you. I'm sure you've got your hands full – but Becky said you worked on the Natasha Joseph case six years ago. I've read the file, but I thought it worth tapping into your encyclopaedic memory.'

'I don't know about the encyclopaedic bit, but I do remember that case well. Man lost his wife and child in one night. We got called out to examine the car when they knew a child was missing. But I'm not sure I can help, Tom, because there was nothing to find – no blood, for sure – other than the mother's, of course. And she had catastrophic injuries; her neck was broken.'

'I've been wondering how the girl got out of the car, because presumably the child lock was set. What conclusion did you come to?'

'We never got any real answers to be honest. The door next to the kid's seat did have the child lock set, but the other side didn't, so she could have got out that way. We did wonder if somebody had rescued her and maybe kept her – but we didn't find any evidence to support that theory, so we concluded that she must have got out of the car to try to find help and then wandered off.'

Jumbo hadn't been able to offer any more insight than that, which was more or less what Tom was expecting. Had there been anything else, it would have been in the file.

So where the hell did the child go?

He still had no answers as he pulled into his drive and noticed with a twinge of disappointment that Leo's car wasn't there. She must be running late. Tom grabbed his things from the back seat, walked briskly up to the front door and put his key in the lock, listening for the beep of his alarm. He walked to the control box and switched it off.

Ever since a break-in at his cottage in Cheshire the previous summer, Tom had become extra cautious. It had seemed at the time that the burglars were after something in his brother Jack's papers, and now those same papers were here – in this house.

Tom knew he was never going to be completely relaxed until he had bitten the bullet and been through the papers to see if he could work out why anybody would want to steal them – unless, of course, he was too late, and they had found what they were looking for back in the summer.

He went to the kitchen cupboard and grabbed a glass, poured himself a generous measure of Glenmorangie and took it through to the sitting room. He sat on the sofa, but quickly abandoned the comfort of its soft cushions and slid down onto the rug, his back propped against the seat he had just vacated. He reached out to the coffee table for a remote control and pressed a button to choose a song at random.

Tom had Jack to thank for his eclectic taste in music. From Tom's early teens to the day Jack died the two brothers had enjoyed many a heated discussion about which genre of music was the best. Tom could remember clearly the first night that Jack had told him to come to his bedroom to be 'educated'. He had sat cross-legged on the bed trying to argue that Jack's taste in music was terrible, until in the end Jack had pulled out a couple of cans of beer from under his bed and thrust one into Tom's hand.

'Drink that, chill and listen,' he'd said to a slightly surprised but delighted thirteen-year-old Tom.

It was a habit that had stuck with them for the rest of Jack's life. A couple of times each year they would get together, drink beer and listen to music. Tom rarely drank beer on any other occasion. It was a Jack ritual, and somehow the taste went with the event.

He took a sip of his Scotch. He seldom allowed himself time to think about Jack, and he was afraid that scrutinising his brother's papers would open a kind of Pandora's box. The documents had been with Jack's solicitor for years as Tom continued to ignore them, and he was wary of the memories – not all of them positive. Memories were the hardest thing to deal with.

The truth was that Jack had been a law unto himself. He had abhorred any kind of discipline or control, and his staggeringly astute brain was constantly searching for the next challenge – until finally he found the one thing that would continue to grow in complexity and stimulate his fertile mind. The computer. As he got older, it became an obsession. From the day he bought himself a ZX Spectrum Jack rarely left his room.

Tom had been in awe of him. This boy with the wild black hair tied back into something approximating a ponytail, with pale-blue eyes that seemed to burn every surface they touched, was actually his *brother*. Jack was only three years older than Tom, but he seemed light years away in attitude. He always called Tom 'little brother' – almost as if he couldn't remember his name. But those special nights when Tom was allowed into the secret world of Jack's bedroom where clothes lay in heaps on the floor and AC/DC blasted out from homemade speakers were never to be forgotten.

Tom took another mouthful of whisky, forcing his mind away from Jack and onto things that mattered now – like a young girl who had suffered God knows what and had been left to die in a cold, damp wood.

He pulled his phone out from his trouser pocket and pressed a key.

'Lucy? It's Dad. I thought I'd give you a quick call and see how you're doing.'

9

Ollie sat quietly in his chair, munching on his favourite cheese on toast – for the moment oblivious to the tension around him.

Tasha hadn't spoken again, but they had to get through to her somehow.

'Tell her the truth,' Emma said. 'Explain to Tasha why we have to tell the police that she's home.'

David put his head on one side, as if to say 'Must I?', but he knew he had no choice.

'Tasha, the police came to see me today, to ask me about you.'

Tasha's eyes were instantly round with fear, her eyes flicking between David and Emma.

'I'm not supposed to tell anybody about this, because the news isn't going to be made public until tomorrow, but a girl's body was found this morning in some woods. The police thought it might be you.'

Tasha dropped her head. Her hair fell forwards to cover her face, but Emma was sure she had glimpsed what looked like tears in the girl's eyes. She made a noise that sounded like a hiss.

'Hey,' Emma said, 'it's okay, Tasha. They just didn't know who it was, and the girl was about your age so they wanted to check with your dad. That's all.'

Tasha didn't look up.

'Tasha, what is it, darling?' David said, standing up and moving towards her.

As he leaned forwards to put his arm gently round her shoulders, Tasha threw herself to one side.

'Don't *touch* me,' she said. She kept her body angled stiffly away from her father until he withdrew his arm. If there had been tears in her eyes, there was no trace of them now.

Emma felt David's hurt as if it was her own, but her biggest concern was Ollie. He shouldn't be here for this. He looked startled for a moment, then his face crumpled and his mouth turned down as fat tears slid down his flushed cheeks. He should have been in bed ages ago, but Emma hadn't wanted to be separated from him even for a moment.

'Tasha, I'm really sorry that you're upset, but I am going to have to take Ollie out of here. All of this is so distressing for him and he's not coping well. He looks feverish. I won't call the police. Okay? Not until we've worked things through with you. I promise – and I don't break promises.'

Without waiting for anybody's permission, Emma lifted Ollie from his chair and pulled him close.

'Come on, little man. Let's get you all snuggled up in your cot. It's okay. Shhh, sweetheart.' Emma kissed his hot skin.

As she turned towards the door, Tasha jumped up.

'I'm coming,' she said.

Emma was about to object, but one look at Tasha's face and she knew she couldn't. The girl was determined to follow her. Emma shook off her anxiety and told herself Tasha was just a child.

What would Caroline do?

'Why don't we all go? We can show you where you're going to be sleeping, and you can have a look round with your dad while I get Ollie settled.'

'Good idea,' David said, seemingly grateful to be doing something that gave Tasha's presence a sense of permanence.

There was one tricky moment when they reached the top of the stairs. The spare room where Natasha would be sleeping was the first door on the right, but when Emma opened it with a smile, saying, 'Here you are, Natasha,' the girl walked straight past her and along to the next room – now Ollie's. She pushed the door ajar and stood still – looking in.

David ran his hand through his hair again, his face etched with guilt. 'We should have put Ollie somewhere else – left her room as it was,' he whispered. 'That was a mistake, Em. She's going to feel that I'd forgotten her.'

Emma said nothing. That was so typical of David. Instead of giving his daughter a rational explanation for the change of bedroom, he would be worried about whether she resented it – resented him.

Now wasn't the time to argue, so she spoke to Natasha.

'That's Ollie's room now, love. Go in and have a look if you like, but it's a bit small for a teenager, so this will be your room. We can change it, of course, but it's got a double bed and it's a much bigger room. What do you think?'

Natasha turned back towards them, her face expressionless, walked into her room and closed the bedroom door.

❖

By bedtime, Natasha had still not reappeared. David had knocked on the door to tell her that they were having dinner if she would like some, but she hadn't answered him. Emma had gone up herself ten minutes later. She had tried the door, worried that Natasha was in there alone and would undoubtedly be distressed by all that had happened. She was only thirteen after all. But something was pushed hard against the door and it wouldn't budge.

Emma imagined Tasha curled up on the bed, confused and upset, and felt her heart break for the girl.

'Tasha, please let me in, or at least let me know you're okay.'

As she had expected, there was no response. What if Tasha had gone? Could she have climbed out of the window? Emma didn't think so, but what if she had harmed herself in some way?

'Natasha, if you don't open this door or speak to me, I'm going to have to get your dad to force his way in – either through the door or if necessary through the window. Now, tell me that you're okay.'

'Go *away*,' came the shout from inside.

'Okay, sweetheart. I just wanted to know that you're not ill or anything. I know this must be incredibly hard, Tasha – we want to help you. Shall I bring you some food if you don't feel like coming down?'

'I told you to go *away*.' No longer a shout, there was a level of determination in the tone that brooked no argument.

Emma had rested her forehead against the door. She had no idea what to do, and Tasha still hadn't told them why she was prepared to run away again if they called the police.

'Okay, I'm going to go downstairs. If you want to have some dinner, it's steak pie and roast potatoes.'

David had eaten his dinner in silence, disappointment that Tasha hadn't joined them evident in his expression, and Emma could find no words to comfort him that didn't sound like empty platitudes. How could she possibly understand how he was feeling? His ready smile had seemed like a distant memory tonight, and she wanted to share his pain, joy and confusion. But she couldn't reach him. He was somewhere else – somewhere that excluded her.

One thing she did know, though. Something was very wrong about all of this. Why wouldn't Tasha tell them where she had been living? Why was she frightened of the police?

Emma had no answers, and after they had finished dinner and cleared up she had taken a slice of chocolate cake and a large glass of milk and left them outside Tasha's door.

She wanted to tell David that tomorrow she was going to call the police, whether Tasha liked it or not. Somebody had kept her from her family for all this time, and there was no guarantee that she was the only one. What if there were other girls like her, hidden away from their families? And how had she got back? They were two miles from the nearest town, and there were no buses.

Emma couldn't help feeling they weren't asking the right questions.

'Let's go up,' Emma said quietly, reaching for David's hand.

He gently pulled away.

'Do you mind if I stay downstairs for a while, Em? I'm going to pour a brandy and have a few moments. Is that okay?'

Emma was sure that David needed time to think about Caroline too, and she couldn't blame him for that, today of all days.

'Of course. I'll still be awake when you come to bed if you want to talk some more.'

He kissed her gently on the lips and she turned to make her way upstairs.

As she passed Tasha's bedroom, she was disappointed to see that the cake and milk were still sitting on the small table on the landing, but to her surprise the door was slightly ajar. She knocked quietly.

'Tasha,' she said in little more than a whisper in case the girl was asleep. There was no response. She pushed the door a little wider to check that her new stepdaughter was okay. The room was empty.

Emma spun round. The door to the bathroom stood wide open; she was clearly not in there. And there was something else. The door to Ollie's room was closed. It was *never* closed.

She flew along the landing and flung open the door to his room. The nightlight cast faint images of stars, bubbles and fish around the room, projecting a pale green light on the dark walls – and over the figure standing at the end of Ollie's cot, leaning in towards him.

10

Day Two

The sky outside Ollie's bedroom window was bright with morning sunshine, although rainclouds were already gathering, their brooding darkness hovering malevolently on the horizon.

Emma stared sightlessly at the garden. Today was going to be a better day, she decided, even though her body felt heavy and lethargic after little sleep. But she was going to have to fight that. Her family needed her.

She had spent the night on a chair in Ollie's room, terrified to leave him alone. At least she had started the night on the chair. In the end, though, she had stretched herself out on the rug in front of his cot. If she fell asleep, she didn't want anybody getting past her, getting to her baby.

When she had found Tasha leaning over his cot the night before she had screamed at the girl in her fear. 'What are you doing? Why are you in here?'

Natasha had stared at her without moving for a few moments – her eyes blank. Then she had pushed past Emma and walked calmly back to her own room, where she had barricaded herself in again. For the rest of the night, Emma had been alert to the slightest sound, but there had been no repetition of that terrifying moment, and her baby had slept peacefully until a few moments ago.

Emma turned to pick up Ollie out of his cot and took him over to the window seat, cuddling his warm little body to her. She wrapped her arms a bit tighter around her son and kissed the top of his head. What would he be making of all this? Ollie was used to a life free from tension but now he could probably sense his mother's anxiety, seeping from her pores. Emma felt tears starting to leak from her eyes again and shook herself crossly. Getting upset wasn't going to help anyone.

She forced her shoulders down, waggled her toes in an effort to relax the muscles in her legs and took some deep breaths.

'Be positive,' she whispered.

Despite the events of the night before, she had to try to act as if nothing had happened. She was sure she had panicked unnecessarily. Probably the girl had simply wanted to look at her little brother. Emma needed to make things right – for everybody's sake.

She pushed herself off the window seat and carried Ollie in his pyjamas towards the stairs. 'So what's today going to bring, my little Ollie?' she said, giving him her best smile.

She paused outside Natasha's door and knocked.

'Tasha, Ollie and I are going downstairs for breakfast. Your dad's in the shower. Do you want some scrambled eggs?'

She waited in silence and was surprised when the door opened and Natasha came out. Seeing her wearing exactly what she had worn the day before reminded Emma that she needed to buy some clothes for the girl, and maybe a few things to brighten up her bedroom.

Natasha's face was blank, but her eyes were tired and bloodshot. Had she been crying?

And it's my fault. It's because I shouted at her. Emma felt a rush of blood to her cheeks and turned towards Ollie to mask her guilty confusion.

'Say good morning to Tasha, Ollie.'

'Tassa, Tassa, ay, ay,' Ollie said, beaming at his half-sister and waving his arms in the air. She looked away.

Emma felt her brows knitting together in a frown at the girl's indifference and forced herself to act naturally as she led the way into the kitchen.

'Sorry – he can't make a *sh* sound yet. Okay – juice for Ollie, and I guess you would like some too,' Emma said, deciding that for now the best policy was not to demand a response.

She poured juice into Ollie's beaker and some into a glass for Natasha.

'Go and sit down at the table, Tasha. I'll bring your breakfast over when it's ready.'

She turned to the fridge, took out some eggs and pushed two slices of bread into the toaster, working entirely on autopilot, her mind elsewhere.

Emma had spoken to David about the police again, and she had finally managed to convince him to call them. When he had first woken up, David had asked where she'd been all night. She knew if she told him the truth about why she slept in Ollie's room he would have said she was overreacting, so she told him she was worried about Ollie having a temperature, and it seemed easier than disturbing David every time she got up to check on their son.

It was a lie. She had never lied to her husband before.

She felt Tasha's eyes on her and somehow got the feeling that the girl could read her every thought. Her eyes narrowed slightly as if she hated Emma with every cell in her body. Did she resent her for taking her mother's place? Emma felt a shiver run down her spine. If she despised them so much, why was she here?

David chose that moment to walk into the kitchen, trying his best to raise a cheery smile, and went straight to Natasha.

'Hello, darling,' he said, beaming at her. 'It's lovely to see you up and having breakfast. Did you sleep well?' He put his arm round her shoulders, pulling her gently towards him so he could kiss the top of her head. Natasha resisted with all her strength, and when David released her the force of her resistance caused her to tumble slightly to the side, her arm sending her glass of juice flying.

Natasha jumped up from the table.

'Stop touching me,' she said quietly, her eyes burning and her jaw clenched. 'I don't like it.' Kicking the chair viciously to one side, she left the kitchen, slamming the door behind her.

Emma didn't know what to do, but she couldn't bear to see the pain in David's eyes. She knew that he was suffocating the girl, but could she blame him? She waited a few moments.

'Shall I go and get her?' she asked, keeping her voice low and even. 'We promised not to contact the police without telling her, but it's going to look really bad if we don't. What do you want to do, love?'

David shook his head.

'You're right, of course. I'll go and tell her. But I'm going to lock the front door so if she decides to run she'll have to come through here. And I'll stop her. I don't know what else to do, but I can't lose her again now.'

11

The incident room was humming when Tom arrived. Becky appeared to have everything under control and the press had now been briefed about the discovery of the young girl's body. Detective Superintendent Philippa Stanley had decided to be the spokesperson. Tom wasn't surprised. Philippa was very keen on raising her public profile, and she was welcome to it as far as Tom was concerned.

He knew what would happen now. All those children that hadn't been reported missing would become top priority in their parents' eyes, the belief that their daughter would come home 'when she's ready' suddenly not being quite such a sure thing.

Tom hadn't slept well. Thoughts of Jack and the dead girl were enough to disturb his sleep, but on top of that he and Leo had discovered something in his brother's papers the previous evening and he couldn't rid himself of the idea that it might be significant.

He hadn't wanted to go through Jack's documents last night, but when Leo had arrived home she had encouraged him to stop putting the task off indefinitely.

'Procrastination, Tom.'

'Yes – I know. It's the thief of time.'

Leo had given him a smug look. 'I wasn't going to say that – I was going to say makes easy things hard, hard things harder.'

'Have you just made that up?' he had asked with a smile.

'No – but the threat of these documents is always there, hanging over you. Until you know if there's anything worth finding – or any evidence that something's already been taken –

they're going to grow into a bigger and bigger burden. Come on – I'll help you. Let's get the job done.'

He had looked at Leo, dressed in one of her monochrome outfits of black jeans and a loose black-and-white striped shirt, and thought about what he would rather be doing. In the end, though, he had caved in.

'Okay, you win. I'll get the boxes.'

It had seemed like a fairly mundane task to begin with – nothing more exciting than documents detailing Jack's presentations to prospective clients. None of Tom's fears of being assaulted by memories were realised until Leo had discovered an SD card, trapped under one of the cardboard flaps at the bottom of the box. She had wanted to load it onto her laptop there and then, but Tom had hesitated, fearing that it might be a video of Jack playing his guitar badly and singing along to Def Leppard. He hadn't been sure he could cope with that, so he had suggested they had done enough for one night and put the card to one side.

It was no good, though. The damned thing was burning a hole in his pocket. The best option by far would be to take a look now in the privacy of his office and just *deal* with whatever was on it. He pulled the card out and slotted into the side of his laptop.

There was one file. SILVERSPHERE.xls. Tom stared at the screen. An Excel spreadsheet – and he recognised the moniker Silver Sphere only too well.

It was Jack's hacker alias. As a teenager Jack had started hacking for fun, to show that he could beat the system. He had truly believed that nothing could defeat him.

Tom clicked on the file to open it. Nothing happened for a second. Then a box popped up.

Please enter your password.

Tom stared at the screen for a moment, and then with a disappointed sigh he ejected the card and put it back in his pocket.

❖

Tom was on his second cup of coffee of the morning when he looked up and saw Becky hovering near the door. His spirits lifted slightly as, not for the first time, he was struck by how much she had changed. There was no comparison between the person in front of him now and the one who had arrived in Manchester a few months previously. Gone was the pale, almost haggard face of a young woman fighting to recover her confidence at the end of a doomed relationship. Now her cheeks were pink, and her eyes glittered with a genuine interest in life. She had regained all of her natural ebullience. Today her outfit matched her smart and sassy personality; her black trouser suit was well cut with a jacket that showed off her slim waist and under the jacket was an emerald-green shirt and a slim gold chain at her neck. She had grown her hair out of its neat bob, and it bounced shinily on her shoulders.

'Okay if I come in?' she asked. 'Only you looked miles away. Ooh – I see you've found your pig.'

Tom had to think for a moment. What pig? And then he followed Becky's gaze to the doorstop.

'Ah yes. The missing pig. Our good friend DC Tippetts had borrowed it.'

'What the hell did Ryan want with your pig?' Becky asked.

'Don't ask. I didn't believe his excuse for a second. Anything of interest in the calls on the missing girl?'

Becky pulled a face as she sat down.

'Not really. As you might expect we've got a stack of names to sort through because people are saying that their sixteen-year-old only looks twelve, or are we sure the girl was white, etcetera. But we've had some news from Jumbo. He's writing the report now but wanted to give me the heads up.'

Tom pushed the crime statistics that he had been studying with little interest to one side and leaned forwards.

'What's he got?'

'They did a fingertip search in the pile of soggy leaves around where she was found and unearthed a syringe.'

'Oh no,' Tom said, his chest feeling heavy with sorrow for the child. 'Do they think the poor kid did it to herself, or did some bastard take her there and give her too much of the stuff?'

'They're not sure. It may even be unrelated. We won't know until we get her tox results, and even if we put a rush on, they're going to be a couple of weeks. As you may have noticed, though, that lovely tunnel held all sorts of delights – including the odd syringe if I remember rightly. It could just be coincidence that there was one near the body. Anyway, Jumbo's team are collecting evidence from the tunnel too.'

Tom pulled a face.

'They're going to struggle to get any fingerprints from the body, but there are some on the syringe. No match to anybody as yet. They couldn't find any footprints – but then they didn't find the girl's either. Everything had been blown about a bit in the weather for the last couple of days.'

'Do they know what was in the syringe?' Tom asked.

'Ketamine.'

'*Ketamine*? I wasn't expecting that. What theories have we got, then? Some bastard knocked her out so that not only had he bagged himself a kid, but a comatose kid into the bargain?'

Becky winced.

'Ket's an unusual choice, I agree. But even if she was injected, it might only have put her into a deep sleep. So she's just as likely to have died from hypothermia. She had zero body fat from what I can see on the photos. You were away last week, but before we got all this wind and rain it was bloody freezing. They reckon it's been the coldest March in Manchester since 1962, and the temperature dropped to minus six overnight.'

There was a tap on the open door and Tom glanced up to see DC Ryan Tippetts standing in the door.

'Boss,' he said. 'It's Natasha Joseph.'

Tom looked at Becky's face as she grimaced at the thought of passing on the sad information to the girl's father.

'Thanks Ryan. That's confirmed is it?'

The detective looked confused for a moment, then his face cleared.

'Oh. I see what you mean. No, the *body* isn't Natasha Joseph. She's turned up at home. Just walked in the door, apparently. Yesterday.'

'Yesterday!' The word burst from Becky's lips as she spun round to face DC Tippetts. 'Why the bloody hell didn't they tell us?'

'Don't shoot the messenger,' Ryan said, holding his hands up. 'That's all I know. Oh – except that the kid's refusing to speak to the police. She says that if we're involved she's going to do a runner.'

Becky shook her head in disbelief. 'Oh that's *great*. Thanks, Ryan.' She turned back to Tom. 'Well, bugger me. That's a bit of a turn-up. What are you thinking?'

'I'm wondering where the hell *she's* sprung from after all this time. We find a body we think might be hers, and then she suddenly comes back? That's quite a coincidence!'

Nothing about this felt good to Tom. The Joseph girl had been missing since she was six years old, so somebody had been sheltering her. Why had they let her go now?

'How do you want me to play it?' Becky asked.

'You need to pay the Josephs a visit. We need to be certain she is who she says she is. If she refuses to speak to you, tell the Josephs we'll give her a couple of days to settle in, but then we're going to have to talk to her. And take a family liaison officer with you – one that's been trained to interview kids. We need to know where the hell she's been, who's been hiding her for all these years, and why.'

12

It felt safe in the bedroom now the door was barricaded shut again with a chest of drawers. She hadn't known if she would be strong enough to shift such a big piece of furniture, but somehow she had managed, and it got a bit easier each time. She had found somewhere to hide stuff, but she still couldn't risk them coming into the room whenever they wanted.

David – he wanted her to call him Dad but he could dream on – had given her an old mobile of his so she could 'call her friends'. That had almost made her smile. It was a bit of a crappy old thing, but he seemed very pleased with himself for his thoughtfulness.

She wished he wouldn't touch her. It made her flesh crawl.

She knew Emma had searched the pockets of her duffle coat when she had finally taken it off the night before. She had slammed her bedroom door but sneaked out to watch Emma glancing guiltily over her shoulder as her hands delved deep into the pockets of the coat where she had hung it in the hall. Emma probably expected to find a phone. As if Natasha would have been stupid enough to bring one into the house yesterday.

Emma wouldn't have told David what she'd done, though. He would have thought it was a terrible thing to do. But Emma didn't trust her. And that might be a problem.

Last night, when everybody was in bed, Natasha had crept downstairs. She had switched a lamp on and looked at the painting in the hall. She had forgotten what her mum looked like.

How could she have forgotten?

She was beautiful. And she had loved Tasha so much. Tasha

could just about remember how that had made her feel, but she hadn't felt like that in a very long time.

Now David had called the police and she was going to have to think on her feet. It wasn't supposed to happen. She knew there were policemen who would pass on anything that they were told to, and she knew that would mean trouble. She had tried every trick she could think of to make David change his mind, but Emma wouldn't budge.

David would have been easier to manipulate on his own. He was a man with guilt hanging over him, weighing him down. She might have managed to persuade him to keep the police out of it. Emma was much tougher. She said they had to tell the police because of the girl – the dead girl. Tasha stifled a sob. Could it be...? No. She mustn't even *think* that.

Emma had won the battle, though, and convinced David to make the call. Emma thought she knew the difference between right and wrong.

She might know about right, but she knew nothing about wrong. She hadn't the first *clue* about wrong.

Tasha smiled to herself. It was only a matter of time.

13

Becky looked at the open fields surrounding David Joseph's home. The red-brick house itself was attractive in a solid kind of way, but she wouldn't want to live out here. The idea of living in the countryside didn't appeal to her at all, and if she ever changed her mind it would have to be for a house with stunning views. This was all a bit flat and featureless for her taste. And as she was a city girl, the vague whiff of manure didn't do much for her either.

The front garden of Blue Meadow House looked pretty much like all gardens in March – generally quite drab but with some cheerful yellow daffodils offering a promise of the warmer months to come. In spite of their burst of colour, as she surveyed the shadows cast by the dark clouds that had chased away the brief morning sunshine, it seemed at this moment that Grey Meadow House might have been a more appropriate name. At least it had stopped raining.

Becky pushed the doorbell, glancing sideways at the quiet, confident profile of Charley Hughes, a young DC who was specially trained in questioning children. She had cropped blonde hair and her features appeared to have been skilfully sculpted, with sharp cheekbones, wide-set hazel eyes and a generous mouth. It was one of those faces that on first sight seemed merely attractive but which became increasingly interesting.

'I'm really keen to see how you handle this one, Charley. It's hard to believe Natasha Joseph has been missing for over six years, and nobody has seen hide nor hair of her in all that time.'

'I'll do my best,' Charley responded. 'But I gather she doesn't want to talk to us at all, so we may get no further than checking that she is who she claims to be.'

Any further conversation was brought to a halt as a woman with a pale face who looked to be around forty opened the door. Her eyes had the haunted look of a person under stress.

'Good morning,' Becky said. 'Mrs Emma Joseph? I'm Detective Inspector Becky Robinson, and this is Detective Constable Charlotte Hughes.'

The woman nodded. 'Please come in.' She held the door open so Becky and Charley could step into the wide hallway. At the far end was a beautiful antique wooden table with a bowl of fresh flowers adding a touch of brightness against a pale beige wall. But it was the portrait above the flowers that drew Becky's eye. It was a painting of a lovely young woman, little more than a girl really, sitting on a chaise longue with her feet tucked up next to her. Emma Joseph intercepted Becky's gaze.

'That's my husband's first wife, Caroline. Tasha's mother.'

Becky glanced at the woman standing before her in the hallway, looking to see if there was any trace of resentment that the portrait of the former wife was still hanging in pride of place, but she saw none. Just a hint of sadness.

'Tasha's with her father. I'll take you to them.'

Becky didn't move. 'Before we meet her, Mrs Joseph, can you fill me in on yesterday? I gather you just found her in your kitchen?'

Emma Joseph lifted her hand to tuck away some stray strands of hair that had escaped from a loose ponytail behind her ears.

'It was very odd. I'd been upstairs with Ollie – my little boy. I came down to the kitchen, and there she was. Standing there, saying nothing.'

'How do you think she got in, Mrs Joseph?'

'She must have gone round the side of the house and come in through the back door. I never lock that door when I'm in all day. Maybe not the brightest decision, stuck out here, but…' She shrugged as if to say 'That's just the way it is.'

'And what has she said to you – about how she got here, where she's been?'

'Nothing. We can't get anything out of her, other than the fact she didn't want the police involved.' The woman shook her head and looked Becky in the eye. 'She just *appeared* – from *nowhere*. How did she find her way to us?'

'She hasn't told you?'

'Not a word. She won't even talk to her dad.'

'Okay, Mrs Joseph. One more thing, if you don't mind. Before you came downstairs and found Natasha in your kitchen, do you remember hearing anything at all out of the ordinary outside?'

For a moment, Emma Joseph look puzzled, but she was a smart lady. 'Oh, you mean like a car or anything?'

'Well, you're quite a long way from a bus route here, and with all these lanes I am struggling to think how she would have got here on her own.'

'Me too,' Emma said. 'I didn't hear a thing, though. The tractor in the next field was making so much noise I wouldn't have heard if a Sherman tank had rolled up, to be honest. But if you think somebody brought her here, why would they keep her for six years and then bring her back?'

Becky took a deep breath.

'I've no idea. It doesn't make any sense at all, as far as I can see.'

❖

Emma Joseph pushed open the kitchen door and Becky caught a quick glimpse of a wonderfully comfortable-looking kitchen and living room – something she would expect to find in a style magazine – before her eyes came to rest on a man with his back to them, hands in his trouser pockets, staring out of a floor-to-ceiling glass door into the back garden. Although of average height and slender build, his hunched shoulders gave him the air of a person much older than the attractive, confident man Becky had been introduced to just the day before.

What a twenty-four hours he had had. Becky could still remember how the colour had seeped from his skin as he had slumped back into his chair at the news that a girl's body had been found. It should be a time for celebration now, but all Becky could feel around her was confusion and disappointment.

The only movement in the room came from the little boy in the high chair. He turned his head as they came in, and his baby face lit up when he saw his mum. He was playing with some brightly coloured plastic eggs and banged one on his tray with delight at her appearance. Becky looked at Emma and saw her worried frown soften as she smiled at her son briefly, before turning back to her husband.

'David,' she said gently. 'The detectives have arrived.'

Tearing his gaze away from the garden, David Joseph turned his head, then with one last lingering look into the garden turned round and walked towards Becky and Charley, reaching out to shake them both by the hand.

'Thank you for coming. I know we should have called you sooner, but Tasha seems so fragile and she was adamant that the police mustn't be told she's here. She said she'd disappear again if we called you.'

'But she's still here?' Becky asked.

David nodded. 'I locked all the doors while we talked to her and explained why we had to call you. We told her about the girl – the one you found yesterday. That seemed to upset her a bit. I promised her that you only want to check that she really is my daughter – even though I don't have a single doubt myself – just so you can close the case.'

Becky knew it wasn't the time to argue, but if David Joseph thought this case was closed, he was way off the mark. Wherever his daughter had been, she had been somebody's secret for more than six years. In Becky's experience, that painted pictures of a life she didn't want to imagine for this child.

'We'll keep it simple for today, Mr Joseph, if that helps. Where's Natasha now?' Becky asked.

He turned and walked back towards the window, the three women following him. Through the glass they looked out at trampled flowerbeds and a muddy lawn that looked as if the local football team had recently played a match on it. But there was one patch of grass that was intact at the far end of the garden, and in the middle was a child's swing. Becky could see a slight young girl hunched up, pushing herself backwards and forwards with one foot on the ground, her arms hooked around the chains. She appeared to be staring into the distance, her eyes unfocused, her mind somewhere else entirely.

'She's been out there since we told her we were going to call you. I've been watching her to make sure she doesn't run off. When she was little, she spent hours on that swing. She used to say that one night she was going to swing so high that she would touch a star.'

'May we speak to Natasha?' Becky asked.

Before he had a chance to answer, Emma interrupted.

'David, if you don't mind, I think I should take Ollie somewhere else. He must be wondering what on earth's going on.'

He glanced at his wife vacantly and gave a slightly bemused shrug.

'Yes, of course. I don't think you're needed here.' He looked from Becky to Charley. 'Is she?'

Becky saw the expression on Emma's face and felt the other woman's sense of rejection.

'I think it's fine,' Becky said. 'But we will need to talk to you again to make sure we've got all the facts. And I think you're going to be vital going forwards, so if your baby has a nap any time soon, do come back and join us.'

Emma flashed a brief, grateful smile to Becky as she left the room with Ollie shouting his indignation at being taken away.

David slid open the door and stepped out into the garden, picking his way through the mud to approach his daughter. Becky and Charley gave him a moment alone with her. He crouched down so he was level with her face; they could see he was speaking but couldn't hear what he was saying. Natasha didn't look at him. They saw him reach out a hand to touch her arm and couldn't miss the fact that she flinched and jerked her arm away.

'What do you think, Charley?' Becky asked.

'If I'm honest, I don't get it. She's come back, but she's rejecting everybody – especially her dad, from the look of things. Until we know why she's suddenly come back *now*, I don't think it's going to make any sense.'

'Come on. He's fighting a losing battle. Let's see if we can get a DNA sample and follow Tom's advice – leave them in peace with all the contact numbers they need. At least for a day or two.'

The two women followed David across the garden. As they approached the child on the swing, Becky focused on Natasha, who seemed too small and slender for a girl who had just turned thirteen. Where her arms stuck out from the sleeves of her jumper, Becky could see wrists that were so narrow they looked as if one squeeze would break them. But then she looked at the eyes, and they told a whole different story. These weren't the eyes of a child. There was a hint of bitterness in her hard gaze, a knowing kind of resilience. Despite that, Natasha's pupils were slightly dilated – a classic symptom of fear.

What's she frightened of?

'Hi, Natasha. My name's Becky, and this is Charley. We know you don't want to talk to us. Your dad's explained, and we're not going to push you.'

Natasha had found a loose thread in the sleeve of her

slightly grubby red jumper and was pulling it and watching with fascination as it unravelled.

'It's very quiet round here, isn't it?' Charley said. 'You can hear the birds singing now the rain has stopped. Could you hear the birds where you've been living?'

Becky detected a small movement of the mouth, but it wasn't to speak. It was a smirk of derision. Charley laughed gently.

'I guess from your expression that's a no, then, is it?'

The girl remained mute.

'Do you think you could tell me a bit about where you were living?'

No answer. David made a move to put his arm around his daughter, but she pulled away.

'Sweetheart, these ladies want to help you. You're not in trouble at all. They just need to understand a bit about where you've been and how you got here.'

Natasha's eyes flicked from Becky to Charley and back again. For a moment, Becky thought she was going to tell them something – something important. But David reached out to touch her again and the spell was broken. She put both hands on the seat of the swing and pushed herself off, turning to her father.

The low tone of Tasha's voice seemed to echo around the quiet garden.

'I told you not to call the police. You should have listened to me.'

As the girl turned and walked towards the house, Becky raised her hand and rubbed away the tingling sensation at the back of her neck.

14

Emma looked in the cloakroom mirror and was dismayed by the pallid, blotchy face that stared back at her. What a mess they all were. David had looked even more ravaged by emotion since Tasha's behaviour in the garden. Two deep lines were carved into his cheeks, and his eyes were bloodshot and puffy. Poor David. She knew he must be alternating between the delight of having his daughter back and the agony of her rejection, but Emma had no idea how to help. She was failing them.

Even Ollie was affected. He was fascinated by his new sister, but the constant feeling that they were all on the edge of a precipice was changing her placid, happy son into a slightly fractious baby. He cried more readily and seemed too conscious of Emma's own distress.

After the police had left earlier, gaining nothing but a DNA sample from Tasha, Emma had tried to do all the right things. She had nipped out, taking Ollie with her, to buy some new clothes for her stepdaughter, trying to think what girls of that age liked to wear. She was going to play it safe with skinny jeans and baggy T-shirts until maybe Tasha could come with her to chose for herself.

When she took them up to Tasha – once more isolated in her room – she had tried to talk to her about the clothes she had chosen, and how they could go shopping together in the future. Nothing elicited a response and Emma wondered if maybe the girl resented Emma's intrusion into their lives. In Tasha's eyes, this was Caroline's house, not Emma's.

She had sat down on the side of the bed, but Tasha had immediately swung her legs over to the other side, her back to Emma.

'I know it must seem strange, Tasha, finding me in this house, married to your dad. But we didn't get together until a long time after your mum died.'

In spite of the fact that she had shown no interest in what Emma was saying, Tasha hadn't rushed from the room, so Emma kept talking, hoping she could break down some barriers.

'I met your dad through my fiancé,' she had told Tasha. 'He was doing some work for your dad's company, and we went to a few charity events together. Your mum was there too. She was very beautiful, Tasha. I really liked her. We nearly always found that we were at the same table, and we had some good times together. She talked about you a lot, told me that you were the best thing that had ever happened to her.'

Emma risked a glance at Tasha. Her back was rigid. She was listening, though.

'I didn't know about the accident for a long time. My fiancé and I had split up, and I took myself off to stay with my dad in Australia. I didn't want to know about anything or anybody for quite a while. When I came back to Manchester, there was an article about you in the paper. It was a year to the day that you had disappeared and your dad was making another plea to people to try to find you. I got in touch to offer him my sympathy. He tried so hard to find you, you know. He was shattered, Tasha.'

That was the wrong thing to say. Tasha hadn't turned round, but her voice was harsh, as if the words were being dragged from deep inside her.

'You really don't know, do you? You actually believe what you're saying.'

Emma was shocked. Every word of her story was true. She tried to interrupt, but Tasha shook her head.

'Whatever happens next, it's his fault. You need to remember that.'

What did she mean? Tasha had refused to say.

That was three hours ago, and now they felt like a family divided. David was in their rarely used sitting room, Emma and Ollie were in the kitchen, and Tasha had barricaded herself back in her room.

Emma's profound sense of failure was compounded by her own feelings about this stranger who had exploded into their lives. All she wanted was to return to the peace and harmony she had known just days before, and she hated herself for the thought.

She took a deep, shuddering breath and blinked away the burning sensation at the back of her eyes. She wasn't going to cry. Ollie couldn't see her upset again – it wasn't fair on him. She picked her baby up from where he was playing on the floor, ignoring his disgruntled 'Ay', and hugged his warm little body to her, hiding her red eyes by holding his head close to her chest.

She took him into the sitting room at the front of the house, quickly wiping the heel of her hand across her cheeks. She could hold on for a moment longer. But when she saw David sitting on the sofa, staring at the wall, her forced composure nearly shattered. He looked round hopefully, but seeing his wife and baby, he turned back, disappointed. She understood. She knew with all her heart that it wasn't a lack of love for them, it was simply that – more than anything – he wanted his daughter to come to him.

She put Ollie on the rug, knowing he would crawl to David. Perhaps time with his son would help, and Emma knew she had to be alone for a moment, to let the lid off all the emotion she was bottling up inside her.

Without a word, she turned and left the room, holding her breath until she reached the sanctuary of their bedroom. She didn't want Tasha to see her distress any more than she wanted Ollie to, although the girl's bedroom door was still shut.

She walked into the bedroom and closed the door, biting back a sob. Sitting on the edge of the bed, she pulled open her bedside table drawer, groping for her tissues. They weren't there.

Emma wiped her tears on a corner of the duvet, and peered in to the drawer. The tissues *were* there – but they were on far side of the drawer, not next to the bed where Emma always kept them.

That's funny, she thought, her tears forgotten.

She stood up and walked over to the dressing table, pulling out the top drawer. The contents were as messy as usual – but she could see instantly that this wasn't *her* mess. David always said he didn't know how she ever found anything in the jumble of unused lipsticks, eyeshadows and facecreams, and yet she always knew exactly where everything was. Nothing seemed to be missing, but there was no doubt everything in this drawer had been moved.

She opened each of the other drawers in turn. Every one was the same. Nothing obvious had been taken, but every item had been touched, moved, examined. And then replaced.

It could only have been one person, and Emma had no idea what to do about it.

Who *was* this child? What had she *become*?

15

By the end of the day, Tom's head was spinning. It had been his unpleasant – but necessary – task to attend the post mortem and he had not been at all surprised that the pathologist had found signs of sexual trauma, but no semen. Sadly, because of the state of the body, it wasn't clear whether the sexual activity had taken place around the time of her death, or in the days leading up to it. There were plenty of used condoms in the nearby tunnel, but who knew whether any would turn out to be relevant to the girl's death.

She still hadn't been identified, and the list of candidates was growing since Philippa's news bulletin that morning. It seemed Becky might have been right about the cause of death being hypothermia, though.

'It's always somewhat problematic to identify hypothermia as the definite cause of death,' the pathologist had said. 'But I've ruled out just about everything else. We won't be certain until the toxicology results are in, of course. The fact that her anorak was thrown to one side and the front of her nightdress ripped does support this theory. I'm assuming this was a case of paradoxical undressing – very common with hypothermia deaths.'

Tom wasn't so sure about the pathologist's explanation. He had come across this rather bizarre effect of hypothermia before, where the victims feel as though they are burning up and remove their clothes, but there was an equally plausible theory.

'Isn't it just as likely that she was drugged, raped, had her clothes ripped and was left for dead? And the cold got her in the end?' he had asked.

'It's possible, yes, but let's wait and see and not make any final decisions until we get the tox results. She may have injected the ketamine herself, and we still don't have an answer to that.'

Fortunately, suicide was very rare for children of this age in England, and yet they couldn't rule it out. It appeared this girl had left home without, as far as they could tell, any money or clothes, suggesting she had either been taken from her bed by somebody – maybe under duress – or she had run away of her own volition in the middle of the night.

Becky had contacted the child sexual exploitation team to see if they had any information that might relate to the girl, but Tom couldn't shake the thought that somebody had *dressed* her in that white nightie. He struggled to believe she had chosen to wear something so old-fashioned herself.

He was about to pack up his files and turn off his computer when Becky herself appeared in his open doorway.

'Time for a quick catch-up?' she asked, walking in and sitting down in anticipation of his answer. 'Natasha Joseph – she's saying nothing, and her attitude to the police is not good. Having said that, there was one point when I thought we might be getting through to her. But it was a fleeting moment. We have no idea where she's been or how she got back.'

'What options have you considered?' he asked.

'Given that we are getting nothing from her right now, I think we need to go back to the accident.'

Tom nodded. 'Agreed. Go on.'

'Okay. I've been over the reports several times, and it seems that Caroline Joseph steered the car across to the other side of the road. There was no sign of a skid until after she came back down from the bank. Why would she steer to the other side of the road?'

'I can only think of two reasons,' Tom said. 'Either she was avoiding something – maybe an animal on the road – or she was distracted. We know she received a call on her mobile seconds before the crash, so maybe she lost concentration. Unfortunately, the call was from an unregistered mobile, so we don't know who she was speaking to, but whatever happened, the car ended up upside down.'

Becky nodded. 'Everybody has always assumed Natasha climbed out of the car and ran off, frightened by what had happened. They thought she must have been lying dead in a ditch somewhere, or fallen down some unknown pothole, crawled into a disused shed, whatever. The view was that everywhere possible had been searched, but there's no such thing as one hundred per cent coverage. So now we know she *wasn't* lying in a ditch somewhere, we have to assume that somebody took her in. Maybe somebody who wanted a child – and apparently she was a beautiful little girl – found her, and kept her. They would have had to hide her – because there's no doubt at all that they would have known who she was, given the media coverage.'

'What about abduction from the scene?' Tom asked.

Becky leaned back and dragged a strand of her dark hair across her face, twisting it around her finger. For a moment, Tom thought she was going to put it in her mouth, the way his daughter Lucy did when she was thinking. Becky must have caught his amused glance, because she dropped the hair and leaned forwards again.

'I wish I knew, but it seems highly unlikely that somebody wanting a child so much would just happen to be driving past on that particular road at precisely the right moment. The whole situation is extraordinary. The only other thing I wondered is whether Natasha witnessed something that had happened. Maybe some drunk caused the accident, and, fearing that the child might be able to give evidence, they thought the best thing would be to take her. If they were really drunk, that might have made sense.'

'It's as plausible as any other scenario at the moment. What ideas do you have about why she's back now?'

'Maybe as a young child she couldn't remember where she

77

lived. Maybe something reminded her, gave her back the memory of her home. Perhaps she thumbed a lift, but it's an isolated spot, so there wouldn't be much in the way of traffic.'

'Or then again, maybe somebody brought her back – her appeal had gone.'

'Possibly. That might make more sense, given that she's rejecting her family. If she'd chosen to come back, why the hostility?'

'Because she feels as if she doesn't belong? She's a stranger to them, and them to her. Perhaps she's not rejecting them. Perhaps she's scared of *being* rejected. The only person who's going to be able to tell us is Natasha. And she's saying nothing.'

❖

Leo's car wasn't in the drive when Tom got home, but he didn't think she would be far behind him. For the second night running, he hadn't felt like cooking and she had agreed to pick up the one takeaway that he loved. Fish and chips.

He had been in the house for about twenty minutes when he heard the front door slam. He walked into the hall towards where Leo was shrugging off her coat.

'Bloody raining again,' she muttered, hanging the wet jacket on a hook. She turned and gave Tom a dazzling smile, holding up a white carrier bag from which steam seemed to be emanating.

He pulled her to him and felt one arm travel up and round his shoulders, holding the nape of his neck and pulling his mouth towards hers. He could feel every inch of her body pressed against his, and was about to relegate the thought of food to the bottom of his list of priorities when Leo pushed back slightly, nipping his bottom lip gently with her teeth.

'Food first. Come on. Nothing worse than soggy cold chips.'

Tom groaned. 'You're a hard woman, Leo Harris.' She raised her eyebrows and looked at him, saying nothing. He grabbed the bag of fish and chips and led the way into the kitchen.

Not bad, Tom thought as he greedily devoured a piece of crispy battered haddock, although in his mind the flavour had never been quite the same since the days when everything was cooked in dripping. One of the tastes of his childhood. An image of Jack leaped into his mind. Fish and chips had been his favourite meal, and the one thing guaranteed to bring him out of his bedroom.

'You're miles away, Tom. Are you worrying about work?' Leo asked.

Tom smiled. 'No, it's the food – fish and chips bring back a lot of memories of when Jack and I were kids. It was the one meal we were allowed to eat on our knees when *Blake's 7* was on the TV. We were both addicted.'

'To the chips, or to *Blake's 7*?'

'Both,' Tom answered with a smile.

'You've never talked about Jack much, you know,' Leo said. 'You might not want to talk about how you felt when he died but as I've been helping with the papers, can you at least tell me how he first got started in the world of computer security?'

Tom took a sip of his wine. Having spent years trying to avoid talking about Jack, his nerdy brother, it was a difficult habit to break.

'It's hard to know where to start, really. He was a bit of a law unto himself, but once he was bitten by the computer bug, he became a gaming fanatic whose only desire was to hack the code to find out how each game was constructed so that he could build something bigger – better. We always thought he would end up as a games programmer, but he was bored with that by the time he was sixteen. Then something happened which seemed to refocus him.' Tom paused for a moment, remembering the day that everything seemed to change. 'He knew this kid from school – quite how he knew anybody from the odd day or two that he bothered turning up for lessons by that point, I don't know. I think the lad's name was Ethan – that's it, Ethan Bentley. Jack used to call him Posh Guy because he had the same name as a posh car, and, unlike the rest of the kids at our school, he had a wealthy dad who ran a rather dodgy hotel – called Bentley's, obviously.'

'Dodgy?' Leo asked.

'Everybody knew about Bentley's. They didn't exactly rent rooms by the hour, but it was certainly the favourite hotel for the great and the good of Manchester when they were having an affair, or just fancied something a bit different.'

Leo screwed her face up in distaste as Tom continued.

'I think Mr Bentley procured various services that nobody would want to be caught acquiring for themselves, if you get my drift. Ethan came to see Jack – told him that somebody had hacked into his dad's computer system and accessed customer records. Fortunately, the hacker had only managed to get one or two bits of information, but he was blackmailing the dad – asking for money – said he would reveal the names to the press. So Ethan had a word with Jack, who went in and made Bentley's computer network watertight. Jack said it was a doddle. Ethan's dad told all his top customers that he could now guarantee their privacy thanks to his wonderfully secure system, and then a few of them contacted Jack to request his services. He went from strength to strength. Ethan, or Posh Guy, was always round at our house after that.'

'You scowled when you said that, you know. Didn't you like him?'

'He was pretty vile to me – told me to fuck off if I ever went into Jack's room when he was there.'

'Charming. What did Jack do?'

'Confrontation wasn't his thing. He just looked a bit sheepish as if he wanted to say something but couldn't. He used to mutter, "See you later, little brother," or something to take the edge off it.'

'Oh well, in spite of keeping such bad company, Jack certainly made good – with knobs on.'

Tom was quiet. This was probably the moment when he should have told Leo about the file on the SD card, and the fact that it was password protected. Not to mention the other fact – that the filename was Jack's hacker alias. But he couldn't. Not yet, at least. He knew she would push him to check it out, and he wasn't entirely sure he wanted to.

16

Day Three

The kitchen seemed a cold place to Emma the next morning. She and David had had a row before he left for work and since then the warmth had seeped from her bones. She couldn't remember them ever falling out in all the time they had known each other. Theirs was a marriage without turbulence or stress, and they had both eagerly welcomed the peace of an undemanding relationship.

Last night they had held each other tightly and she had listened as David talked about how he felt.

'Every time I look at Tasha I see Caroline, and the guilt comes rushing back,' he'd said.

Nobody could have known what would happen to Caroline and Natasha that night, and Emma had spent years trying to convince David that life was a series of coincidences – some good, some bad. A split-second decision to go a different way home could result in a person meeting the love of their life, or tripping over a kerbstone and ending up in hospital. Life was made up of these alternative paths, and on the night in question David had made the decision not to go with his family for valid reasons. Now, it seemed he was questioning that decision all over again.

As they had lain whispering in the dark room, Emma had tenderly stroked David's hair in a way she knew he loved. He was beginning to relax into sleep when Emma felt her body tense. She'd heard something.

David muttered, but she had stroked his hair again, murmuring 'Shh' against his ear as he drifted off.

The open doorway was lit by a faint glow from the night-light on the landing and Emma watched the space, mesmerised. Nothing. But still she watched, holding her breath.

She counted. If she saw nothing after she had counted to ten, she would relax. She reached ten, and there was still nothing. She counted again.

David snored softly against her shoulder, but Emma was on her side, facing the door. And then she saw it.

Soundlessly, a shadow, backlit by the nightlight, came to stand in the open doorway. It took first one step and then another into the room.

Despite the baggy pyjamas, Emma recognised the slender figure of her stepdaughter. She could hear her own pulse, pounding on the pillow, but for some reason she waited.

Tasha took another step and Emma could just make out the whites of the girl's eyes, firmly focused on David's back. Finally Emma spoke, her voice sounding unnecessarily loud in the silent bedroom.

'What do you want, Natasha?'

The girl stood still for a second, then turned and walked calmly from the room without saying another word.

Emma leaped out of bed and rushed to fetch Ollie. He could sleep in their bed tonight. She wanted her family together, in one room.

When David had woken up this morning and found Ollie with them, he had accused her of being ridiculous.

'You're neurotic – do you know that? I appreciate she's not your child, but she's mine and I love her. All I ask is that you respect that and don't treat her like some alien in our midst. So what if she came into our room. When Ollie's thirteen, will you be frightened if he wanders into our room in the middle of the night for something? No, I thought not. You'd assume he'd had a bad dream, or wasn't feeling well. Did you even ask?'

Emma felt a rush of guilt. But it hadn't been like that. Natasha had *advanced* into the room. But how could she explain? David didn't give her the chance.

'Keep an eye on her for me today, Emma. I don't want to lose her again. And don't drive her away.'

What did he think she was going to do – throw Tasha out while he was at work? But some of what he said rang disturbingly true. Perhaps she was being neurotic. Perhaps she did resent the girl for upsetting her peaceful life.

She groaned and rubbed her tired eyes. Ollie was silently watching her from his high chair. She didn't think he had ever seen her sad until this week.

Emma heard footsteps on the oak boards in the hall and quickly rearranged her expression into a neutral one. In the reflection from the window she saw the kitchen door opening. Natasha stepped into the room and just stood there. Emma could only think how difficult it must be for this poor child to walk into a room in a house that didn't yet feel like her home.

'Morning, Tasha,' Emma said, forcing a happy tone into her voice, busying herself with Ollie so that she didn't have to look at her stepdaughter.

'Where's…' It was clear to Emma that Natasha didn't know what to say. She had yet to bring herself to call David 'Dad' and although she could see it hurt him, he'd told her she could call him David if she was more comfortable with that. It seemed, though, that this had left her not knowing *what* to call him.

'Where's your dad?' Emma supplied helpfully. 'He thought it was time he went back to work. He came to tell you this morning, but you were fast asleep and he didn't want to disturb you. He's only going to work until lunch, though. He'll be home in a couple of hours to eat with us. Is there anything you'd like to do this morning?'

Emma finally looked properly at Natasha, who shook her head.

'Right – breakfast. Do you want to make the toast, or help Ollie with his yoghurt? He likes to use his spoon, but most of it goes all over his face.'

Ollie was beaming at Natasha. 'Ay, Tassa,' he shouted and laughed, pointing his spoon at her.

Emma watched Natasha's face closely. She stared at Ollie and for a moment her customary frown smoothed out. But then it was as if she pulled herself together and with a determined walk she went over to the bread bin and slotted two slices of granary loaf into the toaster, her back to a disappointed Ollie. It was clear that Ollie had taken to his sister, despite the fact that she was ignoring him and was watching the toaster as though it could offer more interest than anything or anybody else in the room.

Emma fed Ollie the last of his yoghurt, wiped his face, and put him on the floor. He set off at a fast crawl, straight to Natasha. He grabbed her leg and started to pull himself up. He was so close to walking now.

Emma watched carefully. She saw Natasha glance down and smile fleetingly before munching on the toast, her back still to the room.

'Tassa,' Ollie said, pulling on the girl's jeans and looking up at her. He wrapped his arms round her leg and put his face against her calf. 'Ahhh,' he said, as if she was hurt and he was hugging her better.

What can Ollie see that I can't? Emma wondered. *Have I been too hard on the girl?* She saw Tasha look down again with an expression she couldn't read. Then she saw the girl close her eyes and give a tiny shake of the head before she turned back to her toast, ignoring her little brother.

'Come on, Ollie, let's get that nappy changed and get you dressed,' Emma said, scooping Ollie off the floor and ignoring his disgruntled shout. 'Do you want to come, Tasha? He puts up quite a fight.'

Natasha didn't turn round, but Emma could see her head shaking.

She felt sorely tempted to say to her, 'Can you answer me, please,' if only to take a small chunk out of the barrier that the child had erected, but she knew David would be furious. She didn't know whether her irritation was natural, or whether it was because she was only the girl's stepmother. Perhaps if Tasha was her own child she would feel differently about this rudeness.

'Help yourself to more toast, then, if you're not coming with us. We'll only be ten minutes.' Emma could hear the false jovial tones in her voice and knew with every bit of common sense that she possessed that this was wrong. She should just be herself.

She pulled the door closed behind her, but not before she had seen Natasha watching her, her thin body tense, her eyes flicking nervously between Emma and the clock on the wall. Was this a sign that she was anxious for David to be home? Or was she working out how long they had to be alone? Emma felt a cold prickling down her spine.

'Mummy's being ridiculous,' she whispered to Ollie as she carried him out of the room.

❖

Natasha stood in the kitchen, listening to Emma's soft footfalls as she walked upstairs. She could hear her singing quietly to Ollie as he shouted encouragement.

She hadn't missed the look that Emma had given her as she had gone out of the door and hoped her own face hadn't given too much away.

She glanced out of the window. This had worked out better than she thought. Was it time yet?

Natasha was nervous. It had all seemed so simple, but suddenly it didn't any longer. Suddenly it felt huge, as if a massive truck was hurtling towards her and she couldn't get out of the way.

She had been so confident, so sure she could do this. But now?

Then she thought of why: why she had believed it would be easy; why it was the right thing. And she thought of the alternative. Her nerves calmed a little.

She looked at the clock again.

Tasha knew Emma was perfectly capable of changing Ollie's nappy in a matter of minutes, but as he had just finished breakfast and was still in his pyjamas, there would be the battle of getting him dressed. She also suspected Emma might take as long as possible to avoid having to spend too much time down here. With her.

That was good, wasn't it? It was much better if Emma hated her.

Was the time right?

She tiptoed over to the door and pulled it ajar slightly. From upstairs she could hear Ollie's shouts of protest, and Emma's gentle laugh. Somehow Natasha knew that Emma would be tickling her son's tummy.

She closed the door quietly and checked the clock for the final time.

Her arms stiff by her sides, she clenched her fists.

'You can do this,' she muttered. 'You can *do* this.'

17

Since the appeal had gone live for information about the young girl whose body had been found in the woods, Becky and her team had been inundated with calls from people who claimed some girl they knew hadn't been seen for a few days. Despite the level of detail about age, ethnicity and hair colour, further investigation almost always revealed that the child they were referring to was black, or seventeen – or in one case was even a boy. Unfortunately, if a child really was missing it had to be checked out – not to help solve this case, but because another child might be at risk. Inevitably, the vast majority of calls turned into a wild goose chase.

'It's not a bloody *game*,' Becky muttered, to nobody in particular. The trouble was that they couldn't issue a photo – it would be too disturbing. They were hoping to get the DNA results for Amy Davidson back soon – even if only to rule her out – but this list of possible candidates was sadly growing longer with each call they received.

The one thing they had been able to do, though, was circulate photos of Natasha Joseph around the local forces, in case she had appeared on anybody's radar. They still needed to know what had happened to her, and where she had been. For once, it seemed there was some news.

'I think we've got a real lead this time.' Nic Havers was waving a piece of paper at Becky, looking pleased with himself. 'Have you got a moment?'

'Course I have.' Since joining CID, Nic had a perpetual smile on his face, and to Becky he looked like an overgrown puppy with the most enormous feet and the eager face of a child at Christmas.

'I've been speaking to British Transport Police,' Nic said. 'They think they have Natasha on camera. In fact, they've been looking for her, waiting until the next time she steps on one of their trains to keep an eye on her – possibly arrest her.'

Becky looked surprised.

'What do they think she's done?'

'They want to come in and talk to us about it.'

'Well done, Nic. I'll give DCI Douglas a call to see if he wants to join us. When are they coming?'

'Now, apparently.'

Becky raised her eyebrows in surprise and reached for the phone.

❖

As she waited for Tom and British Transport Police to arrive, Becky walked across the incident room to have a word with Charley.

'Now you've had a bit of time to think about it, what's your take on Natasha, Charley?'

The young detective chewed her bottom lip and gave a small shake of the head.

'I think she's confused. She probably felt secure with the people she's been living with. However they treated her, that's what she now considers to be the norm. My guess is that she would prefer right now to be back where she understands the rules.'

'You mean she could be suffering from a kind of Stockholm syndrome – you know, a younger version of Patty Hearst?' Becky asked. 'I'm not old enough to have been around at the time, but Hearst was kidnapped in her late teens. Within a few weeks of her abduction she joined her kidnappers and even took part in a bank raid with them. So if just weeks of mind control, imprisonment and abuse made a nineteen-year-old feel she belonged with her captors, what impact could six *years* of that life have on a child as young as Tasha?'

Charley's look of revulsion at the idea didn't escape Becky. She clearly had a lot to learn. Expect the worst and be surprised if it's not as bad as you think was Becky's motto. That way people ceased to have the ability to shock and appal you.

Becky's thoughts were interrupted as the door to the incident room opened and two men in British Transport Police uniform entered. Both well over six feet tall; one of them had shoulders like an American footballer and a face to match, with a squashed nose and a wide forehead. Becky didn't think she would like to argue with him about non-payment of her train fare.

Tom Douglas was right behind them, and she walked across to meet her visitors.

Once the formalities had been completed, the big burly policeman, who had introduced himself as PC Mark Heywood, asked if he could use Becky's computer to access the CCTV footage he had uploaded. It took no more than a few seconds for Heywood to pull up a grainy picture. He clicked the play icon.

The sequence lasted a few seconds.

Tasha, Becky thought. A young girl with fair hair wearing a dark duffle coat was walking through the train. A dark-haired lad who looked to be in his mid-teens was walking towards her and stood to one side to let her pass. She glanced at him with a half smile, but didn't speak and walked on, out of shot.

'Is that your girl?' Heywood asked Becky.

'Yes. I'm as certain as I can be from this video that the girl is Natasha Joseph. But why have you got this footage?'

'We'd been alerted to something going on on routes to the north of the city, so we pulled in the CCTV from the trains for the relevant period. That's where we found your girl.'

'When was this, and what's she done?' Tom asked.

'She boarded a train to Leeds at Manchester Victoria a couple of weeks ago. She got off at Boswell Bridge – we can show you that.' He clicked again. It was a view of a small, provincial-looking station. Natasha was standing on the platform talking to a slightly older lad and she pulled off her backpack and put it down on the bench. A few minutes later she walked away and the boy picked up the backpack, disappearing in the opposite direction.

Becky knew exactly what this was and didn't really need to ask.

'Drugs?' she said.

The policeman slowly nodded his head.

18

When she was pregnant Emma hadn't wanted to know whether she was having a boy or a girl, so had decorated Ollie's nursery in a pale sage green and bought a wonderful huge tree stencil to paint in white on one wall. It was a warm and cosy room, and Emma was loath to leave it and venture back into the chilly atmosphere downstairs.

The addition of a window seat in the room had been inspired, and she spent a lot of time sitting there with Ollie, pointing out the birds, the trees and the occasional aeroplane, but her favourite chair was the wingback recliner that she had bought for when she was feeding Ollie in the middle of the night. It was so comfortable that she had often pulled a throw over herself after feeding him and had fallen asleep there.

Hiding up here was ridiculous, though.

'Come on, little man, we're all done.' Emma pulled Ollie's last sock on and gazed at her son for a moment. Ollie still felt a bit hot and seemed tetchy and unsettled. She had to find a way to get back to some sort of normality for her son's sake.

With a sigh, she picked him up and made her way downstairs, mentally rehearsing her tone of voice and how to be non-confrontational with Natasha.

'Okay – I'm going to make a cake. Would you like to help?' she said in a jolly voice as she pushed open the kitchen door.

She smiled at Ollie. 'Are you going to help your sister and me make a cake, Ollie?'

Emma walked towards the table, expecting to see Natasha

sitting there, eating her breakfast. She looked over her shoulder to the other end of the room.

She stopped dead and turned round. The kitchen was empty. Natasha had gone.

❖

'Oh God, where is she?' Emma whispered to herself, trying to hide her anxiety from Ollie, who was resting on one hip as Emma made a tour of the downstairs rooms.

'She must be upstairs. Must have gone up while I was dressing you, Ollie.' Emma tried to rush up the stairs, but carting Ollie's eleven kilos around was beginning to take its toll.

She pushed open the door to Natasha's room. 'Tasha,' she shouted, her breath catching. 'Are you there, love?'

No answer. But on Natasha's past performance that meant nothing, so she was going to have to look. She dashed around all the upstairs rooms – even checking her and David's en suite bathroom and walk-in wardrobe. There wasn't a sign.

'Where are you, Natasha,' she muttered, taking the stairs down as quickly as she could without putting Ollie at risk.

She checked the places she hadn't thought to look in downstairs – the cloakroom and even the understairs cupboard. But Natasha wasn't here. She wasn't in the house.

'Shit,' she muttered, glancing worriedly at Ollie. But he was too bewildered by all the rushing around to pick up on anything she said. Poor baby.

She hurried into the kitchen and looked out at the garden. It was empty of all but the builders' rubble.

Grasping the handle to the back door, she jerked the buggy from the porch into the kitchen and pushed Ollie into it.

'We're going to have to go and look for her, sweetheart. Okay?'

'Kay,' Ollie smiled. He didn't know what was going on, but he sensed excitement of some sort.

Leaving him where he was, Emma went into the back porch to grab her red fleece. It wasn't there.

'What the *hell* have I done with it?' she said. She grabbed David's dark-grey gardening fleece with the paint stains and holes in, and a blanket to put over Ollie. Shoving her feet into a pair of wellingtons, she went back into the kitchen and tucked the blanket around her son.

'Stay under there, poppet. We're not going to be out for long.'

Kicking the door wide with the heel of her left foot, she manoeuvred Ollie through the porch and down the back steps.

Running as fast as she could, she made her way along the side path by the impenetrable high hedge that bordered a narrow track into the fields beyond. They were halfway along the path when she heard a voice from the far side of the hedge. She heard four words.

'It wasn't my fault.'

She stopped to listen. It was Tasha's voice. She desperately wanted to hear what else was said, but Ollie heard the voice too.

'Ay, ay, Tassa,' he called at the top of his little voice.

The talking stopped, and Emma started to run. She wanted to know who the hell was with Tasha. She raced along the path, Ollie bumping up and down in his buggy. But as she reached the side gate, Natasha came into view wearing Emma's fleece, her face red, her eyes shining – but whether from anger or unshed tears, Emma couldn't tell.

'Who were you talking to, Natasha?' she asked, trying to keep her tone as level as possible.

'What?' Natasha answered rudely, avoiding Emma's eyes. 'You must be hearing things.'

Emma left Ollie in his buggy and walked towards Natasha, aiming to get past her to check for herself. But Natasha leaned back against the gate, both elbows resting nonchalantly on the top.

'Move,' Emma said. Natasha's mouth settled into a hard line and she shook her head.

'*Move*, Natasha,' Emma repeated. The girl stared defiantly back at her.

Pushing Ollie to one side, where she could keep him in view, Emma ran along the path at the front of the house, down the drive and through the gate, never letting Ollie out of her sight. By the time she was in the lane, it was empty. There was nobody there.

She heard a mirthless laugh behind her.

'Come on, Ollie,' Natasha said, grabbing the buggy and turning it back towards the house. 'Let's go in.'

'Leave him!' Emma shouted. 'Don't touch him.'

Emma stopped dead. *Why had she said that*? She didn't know, she didn't care. But all of a sudden, she didn't want Natasha to be alone with her baby.

19

'Why did you let her out of your sight? You know how vulnerable she is right now. What were you *thinking*?' David was pacing the kitchen floor, one hand repeatedly scraping the hair back off his forehead.

'For God's sake, David, she's thirteen years old. She's not a small child who's going to wander out onto a busy road, and I would have thought the last thing she would want is to be treated like a prisoner. We don't know how she's been treated in the past, but that would seem to me to be counterproductive if we want to bring her into this family.'

'What do you mean, *if* we want to bring her into this family. She *is* in this family.' David had stopped pacing and was glaring at Emma. She silently cursed herself.

'Sorry. That was a bad choice of words. Of course she's part of this family, but I meant that if we want her to *accept* that she's part of this family.'

'Well maybe if you stopped treating her like a stranger it would help,' he said, his voice petulant.

Emma was about to launch into her own defence when her frustration evaporated. Irritating and irrational as David was being, she couldn't imagine how he must feel at the moment. And she couldn't in all honesty ignore her own negative feelings – however fleeting – about her stepdaughter.

She took two steps towards him and reached out her hand for his.

'Let's stop this, and we should try to keep our voices down.

Ollie's asleep,' she said, turning to look at her son. 'He was so upset by all the shouting. It's taken nearly the full hour since I phoned you to get him settled.' To Emma, even in sleep Ollie looked fretful. He kept moving his head from side to side, and his cheeks were so red. She needed to calm everything down for his sake, if nobody else's.

'The important thing is that Tasha came back,' Emma said, squeezing David's hand gently. 'She said she wanted a bit of fresh air and so she'd gone for a walk down the lane.'

'You said she was talking to somebody. What if the people that took her had grabbed her again? What then?' David said. Emma could feel a slight tremor run through his body, and she gently pulled him towards her and put her arms around his waist.

'That's exactly why I ran after her,' she said. 'Look, I've thought about this a lot. Somebody must have brought her back.' She paused at his impatient look but made herself go on. 'Think about it. How could she have got here on her own? That afternoon when she appeared in the kitchen, she wasn't wet. It hadn't stopped raining all day, so she can't have walked here. I really think they must have decided to let her go, for reasons that we don't understand yet, but we will. And yes, I did think I heard her talking to someone out in the lane but I wasn't fast enough to see who it was, and I could have been wrong.'

She pulled David closer and he rested his cheek against hers. 'There's so much we don't understand. Why won't she talk to us? She's my daughter.'

As Emma searched for some words of comfort, their momentary silence was interrupted by the strident peal of the front door bell. She glanced at David and raised her eyebrows in question.

'I'll get it,' he said. 'And I'll get rid of whoever it is.' He smiled at her – the first normal smile she had seen in days and she felt a layer of anxiety fade away. But it did nothing to eradicate the underlying fear that had no name – the one she couldn't even voice to her husband.

She could hear David's footsteps coming back along the hall and could immediately tell that he wasn't alone.

The door opened. 'It's the police,' David said, ushering Becky Robinson and Charlotte Hughes into the room. 'They want to talk to Tasha again.'

❖

Becky sensed a slight change in atmosphere when she entered the Josephs' kitchen. Emma and David appeared more in control, no longer reeling from events. She felt sure she was about to disrupt their fragile peace.

'Inspector Robinson, what can we do for you?' Emma asked, a puzzled expression on her face.

'I'm sorry that we have to disturb you. I know we promised to leave you alone for a couple of days, but something's come up with regard to Natasha, and we need to bring you up to speed. And please – call me Becky. This is Charley. It will probably make Natasha more comfortable if we drop the formality.'

'Do you mind if we go into the other room,' Emma said. She nodded her head towards Ollie, and Becky smiled at his cute face. Babies were at their most adorable when they were asleep, as far as she was concerned.

'Of course. Is there somewhere with a table?' she asked.

David led the way into a formal dining room that Becky hadn't seen before. She couldn't imagine it was used much, given they had such a huge table in the kitchen cum living room, but maybe the less friendly environment would suit her purposes.

David indicated that they should all sit down and slowly, with as much detail as possible, Becky explained what they had seen on the CCTV on the train and at the station and the conclusions they had drawn.

'Are you sure it was Tasha?' David asked.

'Yes, we are – although of course we'd like your confirmation.'

Becky opened her briefcase and took out four large still images, grabbed from the footage. They were the best shots of Natasha's face and body.

David looked at the images, and then up at Becky. He didn't need to confirm anything – his face said it all.

'But I don't understand why you've assumed this has anything to do with drugs. You've got a thirteen-year-old girl on a train – something I expect lots of kids do to get to school – and she gets off and talks to somebody and forgets her backpack. Why drugs?'

Becky decided not to comment on the fact that they had no evidence to suggest Natasha had ever attended any school – travelling by train or otherwise.

'Well, I don't want to scare you – but initially British Transport Police thought it was either drugs or guns. We're now reasonably certain it's drugs because of where she was going and the station she got off at. They've been monitoring that line for a while, and the pattern's been consistent. The trouble is, they don't want to arrest the kids – they're no use to them really. They want the bastards who are controlling the kids, and that's a bit harder to achieve.' Becky looked at the faces opposite and saw nothing but confusion. They deserved an explanation.

'Somebody will have been using her as a runner – maybe regularly, maybe only this once, we don't know. Kids like Natasha are used as mules – but it doesn't mean that she was managing any kind of drugs operation herself. It does suggest, however, that wherever she's been living there was an association with gangs or maybe an organised crime group.'

David's skin had turned pale and waxy. 'Why would these gangs use kids to do this? Tasha only turned thirteen a couple of weeks ago.'

'They need to be creative, it's too easy for us to catch them otherwise. Look, we're trying to track down the boy she left the backpack with, and I'm confident we will. Then we should know more.'

Becky saw David's expression. Images of the life his daughter had led, a life he had failed to protect her from, must be haunting him.

'Can we talk to Natasha now, do you think? Of course this sadly means she is a suspect in a crime, so you should stay, David.'

Emma stood up.

'I'll tell Tasha to come down and then I'll go and sit with Ollie. I'll leave you to it.'

David's arm shot out and he grabbed Emma's hand in his.

'No, Em. It's time Tasha started to see us as a unit – we're both supporting her, and we're on the same side. If Ollie's awake that's fine too.' Becky saw the doubt in Emma's eyes, as did David it seemed. 'Please, Em?'

She gave him a smile full of such understanding and warmth that Becky felt a stab of envy.

David tried to make conversation with Charley and Becky while they waited. He was clearly distracted, listening for signs of his family coming downstairs, but none of them heard Natasha enter the room. She was so slight that, walking barefoot, she hadn't made a sound, and then suddenly there she was, standing stony-eyed in the doorway.

For a moment, the sight of this strange girl silenced them all, but the trance was broken as they heard Emma approach along the hallway and she followed Natasha into the room, clutching a sleepy Ollie in her arms. He immediately leaned sideways to clutch at Natasha's jumper, trying to attract her attention. She ignored him.

'Sit down please, Tasha,' David said. 'Becky and Charley want a chat with you.' David looked towards his wife, who was heading back towards the door. 'Em? Are you coming?'

'I'll be there in a second – I'm just going to make a drink for Ollie and Tasha.'

Becky smiled and said hi to Natasha, neither expecting nor getting any response. Sitting down, Natasha pulled the sleeves of her jumper down over her hands and, head bowed, she played with the same loose thread as she had the last time they had seen her, watching more of the sleeve unravel.

Becky turned the photos of Natasha back over and pushed them across the table.

'Can you take a look at these photos, Tasha,' Charley said, her voice gentle.

Natasha raised her eyes to Charley's and for a second Becky was sure she glimpsed a vulnerability, a plea for understanding, before the shutters came back down.

She lowered her head to look at the pictures, and Becky didn't need to be a child psychologist to recognise the expression that passed over her face. Even with her head down, Becky saw Natasha's eyes open wide for a second, the top teeth come down over the bottom lip. And now she wouldn't meet anybody's eyes, staring instead at a teapot in the centre of the table.

'Do you want to tell us about this, Tasha?' Charley asked. There was no answer.

'What was in the bag. Can you tell me that?' Becky continued. 'We're asking you to tell us the truth, Tasha.'

David spoke. 'Tasha, can you please answer Inspector Robinson?' Becky wasn't sure whether her title was being used to scare Natasha or not, but it didn't seem to have much effect. They all stayed silent, and when David looked at Becky she shook her head slightly. He got the message and resisted his obvious temptation to try to persuade his daughter to talk.

Nobody spoke for over two minutes.

'It was books.'

'Yes? What sort of books – novels, schoolbooks?'

'Just books.'

'Okay – so why did you leave the backpack?'

'Forgot it.'

'Did you report it lost?'

A shake of the head.

'Whose books were they?'

'Mine.'

'What kind of books did you have, Tasha?'

A shrug.

'Who was the boy at the station you were talking to? Did you know him?'

'No.'

'Why did you talk to him, then?'

A shrug.

'Tasha, we know you caught the next train back. You never left the station, in fact. You arrived on one train, spoke to the boy, dumped your backpack and caught a train back fifteen minutes later. So why did you go all that way?'

'Supposed to meet a friend.'

'What's the friend called?'

There was a pause. Natasha looked as if she thought about shrugging again, but seemingly realised that she should have known the name of her friend. The pause went on for quite a few seconds.

'She's called Serena.'

'Does Serena have a surname?'

'Dunno – she's just Serena to me.'

And so it went on. Round and round in circles. They got nothing else from her. She didn't know where this Serena lived, had no means of contacting her and, when pushed, Natasha answered, 'She's moved.'

Becky had one more card left to play. She reached into her briefcase and pulled out another photo.

'Who's this, then?' she asked.

Natasha gave it an indifferent glance, clearly expecting to see another photo of the boy at the station. But it wasn't. It was somebody else entirely.

The girl didn't look up, but Becky saw her mouth open slightly and every muscle in her body went rigid. She waited, perched on the edge of her seat for no more than ten seconds. When she looked up, her face was wiped of expression.

'I don't know him,' she said.

Her ability to present an impassive face was remarkable for one so young, but as far as Becky knew, nobody had the ability to control when their pupils dilated.

20

'Boh, boh, beep, beep,' Ollie said in his singsong voice as Emma carried him upstairs for his bath and bed. He seemed wide awake at the moment, his head bobbing from side to side, as if there were a tune in his head somewhere but he hadn't yet learned to make the right notes. Fortunately, Emma knew that as soon as she put Ollie in his cot, he would go to sleep.

And long may it continue, she thought, given that neither she nor David seemed to have had a decent night's sleep in days.

As soon as the police had left after dropping their bombshell, David had called his daughter back downstairs to the dining room. They had tried to speak to her about the drug trafficking, but once again had failed to make any progress.

'Tasha, nobody's blaming you for any of this. We know that sometimes people live in environments where drugs are commonplace, and that children can be made to do things they wouldn't do out of choice. You won't tell us about your life over the last six years, but anything you were forced to do is absolutely not your fault. Do you understand?'

David had been calm and reasonable with Natasha, but it hadn't helped. In the end he had decided to go back to the office to work on a report he said he had been struggling to finish. Emma didn't believe him. He wanted to go somewhere quiet and lick his wounds. He would be back for dinner, but for a while Emma had just enjoyed spending some time playing with her baby and pretending that everything was normal. Tasha, of course, was in her room and couldn't be tempted downstairs.

Emma laid Ollie tenderly in his cot and bent down to give him a kiss, breathing in the aroma of baby powder and nuzzling her nose against his soft skin. She sat down in her comfy chair, just looking at her son as he drifted off to sleep. This had always been her idea of bliss, watching his eyes flutter for a while until they were fully closed and he was fast asleep. But the disruption created by Natasha's arrival had ripped that gentle peace apart. It wasn't the child's fault, but in spite of that – and hating herself for the thought – she wished she had stayed hidden.

The room suddenly felt hot and airless, guilt at her selfishness causing her cheeks to flush. She stood up and opened the window slightly, pulling the curtain across so that there was no danger of Ollie being in a draught.

Through the open window she could vaguely hear a voice, although she could hardly make out any words. Maybe she had left the radio on downstairs.

Then she heard one word. 'When?' She stayed completely still, her ears straining to hear more. There was silence for a few seconds. '*Please* – make it soon.'

Although the voice was using a pleading tone she had never heard before, there was no doubt in her mind that this wasn't the radio. It was Natasha.

❖

'David, she was talking to somebody,' Emma whispered into the kitchen phone, terrified that Natasha would come downstairs and hear her reporting back to David. 'Yes, of course I'm sure. She sounded upset, but when I knocked on her door she refused to answer. I didn't want her to know that I'd heard her, but when I tried the door she'd put something behind it again. I asked if she wanted to help me make a pizza, but I got no response.'

'I was hoping this would happen,' David said, and Emma could hear the smile in his voice. 'Not that something would upset

105

her, of course, but that she would use the phone I gave her to contact somebody from her other life.'

'What, so we can trace them?' Emma said, hope in her voice.

'Yes, I'm tracking all her calls. I put an app on the phone before I gave it to her. I can see who she's called, read her texts and find out where she is at any given moment.'

'Why didn't you *tell* me?' Emma asked, uncertain whether she should applaud David's cleverness or be appalled at his duplicity with his daughter.

'Because I didn't know if you would approve. If you thought it was wrong thing to do, I wouldn't have put it past you to tell her.'

Emma was speechless.

'Don't give me the silent treatment, Emma. If she'd gone missing again, I wanted to know where she was. I'm not losing her again, and don't forget that when she wandered off you were out of your mind with worry.'

'I know,' Emma said softly. If somebody had taken Ollie from her she would want to rip their throat out with her bare hands, so she could understand how David must feel.

Emma could hear David typing something into his keyboard.

'I checked this morning, and up to now she hasn't used her phone for anything. But it should show up now. Here we go.'

There was a pause.

'Huh. That's odd. Emma, are you sure you heard her talking? It couldn't have been the radio?'

'I'm positive. Why?'

'Because I'm checking her records now, and she hasn't made any calls. Her phone hasn't been used at all since the day we gave it to her.'

❖

It's all going wrong. I've screwed up.

Natasha was staring out of her bedroom window, seeing nothing. It had all seemed so easy to start with. Anything was better than the alternative. She would have been thrown in The Pit if she had refused – just for as long as it took to make her do as she was told – and then she would have gone the way of the others, ended up like Izzy.

She felt the back of her eyes sting but fought it. She might be wrong about Izzy. Maybe it wasn't her body that the police had found. She should never have told Izzy about the job, though. It was dangerous and stupid. But she had needed somebody to tell her she was doing the right thing.

Now the police had that CCTV footage on the train. She'd been such an idiot, smiling at him like that. If it ever got out – got back to *them* – they would kill her. They would never trust her again.

Emma didn't trust her either. For one awful moment when Natasha had come back into the house that morning, she had thought Emma was going to search her pockets. But she had refused to take the fleece off and had escaped up here, still wearing it. She had managed to hide everything, but it had been close.

Tonight she was going to have to sneak downstairs when they were asleep and do what she'd been told to do. The kitchen and the sitting room. Those were her instructions. She knew what to do. She'd already sorted David and Emma's bedroom, and everything seemed to be working just fine.

Natasha knew she should be happy – this was payback time. But now the police had come nosing around, and she wasn't supposed to let that happen. She would be punished. Surely she'd suffered enough?

And whose fault is that? a little voice whispered in her ear.

She knew the answer. She knew who was to blame for all of it.

She was getting soft, living in this world where people played at being nice to each other. Nobody was nice really. She knew that – she'd seen it all her life. One minute nice as pie, next minute beating the shit out of each other.

Emma played at being nice, but Tasha knew what she really thought. She thought Tasha had disrupted her perfect life. Emma had replaced Tasha's mum in this house and now she didn't want to have to live with the daughter, even though she pretended otherwise.

If you think your life's been messed up, Emma – you ain't seen nothing yet.

Tasha's mum really *had* been nice, though, and Tasha had to hang on to that. She had to remember she wasn't just doing this for herself. She was doing it for her dead mother.

You didn't deserve to die, Mum.

21

Tom was struggling to concentrate on his work and he really needed to get his focus back. He kept thinking about that SD card and the spreadsheet. He had finally told Leo about the password-protected file the night before; he had no idea why it worried him, but it kept niggling away like an itch he couldn't scratch.

'Oh, for God's sake,' he muttered, pulling his phone towards him and pressing the number for Becky's extension.

'Becky – update, please. My office.' Quite why he was taking it out on Becky, he didn't know. He took a deep breath.

Becky's normally cheerful face was looking worried as she poked her head round the doorframe.

'Is it safe to come in?' she asked, flushing slightly as if she regretted her slightly facetious tone.

Tom gave her a lopsided smile of apology, and Becky pulled over a chair and sat down.

'Okay, here's where we're at,' she said, consulting the file she had brought with her. 'The local guys have tracked down the boy Natasha spoke to briefly at the station and they found nothing on him at all. They asked why he'd taken the backpack she'd left on the bench, and he said he'd taken it to ask his mum what to do with it. The station was an unmanned one, so he had nobody to give it to. But he said he bumped into some mates on his way home, so he dumped it.'

'Course he did. No doubt he can't remember where exactly.'

'The locals think he's taking orders from somebody, but their guess is that he doesn't know who. They think the kids have been shipping skunk grown somewhere in Manchester. Oh, and this isn't random. It's organised.'

Tom had suspected that would be the case, and he sighed inwardly. Serious and organised crime was a daily reality costing the country billions each year, causing immense damage to communities and individuals through violence, drug use and child sexual exploitation. He hated it, and all those involved in it, with a passion.

Becky was watching him carefully, and he adopted a neutral expression, signalling that she should continue.

'We showed Natasha a picture of the other boy on the train – do you remember him? The lad that looked like a young and slightly chubby-faced Tom Cruise before he got a chin. Not only did she recognise him, but the fact that we had his picture and we'd seen her smiling at him seemed to scare her. Anyway, Transport Police think they may have a lead on him. He's been seen before. There was a definite sense of a message being passed between him and Natasha. If he's part of the same gang, we're hoping we can find a link and discover how Natasha fits into the picture. But all this new information has got me thinking.'

Becky leaned forwards and rested her arms on Tom's desk.

'The most logical interpretation of events six years ago is that Natasha was found in the aftermath of the accident – a cute little girl – and somebody decided to keep her. So why let her go now? Did she escape from whoever had her, or did they want to be rid of her? I keep going round in circles, but the drugs give the initial abduction a much more sinister slant, don't they?'

Tom tilted his chair back to listen to Becky's ideas, his gaze on a blank area of innocuous beige wall, his mind one hundred per cent on Natasha Joseph.

'Being realistic, Tom, what are the chances that this little girl, on a dark winter's night on a country lane, just happened to be picked up by members of some organised crime group? A crew smart enough to use kids as mules to get their skunk out to the sticks? What – were they out on a jolly that evening and happened upon her? There's more chance of being hit by a flying tortoise, I'd have thought.'

Tom smiled. 'You're right, but it could have been some local scumbag who found her. Somebody at the bottom of the pecking order? Maybe thought he could use her – demand money from her father for her safe return. That would make sense, although with all the police activity at the time, they would have had to wait a while to have any chance of success.'

'All I can say is that if she's been living with somebody associated with organised crime at any level, it must have been a shit life. You'd have thought she'd be seriously relieved to be out of the place, wouldn't you? As it is, she seems to be hanging in there by a thread at the family home.' Becky paused. 'But I still keep going back to the night of the accident. What if we're missing the obvious? What if she was a target?'

'The idea had occurred to me, but a **target** for what?'

Becky shrugged. 'No idea, at the moment. Whatever happened and whoever took her, we need to know whether they let her go or she managed to escape. If she's run away, they'll be looking for her. If she's been running drugs for them, the chances are she knows too much. We need to seriously consider if this child is in danger.'

❖

Tom and Becky's discussion had finally been brought to an abrupt halt when Becky realised it was time for the evening briefing. Tom went with her and sat at the back of the incident room, watching her run through the evidence on the dead girl, giving the team instructions on the next steps.

She was good. Thorough, and always prepared to listen to ideas from members of her team.

Tom quietly left the room before the meeting ended, giving

Becky some space. There was little more he could do that evening, so he grabbed his coat and gave Leo a quick call to say he was on his way.

It had taken Tom a long time to pluck up the courage to start a new relationship after his marriage failed, but then he had moved into his Cheshire cottage and fallen for Leo Harris – the sister of his next-door neighbour. Tom smiled at the thought. He had, without a doubt, chosen the most difficult, commitment-phobic woman in the north of England. There were times when it felt as if she would never entirely trust him, and Tom wasn't always sure he could live with that, but Leo's father had led a double life with two wives for many years, and it was understandable that she found it difficult to have faith in a man.

Tonight they were going to meet at Leo's apartment because she was working on a paper for her psychology degree, so Tom had agreed to call round and cook her supper, spend a couple of hours with her and then leave her to get on with her work.

He had stopped at the supermarket on his way to Leo's and bought the ingredients to make a quick stir-fry, and as he let himself into the apartment he thought, not for the first time, how well Leo had chosen her home. A large open-plan space in an old converted warehouse, the defined cooking, eating, relaxing and working areas all blended together against the bare brick walls and the polished wooden floors.

Leo was focusing intently on her computer screen but turned to flash Tom a smile. She started to push herself up from her seat, but he walked over and bent down to kiss her.

'Carry on with whatever you're doing. I'll make a start on the supper. Do you want a drink?'

Leo reached out an arm and wrapped it around Tom's hips, pulling him closer. She rested the side of her head against his waist.

'You're my saviour, you know that, don't you?' she said.

'What, because I've made you realise that not all men are bad?' Tom stroked her hair gently.

'No,' Leo swatted him on the bottom. 'Because you feed me – without you I would live on toast and yoghurt.'

'Hah – well then I'd better get on with it. Are you going to take a break now or wait until the food's ready?'

Leo pushed the keyboard away from her and stretched.

'I think I'm ready for a break, and there's something I want to talk to you about.'

Tom raised his eyebrows.

'I'll talk. You cook.' Leo stood up and started to push Tom towards the kitchen area, taking a seat at the breakfast bar.

He grabbed a beer from the fridge, and lifted one towards Leo, but she shook her head.

'If I drink, I'll never finish my paper. But I want to talk to you about Jack and the SD card.'

Thoughts he had been pushing to one side started to invade Tom's headspace, and he was momentarily irritated with Leo for spoiling the evening. He almost wished he hadn't told her about the file.

'Don't pull that face, Tom. I know you're trying to ignore this. Now that we've found something potentially interesting you're trying to shove it back into that box marked "no-go area".'

Tom opened a cupboard and started hunting around for the soy sauce, but he didn't respond.

'Don't you get it? Until you've solved this problem and found out what somebody was looking for in Jack's papers, it's going to be lurking at the back of your mind. We need to unravel the puzzle – find out the truth – and then you can deal with it. Squashing it isn't dealing with it.'

'Bloody hell, Leo – are you treating me like one of your case studies now? Am I some kind of psychological phenomenon?'

'Oh piss off. Of course you're not. I'm only thinking of you. You know that.'

Tom could sense Leo's exasperation, and she was right. He said nothing and waited, knowing she hadn't finished.

'Okay – talk to me about passwords. Do you or any of your techie guys know how to break them?'

Tom smiled at that. If Jack had wanted to make something impenetrable, nobody would be able to break it. He was being unfair to Leo, though. He had a fair idea of what the password might be – he just hadn't been sure he wanted to open the file, for reasons he couldn't explain even to himself. It was something to do with the name Silver Sphere.

Leo was looking at him closely.

'What aren't you telling me?' she asked.

Tom pushed the carrots he was chopping away from him and rested his hands on the worktop.

'Jack had a method with passwords. Simple, but effective. He taught me years ago, although he may very well have changed the way he did things before he died. But I guess it's worth a shot. I've used a version of it ever since – but with a few modifications of my own.'

Leo looked at him with her mouth slightly open and her eyes wide, as if to say: 'Were you ever going to tell me this?'

'Okay,' Tom said. 'I should have mentioned it before, but I had to try to remember how Jack's version works.'

Leo waited for about ten seconds. 'Well – go on then,' she said.

'You take the name of the file or of the website that's asking for a password – in this case SILVERSPHERE – all one word. Then you replace every alternate letter with a symbol or number. I'm not sure if I can remember them all, but the password would start with the original letter – a capital S in this case – and then a symbol for the letter I – which I'm fairly certain is an exclamation mark. Then capital L, and I think he used the backward arrow for V. But I can't remember what he used for R. H was definitely the hash tag – oh no, we don't need that, do we. We need P. I think that was the pounds sign. E was the euro – can't remember what it was before we had euros, though.'

'You lost me at backward arrow, I'm afraid,' Leo said.

Tom walked over to the table and picked up a pen.

'Okay, here we go,' he said.

S!L<E?S£H€R€

'The good thing about it is that you can have a different password for every site, but you never forget what it is – as long as you remember the symbols, of course.'

'So is that it, then?' Leo said.

'Sadly no. I can't remember what he used for R. It has to be a standard symbol, or it won't be recognised.'

Tom stared at Leo's keyboard for a moment, mentally going through each of the possible symbols.

He pulled the SD card out of his trouser pocket, slotted it into Leo's computer and clicked the file icon.

'I think I know what it is,' he said, his voice soft and hesitant. 'I think R might be a right hand bracket.'

He typed in the password, pressed ENTER and waited.

It was wrong. The password was rejected.

'Bugger. I was sure it was a bracket.' Tom said, drumming his fingers on the table. He looked at the keyboard again.

'I have an idea,' he said, quickly making a change to the password. He pressed ENTER, and an Excel workbook opened on the screen.

'Bingo. It was a curly bracket, not a normal one,' he muttered, as the screen displayed the first page of the file.

Honegger, Wyss & Cie

A/c no 53696C76657220537068657265

It was a title page, and it meant nothing to Tom. But there was a separate tab and he clicked on that. The second page displayed three columns – dates, names and numbers. There was a pound sign above the numbers column.

Leo was leaning over Tom's shoulder.

'Scroll down a bit,' she said. He knew what she was looking for. The total.

At the bottom of the number column, under the pound sign, there was a figure of a little over four million. The last date in the list was four years before Jack had died.

Leo looked at Tom and shrugged, her interest gone. 'Given that you've already had all of Jack's money, I guess this is just a record of some of it. Not as exciting as we thought,' she said, walking to the kitchen to fetch Tom's beer bottle.

Tom opened a search engine window and typed in the name Honegger, Wyss & Cie. The answer didn't surprise him. A Swiss bank. That explained why there was no account name – only a number. And in Tom's experience, people only had numbered accounts when they had something to hide.

And Leo was wrong about the account. Tom had never seen it before. It wasn't included in Jack's estate, so even his solicitor had known nothing about it.

What were you hiding, Jack?

Tom looked at the list of names and felt his skin grow cold.

The first entry was Bentley. The amount two thousand, five hundred pounds, the date was November 1982.

Tom suddenly knew exactly what Jack had been hiding; this was one secret his brother had buried deep.

'No, he's not asleep. There's been a bit of a miracle this afternoon. Don't hold your breath – it might not last.'

'What do you mean?' Emma asked, grinning at David's obvious pleasure.

'Tasha is not only out of her room, she offered to take Ollie off my hands for a while. She's taken him for a walk. Given what you said yesterday about giving her some freedom, I decided you were right, and so off they went.'

Emma froze. She felt tiny spikes of pain as every inch of her flesh rose in shivering goosebumps.

'What do you mean? Where's she taken him?' She could hear her own voice, measured and reasonable. But there must have been something in it that David recognised, because he turned to her with a flash of irritation twisting his mouth.

'For God's sake, Emma, she's old enough to take Ollie for a walk in his pushchair isn't she? She's been gone for about half an hour, so she'll be back soon. And you know how Ollie adores her. A relationship between those two is just what we need to bring her on side with the rest of us.'

'Where did they go, David?' Emma's voice still sounded calm, but inside she could feel a strange pressure in her chest.

'Only down the lane. I told her to stick to the one and only bit of the lane that has a pavement, and not to go on the narrow parts. She understood that.'

'So why didn't I pass her, then? I came back that way, and there was no sign of her at all. Where are they?' Her voice was rising and her legs started to feel weak, as if they could no longer hold her.

'Stop it, Em. She might have pulled into the farmyard to show Ollie the animals. If she's not back in ten minutes, I'll go and look for her. Okay?'

'No, it's not bloody okay. Go *now*. Find her, David. Just find her.'

David's mouth opened slightly and his brow knitted together in a look of incredulity at Emma's raised tones.

'Jesus, Em, are you overreacting or what?' David took a step towards the back of the chair where his jumper was scrunched up, snatched at it and went to pull it over his head. But then he turned to Emma and smiled.

'Hear that? The side gate. Oh – and look out of the window. Here's Tasha with the pushchair. You see? All's well that ends well.'

He gave Emma a smug smile, and she felt her taut muscles begin to relax as David walked over to the door and opened it.

'Hi, Tasha, I was about to come and meet you. Make sure you'd found your way home.' Emma saw David wince as he realised how inappropriate those words probably were. 'Ollie asleep then?' he asked leaning forwards to look in the buggy.

He lifted his head and turned to Natasha, a look on his face that Emma couldn't interpret.

And suddenly she knew.

She flew over to the door, grabbed the buggy and pulled the hood down.

Emma felt a scream building in her chest, bursting to escape the confines of her ribs, her lungs.

'Where is he? Natasha, where's Ollie?' Emma gasped, fear turning her muscles weak. She clung on to the back of the buggy for support as she looked at Natasha's bowed head, a peculiar half-smile just visible on her face. She wanted to shake her, slap her, anything that would make her say what she'd done with Ollie.

David beat Emma to it. He walked over to his daughter and grabbed her by her upper arms.

'It's okay, Tasha. You just need to tell us so that we can go and get him. Come on, love. Tell us where he is.'

Natasha looked up, straight into Emma's eyes. Her pale face was wiped of expression, and her eyes were like empty pools.

'Gone,' she said.

23

'*Gone.*'

The sound of the word reverberated around Emma's head, echoing, but not making sense. What did she mean 'gone'? She bent down to look in the buggy again, sure that she must have been mistaken. She raised her eyes to Natasha's, and the girl returned her gaze. David stood immobile to one side, staring at his daughter. They were all still – frozen – as if part of some hideous tableau.

The silence was broken by a guttural cry of pain that Emma knew was coming from her, but which she had no power to stop. She flew at Natasha, wanting to strangle the life out of her, but Natasha used the buggy as defence, twisting it to the side to prevent Emma from reaching her in the open doorway, her cold, flat eyes suddenly burning.

David stood transfixed, still staring blankly at his daughter, neither trying to defend her nor helping Emma to reach her.

From nowhere, Natasha seemed to gain strength and she pushed the buggy to one side, raising her arm towards Emma.

'Sit down,' she yelled over Emma's screaming. 'If you want to see that baby of yours again, sit down *now.*'

Emma didn't want to listen. She pushed Natasha out of the way and ran out through the back door, her eyes wildly searching the garden in case Ollie was there. She turned quickly and sprinted down the path, swivelling her head from side to side in case her baby was here, hidden under a shrub.

'*Ollie,*' she screamed, desperate to hear his little voice shouting back to her.

There was nothing.

She raced out of the gate to the road. Nobody. Not a car in sight either.

The lane, she thought. *He must be on the lane.*

She ran along the front of the house, calling her baby's name, sobbing between her shouts. The lane along the side of their garden was empty too.

Emma crouched down in the road, her arms wrapped around her body.

'*Ollie*,' she shouted again, holding her breath, listening for his response.

Silence.

She didn't know how long she had been there, crouched on the lane, when she felt David's arms go around her. He lifted her gently and led her back towards the house – towards Natasha.

'What's she done, David? What's she done with Ollie?'

David had no answer to give her.

Emma wanted, more than she had ever wanted anything in her life, to kill this child of her husband, and as David steered her through the door, she flew at Natasha, her hands like claws. David grabbed Emma's flailing arms and pulled her to him again, wrapping his arms tightly around her while she sobbed and raved.

'Shh, Em. We've got to listen to her. If she's hidden him somewhere, we need to listen – so we can find him as quickly as possible. Please, Em, sit down and hear what she's got to say. Please. I want to find him as much as you do. Come on, darling.'

David led her, shaking, shivering with sudden cold, to a chair. She could feel the tremors running through his body too, as she collapsed into her seat, tears streaming from her eyes. She bit down hard on her bottom lip, trying desperately to control herself until Natasha told her where her baby was. Then she could go and get him. This nightmare would surely be over in a few minutes? She continued to stare in horror at Natasha –

a girl she didn't recognise – hoping it was all some elaborate game.

David sat beside Emma, grasping one of her hands in both of his, and Natasha moved to the other side of the table, her eyes flicking wildly from David to Emma and back again, never resting on either of them for more than a second.

'What have you done?' David asked, his voice sounding calm, but Emma could hear the wavering tones that he was trying so hard to suppress.

'Ollie's safe, David. Your precious son's okay. Is this what you were like when you lost me?' She paused for a second, with a twisted smile. 'Nah – didn't think so.'

Emma couldn't contain the groan that escaped from her swollen lips. This was the most they had ever heard from Natasha, and her soft, slightly high-pitched voice with its Manchester accent sounded like a child's voice. The words were the words of a thug.

'Tell me you haven't hurt him,' David said, his voice soft, pleading. 'He's only a baby. Have you hidden him somewhere? What do you need us to do? *Tell* me, Tasha, then we can go and get him.'

Natasha laughed. Actually laughed – but it was a sound that conveyed no humour.

'He's not outside, David. I told you – he's gone. They took him.'

'Phone the police,' Emma said to David without taking her eyes off her stepdaughter.

'Natasha, I'm your dad. I'm not just David – I'm your *dad*. Whatever the problem is, tell me and we'll fix it. But for now we have to find Ollie, and I'm going to call the police. I'll make sure you're not in trouble. Okay, sweetheart? We know you've had a difficult time, but I promise we'll sort it.'

He picked up his mobile, which was lying on the table – not taking his eyes of his daughter.

Natasha said nothing as David pressed the screen of his

mobile. He stared at the phone, and pressed the screen again, then looked up at his daughter, his puzzled frown bringing a hint of a smile to her face.

'Won't work, David. Yours neither, Emma. I know about phones, see. I've spent years nicking them, fixing them. Your stupid app was never going to catch me out – I'm an expert.'

Emma stared silently at the stranger in front of her. But Natasha hadn't finished.

'And don't go thinking you can sneak into your bedroom to call. The landlines are disabled – except the one in here. You can answer it – in case them detectives call – but you can't call out. My job's to make sure you don't phone the pigs. You got that?'

Emma's last hope disintegrated, shattering what little faith she had left in this girl into shards that pierced every organ of her body like broken glass. This wasn't a hasty decision, a fit of jealousy from the returning daughter – this was carefully planned.

'I'm the only one with a phone now,' she said, holding a mobile that Emma had never seen before in the air. Was that what she'd had in the pocket of the fleece yesterday? Natasha hadn't finished, though.

'I'll tell you what you've got to do as soon as they tell me. Then Ollie can come back and I can go home. You got that, David?'

David didn't move. He put his phone down and stared at his daughter, his face stark in the bright kitchen lights.

Emma closed her eyes and focused on an image of her baby boy. *Ollie.* She was screaming inside for her son; sound and vision around her merged as one and spun, out of control, as she felt herself falling against her husband, curling herself into a tight ball, a low moan of despair echoing around the kitchen.

❖

They were getting nowhere. For twenty minutes they had shouted, pleaded, begged, but Natasha would say nothing more than she had already, and she would no longer look them in the eye.

She sat, nursing her mobile, as if that was where the answer lay. David had tried to take it from her, to see who was listed, but she had sneered at him for being so stupid, and he had backed away, his eyes blazing, as he seemed to realise how close he had come to hurting one of his children in order to save the other.

Now Emma stood at the far end of the kitchen, anger, desperation and the agony of loss fighting for dominance in her heart and her mind. She had never in her life wanted to physically hurt anybody, but Tasha wasn't her child and she didn't know if she could control herself. She wanted the girl in her sight, but as far away as she could get. She felt a crushing urge to grab Natasha by her hair and drag her, howling in pain, outside to search for Ollie – her baby. What would he be feeling now? Would he know what was happening? He would know that his mummy wasn't there. Would he be scared? And he had been so hot – she was worried that he was coming down with something. Would they care?

'Ollie!' The cry erupted from deep within her, the impassioned wail of a pain too intense to contain within her body. She marched over to Natasha and, bending at the waist, thrust the whole of her upper body towards the girl. 'Ollie loves you, you little bitch!' Emma screamed – a word she hated even as it spewed out of her mouth. But that was nothing, *nothing*, to how she was feeling. There were no words strong enough. She moved closer, arms outstretched towards Natasha, hands poised to grab her.

'Em, stop it,' David said. 'It's not going to help. Look at her face.' There was little doubt that David was right. 'Why do you hate us, Natasha?' he asked.

For a moment her gaze wavered. She glanced at Emma, but when she looked back at David her eyes hardened once more.

'You don't know?' she asked. A humourless laugh escaped her lips.

'No – of course I don't know. Tell me, for God's sake,' David pleaded.

She shook her head. 'You might fool Emma – but you don't fool me.'

Emma stood still and stared at this girl – her calm, obdurate stance belying her youth. What was she talking about?

She couldn't read David's expression. His brow was furrowed and the corner of one eye twitched.

'You need to make her talk, David. She has to tell us what the hell is going on. Take that bloody phone off her that she's guarding with her life.'

Natasha shook her head.

'If you take the phone, you'll be sorry. I've got to call in an hour to let them know I'm safe and that you've not hurt me or called the pigs. If I don't call, you'll never see Ollie again – so *back off*, Emma. You too, David. You don't know who you're messing with.'

Sadly, Emma knew she was right.

She hadn't told them why, though. Why would anybody want to harm Ollie?

Emma couldn't stand it any more and ran for the door. She had to get out of here.

'Let her go, David,' she heard Natasha say. 'She's no use to us anyway.'

Who in God's name was the 'us' she was talking about?

The only place that Emma wanted to be right now was in Ollie's room, but when she walked through the door it felt cold. It was almost as if the room had greeted her with the expectation of welcoming its usual inhabitant, but when it was only Emma it seemed to settle back with a sigh.

Emma tried to think of everything that had happened since Natasha had arrived, but she couldn't focus for more than two minutes without her mind switching back to Ollie. She just wanted to hear him shout 'Ay, ay' again, and clutch his warm, chubby little body and feel the velvet softness of his cheek against hers.

She sat in her nursing chair, arms wrapped tightly around her body, each hand on the opposite shoulder as if to simultaneously comfort herself and hold herself together, remembering all the nights that she had sat here beside her son.

She had to do something. She had no idea what, but she couldn't sit here and do nothing, knowing that her baby would be missing her as much as she missed him.

David had said that they must listen to Natasha and do whatever she said. In the end, that was the only way. But not for Emma. She couldn't stand idly by and hope that this would all resolve itself. What could they, whoever 'they' were, possibly want? She and David didn't have enough money to pay a hefty ransom, but if it was money they wanted she would find it from somewhere.

Emma suddenly sat upright. There was one person she knew who had money, money that he had tried repeatedly to give to her years ago but which she had refused, because at that time speaking to him would have been too painful and she was too proud to accept what would have felt like a redemption payoff.

If only she could contact him. But how?

Emma leaned back in the chair and picked up the koala bear that her father had sent Ollie for his first birthday. He loved this bear and would sometimes sit on the floor and chatter to it in his strange, delightful, baby talk.

Through her pain a thought kept jabbing away at her. She looked at the bear; there was something she should remember, something to do with her trip to Australia with David just after they were married.

Suddenly she was on her feet, practically running to her own bedroom. There was no lock on the door, but she couldn't risk Natasha coming in, and she wasn't even sure if David would agree with what she was about to do. She didn't care. She bent down and turned an old wooden doorstop around, jamming it under the closed door. It hit her like a hammer blow that they wouldn't be needing it that night to hold the door open so she could listen for Ollie, never entirely trusting the baby monitor. There *was* no Ollie.

She bit back the howl of anguish that wanted to burst from her lips. *Focus, Emma. Get him back.*

She climbed on a chair and reached into the top of the wardrobe to grab an old shoebox. Jumping down, she upended the box on the bed and there it was – the pay-as-you-go mobile her father had given her so she could call him while they were in Australia without it costing a fortune. Her dad hated wasting money. She didn't know if the SIM card was still active, or if there was any money left on it, but it was less than three years since their visit and she couldn't believe they had used every penny that was on there. She pressed the on button, but nothing happened.

Stupid, stupid. Of course the battery would be flat after all this time. She sifted through the odds and ends that had been stuffed into the box. Somewhere, there had to be a charger. If they wanted money – she would get it. Pride wasn't going to stand in her way now. She just hoped and prayed that he had kept the same mobile number.

24

Tom's mobile was ringing when he returned from the early-afternoon briefing session. It hadn't been a particularly productive meeting. They had chased every loose end they could find to trace who the dead girl was and were still absolutely nowhere. The DNA analysis from Amy Davidson had come back negative, so whoever the dead child was, it wasn't Amy. She was still missing, and Tom had requested an increase in the size of the team. Somebody had to know who this child was. How could a girl so young not be missed?

He picked up his phone.

'Tom Douglas.'

'Tom, it's Leo. I hope it's okay to disturb you, but I wanted to have a word with you about that account of Jack's. I was looking at the list again this morning, and I'm fairly certain that quite a few of the names were also on the client list I was looking through the other night. Do you want me to pop round to your house and compare the two?'

Tom was silent. He had already made the connection himself but wasn't prepared to share this with Leo yet, if ever. The other thing he knew was that the transaction dates of the money in the Swiss account all pre-dated the contract dates of the matching clients.

'Don't worry,' he said. 'You enjoy your day and I'll have a quick look when I get home.'

'Did you have any joy with the bank?' she asked.

'Yes. They're going to call me back. They've warned me that if it turns out the account really is Jack's then unless I am specifically named in the account records as the beneficiary of his will, I won't be able to access the funds. Not that I want them, but at least they could go to charity or something. They're going to check and see what the instructions are.'

'And one other question, then I'll let you go. This girl that's come back from oblivion – she's Natasha Joseph. That's right, isn't it?'

'Yes it is. Why?'

'Her dad's David Joseph – the owner of Joseph & Son in Manchester?'

'The very same. David's the son, but I think his dad's been dead for some years – why are you asking?'

'He seems to have been one of Jack's clients and he's on both lists. An initial deposit of ten thousand pounds into the Swiss account. But I remembered his name from looking at the client list the other night because of the story of his daughter.'

Tom was about to respond when his phone buzzed.

'Sorry, but I'm going to have to talk to you about that another time. I've got a call waiting, and it looks like a foreign number so I'd better take it. See you this evening.'

Tom hung up on Leo and picked up his mobile. It was a number he didn't recognise.

'Tom Douglas,' he said.

A voice began to whisper down the line, almost too low for Tom to hear.

'Please don't speak. I haven't got much time and I don't know how long the credit will hold out on this phone. It's Emma. Jack's Emma. I know it's been a long time, Tom – but I really need your help.'

❖

'Okay, Tom, you know the drill. Nothing on open computers, no public phone conversations. Pick your covert team and let me know who you've got. But before you start the ball rolling, tell me quickly how you know Emma Joseph and any background you have.'

Tom had been relieved to find Philippa Stanley in her office after he had put the phone down to Emma. The 'no police' directive meant this had to be handled by a specialist team, and while he was glad that Becky could be included, he would need support from his superintendent to pull the right people together.

He leaned forwards in his chair, his forearms resting on his thighs, still reeling from the shock of hearing from Emma after all this time and discovering that she was Natasha Joseph's stepmother. He felt he should have known that. He had only been thinking about her the night before when he was talking to Leo about Jack.

'I haven't seen or spoken to Emma for years. She was my brother Jack's fiancée and they were good together. I don't know what happened to them. Everything seemed fine, and then all of a sudden Emma was dumped and Jack wouldn't tell me why. Emma ran off to Australia to stay with her dad.'

'And then Jack died, is that right?'

'Yes – in a speedboat accident in the Adriatic. I tried to contact Emma – basically to give her some of Jack's money because, in my view, by rights it was hers anyway – but she wouldn't touch it. I never heard from her again. I've never met David Joseph – Natasha Joseph is Becky's case – so I had no idea his wife was Jack's Emma.'

'Well, on one level that's good news. Although you once knew her, it seems that you're not closely connected. If you can assure me that she is a distant connection, and she trusts you – which is the vital point – you can continue leading the investigation.'

Tom scratched the side of his head, doing his best to avoid the question.

'Emma didn't contact me because I'm a policeman. She phoned me because she's assuming there's going to be a demand for money and she wanted to know if I'd pay the ransom, which I'd be more than happy to do. But there's been no demand, and when

I explained that – as a policeman – I had to report this, she went ballistic. I calmed her down, but she hasn't entirely bought into police involvement, so we need to tread carefully. And she hasn't told her husband she's been in touch with me – at least not yet.'

Tom would ideally prefer to get the whole family to somewhere safe – out of their own home. A ransom negotiation would be far more likely to succeed under police control, no matter what the Josephs had been told.

Tom was certain that this wasn't about a simple payoff, though. There were people with far more money than David Joseph not a million miles from Manchester, so why choose him?

'What do you think's going on, Tom? What's your famous gut telling you?' Philippa gave a half smile. Tom knew she had no time for instinct over evidence, but she understood that for Tom, talking about his hunches often resulted in some lateral thinking that produced results – although she would never attribute it to 'gut'.

Tom explained his doubts about this being a kidnap for ransom, and Philippa nodded her agreement.

'I could be wrong,' he said, 'and I haven't even hinted at this to Emma, but it has all the hallmarks of a classic tiger kidnap and my gut says that David Joseph is going to be asked to commit a crime on behalf of this gang. Natasha has to stay to see it through because if we turned up to interview her and she was missing, the plot – whatever it is – would fall apart.'

Philippa leaned back, folding her arms, as if suddenly it all made sense.

'Now we know why Natasha said she didn't want them to call the police. That must have rattled a few cages. But it seems that whoever took her trained her well. From the little Mrs Joseph was able to tell you, it sounds as if the kid's as cold as ice. What are we doing about keeping in touch with Emma?'

Tom had decided to involve Gil Tennant, the technician he trusted the most. Nobody would suspect for a moment that he was a policeman. He looked as if a strong puff of wind would blow him over, and if he dressed true to form he would probably be wearing pink trainers with a matching fleece.

'Gil's going to find out how to add credit to Emma's phone from the Australian telecoms company, and I want him to go out to the Josephs' house and check if there are any bugs. I'm praying there wasn't one in Emma's bathroom. She's obviously watched too many movies, though, because she'd taken the phone into their en suite, switched on the taps and spoken from the shower cubicle, so I'm fairly confident she wasn't overheard.'

'And her husband doesn't know she contacted you?'

Tom shook his head, thinking of Emma's comment. 'He's already suffered the pain of losing one child, so I think he'll want to do whatever they say rather than risk anything happening to Ollie.'

Philippa raised her eyebrows. 'Can Emma Joseph handle this?'

'She's going to have to. If we're going to get her son back, she hasn't got much choice.'

25

The edges of Emma's vision were obscured by a grey mist which seemed to be slowly thickening so that only one object was still visible in full iridescent colour: the resolute, impassive face of her stepdaughter.

Natasha was sitting facing Emma across the table, seemingly indifferent to the torture she was putting them through. David marched from one end of the kitchen to the other, running a hand through his fine hair.

'Why have you done this?' Emma hissed between clenched teeth, her throat raw with tears. David looked anxiously at his wife.

The only thing helping her to keep it together was the fact that Tom Douglas now knew what was happening. Somebody outside these four walls, other than the bastards who were holding her son, knew the torment she was suffering. Tom was going to help. She had nearly screamed when he had said he was going to have to make it official, but now she was relieved. It no longer felt as if it was her sole responsibility to get her son back. David, of course, wanted him back every bit as much as she did, but his pain had a different dimension – confused as it was by the horrific actions of his daughter.

It had been a struggle to resist sitting by the phone in case Tom called her back, but she had hidden it in Ollie's room – somewhere she doubted Natasha would look – and switched off both sound and vibrate. Tom had come good, as she had been certain he would. First a text to say that she now had plenty of credit on the phone, and then a second text to ask her about their alarm company: would David know when they last came to do some maintenance?

An hour or so later when the front doorbell had rung, she had only just prevented David from answering it, certain that he would turn away whoever was calling. A dapper little man had stood on the doorstep with a clipboard and a bag of equipment and said he would only be fifteen minutes doing a routine check on all of the alarm equipment. He had asked them all to leave the kitchen while he tested the infrared detectors, and Emma had seen David's look of incredulity that she had allowed this to happen, now of all times. But she had shrugged and dropped her head as if to say, 'I'm not thinking straight.' David had reached out to hug her and a momentary warmth had filled the cold cavity in her chest.

The engineer had left, and since then they had once more been locked in emotional combat.

'Natasha, I asked you a question. Why have you done this?' Emma said again, this time opening her mouth wide and letting the emotion flow from her and settle around Natasha.

'Your precious baby will be home soon if you do what you're told. And then I'll be out of your hair. Now shut the fuck up, will you?'

David stopped his pacing. 'Natasha,' he said with such a note of horror that, under any other circumstances, Emma would have smiled. How could he be shocked at nothing more than an arrangement of four letters of the alphabet from a girl who had abducted his son?

'I'm going upstairs,' Emma said. 'I'm going to sit in Ollie's room for a while. Please don't follow me. I don't want to speak to you – either of you.'

She sensed rather than saw David's look of hurt. But unless she made him feel unwelcome he would want to be with her to try to offer her comfort, while at the same time trying to find excuses for Natasha's behaviour. She didn't want to listen to any meagre defence that David might construct in order to justify his daughter's actions, and she couldn't have him there if anything arrived from Tom.

She hoped and prayed it would.

❖

Less than a mile from Blue Meadow House, the Joseph family home, Tom sat in his car in a lay-by, waiting for Becky. He had sent her to check all the lanes in the vicinity of the house for any unusual activity before he got too close. He needed to find somewhere that Emma could reach on foot, as he was certain Natasha would have been instructed to stop them using their cars.

Gil had called to say he found bugs in the kitchen, sitting room and in David and Emma's bedroom. Tom hadn't wanted the bugs removed; they had to be left in place, as if everything was going to plan.

According to Gil, they were GPS bugs, activated by sound. In theory the police should be able to monitor signals from the house to the receiver, allowing them to trace where the receiving equipment was. But these were no amateurs and they would be bound to be employing counter-surveillance techniques of their own.

He needed to know if the outside of the house was under surveillance. Although the fields around Blue Meadow House didn't offer too many places for a watcher to hide, Tom knew only too well that on a job like this some guy might lie for hours in a cornfield to keep eyes on a property, so he'd organised a chopper with infrared detectors to circle the area. The news was good. Nobody was concealed in the fields.

Becky's black Golf slid into the lay-by behind Tom's five-year-old navy-blue BMW – a car he reserved for work – and she hurried to his passenger door and jumped in.

'Bloody freezing out there. Rather Emma than me, walking to meet you. Are you going to wait in your car?'

'No such luck,' Tom said. 'If she's seen getting into a car, that would be game over. I'm going to meet her in the wood down the road from them.'

'It's getting dark out there. She's brave, isn't she, going into a murky wood on her own?'

'Desperate, I think. I doubt she'll notice the dark or the cold. Anyway, what did you find?'

'Nothing. The only cars around seemed to be going about their normal business and there weren't many of them. I've got the numbers of all of them. I'm about to run a check on them now. But no parked cars, nothing ringing any alarm bells. They're obviously trusting technology and Natasha to keep control.'

Becky glanced at Tom and he could see concern written all over her face.

'Are you okay with this, Tom? It's bad enough when we don't know the victims, but this must be difficult for you. What's Emma like?'

Tom gazed out of the side window, away from Becky.

'She was a totally steadying influence on my rather bonkers brother. And then he dumped her.'

Tom didn't add how supportive Emma had been to him when his own marriage to Kate had failed a few months before Emma split with Jack, or how, over the years she'd spent with his brother, Emma had begun to feel like the sister he'd never had.

'She's a giver, if that makes sense. Always willing to help others, but she finds it very difficult to accept anything from people. I'm sorry we lost touch – especially now.'

'This time she's reached out to you, though, hasn't she? I'm worried that you can't be dispassionate about this case, Tom. Does Philippa know how close you were?'

Tom turned back to Becky and narrowed his eyes. 'I'm not close to her. She's somebody I used to know, which is why she was able to make contact with me. I've no personal interest in this case, other than making sure a baby boy is returned to his mother. Are we on the same page here, Becky?'

'Got it,' Becky said. 'But if you have to have that conversation with anybody else, you need to be a whole lot more convincing.'

26

The comfort of the chair in Ollie's room was doing nothing to soothe Emma. She pulled the phone out from the folds of the blanket she was clutching – a safe hiding place should anybody decide to follow her in here. The screen was blank. But then it was probably only about ten seconds since she had last checked.

She stared at her son's empty cot. She should have been giving him his bottle now, feeling his warm body snuggle against her as he looked up at her with his big eyes, just showing the first hint of sleepiness. Who was looking after him? They wouldn't know that he hates apples but loves pears, would they? Would he be warm enough? Had David put his coat on before Tasha took him out?

Her hand seemed to be set to automatic, dragging the phone from under the blanket every few seconds, then pushing it back. Out it came again – and this time the screen lit up. Emma felt a leap in her chest.

> There's a small wood about half a mile from your house on the road that leads to Willow Farm. Get away from the house and meet me there when you can. You might need a torch. I'll wait for as long as it takes. Your house is bugged. Careful what you say. Tom.

Thank God.

And thank God she had taken what had seemed the ridiculous precaution of speaking to Tom from the shower.

How was she going to get out of the house, though? She knew

Natasha would have something to say on the subject, as David probably would. She had to make a stand and stick to it. The thought of somebody listening to her every word, every nuance, terrified her. Even if she could convince her husband and step-daughter, would she convince the listeners? But this was for Ollie. She *had* to make it work.

Emma switched the phone off and buried it right at the bottom of Ollie's toy box, trying not to look at all his favourite toys.

She pulled herself upright using the side of his cot as support, and took a deep, steadying breath.

'Right. Let's do it.'

She marched determinedly downstairs, grabbing her coat from the rack in the cloakroom.

Her resolve weakened when she pushed open the kitchen door. David was on his knees next to Natasha's chair.

'Natasha, please, darling. Tell us where he is. We'll make sure you don't get into trouble. I love you, Tasha – I've always loved you. I lost my little girl once and it was as if my heart had been cut out. Please don't make me lose you again, and Ollie too. Please, darling.'

Emma looked at Natasha's face, and for a moment she saw something there. A flicker of uncertainty, just for a second. Tempted as she was to rush over and join in the begging, she knew it wouldn't work. To Natasha she was nothing, so her only choice was to play bad cop.

'You're wasting your time, David. She's a heartless little cow.' She walked towards the table and leaned forwards, resting her hands on the smooth surface and pushed her face towards Natasha. 'Your baby brother adores you, and you know it. Ollie shouted your name all the time. "Ay, ay, Tassa." Do you remember? He wrapped his chubby little arms around your leg, and he kissed you before he went to bed. Those lovely baby kisses. He would have loved you if you'd let him – and this is what you do to him. How do you think he's feeling now, with somebody who doesn't know him? Somebody who isn't cuddling him and laughing when he thinks he's being funny? He won't only be crying for his mummy and daddy, though, will he? Not any more. He'll be crying for you, "Tassa" – the one who's betrayed him. He'll be missing you too.'

Emma saw a distant echo of her own distress in Natasha's eyes and couldn't decide whether to push further against the girl's defences or leave her with time to think. But Tom was waiting. She'd get back to Natasha later.

'I'm going out,' Emma said, pushing her arms into her coat.

Two pairs of eyes swivelled towards her in surprise. Natasha jumped up and quickly ran her hands over Emma's body.

Bloody hell, she's searching me. And she knows how to do it.

Thank goodness she had left the phone upstairs. Her heart started to thump at the thought of how disastrous that could have been.

'Don't go,' David said, looking wretched, still in his supplicant position. 'We need you here, Em. We need to talk this through.'

'No David – she's not going to listen. She's had all feeling drummed out of her. Anyway, how do we know she's telling the truth? How do we know that anybody's taken Ollie? How do we know that she didn't do something to him when she took him for a walk, and that she's made all this up to put us off the track? I'm going out to look for him.'

Emma stared at Natasha.

'Have you hurt him, Natasha? Have you left him somewhere out there? Have you hurt your baby brother?'

Natasha turned away from Emma.

'No, I wouldn't,' she said quietly. 'I wouldn't hurt Ollie. He's safe. You'll get him back – just do what we tell you. He's not out there. I promise.' Natasha's voice faltered on the last word.

Oh my God, she's going to cry.

David was by Natasha's side instantly, reaching out to hug her – and the spell was broken. She pushed him away, face hardened once again.

'You need to stay here, Emma,' she said. 'They won't like it if you leave the house.'

'Tough,' Emma said, aware of David's head shaking as if telling her not to go. 'I don't believe anybody's got my son. I believe there's only you, Tasha. So I'm going to check – to see if I can find my baby. I should have done it hours ago.'

❖

Tom could hear rustling in the undergrowth and knew somebody was approaching along the leaf-strewn path. It was a small wood – not much more than a copse really – but it would provide some cover from the road. Becky was right, though. The weather was wicked, and Tom blew on his fingers, wishing he had remembered some gloves.

Covering most of the torch with his fingers, he shone its diffused beam towards the path, and there she was.

He wanted to say she had hardly changed, and he suspected that a week ago those might have been the first words from his lips, but today it wasn't true. Her face was devoid of a scrap of colour, unless you counted the blue smudges underneath her eyes, and her tight ponytail made her pale face appear stark and angular, with none of the softness of features that Tom remembered.

She rushed to Tom and he enveloped her in his arms, holding her close. Her arms round his back were like limbs of steel, as if holding him this tightly would relieve the pain. In his grief over the loss of Jack he hadn't appreciated how much he had missed this woman. She had helped him draw closer to his brother, and for that he couldn't thank her enough.

'I'm so sorry about all this, Emma. It must be hell for you, but we're going to do everything we can to get Ollie back,' he murmured close to her ear.

Emma pushed him away gently and glanced nervously over her shoulder into the blackness beyond the torchlight.

'Do you think anybody will have followed me?'

'No. We've had a good look around and there's nobody watching the house. If anything, they'll be watching the exit points to the lanes that lead from here. Becky's paying David and Natasha a visit now with some fabricated new information about the boy on the train. She'll keep them there, and if there are any problems she'll call, so don't worry.'

Emma's eyes widened. 'Becky knows? What if you've got a mole or something inside the police?'

Tom gently held Emma's arms and looked down into her troubled eyes.

'It's okay. We have a procedure for this. Nearly every kidnap begins with the words 'Don't tell the police' and we know exactly what to do. At the moment only four people know – me, my boss, Becky, and the guy who came to check out the bugs earlier. We're putting together a team, but until we know what we're dealing with we'll keep it small and on a need-to-know basis.'

Emma nodded and sank back against Tom's broad chest, wrapping her arms around him again. He could feel her body shuddering slightly, whether from cold or fear he didn't know, but he tightened his hold, wishing he could pass some strength from his body into hers.

She pushed back again, unable, it seemed, to stay still. He felt the cold hit his chest where he had held her against him and pulled his coat more tightly across his body.

'Tell me everything that's happened.'

'There's not much that you don't know already. I guess you're up to date on Natasha's reappearance? She's been incredibly distant since the word go. She's refused to tell us where she's been living, how she got back, whether she's been unhappy. She clearly blames David for not being with them that night. It's as if she wants to make him suffer – as if he hasn't punished himself enough.'

'Has she given you any hint at all of what's going on?'

Emma shook her head. 'She says there's something that we have to do, and we're going to be told soon. Then we can have Ollie back.' Her voice broke on a sob. 'She's just a kid, Tom. How is this possible?'

He didn't have the heart to tell her about the number of young criminals he had to deal with on a regular basis, most of them every bit as tough as their adult counterparts. And anyway she didn't want a response. She wanted to talk, to try to find some release by sharing her fears.

'David pleads with her. He doesn't want to yell and scream, because he thinks she's damaged. But I've made a bit of a break-through, I think. Ollie absolutely adores Natasha, and although she tried to keep herself distant from him, he's a lovely baby and I saw her face soften a few times when he was trying to get her attention. I'm hoping that might be what breaks her – God knows, something's got to.'

Tom nodded. 'Listen, Emma, we don't know how the next few hours or days are going to pan out, and my view is that we should take you all to a safe place and negotiate Ollie's safe return.'

Emma grabbed Tom's arm.

'No, Tom. *No.* I know that by telling you I've broken their rules, and that was a huge risk. But I need them to think we're going along with what they want. That's what David wants us to do – agree with everything, and just get this thing over.'

'Okay, but you need to remember the house is bugged – the kitchen, the sitting room and your bedroom – so if you do decide to tell David at any point about your contact with me you need to make sure you're not overheard.'

Emma nodded and let go of Tom's arm.

'So how are you going to get Ollie back? They haven't asked for any money yet. How long are they going to wait?'

Tom didn't feel this was the appropriate time to tell her that it might not be money they wanted. That would scare her even more.

'We've got some ideas and we're going to be very cautiously checking them out. But we're not talking about a random gang of chancers, so we need to handle it with care. We're trying to track down the lad Natasha recognised on the train. If he's part of the same gang, he might lead us somewhere.'

'What can I do – should I be trying to sort out some money?'

'Don't worry about money. Leave that to me. Forget it and focus on trying to get Natasha to tell you anything at all. Every little bit of information you can glean from her could be useful. Tell me anything – however trivial. Until then, just act as if you're following instructions.'

Tom put his hands on Emma's shoulders and looked down at her tear-streaked face.

'You're doing great, Emma. Keep plugging away at Natasha's conscience. You might get through to her.'

Emma nodded, leaned in to give Tom a final hug and whispered, 'Thanks,' in his ear.

She turned to go, leaning forwards as if the pain racking her body was making it difficult to stand upright.

'Emma,' Tom said softly. 'I'm so sorry about the way Jack treated you. I've never understood it and I'd always thought I'd have the time with him to force him to explain it to me. I never expected the daft bugger to die like that. Did you ever understand why?'

Emma's body straightened, but she didn't turn round.

'Why he dumped me, or why he died?'

Tom frowned. What did she mean, why he died? Emma didn't wait for his response and half turned back towards him, not meeting his eyes.

'Do you know he dumped me by email? Did he ever tell you

that? No – I bet he didn't. We'd rented a place in Croatia for a year if you remember, and Jack had come over to England to work on one of the random projects he'd taken on since selling his business. That's when he met Melissa – the woman he left me for. So it was one brief note, and goodbye me.'

'Bloody hell. What a dreadful thing to do. I'd never have expected that from Jack. You two always seemed so close.'

'We were. We had our issues – what couple doesn't after ten years? But nothing that couldn't have been sorted out with a bit of compromise on both sides. I absolutely never saw it coming.'

'Did you ever hear from him again?'

'Oh yes.' Emma lifted her head, staring past Tom as if she could see something in the far distance that was only revealing itself to her. 'I heard from him once more – the day before he died. It was as if I'd lost him twice.'

This time the pause was longer, and Tom somehow knew her next words were going to hurt. She turned her head until her eyes met his.

'The reason I haven't been able to see you since then, Tom – the reason I've ignored you all this time – is that I couldn't see you without telling you. Now I think I must. Jack wrote to me the day before he died to say goodbye. I'm sorry, but the truth is, his death was no accident. Jack killed himself.'

27

The road seemed to stretch endlessly before Tom as he walked quickly, head down, back towards where he had left his car. In the open air he felt exposed, unable to focus his thoughts as he struggled to come to terms with all that Emma had told him. He knew he should be concentrating on the missing baby, but he made a deal with himself. A few minutes – that was all – to try to adjust and to reconcile everything he had ever thought about Jack's death with the truth.

Emma had turned to leave after she had broken the devastating news, but Tom had reached for her arm and held her there – perhaps unfairly in view of everything the poor woman was trying to deal with.

'I know this is the least of your worries now, Em, but is there anything else you can tell me? What did he say?' Tom could hear the despair in his own voice. Suicide had never been something he had found easy to deal with in his job. It spoke of a level of hopelessness that was outside his comprehension. Even in the bleakest moments of his life he had managed to retain the hope that each day, things would get a little better.

Emma had reached forwards and rested the palm of her hand against Tom's cheek, to his shame adopting the role of comforter when her own life was in such turmoil.

'Jack said he'd made many mistakes in his life and that the day of reckoning had finally arrived. He'd made a decision that he knew was going to cause pain, but as far as he was concerned it was the only way out of an existence that had become unbearable. I'm so sorry, Tom.'

Tom had wanted more than anything to keep Emma there and ask her more questions, but one look at her face – concern for him mixed with desperation and fear for her baby – had jolted him back to reality.

'Thanks for telling me,' he'd said, covering her hand with his own and gently removing it. 'It's a lot to take in, but there'll be time for that when we've got Ollie back. Go, Em. Get back to David and keep in touch. We're going to find Ollie and bring him home. I know it's wrong of a policeman to make promises, but I'll move heaven and earth to get you your baby back.'

With a last swift hug they had parted, Emma walking back towards her home, and Tom moving in the opposite direction to exit the small wood at the far side a few minutes later.

His car was in sight now, and his fast walk turned into a slow jog until he was able to press his remote to unlock the doors and slide into the driver's seat. It felt like reaching sanctuary, a place where he could pull his thoughts together.

Tom leaned forwards, his head resting on arms folded across the steering wheel.

'*Why*, Jack?' he muttered.

For all Jack's wayward behaviour, he'd had a wicked sense of humour, and had relentlessly 'taken the piss out of life', as he had put it himself. In spite of his success and his obvious brilliance, Tom had known there was a darker side to his brother and although he had never understood it, he had always believed that Jack lacked confidence. He had mockingly called Tom 'White Hat' – when he wasn't just calling him 'little brother' – because he always thought Tom was one of the good guys – Jack's polar opposite.

Realising that understanding Jack's motivation for taking his own life was not going to come to him in a flash, Tom leaned back, his head against the headrest, and closed his eyes.

Whatever it was, why didn't he come and talk to me about it?

It was no good asking that question now. He would never know.

Opening his eyes, he leaned forwards again and put the key in the ignition. Time to think about the baby now – to focus on the living and not on the dead.

28

'Where've you been?' The words burst from David as Emma walked into the kitchen. Deep lines of stress were etched into his usually smooth forehead, and she could see he hadn't coped well with her absence.

'I walked down as far as the wood. There's a bit of tree trunk that some kids must have dragged into the clearing to use as a seat, so I sat there for a while.'

David looked horrified.

'But it's dark out there. Weren't you frightened in the wood on your own?'

Emma closed her eyes.

'My child has been kidnapped. I can't imagine any single thing that would be more terrifying than that. I'm not sure I'll ever be frightened of anything normal – like rats, or hurricanes, or marauding gangs of youths – ever again.'

She was being hard on him and that wasn't fair.

'You shouldn't have gone out. We'll only get Ollie back if we do exactly what they say. So stick to the rules, please, Emma. And then, when it's all over, we can get help for Tasha. We just need to hang on in there.'

Sometimes she thought of David as an ostrich, burying his head in the sand and forcing himself to believe that all would be well. It was one of the few things about him that she found frustrating. It wasn't so much optimism as an inability to face reality and a tendency to look for the easy way out.

It wasn't going to work this time. There was no easy way out.

On her walk back to the house after meeting Tom, Emma had decided on a two-pronged attack on Natasha, the aim being to confuse her. She knew David would be cajoling her, which she was fairly certain Natasha would be able to resist. What she might find less easy to resist was kindness, the feeling of a home into which she was welcomed. And then, just as she was slightly thrown off-guard, Emma would introduce Ollie back into the picture.

'Right,' she said. 'Nobody in this house has eaten a thing since this morning. Whatever's going to happen, we can't be fainting by the wayside – so like it or not, we're going to eat.'

She pulled a Bolognese that she had made a few days earlier from the freezer, and stuck it in the microwave to defrost. She wanted life in this house to feel good to her stepdaughter, like a real home should feel. Then she might be less inclined to rip it apart.

David said nothing and set about laying the table. She saw him head towards the wine.

'Sorry, darling, but I think it's a really bad idea. What if you have to drive somewhere tonight and you're stopped by the police?'

A look of irritation crossed David's face.

'It's tomorrow,' Natasha said – the first bit of information she had volunteered.

'What's tomorrow, Tasha?' David asked, adopting a nonchalant tone as if this were an ordinary conversation.

But she merely tutted and raised her eyebrows.

David and Emma exchanged a glance and carried on with what they were doing. They ate dinner in virtual silence, all three of them pushing their food around their plates. As a strategy it had failed completely, and the thought of food actually made Emma feel sick. There was one more thing she wanted to try, though.

At the end of the table sat Emma's laptop. She pulled it towards her, making sure that the screen was visible to everybody at the table, and tapped the space bar to bring it to life. She clicked an icon on the screen, and suddenly the room was full of Ollie – laughing, crawling. Emma remembered shooting this video on her phone. She knew what was going to happen next and she swallowed the vast lump that was lodged in her throat. She couldn't cry now – it would ruin the moment.

First a pair of shoes came into view, then the legs of a person sitting on the leather sofa at the far end of the kitchen. Emma had zoomed out to get the full view of Ollie grabbing Natasha's jeans and pulling himself upright. 'Tassa, Tassa,' he shouted with a huge smile as his face drew almost level with hers. Emma had managed to capture the one second when Natasha had allowed herself to smile at Ollie before her face settled back into her habitual scowl.

The three of them watched, almost mesmerised, until Natasha reached out and slammed the laptop lid shut.

'It won't work, you know. I'm not stupid. Do you think I'm a normal kid who does what she's told, scared of getting in trouble and being grounded?' She gave a cold laugh. 'When you come from where I do, what you're scared of is being thrown in The Pit, starved until you'd do anything – yeah, anything – for a piece of bread. Or worse, you're scared one of the big guys – the real evil bastards – is going to deal with you. Do you know what they call these men? No – I bet you don't. They call them *enforcers*. So you see, a bit of mince and a family photo really, really doesn't cut it.'

Emma wasn't able to pull her eyes away from Natasha's. An image of this girl's life for the past six years was painted clearly in her mind and suddenly she felt no hope at all.

29

One look at Tom's face as he walked towards her, and Becky knew something had happened. Tom had what Becky's mum would call an open face; wide blue eyes that looked straight at you, and a relaxed, confident expression. Not tonight, though. His face seemed narrower, his eyes slightly downcast with a smidgeon of a wrinkle between his brows. His skin seemed paler too, and his generous mouth was set in a straight line, as if his teeth were clenched. Forlorn was the word that sprang to her mind.

He was a good-looking bastard, by anybody's measure. Six foot tall or more with those wide shoulders and broad chest, he usually had an easy way about him that felt comfortable and secure to be around. Mind you, he had a temper. On more than one occasion Becky had seen him come close to losing it with a suspect – particularly when kids were the victims. And he could be a bit gruff and direct when the mood took him. But all that just added to the interest, in her book. Not that she should be thinking that way. After all, he had Leo – studying for a degree in psychology, no less. Smart as well as beautiful, it seemed.

'Cup of tea?' she asked, squashing the twinge of irrational resentment of a woman she had never met. Tom barely registered her question, giving her a distracted look as he marched into his office. Taking that as a yes, she diverted into the kitchen.

'How did it go with Emma, then?' she asked five minutes later as she plonked a mug of tea on Tom's desk.

'Nothing much to tell you, really,' he replied shortly, staring at the drink in front of him.

'I sat with David and Natasha, as instructed,' she said, thinking that if she jabbered on for a bit it might give him time to pull himself out of whatever was bothering him. 'Course, I was careful because of the bugs, so I asked her questions about where she'd been living. I knew she wouldn't tell me anything. She walked out – so I followed and cornered her in the hall – a bug-free zone. I said we'd had some new information, and I wanted to run some names by her. She was quite sneery about it, as if to say, 'Do you think I'd tell you?' but it didn't matter because I made them all up. I did, however, think there was a flicker of something when I mentioned the name Rick or Richard Harvey. Whether it was the first name or the last I don't know – but if I had to put money on it, I would say that it was the name Rick that did it. I'd only wanted to unnerve her – so that was a bit of a bonus.'

Becky waited. Tom had been looking at her throughout, but his eyes were distant, unfocused.

'Good. Well done, Becky.' Tom closed his eyes for a second and she saw his shoulders move up then down as if he was trying to get himself under control.

'We've got bugger all to go on, if we're honest about it,' he said. 'What exactly *do* we know?'

And so it had begun, the trawl through the information on whoever had taken Natasha in the first place, who had brought her back and who had taken Ollie. They had just about nothing.

Tom's phone beeped in his pocket. He pulled it out and read the screen, suddenly pushing himself forwards, sitting upright in his chair for the first time.

He raised his eyes from the phone and looked straight at Becky. Her heart rate increased. Tom's expression said it all.

'A text from Emma. It's moving. Whatever they want, whatever is planned, according to Natasha, it's going to happen tomorrow,' he said.

❖

Alone in his office once more, frustration was coursing through Tom's veins. He had now selected and briefed a small team to work on the kidnap, and they were pursuing every line of enquiry they could think of, but he felt they were working completely blind.

His personal mobile phone rang.

'Tom Douglas,' he answered.

'Hi Tom, it's Leo,' Tom breathed out slowly. He had forgotten to tell Leo he wouldn't be home – maybe not at all – tonight. He realised he had no idea how she would react on the rare occasions that he might have to be secretive.

'Bollocks. I'm sorry, Leo – I'm a useless cretin. Look, I'll call you back. Sorry – we can't use my personal mobile at the moment. Give me two minutes.'

He hung up. This was the number that Emma would use if she needed him, and he couldn't be tied up talking to Leo if she wanted to get through.

He quickly dialled Leo's number on his office phone.

'Sorry,' he said. 'I need to leave my other line free.'

'Is it Lucy?' Leo asked, the concern showing in her voice. She had met Lucy a few times, and they were getting along better on each occasion. There had been a slight wariness on Lucy's part to start with, but Leo had been sensitive to any possible jealousy.

'No, nothing like that. It's work, but I can't go into it. Sorry.'

There was a brief silence – as if for a moment she hadn't believed him. Tom felt an unexpected flash of irritation, although Leo's next words betrayed nothing.

'I wanted to know if I should put my limited skills to the test and make something for supper,' she said. She was a fairly useless cook, but he didn't want to undermine her completely.

'I would love you to cook me supper, but it's highly unlikely that I'm going to be home at all tonight. If I am, it'll be the early hours.'

'What's up? I thought your current cases were all in hand.'

'Hah. Unfortunately crime in Manchester is relentless. There is no such thing as clearing your caseload, I can promise you that. Some bastard is sure to do something that needs attention the minute you think you're on top of things. But this is different. I need to stay and sort this. Sorry,' he said again.

'And you're not going to tell me what it is?'

'I can't.'

'Oh well, I've got loads of reading to do anyway. The question is, shall I stay here – I'm at yours – or should I go home?'

'Let's just say I hope and pray that *if* I get home, and it's a big if, it will be to your warm, naked body in my bed. Is that okay?'

There was a soft chuckle down the line. *That's better*, he thought.

'Wake me when you get in, then. I wouldn't mind some of *your* warm, naked body while we're on the subject.'

For a moment, all thoughts of Jack and Ollie disappeared as his mind conjured up a picture of Leo, her long dark hair spread across the pillow and her beautiful slender body lying waiting for him.

'You've gone quiet, Tom?' she said, the laughter still evident in her voice. 'Glad I've cheered you up. You sounded very grouchy when I called. Oh – before I go, you've got a message on your answerphone. Do you want me to play it to you?'

His mind now firmly back on the job, Tom answered. 'Yes please.'

He heard Leo's footsteps on the bare wooden floorboards of his hall, going softer as she walked across the rug. Then a click.

'This is a message for Mr Tom Douglas. My name is Raoul Charteris calling from Honegger, Wyss & Cie in Switzerland. We have received your request regarding the account beginning with the numbers and letters 53696C766. It appears you are the beneficiary named on the account. However, there are some irregularities regarding the account that we need to discuss with you before we can proceed further. Please give me a call on +41 43 733 5360 at your earliest convenience. I'm keen that we speak as soon as possible, Mr Douglas, so this number will get through to me at any time.'

30

The night was very still, and through the open curtains of Ollie's bedroom window Emma could see a thin crescent moon and a sprinkling of stars. She wanted the window and the curtains to be open. She needed to see the sky and the moon that would be looking down on Ollie, smell the air that he would be breathing, wherever he was. Somehow, by closing the curtains it was as if she was creating a cocoon of comfort that excluded her son, so she had pushed them as far back as possible, feeling that she could reflect her thoughts and love from the stars down to her baby.

She had started the night lying next to David, hoping they could give each other some support, but that was harder than it seemed. How could she sympathise with his feelings for his daughter – the girl who had stolen Ollie? They seemed to be separated by a chasm a mile wide.

David had eventually fallen into a fitful sleep. She didn't know how he could but she also knew he was exhausted, and she suspected from the smell of his breath that he had resorted to drinking brandy to numb his pain. Since they had known that 'it' was going to be tomorrow, there had been no reason for David to resist the lure of alcohol. She couldn't drink, though. What if Ollie needed her?

She had to feel close to her baby. Ollie's bedroom was where she wanted to be, and as soon as she was sure David was sleeping, she had escaped their bed and rushed to the place she felt closest to her son.

Emma wondered what was going through Natasha's head

now. It was so hard to reconcile the young, frail-looking girl with the kid standing before them, telling them that nothing they did would frighten her.

Then she reminded herself that children much younger than Natasha were fighting wars in the Middle East and being trained to kill, and she'd seen a documentary on the television that said as many as five hundred children in the UK under fourteen had been found guilty and sentenced for violent crimes in the last twelve months. Much as it beggared belief, perhaps Natasha's behaviour wasn't as incredible as it seemed.

Emma pulled a blanket over her legs. She didn't really know why she had got ready for bed at all. Even though she had hardly slept since Natasha had arrived days ago, she couldn't bear the thought of closing her eyes. What if she missed something important? What if they brought Ollie back and couldn't get in – left him outside crying – and she was asleep? Or what if he was ill and they panicked? She had to be awake, alert, ready for anything if it meant getting Ollie back.

Just one thin wall separated her from the cause of their problems. One wall. There was no doubt that Natasha would have barricaded herself into her room, but Emma formed thoughts like spears to penetrate the wall and get inside Natasha's head.

'How could you do this to your baby brother?' she asked silently, directing the flow of her thoughts by imagining Natasha's sleeping form. 'What did this baby ever do to hurt you? What did any of us do to hurt you?'

Her focus was so intense that she almost missed it.

What was that?

It was a noise. Natasha was moving around in her bedroom. Emma lay still, focusing all of her strength on listening to the sounds from the next room. She could make out a hum that sounded as if it could be a voice, but it was so low that it was nothing more than a distant murmur.

Yes, it was definitely a voice and then Emma heard one word, louder than the rest, but with a distinct edge of despair. '*Why?*' And then nothing. Just the sound of the wind rustling the leaves of the holly tree outside the window.

Emma crept from the chair towards the door. Even though there was no Ollie, she had left his door ajar out of habit. Shutting it would have simply underlined what she already knew: Ollie wasn't there. But now she was glad, because she thought she might hear better. She sat down on the floor beside the open door, pulling her knees to her chest and wrapping her arms around them.

The murmuring had stopped. There was silence for a few moments, then Emma heard a different sound – a drawer being slowly and carefully pulled out.

What was going on?

She sensed, rather than heard, movement in the next bedroom, the sounds so subtle that they were only recognisable because she was listening so intently. But then there was a noise that was clear. It was the sound of Natasha's door opening.

Emma shuffled quickly back from the doorway into the shadow of the room as Natasha tiptoed along the landing, silently creeping down the stairs.

❖

Emma waited behind the bedroom door, listening to the sounds of the house. She was certain that David hadn't put the alarm on before going to bed. She'd asked him not to – in case somebody broke in to bring Ollie back.

It took Emma less than two seconds to decide: if Natasha was going somewhere, Emma was going after her. She didn't know if Tom was wrong and the house was being watched, but right now she didn't care. She wanted to know what Natasha was up to.

Where on earth could she be going? Emma heard the back door open and then close quietly. Please, Natasha, don't take the key and lock the door from the outside, she prayed.

Glancing at her navy-blue pyjama bottoms and thinking they would have to do, she darted into their bedroom, grabbed a black jumper from where she had thrown it earlier and ran down the stairs, not bothering to mask the sound of her footsteps. David wouldn't wake up. He seemed to have trained himself to sleep through anything – including Ollie's occasional bad nights – and Natasha was already gone. Emma just hoped she could catch up with her.

Stopping to grab a pair of moccasin slippers with rubber soles that would make no sound on the road, she quietly opened the back door and slipped outside, pulling the door closed behind her. It was bitterly cold, but Emma barely noticed.

Keeping to the grass rather than the gravel of the drive, she ran to the gate and looked both ways. The moon wasn't very bright, but she could see a moving shadow to her left, heading towards the very same wood where she had met Tom earlier. If she followed now, she would be exposed. She thought quickly. The other side of the road had a steep grass verge and a tall hedge. If she could make it over there, it wouldn't be the obvious place to look if Natasha checked to see if she was being followed. Emma waited a couple of seconds and then risked the quick dash across the road and up the verge, standing still for a few seconds.

Natasha slowed down and glanced over her left shoulder to where Emma had been only moments before. Emma held her breath. Natasha turned back and carried on walking, and as she moved forwards Emma crept along the hedge, keeping her head low. Natasha took the first path into the wood.

Giving her prey a moment or two to get further away from the road, Emma waited until she thought it was safe, then ran back across the narrow strip of black tarmac to the edge of the pathway.

It was completely silent in the wood. There was no wind, and they were too far from town to hear any traffic noise. Emma could hear herself breathing, her breaths short and sharp with fear. The sky was clear with only a sliver of moon to give any light, and the leaves that had littered the paths since autumn were crisp with frost, certain to crunch as she walked. With no other sounds of the night to disguise her movement, she stood stock still.

Guessing that Natasha would be heading to the little clearing where Emma had met Tom, she took a chance and decided to skirt the wood, keeping to the field where the soft grass would absorb the sound of her footsteps, hoping to see and hear everything from the cover of the sparse trees.

Staying low, she crept into the field, keeping to the very edge of the trees. She could hear Natasha crunching along the path. Emma stopped as the sounds grew louder. The girl was heading her way. Suddenly Natasha was in view, not ten metres away, standing still and looking around her. Emma crouched even lower, dropping her head so the weak moonlight wouldn't pick out her white face.

Natasha was on the move again, this time with purpose and direction. She was striding further into the wood and Emma knew she would have to follow. She could hear voices. One was unmistakably Natasha's. The other voice was a man's.

Emma crept closer, watching the ground to avoid the biggest patches of frozen leaves. The voices became clearer.

'You're a stupid bugger, Shelley,' the man said, his voice tense with suppressed anger.

Emma peered around the trunk of the tree. She couldn't see anybody apart from Natasha. Who was Shelley?

'If we fuck this up, it's not just you that's going be screwed – it's me too – and I don't like being messed with. Are you hearing me? I need you to tell me you've got this. And I want to watch your face, because you'd better not be lying to me.'

Emma edged closer still. She could see the man now. He wasn't a tall man, but he was stocky with a belly, wearing ill-fitting jeans and a brown leather jacket. She looked at his face. What moonlight there was illuminated his features; the man's hair was slicked back and greasy, and his face looked oddly scarred until she realised that the disjointed reflections of light from his skin were due to pockmarking, probably from his teenage years. The scowl on his face said that Natasha – or Shelley as he called her – was in trouble.

Natasha bravely looked him in the eye, but Emma could see her hands, clenching and unclenching.

'I told you yesterday, Rory – it's not my fault the pigs came. I *told* David I wouldn't speak to them. But they'd been to see him at work because of that girl who was found dead. They thought it was me.'

'I bet he wishes it had been, now.' The man gave a throaty laugh and spat on the floor.

'Tell me it wasn't Izzy. It wasn't, was it?' Emma heard a note of distress in Natasha's voice. *Who's Izzy*, she thought.

'How the fuck do I know who it was?'

'So you haven't found her, then?'

'I'm not here to talk about your stupid little friend, Shelley. She didn't know when she was lucky, that one, and you shouldn't have told her you were going to take the baby. I thought you knew better.'

'She won't tell anybody, I promise.'

'Not if she's dead, she won't.' He laughed. 'Forget her. We're here to sort out how you're going to manage the filth if they come sniffing again, and I need to know why they came back.'

Emma had manoeuvred herself slowly into a position where she could see Natasha's face, and she saw a momentary glimpse of fear on the girl's face that she quickly tried to disguise. But not quickly enough.

'Jesus, you silly bitch. Do you think we don't know when they come calling? At least you've planted the bugs now so we can hear what they're saying, but what did they want yesterday?'

Natasha looked at the ground and kicked some leaves backwards and forwards.

'Same old,' she said. 'Just trying to get me to tell where I'd been – how I'd got back. Just having another go.'

She was lying. Emma couldn't imagine why, but Natasha wasn't telling him about the CCTV footage on the train.

The man reached out and grabbed Natasha's upper arms. Emma heard a faint squeak of pain, quickly stifled. He shook Natasha hard and pushed his face right up to hers.

'I need to know you've got this, Shelley. You wanted to do it – remember. We had options, but you said you would make it easy for us. What's going on in that head of yours?'

Natasha looked at him, her face wiped of expression. 'Nothing. It's good to see the bastard suffer. It's not Ollie's fault, though. He's a cute baby. Who's looking after him?'

'As if I'd tell you that, even if I knew. We do our bit, they do theirs.' He shook her again, harder. 'And what have I told you about calling the baby by its name? It's just "the baby" – okay? It'll all be over tomorrow night, then you can come home. But if you fuck this up, I'm a dead man, and you know what'll happen to you, don't you?'

'I'm not going to fuck it up. I know what I'm doing.'

'Well, remember – the only person they know is involved is you. Anything goes wrong, I'll be long gone before you have a chance to squeal – and you'll be the one locked up. They'd throw away the key, too – you get life for kidnap, did you know that?'

He let go and pushed her away. Natasha staggered backwards but said nothing, and the man started talking again.

'This job is worth a fucking fortune, and we're halfway there. Tomorrow you'll be told what's got to happen next. When it's over, you walk out. You never have to see him again, Shelley, and they'll never find you.'

Who was he talking about? Who was 'him' – Ollie? David? Somebody else?

One thing was clear to Emma, though. The bastard who

Natasha wanted to suffer was David. How could she hate him so much?

The man called Rory was talking again, and Emma edged a little closer.

A twig snapped under her foot, its sound like a pistol shot in the silent wood.

His head spun round. He was staring straight at the tree Emma was hiding behind, but it was darker here than in the clearing and she was sure he couldn't see her. The man started to walk towards her, and for a moment she thought about standing up and running. He wouldn't catch her – he was too fat. But he would know she'd seen him, and she didn't know what that would mean for Ollie.

The man was getting closer.

'Rory,' Natasha said, her voice an urgent whisper. 'I'd better get back.'

He turned round. 'There was a noise over there. Didn't you hear it?' he asked.

Natasha shook her head. 'There's lots of noises – it's the countryside. You're just not used to it. Probably a rabbit or something. Anyway, I need to go. Emma's a right cow. She snoops around the place in the middle of the night, and I don't want her to know I'm missing.'

He turned and walked back towards Natasha. Reaching out one beefy hand, he fastened it tight around her neck, lifting her slight body off the ground and pinning her to a tree.

Natasha groped behind her to try to hold on to something, stretched out her toes, but they didn't reach the ground. Emma saw the panic in her eyes as she struggled to breathe, gagging sounds coming from her throat. She was going to have to do something if he didn't let the girl go soon.

'There are those above me who aren't as soft-hearted as me – you know that,' he said. Her head hard back against the rough bark, Natasha was looking away from her captor as if fearful of seeing the menace in his face. 'You don't want to get on the wrong side of them, do you? I'm a pussycat in comparison. So do this job, *don't* fuck me around and do it right.'

He slackened his grip on her neck slightly and her head lolled forwards. Instantly he tightened it again, and her head banged hard against the tree. He pushed his face right up against Natasha's and then pulled his arm away quickly. The girl fell to the floor, but was on her feet in a second, like a cage fighter wary of a flying boot.

'Now bugger off before you're missed.'

Natasha started to bring her hand up as if to rub her neck – but seemed to think better of it. Giving the man one last haunted look, she turned round and head down, shoulders hunched, she disappeared into the night.

Emma waited. The man stood and watched Natasha go, spat on the ground again, then turned to head in the opposite direction.

More than anything, Emma wanted to grab a huge tree branch, chase after him and hit him as hard as she could then hold him down and force him to tell her where Ollie was. But she had no chance. He was double her size and she had the feeling he wouldn't hesitate to snap her neck if he thought she was trouble. But there was one thing she could do. Follow him and get his registration number, because he was bound to have travelled by car.

Edging round the side of the wood, she headed towards the road, her plan being to hide at the corner of the wood until the man called Rory had passed her.

Suddenly behind her she heard the roar of an engine. Flinging herself to the ground so she wouldn't be spotted in the blinding headlight, she watched as a powerful motorbike sped past her, her pupils too contracted to be able to read the number plate as it receded into the distance.

❖

Natasha made her way silently back to the house, her feet dragging along the path, brooding on everything Rory had said. Her neck and throat hurt, and so did the back of her head. But the pain was nothing in comparison to the sick feeling of panic in her gut when she thought of the things she had kept from him.

She hadn't dared tell Rory about the photos on the train. She'd been really stupid, looking at Rick the way she had, but he was good-looking and he always smiled at her. Smiles felt like precious gifts in her world, and she held them close until their warmth faded. If the police caught Rick, though – and they were bound to be looking because of her stupidity – it would all be over.

They'll know where he lives, and they'll know about me.

If she'd told Rory, he could have stopped Rick from doing the skunk run, and he'd be safe. But she'd stayed quiet, knowing how mad Rory would have been. He was mad at her anyway for even speaking to the police, and for telling Izzy so much, but if he found out about the CCTV on the train – and worse, that she hadn't told him – that would be it. She'd be thrown in The Pit.

She hated The Pit – after those first few times she had always done everything they asked so she wouldn't get thrown in there. But sometimes it wasn't punishment for something she had done – it was because of what they *wanted* her to do – or maybe because Rory was in a nasty mood. A mistake like this, though, and that's where she'd be. No food, little water, no heat, no light – until she begged for mercy.

There would be no mercy if she screwed this up. Izzy hadn't even done anything, and she'd still got two weeks in The Pit – to make her docile, according to Rory – then she was shipped off to be one of Julie's girls. She'd lasted just a week before she had gone missing, and who could blame her? She was only thirteen, same as Tasha. Those greasy fat bastards who paid Julie for girls like Izzy made Tasha want to puke.

She kicked a stone on the path. She could cope with nicking

phones, ferrying drugs, other stuff like that. But she didn't want to go to Julie's.

It was stupid to think of running, though. Nobody was allowed to escape from this world. Once you were in, you were in for life – a different kind of prison. One without locks on the doors. But run away and it wouldn't be Rory Slater who she had to worry about. They would send Finn McGuinness to find her.

Was that what had happened to Izzy?

He looked so ordinary, did Finn. Smart, even. But everybody understood what he was, and nobody ever crossed him. Rory was bloody terrified of him. And even Finn had to answer to another boss – a name that was never mentioned – a man who Tasha had never met. She never wanted to.

Finn and Rory had made this job sound so easy: make David suffer for what he had done; take the baby for a walk – he won't be away for long. It was easier than most of her jobs. She just had to make sure nobody called the police, and that was a doddle. And when it was all over, she could walk away and go home. Easy.

Except it wasn't. Blanking people was a breeze – she'd done that all her life, or at least the part she could remember. Fixing phones, planting bugs, being bolshie – piece of cake. But she hadn't expected to think Ollie was cute. She hadn't expected him to like her. It felt good when he called her name and gave her one of his smiles. And now everybody was in pieces.

Natasha was staggered by the pain her actions had caused. David kept crying; she'd never seen a bloke cry before, except on the telly. An image of him crying when he had lost her six years ago came into her head, but she pushed it away. She couldn't imagine Rory crying, or Rick for that matter. They wouldn't. Rory had always beaten the hell out of her and all the other kids if they cried for nothing. 'I'll give you something to cry about,' he always said.

They all soon learned, just as Natasha had done.

She'd cried tonight, though. She had cried for the life she should have lived – the life that had been stolen from her and her mum. But she hadn't cried like Emma did. Emma sounded as if somebody was hacking her into small pieces with an axe.

And then Natasha got it. Maybe that was how it felt to really love somebody.

She wouldn't know.

31

'Shit,' Emma muttered as she tried the back door. Natasha must have gone into the house this way and locked it. It was obvious when Emma thought about it. She sat down on a rickety old garden bench, waiting for her heart to stop thudding so she could focus on what to do now.

What if he'd seen me?

Following Natasha had been a risk, but now she had a name. No surname, but Rory was an unusual name and she prayed it would mean something to Tom. It had to. It was the only lead they had.

She started to shiver.

Where are you, my lovely Ollie? Are you warm enough?

The dull ache of loss turned to a sharp pain, and she wrapped her arms tightly round her body, swaying backwards and forwards to try to ease the agony, a soft moan escaping from her dry lips. She went over and over every word she had heard, everything she knew, wondering if she had missed some clue, something that would lead her to Ollie, until finally her mind became blank, numb.

Emma didn't know how long she had been sitting outside, but she couldn't stay out here until morning. Her whole body was shaking uncontrollably now, and she would be no good to Ollie if she made herself ill.

She had no idea how she was going to get back in the house. David had told her that there was a spare key hidden somewhere in case they locked themselves out, but she couldn't remember where it was.

A wave of hopelessness washed over her, and she reached out to try the back door again. It swung open at her touch.

What?

She had been certain it was locked. Her frozen fingers mustn't have pressed down hard enough on the handle.

She pushed the door back fully, and walked into the warm kitchen, kicking off her slippers to let the underfloor heating thaw her icy feet a little. She didn't switch any lights on. The bright spotlights would cast a beam into the garden and Natasha might see them.

Emma knew her way around her kitchen by touch; she made her way over to the kettle and switched it on. The indicator light glowed blue as the kettle came to the boil, giving just enough light for Emma to see the mugs on the shelf above. She pulled one down and turned towards the fridge.

The mug dropped from her hands, shattering into pieces on the tiled floor. Standing right behind her, less than a metre away was Natasha, her grey-green eyes reflecting twin pinpricks of bright blue light from the kettle, a finger against her lips.

Emma's heart leaped in her chest. The water boiled and the indicator light went out, plunging the kitchen back into darkness. A hand reached out and grabbed Emma's sleeve, pulling her out through the kitchen door and into the hall. The kitchen door was closed quietly.

'My *God*, Natasha – what are you doing here in the dark?' Emma whispered, her voice hoarse.

'Why did you follow me?'

'What are you talking about? I wanted a bit of fresh air so I went outside for a few minutes. You can hardly expect me to sleep when you've stolen my baby, can you?'

Natasha stood inches from Emma's face, a trickle of light from the landing painting pale grey patterns on the girl's cheekbones, leaving her eyes and lips black.

'Have you got any idea what would have happened if you'd been found out there, watching us, listening? Do you know what he'd have done if he'd found you?'

Emma shook her head. 'What could he possibly have done that would be worse than he's done already?'

Natasha pushed her face even closer to Emma's.

'He'd have killed you, you silly bitch,' she whispered.

Emma stared at her.

'You've got no idea, have you? These men order hits on people for insulting their *wives*, and you heard him admit to kidnapping your baby. What do you *think* he would've done?'

'And why do you care about that, Tasha?' Emma asked, the stupidity of her behaviour suddenly hitting her.

'I don't. But if he'd killed you, there'd have been a witness. *Me.* And they don't like witnesses. Too messy.'

Emma turned back towards the kitchen, not wanting Natasha to see the fear reflected in her eyes. She spoke with her back to the girl.

'And what would he think if he knew you'd lied to him? Why didn't you tell him that the police have you on camera? I guess he wouldn't have liked that either, would he?'

There was silence, broken only by the ticking of the hall clock.

'Just remember, I saved your life. I won't do it again.'

Emma felt a slight movement behind her and knew that Natasha had gone.

32

It was two o'clock in the morning by the time Tom inserted the key in the front door of his Edwardian semi and made his way quietly upstairs. He opened the door to the master bedroom, and there – as he had hoped – lay Leo, lying as she always did with the duvet up to her armpits but her arms outside the covers and her feet poking out to one side.

Deciding to shower in the main bathroom rather than the en suite so he wouldn't disturb Leo, he emptied his pockets of keys and phones and placed them quietly on the chest of drawers. Tempting as it was to strip off, climb into bed, and gently wake Leo from her peaceful slumber, he wanted a hot shower to wash away some of the stains that today had left on him, and after nearly twenty hours in the same clothes a shower was a necessity as much as a desire.

He'd had precious little time to think about anything for the past few hours other than young Oliver Joseph. All thoughts of Jack that had tried to surface were pushed firmly to the back of his mind. And then there was the bank to think about too. What irregularities could there be with Jack's account? Tom was going to give any money that was in the account to charity anyway, so it was probably just a matter of paperwork, but it might give him a few more answers. He'd already couriered notarised copies of his passport to the bank to prove that he was who he said he was, and he would try to find time to phone them in the next few days.

His mind buzzing but his body exhausted, Tom turned the

shower off, dried himself and walked naked across the landing into the bedroom. He pulled back the covers and slid into bed. He needed sleep, but he needed Leo more and he knew she would welcome him if he woke her. She would drive out thoughts of a missing baby and a dead girl – just for a few moments – and ease the tension in his limbs.

In sleep Leo was beautiful. Her face was turned towards him, one arm stretched above her head. He leaned in and kissed her gently on the mouth as his hand snaked under the covers and found her flesh, warm and inviting.

Without opening her eyes, her arm came down and around Tom, pulling him towards her, and she rolled on her side, wrapping her leg around his thigh.

'Hi,' she murmured, running her hand lightly down his back, coming to rest on his hip.

Tom's mind emptied of everything but Leo as he slowly brought her fully awake, giving her time to come round from whatever place she was visiting in her dreams. He stroked her hair away from her face and kissed her again, then buried his face in her neck to find her collarbone, a place she loved him to touch, and she groaned softly in his ear.

Gradually the groaning sound took on a different tone, and he felt Leo's shoulders stiffen.

'Shit,' he muttered as he recognised the sound of his mobile vibrating on the chest of drawers. 'Sorry, Leo. I can't ignore this.'

Tom could feel Leo's eyes following him as he walked towards the chest of drawers, and he heard a moan of frustration.

'Come back to bed, Tom. You can't leave me now.'

He had no choice. It wasn't a call, though. It was a text.

Tasha's been living with man called Rory. Drives a big motorbike, not a Harley. Calls her Shelley. Ollie's not with him. It's definitely going to happen tomorrow, today now,

174

I suppose. Natasha asked about dead girl asked if it was
Izzy. Don't know any more than that. Emma.

He turned to look at Leo, both palms upwards in a gesture of
hopelessness.

'Who is it?' Leo asked.

Tom shook his head. 'Sorry, I can't say. I have to go, though.'

Leo's frown lasted no more than a second or two.

'Go,' she said, 'before I jump out of this bed and grab you.'

'Sorry,' Tom said again, snatching up a handful of clothes and
making for the door.

'And stop apologising,' was Leo's parting shot.

Tom closed the door quietly behind him and made the call.

'Becky? Sorry about this. My office, half an hour please. Get
the rest of the team too, if you can. We need to work quickly.'

33

Day Five

The side of the bed dipped as Emma slowly became aware that sunlight was flooding in through the open curtains. The early-morning torpor seeped away as the horror of yesterday flooded through her veins, and she sat up abruptly, pain ripping through her – undiminished by the passing hours.

Ollie. I miss you, sweetheart.

David was perched on the side of the bed, and she noticed a mug of tea on the bedside table, its mottled surface telling her it was cold.

'You managed to sleep, then,' David said.

It was true. She couldn't believe that after everything that had happened she had actually slept. Maybe knowing that Ollie wasn't coming home any time soon had lifted the burden of waiting for long enough for her to get a few short hours of restless sleep. But now, he filled her heart and mind again.

Ollie. Emma's whole body craved the feel of his soft skin, the sound of his shouting and laughter, his warm milky smell after his last bottle of the day. How could pain that wasn't inflicted by a physical assault hurt so much? How could emotional distress turn into this agonising emptiness? She could touch the parts of her that ached, but she knew of no analgesic that would relieve the pain.

She didn't have to say any of this to David. She knew he would be feeling it too, and so much more.

'I didn't mean to sleep so long, but I was still awake at four and then I guess exhaustion took over. How are you?'

'Pretty shitty, as I'm sure you are. I must have woken up as you went to sleep. It was your feet that woke me. They were like blocks of ice – you must have had them outside the covers or something. But I couldn't get back to sleep after that, and I thought I'd disturb you with my tossing and turning, so I went downstairs.'

Emma could remember coming to bed, still shivering, her whole body reacting not only to the cold, but also to Natasha's grim warning. She desperately wanted to tell David what had happened, what she had learned and how she had sneaked into Ollie's room to text Tom before she got into bed, but suddenly she remembered what Tom had told her. There was a bug in their bedroom, and anything she said would be heard by somebody, somewhere.

Emma pushed back the covers.

'I'm going to have a bath – I need to clear my head. Come and talk to me?'

'I'll go and make you a fresh mug of tea and bring it with me.'

He leaned towards her and they wrapped their arms round each other in a tight hug. A fraction of the pain seeped out of Emma's limbs, only to return the minute they let each other go.

❖

The bath water was scalding hot, but Emma welcomed the stinging sensation on her flesh. She thought about those deeply religious people who engaged in self-flagellation – something she had always thought of as indescribably stupid. She could almost appreciate it now – maybe the physical pain helped to relieve some inner emotional pain that nobody else could understand.

The door nudged open.

'Christ, it's like a Turkish bath in here. Can I open the window, Em? I can't actually see you through the steam.'

'No, please don't. Sorry – if it's too hot for you, take your jumper off or something.' Emma didn't know if their voices would carry through an open window but she wasn't prepared to risk it.

'I'll leave the door open, then.'

'No, shut it please, David. In case Tasha comes in and hears us.'

She was certain that wouldn't happen, but their voices might reach the bug in the bedroom.

In her mind, Emma had a hundred things to discuss with David. But she wasn't sure that he would be able to handle the fact that she had involved the police. It wasn't worth the risk of telling him.

'Listen, David, I know how much you want to protect Tasha. She's your little girl and you love her. I totally understand that. Whatever she does, your love for her is unconditional and undiminished. But I noticed yesterday that when I talked about how Ollie loves her – when I put the pressure on – she wobbled. Only a bit, but she wobbled. I'm going to work on her from that angle.'

'Work on her? Jesus, Emma, somehow that sounds so callous. You make her sound like a seasoned criminal.'

Emma resisted the temptation to mention drug mules or abducted babies.

'We both want the same thing,' she said in a calm voice that belied her inner turmoil. 'She told us yesterday that whatever they want it's going to be today. I need to lower Tasha's defences somehow and I don't want you to react.'

'Are you sure that's the right strategy? We don't know what they want, yet, and if we upset Tasha too much isn't there a chance that this will all go horribly wrong?'

Emma frowned. 'What do you mean? Surely they just want money from us?'

'I doubt it. I'm not sure that makes sense,' David said. 'Why take *our* child? We're not rich or famous – there must be better options around than us.'

'So what the hell is it?' Emma sank lower in the bath, suddenly cold at the thought that Tom's wealth might not be the solution she had been hoping for. She watched David's face and couldn't push away the thought that he was hiding something from her.

'Maybe they want to coerce us into doing something for them – something criminal.'

What? What could he possibly mean? What if they wanted David to plant a bomb that would kill three thousand people, or walk into a bank and shoot innocent women and children – men too, come to that? Would he be able to do it? Would he hold a gun to a child's head if they asked him to, to save Ollie?

Emma burst into tears and David leaned over and grabbed her – pulling her close, oblivious to the hot water soaking through his shirt.

'It's okay, Em. I can do it. I know I can. But if you feel better trying to get Tasha onside, I'll support you.'

Emma held on to David tightly. She needed to feel his arms round her. She didn't want to let go of everything they'd always had together, but, close as his body was to hers, Emma could sense a wall growing between them. It felt as if David knew what these people were going to ask, and she was more convinced than ever that there was something he wasn't telling her.

34

The early hours of the morning had reaped unexpected results for Tom's team. By 4 a.m. everybody had been briefed and a plan had been agreed.

The name Rory had been the clue, particularly when coupled with the motorbike. Desperate as Tom was to scan the police database to see if anybody by that name had a criminal record, he was wary of doing anything on a computer. If somebody inside HQ was working for this bunch, a search for the name Rory might be flagged. He couldn't risk it.

He and Becky had realised they needed somebody from the organised crime team – somebody with experience of drugs and their dealers. Natasha's behaviour on the train and the suspicion of her involvement in the distribution of drugs was the only tenuous link they had to a criminal gang, so Philippa had recommended a colleague of hers from her inspector days – DS Andy Hughes. He had been working under cover for a couple of years and was just getting back into a slightly less dangerous role as a regular detective. Beard gone, hair shorn to quarter of an inch all over, body toned from hours in the gym, he was unrecognisable. At least, that's what he obviously hoped. Only the depths of his dark-brown eyes gave any hint of the strain of the job he had done for all that time.

His involvement on the team paid off immediately as Tom described the person Emma had seen with Natasha.

'I think I know who this is, sir,' Andy said. 'I'm pretty sure it's Rory Slater – from out Cadishead way. Lives in a big, run-down

Victorian house with his wife – Donna, she's called – and a massive brood of kids. He's small fry – just distribution. He wasn't one of my targets, but I knew who he was. Rory was clearly shit-scared of whoever was pulling his strings. This gang's the real deal, I'm sorry to say.'

'How do you think he ended up with Natasha, then?' Becky asked.

Andy shook his head. 'I don't know. My best guess is that some lowlife found her and thought she might be useful. Perhaps he thought there'd be a price on her head, or something, and he'd be able to cash in. When there wasn't, he was landed with her. Unless you're a complete numpty you don't go trying to extort money from the dad when he's surrounded by police, as David Joseph would have been at that time. And there are so many kids in Rory's house that one more wouldn't be noticed – half of them don't seem to bother with anything as mundane as school. I'm sure he finds other uses for them.'

It had felt like a major breakthrough, but it was disappointing – if unsurprising – to find that Rory Slater was at the bottom of the food chain when it came to this group.

According to Emma, Rory claimed he didn't have Ollie. Tom was desperate to get into that house, though. He had to be absolutely certain that Ollie wasn't there but at the same time, he couldn't risk alerting the gang by ordering a full-scale raid. A more subtle approach was required.

They were going to put the Slaters under surveillance and Becky started to set the wheels in motion.

'Any chance Slater would recognise you, Andy, if you went in as a detective looking into something involving one of his kids?' Tom asked.

'Nope – even my own mum didn't recognise me when I was under cover. I wore contacts to change my eye colour, so it would take somebody a tad brighter than Rory Slater, who's never actually met me, to recognise me as the same pisshead who was in the pub a couple of times when he was there. And he never heard me speak.'

'Okay, we'll set up the surveillance, but I'd like to get a feel for what goes on in that house, and we need to know if Ollie's there. That would certainly make things easier. We'll wire you up, Andy, so we can listen in. You okay with this?'

Andy gave a nonchalant shrug and Tom knew that an assignment like this was nothing to him.

The surveillance team had identified a row of shops opposite the Slater home with vans coming and going all day, so their vehicle wasn't going to stand out at all, and everything was in place by ten o'clock in the morning. Already the wide, toy-strewn front garden of Rory Slater's house in Cadishead was full of kids.

From the van, Tom watched as Andy pushed open a wooden gate that was hanging off its hinges. A couple of the children looked at him enquiringly, but the other three ignored him.

'Is your mum in, son?' Andy asked one of the boys. Tom could hear him clearly.

The boy grunted a noncommittal response.

'Your dad?'

'Nah – he'll be down the bookie's. We won't see him till dinner.' This sounded like a younger voice, and Tom could see Andy crouching down to the level of one of the children. Andy fished a picture out of his inside pocket. It was a photo of the boy from the train.

'Is this one of your brothers?' he asked, keeping his voice level and friendly.

'Never seen him before,' came the reply. Even from the van, Tom could see that the boy hadn't even glanced at the picture. These kids were trained from an early age, it seemed.

A girl of about nine strode up to them and stopped dead, hands on hips.

'Whoever you are, piss off.'

Andy spoke calmly to her.

'Be a good girl and go and tell your mum that I want to see her, will you?'

'No. She don't like bad news. Who are you, any road?'

'I'm DC Hughes.' They'd agreed that he would play down his rank. It was unlikely they would check his warrant card.

'DC short for Dick, is it,' she muttered with a laugh at what she thought was an original joke. She turned and went back into the house, and Andy followed. They could no longer see him, but they could hear every word.

'Nice banner, kids. Welcome home, Shell.'

There was a clatter in the background.

'Steady on, son – we don't want you falling off that ladder.'

There was a grunt in the background and what sounded like 'fuck off' but Tom couldn't be sure.

'That's a nice welcome message for somebody,' Andy said. 'Who's Shell?'

'She's our sister.' It sounded like a little girl speaking.

'Shut up, idiot,' an older voice growled. 'And you – piss off. You shouldn't be in here without a warrant.'

Andy refrained from responding, but Tom could picture his expression of mild disdain. In his experience it was always best when kids tried to rile you to treat them with contempt. Most didn't have the confidence to continue with their abuse if they thought they were being mocked.

'Who's the candle for?' Andy asked

'What's all the bloody noise about?' The voice came from somewhere further away and was quite faint, growing in volume as the speaker got closer to Andy. Nobody answered.

'Mrs Slater?' Andy said. There was the sound of a baby crying and the listeners in the van stiffened for a moment. 'Cute baby,' Andy said. 'What is she, about eight months?'

Clever guy, Tom thought.

'She's nine months, not that it's any of your bleeding business,' the woman muttered, an aggressive note cutting through the wheezing tones of too many cigarettes.

'If you've come about the kids and school, you can sod off. I do me best, but there are twelve of 'em, and I ain't got a car. Sometimes we walk, but I'm not too good on me legs – so tell me what I'm supposed to do, will you?'

'Twelve kids – that's quite a handful,' Andy said conversationally. 'All yours, are they?'

'What's that supposed to mean?'

'Nothing – I wondered if you fostered, that's all.'

'A few are me sister's kids. She doesn't like 'em much, so they've come to live with me.'

Tom made a note to check up on Donna Slater's sister as soon as Andy was out of the house.

'So what do you want, then? My Rory'll be back soon, and he don't like you lot, so best make it snappy.'

'We've only got one question, Mrs Slater,' Andy said. 'Do you know this lad?' There was a brief pause.

'Look at the picture, Mrs Slater,' he said. 'I mean it – look at it properly.'

'Don't recognise him,' was her only response after all of two seconds, followed by a brief bout of coughing.

There wasn't a sound from the Slater's living room. It was as if the children had left, or maybe each child was holding his or her breath to see what Donna Slater would say. Suddenly it was filled with sound again as if a button had been pressed, and Tom guessed that there had been some silent communication between the woman and the kids.

'Thanks for your time, Mrs Slater. Hope you have a happy reunion with your daughter when she gets back.'

'How the fuck do you know about that?' came the angry response.

'Call it intuition, Mrs Slater. Or perhaps it could be something to do with that bloody great banner on your wall.'

❖

A few minutes later, Tom watched as Andy wrestled with the broken gate and start walking towards them. As he walked he started to talk.

'They know the lad. No doubt about it. If you're right and the girl Natasha is known to them as Shelley, they're definitely expecting her home tonight or tomorrow. At a guess, the lad you're interested in from the train was in his bedroom. I saw a little kid get a nod from one of the older ones and sneak off upstairs – I would imagine to tell him to hide. Not that I had any right to search anyway. I don't think the baby was there, though. I think they would have been more frightened by my visit. The kids look scruffy, but not malnourished. Not the healthiest of specimens – you know, a bit grey-looking rather than pink and rosy – but not skinny and I didn't see any bruises. Mind you, they all had jumpers on because the house is bloody freezing.'

Andy walked straight past the van without slowing down or looking at it.

'The kids know what they're about. Not one of them looked at the picture, probably trained that way because they're too young to be able to disguise emotion. I got the feeling that the kids stick together, but when they heard Donna coming they all busied themselves. A couple made themselves scarce. But no sign of Rory. I'll call at the bookie's – see if he's there. I'll let you know if he is. One other thing. They had a candle burning and a picture of a girl propped up behind it. Blonde girl, looked about twelve. See you later.'

Tom gave it five minutes and then exited the van, leaving the surveillance team to do their job. He needed to check how many children should be in that house, whether Donna Slater had a sister and, if she did, whether one of her kids was missing.

❖

Across the road from the Slaters' house, two men sat in a dingy flat above a shabby hairdresser's. The persistent high-pitched cries of women shrieking to be heard above a background of hairdryers from the salon below was only marginally masked by music blaring out from speakers situated just below the floorboards of the first-floor room.

'God, this music is doing my head in,' said one of the men. 'If I have to listen to another track from bloody Adele, I'll go down there and personally pull the plug on whatever's playing that frigging music and crush it underfoot.'

The other guy laughed. 'Well, it says something that you recognise her music, Jim. Not sure I would admit to that if I were you.'

'The wife's favourite – I don't have much choice at home, but I didn't think I'd have to suffer that noise all day as well. Mind you, maybe it's better than the racket those women make. Wah, wah, wah – it's relentless. What the hell do they find to yabber about?'

The question hung unanswered in the dank air of the drab room in which they were sitting. The dirty, yellowed woodchip wallpaper was peeling away from the plaster, its discolouration enhanced by the number of cigarettes the two men had smoked in the week or so that they had been sitting there. An old brown sofa was pushed against one wall, stuffing escaping from the arms. There was a folding card table and a couple of bent-back chairs that looked as if they had been made in about the same year as the row of shops had been built. As rooms went, it had to be one of the most depressing that either of them had seen for a while.

The lack of home comforts didn't matter to the two men, though. They had brought their own chairs. Right now, they were both on high alert, a state that Jim put down to the acrid fumes of cheap hair lacquer that seemed to permeate the room. He was sure it was making him high, but at that moment he had other things on his mind.

'Who the fuck is that?' he asked, peering through the binoculars set into a stand. With one hand he pressed the trigger release for the camera on a separate tripod. He didn't need to check the viewfinder – the telephoto lens was permanently focused on the house opposite.

'I don't know, but I'm more interested in that van parked outside the halal butchers. It's been there for forty-five minutes and nobody's got in or out, and nothing's been delivered. Given its position, I'd say it's surveillance. And I'd say it was on the Slaters.'

'Bloody marvellous. If that's the case, what's that other idiot doing walking right in there? Stupid bastard – he's going to bugger everything up if he's not careful.'

Jim pushed himself back from the window and the wheels on his chair propelled him to the table behind. He grabbed a packet of cigarettes and wheeled himself back to the window.

They watched for a few more minutes until the man came out of the house and walked up the road.

'He's not even glanced at the van, and he's talking. He's wired. Give it a minute or two.'

They waited. Finally the side door of the van slid open, and a tall man in dark-blue jeans and a black jacket emerged on the side away from the Slaters' home.

'Who's that?'

'Jesus. It's Tom Douglas. He's a DCI in the Major Incidents Team. What in God's name is he doing here?'

Jim muttered a string of expletives.

'We've got to stop them before everything goes tits up. *Bollocks.* This is *all* we need.'

The man picked up his phone and dialled a number.

35

The table was covered with the remains of three uneaten breakfasts, and the room smelled temptingly of the bacon that remained untouched on plates. Cooking was something that Emma felt she could do to keep her body occupied while her mind spun in circles. Just sitting had never been something she had managed easily, and any problems in her past had always resulted in bursts of energy. It wasn't only that, though. Unlike David, she was aware that the conversation in the kitchen was being listened to, and much as she was determined to work on Natasha, the girl wasn't going to weaken when she knew she would be heard. And she could hardly drag her off into the bathroom.

She pushed her chair back and started to grab plates.

'I'll do that, Em,' David said. 'I'm sorry we haven't done justice to your breakfast. I think if I try to swallow anything solid it will choke me.'

'I wonder what they've given Ollie for breakfast,' was all she said. 'I hope they understand what babies of his age like to eat. Do you think they do, Natasha? Or will they be feeding him salted peanuts, or whole grapes with pips in?' She looked pointedly at her stepdaughter, who looked pale this morning. The girl had spirit, though, she had to admit, as Natasha gave Emma a defiant stare.

Emma slammed the plates down on the worktop with such force that she was surprised they didn't shatter. She spun round and leaned back against the counter, folding her arms.

'Right,' she said with as much bravado as she could manage. 'We're going for a walk. All of us. Get your coats.'

'What?' A response from Natasha at last. 'I'm not going nowhere. You're not my mother. You can't tell me what to do.' *Bravely said, Natasha,* Emma thought.

'Wrong, Natasha. I'm the grown-up, you're the child. You may be capable of doing some terrible things that even in my wildest dreams I wouldn't stoop to...' Emma ignored David's look of horror, '...but you are *not* going to stop me from going for a walk, and your father is coming with me. If you want to spy on us you'd better come too, or we might escape into town and call the police.'

'Em, what happens if somebody calls?' David asked, clearly wondering what she was playing at.

'Nobody's going to call, are they? They'll phone Natasha on that mobile that never leaves her right hand. The one I presume she smuggled into the house in the pocket of my fleece.'

Without waiting for a reply, Emma stomped off into the hall, returning with three jackets of various sizes. She saw Natasha look askance at the red one that was thrown at her.

'Put it on. It's cold out there, and it was good enough when you needed deep pockets, wasn't it? We need to move – to get some energy back. Come on, both of you.'

Emma opened the door to the back porch, stuffed her feet in a pair of green wellingtons and set off down the path, knowing that David would follow her.

She waited where the path met the lane, and sure enough a couple of minutes later David and his daughter came plodding round the corner, looking like a pair of reluctant hikers on a Sunday ramble.

She turned on her heel and marched off. She wanted them to be well away from the house before she started on Natasha. She waited at the start of a track that led across the fields to an old bridleway she had walked down a few times. Natasha and David caught up with her, and she ushered them onto the track.

'I used to bring Ollie here when he was tiny,' she said

conversationally. 'I used to strap him into a papoose type thing, but with him facing outwards so he could see what was going on. He loved it. I bet your mum brought you here when you were a baby. Isn't that what you told me, David? That Caroline used to love walking with Tasha when she was little?'

After a brief pause, David seemed to realise what she was trying to do.

'We all used to go together at the weekend. Do you remember, Tasha? And when you got your first bike you insisted you could ride it all the way. We said the track was too rough for a bike – particularly with stabilisers on, but you weren't having any of it, and I had to push you. Had a bad back for weeks.' David looked at Natasha and smiled, to show there was no resentment in his words.

'How well do you remember your mum?' Emma asked, as if this were the most normal family out for a walk. 'I told you the other day that I met her – I could see how much your dad loved her.'

Emma had no knowledge of child psychology at all but felt that the more she played on the whole mum and dad thing, the more Natasha might feel a sense of belonging and a commitment to Ollie.

'I lost touch with them, though, when I went to Australia,' she continued. 'Then my ex-fiancé died – I didn't tell you that, did I? I was a mess. It's horrible when someone you love dies, isn't it? You must have felt terrible when your mum died. Do you remember the accident?'

Natasha's face had tightened. She was, after all, only a kid. A kid who had lost her mum in a horrible accident and then had been brought up by that awful Rory man. In spite of everything Emma wanted to hug her. So she did.

It only lasted a second, but she felt Tasha lean in towards her and then push her away and march off in front of them. Emma gave her a minute and then she speeded up too, so she was walking abreast of Natasha, with David slightly behind on the narrowing track.

'When I met your dad a year after you'd disappeared, he was a total wreck. He missed your mum so much, but more than anything he missed you. For two years it was the only thing he ever talked about. He didn't know what had happened to his little girl, and he blamed himself because he didn't go with you that night. Your mum skidded the car and died, and you disappeared. She wasn't a great driver, according to your dad. Maybe she lost control – was it because you were talking to her? Did she turn round to look at you and drive off the road? Is that what happened, Tasha? Because she loved you so much that if you had needed her she'd have turned round, I'm sure. Is that why you're like this – because you think you caused the crash?'

Natasha mumbled something.

'What did you say?' Emma asked.

The girl lifted a strained face.

'It wasn't me,' she shouted. 'It wasn't my fault.' She spun round and stared at David. 'Tell her it wasn't my fault.'

Just for a second, all three of them stood immobile, Natasha and David staring at each other, Emma looking at David's haggard face, a nerve twitching above his left eyebrow. She had to break this tension.

'It was nobody's fault, Tasha. I was simply trying to understand what happened – how your mum lost control of the car.'

Emma reached out a hand to Natasha, but the girl moved out of the way. Turning her back on her father and moving as far away from both of them as she could get, she carried on walking, head down.

Emma felt she was getting nowhere. Surely there had to be something that she could say or do that would get through to Natasha? She was so focused on searching for the right words that she almost missed it when the girl spoke.

'It was the man's fault. The man on the phone.'

Emma carried on walking, not wanting to do anything to stop Natasha from talking. After a second or two, she carried on.

'There was a car right across the road, and Mummy was stopping. Then her phone rang. I didn't think she was going to answer it, but she did. Suddenly she speeded up. I heard her shouting into the phone "Why can't I stop? What's going on?" Then the car went mad – all over the road. She shouted for help – she shouted to the man on the phone, but it was too late.'

'What did she shout, Tasha? Can you remember?'

'Of course I can. I remember everything. I wasn't a baby, and it's not the sort of night you forget in a hurry.'

'So what did she shout?'

'Just a name. I don't know what he said to her, but she shouted his name.'

Emma waited.

'She was going to stop. If she'd stopped, she wouldn't have died, would she? But the man on the phone frightened her. She dropped the phone and went really fast, round the car in the road. Then she shouted to him – but it was too late. It was all *his* fault.'

'Do you remember what she shouted?'

David had turned white.

'Of course I do. It was a name – somebody I didn't know, but I hate him. Jack. That's what she screamed. Jack.'

36

The small team sat in Tom's office, which was stuffy with the stale odour of too many warm bodies and too many half-drunk cups of coffee lying around on every vacant surface. Rory Slater hadn't been at the bookie's, but they had finally tracked him down and put a tail on him in the hope that he would contact his masters. His home phone was being tapped, but there was currently no mobile signal coming from the house. So for the moment all they could do was watch and wait.

They had looked into all Slater's known associates, but that line of enquiry had revealed very little. As Becky said, those they had found were 'run of the mill scumbags', but none was capable of masterminding this – whatever 'this' was.

Becky's nose was glued to her computer screen, and Tom had noticed her rub her tired eyes a couple of times. He knew from experience there was nothing worse than staring at a screen when you'd had precious little sleep.

'Got her,' she whispered, more to herself than anybody else. Despite her low voice, those left in the room turned towards her.

'Donna Slater has a sister – Sylvia Briggs. Two daughters, one son. One of the daughters is thirteen, and she's called Isabella. I think I need to pay Mrs Briggs a visit.'

'Well done, Becky.' Tom cast his gaze round the rest of the room. 'We all know what's at stake here, so let's get on with it. And remember, even though I'd like to think nobody in this division would be in the pay of an organised crime group, with a baby's life at stake we mustn't assume anything.'

Tom's office emptied and he rested his elbows on the desk and his chin on his cupped hands. More than anything he wanted to drag Rory Slater into an interview room and grill him until he admitted where Ollie was being held. But he didn't think Rory would know. The baby would have been handed over to a middleman. Rory would be part of one small cell in a bigger organisation.

Tom turned to his computer to check his email. There would be nothing about Ollie Joseph on here of course, but he had other cases to think about. And he still had the Swiss bank to call back. For the moment, there wasn't a single thing he could be doing to help Ollie, and Becky had the sad case of the dead girl well in hand.

He paused for a moment. It was Saturday, but then he remembered the message – call me any time – and he strongly suspected that for private clients with enough funds there would be access to the bank seven days a week.

He checked his mobile for the number he had used the last time and pressed call.

'Good morning. My name is Tom Douglas. Could I speak to Mr Charteris, please?' Tom hung on for a few moments as his call was put through.

'Mr Douglas, good day to you. Can I go through some security checks with you, please?' Tom hoped he could remember the 'memorable word' he had submitted so that he could pick out the third and eighth letter.

'Okay, Mr Douglas. Thank you for calling us back. As I mentioned in my message, when the account was opened details of a beneficiary in the event of your brother's death were provided, and it is indeed your name that's on the documentation. Of course, if nobody knew there was an account with us it's understandable that we weren't informed its owner was deceased. I'm sorry for your loss.'

'Thank you. You said there were some irregularities with the account that you wanted to discuss?'

'Yes. Do you think your brother may have provided details of this account to anybody else other than you?'

Tom thought for a moment. Emma would be the most likely, but she would have mentioned it when he was trying to give her money all those years ago. Melissa was another option. She'd been living with Jack for about six months before he died, and she had moved heaven and earth to claim ownership of some of Jack's estate because she said she was 'owed' it. If she'd had access to the four million, though, Tom wasn't sure she would have continued to try to get the rest of Jack's money. He had no idea where she was now. He had never been provided with her contact details and hadn't seen her in person since Jack died. All dealings were through her solicitor – a man with too smart a suit for the job he was doing whom Tom didn't trust as far as he could throw him.

'I can't think of anybody. Why are you asking?'

'Well, I'm sorry to tell you that the account is closed. The balance was withdrawn a few months ago – September, to be precise – transferred to an account in the Cayman Islands. I can, of course, provide the transfer details under the circumstances, but I doubt that will help you.'

Damn it. Another banking system with secrecy laws.

It seemed Tom had been right. Whoever had broken into his house in the summer must have stolen the login details of the account in Switzerland and cleared it out.

He was about to question Mr Charteris further when his internal line rang. Making his excuses and asking if it would be okay to call again, he hung up and answered his phone.

'Tom Douglas,' he answered vacantly, his mind running through the options for discovering who had taken Jack's money.

'Tom, we need to talk. My office, one hour.'

'Philippa, I'm a bit busy at the moment. Can it wait, please?' he asked. Sometimes, Philippa's high-handed attitude grated on him, although most of the time he accepted that she was the boss.

But today he had other things to worry about than offending Philippa.

'No. It can't wait. I've had a call from the head of operations for Titan. One hour, please.'

The phone went dead. What the hell did the North West's Regional Organised Crime Unit want with him?

'Bugger,' Tom muttered.

37

The only sounds were birdsong, a distant tractor and the squelching of three pairs of wellington boots on a track that had suddenly become a quagmire. Nobody had spoken since Natasha's shocking revelation that her mother had shouted the name Jack, and each of them was lost in thought.

Emma didn't know what David was thinking, but she could guess. Why would Caroline have called out another man's name just as she crashed? Who was this Jack? Even as she wondered about it, Emma felt a chill creep up her back. Jack wasn't such a common name. But if it was *her* Jack, why had he phoned Caroline? What had he said?

She could sympathise with David's obvious confusion; she felt bewildered herself. Caroline's accident had occurred less than a week before Jack's death and only days before she had received his suicide note. Not that she had recognised it as such when it had arrived. The wording suggested that he was wallowing in some kind of self-pity, and she was so appalled at the way he had dumped her all those months previously that she had dismissed it as a cry for sympathy for all the mistakes he had made in his life. She'd decided he wasn't getting any sympathy from her. He could whistle for it.

And then he was dead, and she knew she should have done something when she received the note – called Tom, phoned Jack to talk it through – anything. Her disgust at his treatment of her didn't mean she wished him any harm.

She had never understood about Melissa, though, who had appeared to come from nowhere, and had been with Jack for the last six months of his life. To this day, Melissa had been one piece of the puzzle in their relationship that had eluded her. His suicide was the other.

Emma was so absorbed in her own thoughts that she had momentarily lost sight of what mattered here and now. She glanced at Natasha, whose eyes betrayed a hint of uncertainty, and Emma felt a glimmer of hope. She still felt as if somebody had put a hand into her chest and ripped her heart out through her ribs, but there was a faint pulse of optimism hovering at the edge of her consciousness.

'Are you okay, Em?' David asked. She glanced across at him, above Natasha's head, and nodded.

'Do you think it was *my* Jack?' she said, knowing the answer before he spoke.

'I can't think who else it could have been, but I have no idea why he was calling Caroline.'

'What was their relationship?'

David's head spun round. 'What?'

Emma closed her eyes for a second. She had phrased that badly and should have known that David would only hear the word 'relationship'.

'I mean, how did she know him, and how come she knew him so well that he had her phone number?'

Looking slightly mollified, David walked on a few yards before answering. If it turned out Caroline had been having an affair with Jack he would be devastated – and so would she.

'You know he sorted out my computer security at work, don't you?' he said after a few moments, turning back towards Emma.

'Of course – that's how I was introduced to you and Caroline at those charity events. But I never thought she and Jack were close – on swapping mobile numbers terms.'

'No, me neither,' David muttered.

'Did Caroline meet him first, or did you?'

'It was me. I went to a seminar about internet security. He was the keynote speaker, and I was impressed. So when I needed to upgrade the system at work a few months later, I called him.'

Natasha had walked on, her head down, lost in her own thoughts. They could leave her to her worries for a while.

'And Caroline?' Emma asked tentatively.

'She used to stop by the office a couple of times a week – more sometimes. After Tasha went to school, Caroline found herself at a bit of a loose end. She wasn't a joiner, if you know what I mean. She didn't like going to the gym or anything like that, and she said being at home all day freaked her out. So she would come into town, have a look around the shops and then come to the office for an hour or so. Jack used to call in every few days to check on the work his team were doing, but that was way before Caroline's accident. By the time she died, Jack had sold his company, and we hadn't seen him for months at social events. I guess after you and he split up he didn't enjoy them any more. I can't think why he would have had Caroline's mobile number, though.'

Emma thought for a while.

'If I had to guess, I'd say that while he was working for you he used the opportunity to get *all* your phone numbers. He was a hoarder of information. "Data is king" he used to say. So I'm not surprised he had her number. I'm more surprised that the police didn't track the call back to him.'

'They knew she'd taken a call just before the accident but they told me it was from an unregistered mobile.'

Emma shook her head. Jack's love of secrecy sometimes went to ridiculous lengths. For a while, as she talked to David about Jack, Emma felt temporarily glad of the distraction, but it didn't take long for the aching void in her chest to return. Caroline and Jack were dead. They had been missed, but the pain of losing them was nothing in comparison to her fear for Ollie.

Up ahead, Natasha suddenly thrust her hand into the pocket

of her fleece and pulled out her mobile, pushing it to her ear. David and Emma both broke into a run at the same time.

She spun round towards them, holding up one hand as a clear 'stop' signal, and brought her finger to her lips.

'Hello, Rory,' she said, looking down at her feet.

Slowly she lifted her head and stared at Emma and David. Her eyes widened, and her pupils dilated.

'*Finn*,' she said. 'I…'

They could hear the rasping notes of a voice from two metres away, although they couldn't make out the words. The tone was one of cold fury.

'Finn, I didn't tell them anything. I never mentioned Rory.'

David started to move forwards, his hand out to take the phone from Tasha, but the girl shook her head furiously.

'I'm sorry I didn't tell Rory they'd seen me. I know I should have, then he could have changed the route. I'm *sorry* – I thought he'd be mad at me.' Tasha's voice had dropped to little more than a whisper, and her eyes were flooded with tears.

'No, Finn, *no*. I promise – the police know nothing about the baby. Don't hurt Ollie, Finn.' The last words were whispered so quietly that the caller wouldn't have heard them. But they were a plea from the heart.

Tasha listened for a few more minutes, ended the call and folded at the knees. David grabbed her, lowering her to sit on the bank on the side of the track.

'What, Tasha? What's the matter? Who's Finn, and what did he want?' It was all Emma could do to stop herself shaking the girl. She reached forwards to grasp Natasha's shoulders, but when she saw the girl's eyes, black with fear, her hands dropped gently and rubbed Natasha's arms.

'I don't know what they'll do to me now. You were right – what you said last night. I should have told Rory about the CCTV. Finn says Rory's being questioned by the police.'

'Good,' Emma said. 'He looked a nasty bastard. Surely that's a good thing?'

'*What?*' David clearly had no idea what they were talking about, but Emma and Natasha both ignored him. Now wasn't the time for lengthy explanations.

'Of *course* it's not a good thing. They don't trust me now. That means I'm probably going to die. Everything could go wrong now, don't you see? And all because of me.'

'What about Ollie?' Emma asked. 'What does this mean for *Ollie?*'

Natasha shook her head again. 'It changes everything. They don't know if it's safe to go ahead with the job. If it goes wrong, I'm dead. Finn's got to see what the boss man says. I don't know who he is – he's like a shadow. I don't think even Rory knows.'

'What's "the job", Tasha?' Emma asked. 'Can't we just give them some money and get Ollie back?' But Tasha wasn't listening.

'It was meant to be over today. You could have had Ollie back and I could go home.' Her head hung down and tears dripped unheeded onto the legs of her jeans.

Emma crouched down in the muddy lane. 'Nobody wants you to go anywhere, Tasha. We just want Ollie back. But we want you too. We're not going to abandon you.'

'Oh, you will. You might not think so, but you will.'

Emma looked up at David, whose face in the weak sunlight had lines carved so deep that he looked twenty years older. She turned to Natasha and put her hands on the girl's shoulders.

'That's not going to happen, Tasha. We're *not* going to let you go.'

Natasha's whole body was shaking with the force of her tears, and her hands were covering her eyes.

'Course you will. You still don't get it, do you? I know you want Ollie, and I know nobody ever wanted me. Even Rory doesn't want *me* – only what I can do for him.'

David fell to his knees in the mud. 'I don't know what you and Emma are talking about, but I do know one thing. You were always very much loved and very much wanted, Tasha. You still are.'

Natasha pulled her hands away from her eyes and for a moment her expression hardened.

'That's not true, is it? I was a pawn in a game. That's what Rory says. It's all I've ever been – a pawn.'

Emma's head was spinning with every word that had been spoken, but for now the only thing she wanted to think about was Ollie. She looked at David as he pulled his daughter towards him. For a moment, Natasha leaned into him – but with a sudden thrust, pushed him away.

'Don't.'

David looked as if he had been shot, a mixture of emotions that Emma couldn't quite decipher distorting his features.

'At least I've done one thing right,' Tasha murmured. 'At least the police don't know about Ollie. Then I really *would* be dead.'

'I think you're being a bit melodramatic, darling,' David said. 'Nobody's going to hurt you when you're with us.'

Natasha looked at him. 'I would have thought you, of all people, would have known better than that.'

Emma walked away from them both. Whatever was going on between Natasha and her father, it was doing nothing to help Ollie, and she didn't have the energy to argue about it right now.

She put her hand in her pocket and felt the solid lump that was her mobile phone – the object she had considered her lifeline. Now its cold touch burned her fingers, and she couldn't help wondering if all it offered was a death sentence – for Natasha, and maybe even for Ollie.

38

Tom could have done without this. Whatever Titan wanted, he was sure it wasn't as vital as finding young Ollie Joseph, and Philippa should know that. Irritated as he was, though, he had little choice but to bow to her command. Much as he had never wanted to rise above the rank of Chief Inspector because he didn't want to be confined to an office even more than he already was, sometimes he wished that he had the power to say 'no' when he was told to do something.

He knocked briefly on Philippa's closed door and pushed it open without hearing her usual call of 'Come' – another source of irritation. She sounded like the Queen sometimes, and, efficient as she was, when she received her next inevitable promotion Tom was certain that she would become so far up herself that nobody would be able to find the real Philippa any more.

Her office reflected her personality – or at least the personality she liked to display. The room was featureless with some random prints on the wall that conveyed nothing about the person who had chosen them. In fact, they had probably been chosen by the decorators. The desk was totally uncluttered, with a stack of three wire trays that, unlike Tom's, weren't overflowing all over the desk. In other words, bland but fit for purpose.

Philippa was dressed in her customary dark suit with a dazzling white blouse, and every strand of her straight auburn hair was in place, the bob just below her ears that never seemed to get any longer or be cut any shorter. Facing Philippa, his back to the door, was a man in a pinstriped jacket who turned to stand as Tom came in.

Beating Philippa to the introductions, Tom held out his hand. 'Tom Douglas,' he said, noting the warm, dry grip of the distinguished-looking man facing him.

'Paul Green', he responded, indicating the chair next to him and sitting down.

Tom sat, and turned to face Philippa.

'What can I do for you both?' he asked.

'Tom, Mr Green would like to talk to you about your possible surveillance of one of Titan's targets, a man by the name of...' Philippa glanced down at her notepad, '...Rory Slater.'

Before Tom had a chance to speak, Green turned to face him.

'If I could explain, Tom – it's okay if I call you Tom?' Without waiting for confirmation, he continued. 'We've had our eye on Slater for some time. I know you're interested in him as the person who may have been harbouring Natasha Joseph, but he's part of something much bigger and we've been running an operation to catch the head of this organised crime group for a few years. We're sure we know who the main man is, but catching him is proving difficult. He doesn't get his hands dirty. He leaves all that to his minions. Slater is bottom of the pile, but through him we're getting closer.'

Green withdrew some photos from his briefcase and laid them on the desk.

'These were taken this morning. You sent somebody into the Slater household, and you've got a surveillance van just down the road. I need you to back off, Tom. This operation is too big to be blown apart by the investigation into a girl who has now reappeared.'

Philippa interrupted. 'You and I haven't had a chance to discuss your interest in Slater, Tom. I gather he's only just come onto your radar.'

'That's right – in the early hours of this morning.' Tom turned towards Green. 'But it's no longer only about a missing girl. Slater is implicated in the kidnap of a baby, Mr Green.' As Tom knew only too well, a child's life trumped just about everything else, including organised crime.

'Shit,' Green mumbled.

The room was quiet for a moment.

'We've had our eyes on this particular group for a long time,' Green said. 'We've known Slater was part of it, and there's a guy higher up the chain that's implicated too – Finbar – or Finn – McGuinness. He's an enforcer and a sociopathic bastard.' Paul Green leaned towards the desk and took a drink from a glass of water before continuing.

'McGuinness has been out of prison for about eight years – he was the driver in an armed robbery – but to all intents and purposes he seems to be keeping out of trouble. His wife runs a burger van in Salford – very popular it is too. We know that Slater picks up the drugs that he sells from the McGuinness burger van, and we want to trace the supply chain back from there. Finn McGuinness keeps a very low profile, but everybody's terrified of him. We've held off doing anything about the burger van until we can get the top man – the man who's running the show – and we think we're getting there.'

Tom filled them in on what he knew of Slater, and how he was implicated in Ollie Joseph's kidnap.

'None of what you said has surprised me, Tom. This gang is highly organised, but also opportunistic,' Green continued. 'They're entrepreneurial. They deal in drugs, firearms, women – anything they can sell on the street. But if an opportunity comes up – something out of the ordinary – they'll go for it.'

'And you think they're going for something now, do you?' Philippa asked.

'We know they are, although we don't know what exactly. We have a CHIS. He's working for them, but at the moment he only has a small part of the picture. It's going to happen soon. He's been on standby for a couple of days now.'

Tom had always thought that CHIS, or Covert Human Intelligence Source, was an absurd term. He was much more comfortable with informant, or even snout, but within Philippa's four walls, political correctness was everything.

'Do you think the kidnap and the job are related?' Philippa asked.

'Could be,' Tom answered. He filled Paul Green in on more of the details of young Ollie's abduction and his belief that money was unlikely to be the motive.

'Tiger kidnap,' Green said. 'That sounds about right for this lot.'

'Our information is that whatever David Joseph is going to be asked to do, it's today. Then the baby will be brought back safe and well, we hope. Given the timetable your CHIS is giving you, it sounds as if they might be linked. What else do we know?'

There was a knock on the door and Philippa barked 'Wait'. But the door opened and Becky poked her head round the door.

'So sorry, ma'am,' she said, giving a slightly nervous grimace, 'but we need Tom. A bit of a problem. Ten minutes ago, British Transport Police arrested the lad Natasha was seen smiling at on the train and they've taken Rory Slater in for questioning too, because he was at the station waiting to pick the lad up.'

Tom heard a groan from Paul Green and he had to sympathise with the man. Years of work could be about to go down the pan. Of course, Transport Police had been excluded from the information about the kidnap and so they believed the focus was still on finding out who had taken Natasha.

'They let me know straight away,' Becky said, 'so I told them under no circumstances to mention Natasha Joseph. Let's hope they were listening, or we're in trouble.'

39

Fear was nothing new to Natasha. For more than six years it had been a daily reality – fear of pissing Rory off; fear of being caught nicking stuff; fear that her life would never get any better. But this was a whole new level of fear. She felt sick. She knew what happened to people who let Finn down. She'd seen it with her own eyes once, when she was somewhere she shouldn't have been. But Emma and David wouldn't believe her. They really had no idea.

Nobody was speaking to Natasha anyway. Nobody knew what to say to her, and she got that. It wasn't supposed to be like this, though. She wasn't supposed to care about any of them – not Emma, not Ollie and certainly not David. She had jumped at the chance to do this job because more than anything she wanted her father to have some idea of the life she'd been forced to live. Then they told her the reward – another year before she would have to go to Julie's – and she would have done anything for that.

Nearly all the girls who went to Julie's had to have some time in The Pit first – Rory said it was to make them obedient – to show them what would happen if they tried to run away. Natasha had been terrified of that hole in the ground at the back of the cellar since the first time she had been thrown in there. She had been six years old, and the darkness had swallowed her whole.

Am I dead? It had been the only thought that her young mind was able to grasp. This wasn't what being alive was like, so it had to be what being dead felt like. Never before had she been left alone with nobody to speak to for days at a time. For hours she had wandered round, bewildered, stumbling about in the dark, touching the damp earthen walls and asking, begging, for somebody to speak to her. But nobody was listening.

The floor and walls of The Pit were icy, and freezing air blew through gaps around the trapdoor. She had cried and cried, but nobody had come.

I didn't know what I'd done wrong – why I'd been put in there.

Then there was the man with a voice that sounded like footsteps on a gravel path – the man who she now knew to be Finn McGuinness. She had heard him talking, but she couldn't remember now what he had said. Apart from one thing.

'Her mam's dead. She's no use to us. Get rid of her.'

She had repeated those words over and over in her head. 'Her mam's dead.' She understood that, but it wasn't for some time that she understood the rest of what he had said.

And if she was no use to them all those years ago, she was even less now. She couldn't do the skunk run and she had screwed up this job. They wouldn't let her go, though. Nobody was ever let go. That only left two options.

'She's no use to us. Get rid of her.'

Or she would end up at Julie's – just like Izzy had.

She didn't know which was worse.

❖

Emma lowered herself onto the grass, immediately feeling the damp penetrate the denim of her jeans but not caring. She reached out and gently took Natasha's hand in hers.

'How are you doing, Tasha?' she asked. Natasha didn't answer. She put her head down and stared at her hands as she pulled on one finger after the other. They were the hands of a child: chewed, torn fingernails and slightly grubby.

'Why did you agree to do this – to take Ollie? Is it the only reason you came home? Why do you want to hurt us so much? Please, Tasha, try to explain and we'll do our very best to understand.'

Natasha cast a sly look at David.

'Ask him.'

David stood up and went to the other side of the track, looking out over the fields. From behind, Emma could see that every muscle in his body was tense. Finally he turned round, came over to Natasha and kneeled down.

'Tasha, staying at home and not coming with you and your mum that night was a massive mistake – one that I've regretted ever since. I was selfish. I should have come. I did everything I possibly could to find you. Ask Emma. Check it out in the local papers. I don't know what else to tell you. I even launched the Natasha Joseph appeal a year later.'

Natasha looked at him, distrust still in her eyes, and started mumbling. 'You're not Natasha Joseph. She's dead. You're Shelley Slater. Shelley Slater. Not Natasha Joseph. Tasha's dead. Her father don't want her. You're Shelley Slater.'

'Is that what they said to you?' David asked softly, stroking his daughter's hair, matted through lack of washing and brushing as she had refused any help from Emma. For the first time, she let her father touch her without flinching.

Natasha nodded and sniffed. 'I wouldn't say it. I wouldn't say Shelley Slater – so they threw me back in The Pit. I had to stay there 'til I said it – then they kept asking me what I was called, and if I slipped up I was thrown back in. It was cold and damp, and I got no food. But Rory was scared he'd be caught with me and he said I wasn't worth the trouble. I don't know how he'd ended up with me, but he said he'd fucked up and I was a bleeding nuisance.'

'You're never going back there, Tasha. I promise you. I may have let you down six years ago, but I'm your dad, and you're staying with us.'

Natasha spun round, her blotchy face going red with anger.

'Have you not listened to me? They won't let me stay.'

'Listen to me, Tasha,' Emma said. 'I know this is really difficult for you, love, but I might know somebody that can help us. He's a friend of mine, and he's really good at sorting out difficult problems. What do you think? Shall we go and meet him?'

Natasha lifted her tear-stained face.

'*No!*' she practically screamed at Emma. 'Don't tell nobody else. If anybody else knows, you won't get Ollie back, and they'll come for me.'

'What choice have we got?' Emma asked. 'Finn says the deal is off – so we need help, don't we? I just have to make a phone call.'

Emma knew she had to get the girl on her side, to make her believe that there *was* a way out for all of them.

'You can't,' Natasha said. 'My phone's monitored, and I fixed yours.'

Emma stood up, brushing the damp grass from her trousers. She had hoped to use Natasha's phone, but that obviously wasn't going to work. She turned round to face her stepdaughter, and put her hand in her pocket. This was a huge risk, and one she sincerely hoped she wouldn't regret.

Her heart was beating fast. She could feel a pulse in her neck throbbing against the collar of her jacket. Slowly Emma pulled the phone out of her pocket and held it towards Natasha on the flat of her hand.

Natasha's mouth fell open. 'Do you have any idea what would happen if they knew you had a phone? Do you have any *idea* what you've done?'

Emma was silent.

'You've phoned the police, haven't you? Did you tell them about Rory? You did, didn't you? You *stupid cow*.'

'Emma?'

She ignored the question in her husband's voice, turning her head slightly to give him an apologetic smile and crouched down in front of Natasha.

'We need their help, Tasha. You think you're in trouble with

Finn and Rory, but they've still got Ollie. We can't wait to hear what they decide. It might be too late for Ollie. Shall we go and meet this friend of mine?'

Natasha jumped up from the bank and pushed past Emma.

'And what if Finn finds out? How do you think him and Rory knew the police had been to see me in the first place? How many bent coppers do you think they have on their payroll? *Jesus*, if you've told the pigs, one of them will have squealed to Finn – you can bet your life on that.'

Resting her folded arms on a five-barred gate, Natasha put her head down and cried silently, her heaving shoulders being the only clue to her tears.

Emma stared at the phone in her hand.

Was it really the answer to all of their problems, or was telling Tasha the most foolish mistake of her life?

40

'Tell me,' Tom said to Becky as he walked into his office and sat down.

Becky was as succinct as possible in repeating what British Transport Police had told her – that the boy who Natasha had smiled at had been seen on another train, this time with his own backpack on. The plain-clothes policeman who saw him had been doing a routine run on that particular line, but he recognised the boy's face from the details that had been circulated, so he followed him. The boy dropped off his backpack, the same as Natasha had. When he got back to Victoria Station, Rory Slater was waiting for him, so they were both arrested. Slater's denying all involvement, blaming it on kids from school putting the lad up to it.

'Why was Slater waiting for him?'

'I asked that. He said he was in the area, but wouldn't say what he was doing. Maybe the lad was supposed to be paid for his delivery? When they recovered the backpack from the boy he passed it to, it had two kilos of skunk inside, so it was worth a bob or two. Slater probably didn't trust him to bring the money straight home.'

'How do we think this changes things?' Tom asked. Becky felt a slight glow of warmth at being consulted.

'As far as Slater is concerned, this is a routine pick-up. He may somehow have found out that we caught Natasha on CCTV, though, and if we don't ask him about her it will be a red flag. So they just need to show Slater and his lad Natasha's picture and ask if they recognise her. He'll say no, and that will be that. There can't be any hint that we know Natasha's been living with him, because he'll wonder why we're not arresting him.'

'Shit,' Tom muttered, drumming his fingers on the desk. Becky decided to give him a moment. 'And he'll know there can only be one reason – that we know about the kidnap.'

The office was quiet for a moment while they both thought about the potential for disaster.

'Okay,' Tom said. 'We need to use this to our advantage. BTP are bound to be sending a search team into Slater's house, looking for drugs. We can send one of our guys with them to bug the place.'

'If they let anything slip about Natasha, we'll have to keep Rory locked up until it's all over, and that's going to be difficult.'

'It's worse than you think,' Tom responded. 'We've been told to keep away from Rory Slater – there's another operation. A big one. We need to sort out liaison between us and the Titan guys. They're not at all happy about this, and I don't blame them.'

'Bollocks – that makes what I've got to tell you even more tricky,' Becky said. 'I went to see Sylvia Briggs – Donna Slater's sister. I asked about her kids. None of them live with her. She says a couple of them live with her sister – Donna. I asked specifically about Isabella. She started running away from home when she was nine and Sylvia gave up bothering to try to find her.'

'There are some truly delightful people in this world, aren't there?'

Becky smiled, although funny it definitely wasn't. She was spared the necessity of responding, as Tom's private mobile began to ring.

Tom listened carefully to his caller for a few minutes.

'Calm down, Emma, there's no need to panic,' he said. 'But we do need to get you all out of that house. It may not be safe, and we need to assess the level of threat. Where are you now?'

Tom's voice was low and urgent, and Becky knew something was seriously wrong.

'Okay. Go home, pick up some shopping bags and get everybody in your car – not David's Range Rover because it stands out too much. Remember to take your purse – exactly as you would if you were going shopping. It needs to look natural. I'll make some arrangements. Call me when you're away from the house and I'll tell you where to go.'

He paused again.

'Oh, and Emma – I need you to wear something quite distinctive – a bright colour and not too tight. I'll explain later. It's just started chucking it down outside, so choose something with a hood. When you call me, don't lift the phone to your ear. Put it on speaker and leave it on your knee. Make sure Natasha takes her phone – it will have a GPS tracker on it, and if they can't find her they'll panic. Right. I need you to repeat all of this.'

He listened silently. 'Well done. I'll see you in less than an hour. Oh, and Emma? You're doing great. Really great.'

Becky had said nothing throughout but had taken notes of everything Tom had asked Emma to do – in case they needed to repeat the instructions later. Tom turned to her now.

'I want BTP to keep Rory Slater until I say they can let him go. The Joseph family is in danger. Out of choice, I'd pull them all out to somewhere safe – but they'll never agree to that. Either way, Rory Slater and his bosses think they're going to get Natasha back – they can't afford to let her go. She's bound to know way more than she realises. We need a plan to keep this family safe, Becky. And we've got about ten minutes to decide what it is.'

41

Unlocking the bathroom door, Emma emerged into their bedroom to see David standing waiting for her.

'Emma,' he started. *Shit*! She hadn't told him about the bugs, not wanting to freak him out too much.

'Oh darling, what are we going to do?' she interrupted before he could get started. She moved quickly across the room and pulled him into a hug, gently whispering 'Shh' in his ear.

He pushed her away and looked at her with such astonishment that she wondered if he would ever trust her again. But he wasn't stupid. He pulled her roughly back into his arms and she let out a small cry of shock, which she quickly turned into the start of a sob. She felt David's lips against her ear.

'I don't think I know you any more.' The words were spoken so quietly that she wasn't sure she had heard him correctly. He sounded so sad, so alone, and she longed to give him the time he deserved to listen to her explanation. She had lied to him, kept him in the dark and was now insisting that he did her bidding. This was so far from the relationship they'd had.

She pulled him into the en suite and closed the door, keeping her voice low.

'I'm sorry, David. Everything happened so quickly and I knew you wouldn't want me to contact the police. But I couldn't stand idly by and watch it all unfold.'

'Don't you think it should have been a shared decision?' he asked, not unreasonably.

Emma forced her shoulders to relax a little. She had to stay calm.

'Probably – but everything's different for you. You're being pulled in all directions – I didn't want to stress you any more than you are already. But the important thing is, there are bugs in the kitchen, our bedroom and the sitting room. They can hear every word we say.'

David pulled his head back, his brow furrowed. 'Are you saying that *Tasha* put the bugs in place?'

Emma nodded. 'Tasha's been brought up in a criminal family, poor kid. All this – Ollie's kidnap, the bugs, the drugs – I suspect none of it's enough to scare Tasha. But she's frightened of those two men – Finn and Rory – so she lied to them about being captured on CCTV. That was her big mistake and now she's terrified. Look, we need to get a move on. We're losing time.'

She put her finger to her lips and opened the bathroom door.

She walked quickly to a chest of drawers where she knew she had a long royal-blue zip-up jumper that she rarely wore because it was too big. She didn't want to see the confusion in her husband's eyes for another second, and he saved her the trouble. The door closed quietly as he left the room, and for a moment she gave herself the luxury of two minutes sitting on the bed, calming her nerves, and then got up to follow him. She paused at the door.

Although her heart and soul were occupied with Ollie and his safety, Emma knew she was going to have to talk to Tom about Jack too. Natasha's revelation that it had been a man called Jack who had phoned Caroline just before she died was weighing on her mind. She reached up to pull the old shoebox from the top of her wardrobe. Opening it, she rummaged around until her hand found what it was searching for and she pulled out two sheets of paper, folding them carefully and putting them into her bag along with her phone.

Act two, she thought as she walked downstairs, gulping down a hard ball of fear.

The kitchen was silent, and she walked over to the fridge and pulled open the door.

'Right,' she said in a determined voice. 'Tasha says nothing's going to happen today. But let's hope Ollie will be back tomorrow. I have to believe that. I have to convince myself that he's staying with grandparents for a couple of days, or I wouldn't be able to breathe. And we need to eat. We're out of food, out of milk, everything. He's not going to come back to a house full of sick, helpless people. We need to go shopping.'

David was staring at the inside of the fridge door, where a two-litre container of milk was nearly full, and the shelves were stacked with fresh food that had been bought just the day before.

Emma looked at Natasha and nodded her encouragement.

'You can't go out. I told you, you can't go anywhere without me,' the girl said, her voice sounding weak and unconvincing. It would be better if Natasha didn't have to speak again.

'Then you'd better come with me to keep an eye on me, hadn't you. We'll all go, then you can make sure I don't do anything... your masters wouldn't like.' Emma was suddenly aware that she had nearly said the name Rory and had only just stopped herself in time.

'David? Come on. You're coming too. A family outing,' she said with a sarcastic laugh that ended in yet another sob.

David went to pick up his keys.

'No, we're going in my car. I want to drive. I *need* to drive,' she said.

David shrugged and threw his keys back on the table as Emma ushered them out of the door.

❖

There was an oppressive silence in the car, and Emma wondered not for the first time how silence could vary so much in pitch and tone. This silence held a high-pitched scream at its heart. Her own head was filled with Ollie, but she kept pushing the thoughts away – mentally stroking his soft hair as she did so – to focus on what mattered. Getting him back.

She could guess what was going on in David's head. He would be worried about Ollie too, but images of Natasha's life over the last six years were becoming clearer and clearer, and he had to face up to the fact that Emma herself had been lying to him.

When they were first together David and Emma had talked openly about the small deceptions they had lived with in their previous relationships and agreed that there wouldn't be a single secret between them. As far as she was concerned, that had been the truth. Until Natasha had walked into her kitchen. Since then, Emma had lied about her feelings and kept secrets from her husband.

She glanced in her rear-view mirror at her stepdaughter. Tasha was slumped against the back seat, her face washed out, her eyes haunted by images of her past and her future. This was a child who needed her mother more than ever, and Emma wished she could summon Caroline here right now.

Emma had called Tom the minute the car was away from the house, doing as he said and keeping the phone on speaker on her knee. He had told her to go to a supermarket – not their usual one, but a different one – and park in the busiest aisle of the car park.

David hadn't spoken until the call had ended.

'Who was that?'

'Tom Douglas.'

'Douglas? *Jack's* brother?'

'He's a friend, David. I called him because I thought there would be a ransom, and Tom's got more money than anybody else I know. Jack's money. We still might be able to buy Ollie back, you know.'

David looked at her, his sad face telling her how unlikely that was.

Arriving at the supermarket, Emma reversed into a space that was hardly wide enough for the car and turned the engine off.

'Now we wait.'

Around them shoppers pushed trolleys past their car, heads down against the rain, holding the hands of children or partners, or sometimes they battled alone with a shopping cart on wonky wheels.

Emma's phone lay on her knee, and she glanced at it every few seconds until finally it vibrated and without picking it up she answered the call and put it onto speaker.

'Okay, Emma – great choice of parking spot, but you need to know we think they're here.' There was a small gasp from the back of the car.

Tom continued. 'They'll have picked up Natasha's GPS on her phone. We've been checking any suspect cars that contain two or more men coming into the car park. We've got a hit on one of the number plates. They're watching, so you all need to be very smart about this, but no need to be frightened. They've turned into the top of your aisle, and they know where you are. Don't, whatever you do, stare at each car as it goes past. The fact that you haven't got out yet might be confusing them, so turn to each other now and start to argue – about anything. I'll tell you when they've passed.'

That was one instruction that probably wouldn't be hard to achieve, Emma thought, as she looked at David's stony face. She knew he was already regretting the fact that he had agreed to this.

Tasha slid even further down in her seat and Emma turned to David, shouting nonsense about the mess in the back garden – the first thing that came into her head that was nothing to do with Ollie. They couldn't hear, but they would see her expression. David stared at her mutely, a look of shock on his face that she knew wasn't an act. She kept it up for two minutes before she heard Tom's voice.

'They've gone past. It's pouring with rain,' Tom said, 'so you can run into the supermarket with your hood up or hat on. Emma and Natasha walk quickly to the back, where there's an entrance to the ladies toilet. Go down that corridor, and somebody will be waiting for you. David – hang back a little, pick up a trolley and make your way to the back as if you're going to meet them.'

'Will they follow us in?'

'I doubt it – they'll just be watching your car for when you come out.' Tom paused. 'You okay?'

'Fine,' Emma answered. 'See you in a few minutes.'

She disconnected and went to open her door. David grabbed her arm.

'Emma – are you sure we're doing the right thing? I don't like it.'

She had no words. She wasn't sure that she liked it either, but if Rory's arrest meant the whole plan had fallen apart, she had no idea what would happen to Ollie. And she wasn't going to take that risk.

She gave her husband the most reassuring smile she could muster, opened her car door and turned to release Natasha from where the child lock was holding her prisoner.

42

Emma and Natasha were met in the corridor at the back of the supermarket by a lady of indeterminate age – she could have been anything from early forties to early sixties in her slightly frumpy uniform and her sensible shoes. She didn't smile at them but eyed them suspiciously as she introduced herself as Mrs Clayton and informed them that Mr Douglas was waiting for them.

Without expecting a response from Emma, the woman marched off, leading the way, but Natasha hung back slightly.

'What's up?' Emma whispered.

'I think she recognised me,' Natasha murmured.

'What, from the newspaper articles?'

'No – I think she used to work at another supermarket near where we lived. It was one of my targets.'

Emma gave her a puzzled look and Natasha tutted.

'I used to nick stuff from there,' she said, as though it should have been obvious.

Emma closed her eyes briefly and reached for Natasha's hand.

The office they were shown into was an airless box, with one closed and locked frosted glass window, criss-crossed with thin wires, situated high up on the wall, letting in next to no light. How anybody worked in here every day was a mystery to Emma. She would go slowly mental.

Tom was standing looking at a noticeboard and much as Emma wanted to go to him and hug him, she resisted. She knew that creating allegiances that excluded David and Natasha on any level would potentially make this so much more difficult.

Tom's eyes met Emma's for a second and they showed nothing. She understood.

He turned to Natasha. 'You must be Natasha. You're a brave girl – we know this can't have been easy for you. Come and sit down. We're going to have a chat to see where we're up to, and what we need to do next. Okay?'

The door opened again and David was ushered in.

'David,' Tom said, reaching out his hand. 'Tom Douglas.'

Tom had arranged the chairs so they were in a group with a low coffee table in the middle. As soon as they were seated, he started to speak.

'We haven't got much time. Anybody in your situation would do a hasty whizz around the supermarket aisles for necessities – it's not a pleasure trip – so we need to be quick. Okay?'

Emma and David nodded. Natasha didn't seem able to look at Tom.

'Natasha, I know you've had a hard time, but if I'm going to help you I'll need to ask you some questions. Is that all right?' Tom waited for a response that didn't come. 'We understand that you've only done what you've been told to. But things haven't gone quite to plan, have they?'

Natasha's eyes were glued to the floor, where she was kicking the toes of her trainers backwards and forwards, her hair obscuring her face – a child again. But there was the trace of a shake of her head.

'We know a bit about Rory Slater and Finn McGuinness. They're dangerous men – and we need to keep you safe from them. But to do that, you're going to have to help us too.'

Emma noticed a tear splash on Natasha's knee. She could see that Tom didn't miss it either.

'You're scared of them, aren't you?' he asked. A small, but definite nod was his answer.

'Well, the only way we're going to get rid of that fear is to get them both locked up, where they can't hurt you any more.'

A sound that was suspiciously like a derogatory laugh came from behind the curtain of blonde hair.

Tom looked from Emma to David, with an apologetic expression.

'Do you know what their plan is, Natasha? You told Emma and your dad that it might be off now – because of Rory Slater being arrested – but what was the plan?'

'Don't know. They said it wouldn't be what David was expecting.'

'Why would your dad be expecting anything?'

'Look – I just did what I was told.'

'Why did you agree to it? It's not an easy job for a young girl like you.'

At that, Natasha looked up and thrust her face towards Tom. 'Do you think saying no is *allowed*? Do you know what would have happened to me if I'd *nixed* it?' Her mouth dropped open slightly, her young face a picture of incredulity. She looked down again and murmured something.

'Sorry, Natasha. What did you say?'

She looked up again. 'I said I *wanted* to do it.' The room went quiet.

'Do you want to tell us why?' asked Tom, his voice quietly persuasive.

'I think we need to move on, Tom. I think it's upsetting Tasha too much.' David looked at his daughter, the worry lines deep on his brow. 'We need to be looking forwards now, don't you agree.'

Natasha made a pfff sound.

Emma watched Tom's face. She couldn't read it.

'Okay – what do you think will happen if whatever they were plotting is cancelled because of Slater's arrest?'

'They'll come for me.' The voice was quiet now, but there was no hesitation. She was in no doubt.

'And if it goes ahead and it's successful?' This time she paused for longer.

'I'll go back. I'll be thrown in The Pit for screwing up, then sent to Julie's.'

Tom gave a questioning look to Emma and David. Emma nodded to show that she understood at least part of what Tasha was saying, but now wasn't the time to repeat it.

'Do you want to go back?' Tom asked. Natasha looked up, glanced at David, then at Emma, and shrugged, dropping her head back down. Poor kid. It was so clear she didn't feel she belonged anywhere.

Emma reached out her hand to Tasha's. 'You're not going anywhere, Tasha. They're not getting you back.'

Tasha snatched her hand away. 'No? What if it's me or Ollie? Then you'd change your tune, wouldn't you?'

Tom shook his head at Emma, and she realised he wanted her to be quiet.

'We're going to make sure nobody hurts you, Natasha. You just have to help me a bit. Let's start with where you've been living. There are lots of other kids there, aren't there? Was it fun?'

Natasha made the scornful pfff sound again. 'No,' she said.

'Did you have a favourite friend there?'

'Izzy.'

'How old's Izzy?'

'Same as me,' she answered quietly. She looked up, straight at Tom. 'Is she dead?'

Emma heard a sharp intake of breath from David and she closed her eyes. Something else she hadn't told him.

'Why do you think she might be dead?' Tom asked.

'Cos they put her in The Pit until she gave in, then they sent her to…' Natasha paused and frowned. 'She said she was going to run away, and I'd told her stuff I shouldn't have. If she'd run away, they'd have caught her. There was that girl you thought was me. Is it Izzy?'

'I don't know, I'm afraid. That's the truth, but we do believe it might be. Where do you think she would have gone?'

'She'd have gone to the woods. When she used to run off from her mam's she went there.'

'You mentioned being sent to Julie's. Who's Julie?'

Natasha looked up, her eyes darting from Tom to Emma and back again. Her hand covered her mouth as she spoke.

'I didn't. I never said nothing about no Julie.' She started to breathe rapidly as she dropped her gaze.

Emma wasn't sure how much more of this Natasha was going to be able to take, but Tom was handling her well. Maybe it was because he had a daughter himself. Until Julie had been mentioned, she had seemed to be opening up to him, but now she looked wary again.

'Let's forget about Julie for now. What I would like to know is how you came to be living with Rory and Donna Slater.'

She looked at David for a long moment, then turned back to Tom.

'It was the night Mummy died.' Natasha's voice caught slightly, and she suddenly sounded like the child she was six years ago. 'The men grabbed me. I thought they were going to hurt me, but one of them picked me up and threw me in the back of a car.' She stopped.

'Why don't you tell me everything you remember from that night. Just do your best.'

Emma watched Natasha's face. She was looking at nobody, gazing, it seemed, at a waste bin in the corner of the room. Her face was pinched, as if she was consciously holding every feature taut. The only sound in the room was the faint hum of an antiquated heating system pumping warm air into the room around their feet. When Natasha started to talk, her voice was low – little more than a whisper – and the three adults in the room all leaned forwards to listen.

'I think I'd been asleep, and I woke up because I heard Mummy talking. She was driving really slow and I could see another car on the road. I thought Mummy had stopped. But then she started going really fast. We went up a bit of a hill and then it was like we were on our side. We came down again, but then we were all over the road – like she couldn't drive straight – and we shot back up this hill and the car turned over. It was upside down. Mummy called out,' she looked up at Emma, 'like I told you, but that was it.'

Tom gave Emma a questioning glance, but she shook her head. She would have to tell him, but unless Natasha said anything now, it could wait.

'Do you remember what happened next?'

'Suddenly there were lots of people. They seemed to come from out of the hedge and they were rushing towards me. I was screaming because they looked as if they were walking on their heads. I was crying for Mummy. Then somebody pulled me out of my car seat.'

Emma risked a glance at David. His face was white and she wished she could reach out and hold his hand, but Natasha was sitting between them. Everything the girl was saying proved beyond any doubt that it was no accident that had killed Caroline. Something had been planned and Tasha hadn't wandered off, as they had always believed. It must have been tearing David apart to listen to this.

'Can you remember anything else?' Tom asked.

'Not really. They were all shouting and swearing at each other. I only remember one thing that I heard. Somebody said, "What are we going to do with the fucking kid?" It was the first time I'd been called that.'

Emma was somehow certain that it wasn't the last.

43

Emma saw Tom glance at his watch. She knew time was short, but he was starting to look concerned.

'Natasha, you've been really helpful, but I need to talk to your dad and Emma for a few moments. I'm not keeping secrets from you, but it's better if there are some things you don't know in case Rory or Finn contact you again. Is that okay?'

Natasha sucked her top lip and turned her head to glance at Emma under worried brows.

'Tom, I'm not sure that Tasha should be on her own. Can I go with her?' Emma asked.

'No need – Becky's down the hall. She'll look after her. Give me a second.'

Tom consulted a post-it on the desk phone and pressed a number. While he was speaking, Emma turned to Natasha.

'You'll be okay with Becky, Tasha. We're all looking out for you, I promise.'

Natasha's eyes filled up for just a second before she glanced away and took some deep breaths. Emma looked at Tom. He was watching Natasha and he shook his head very gently as if the sadness of this child was stabbing at his heart too.

The moment was lightened as Becky pushed open the door and cast her easy smile around the room, her expression the right balance of concern for the circumstances and relaxed confidence that all would be well. She ushered Natasha into the corridor while offering to organise something for her to drink, and the room fell quiet as the door swung to.

Tom was all business again.

'Okay. This is what we're going to do. Emma – when we leave here, you're coming with me. Becky's going to change tops with you, and she's going back with David and Natasha.'

Emma felt her eyes flood with tears and she put her head back, willing them not to spill. She knew that if she let go, she would begin to sob and would lose the last of her control. When she finally spoke, she could hear the broken tones of her own voice.

'You told me you would help, Tom. What right have you got to separate me from my family now, of all times? What if they know that Becky's not me, and it ruins everything?'

'We need somebody in your house, Emma, just for three or four hours. No more.'

'Why?' she asked, lips clenched.

Tom was looking straight at her, his eyes locked on hers.

'We need to do a risk assessment. If it was up to me, I'd take all three of you to a safe place now and start negotiations for your baby's safe recovery. But I'm letting Natasha and David go home because we think the best chance for Ollie is if you appear to be going along with their wishes. Becky will work out the best plan to keep you all safe.'

Emma knew when she was beaten. Already she felt isolated – no Ollie, no David, and to her surprise the thought *no Tasha* sprang into her mind.

'Becky also needs to talk to Natasha – to make sure that she's now on *our* side, not on theirs. We don't have time to be sure about that sitting in this office, and we can't risk being wrong.'

Emma wasn't sure herself. Tasha's motivation for coming here had been fear – but it wasn't clear whether the girl would feel safer helping them, or bowing to the wishes of her masters. At least she understood the gang's rules, and at the heart of all this Emma was certain she was missing something. There was something Tasha was trying to tell her, but couldn't. If only she knew what it was.

'Do you need me right this minute, Tom? I know we're running out of time, but I want to explain to Tasha myself why I'm not coming back. I don't want her to think that somebody else has abandoned her.' Emma caught David's frown in her peripheral vision, but she was focused on Tom, praying that he would agree.

He nodded. *Thank God.*

'Second door on the right, Emma. We're out of here in five minutes.'

Emma stood up and, to her surprise, Tom walked her to the door. He held it open and moved slightly into the corridor.

'Are you okay?' he asked. 'I need some time with you as well. I'll explain later.'

Emma had no idea what he could possibly mean, but she nodded and walked off down the corridor, knowing Tom was watching, making sure she made it safely to the room where Becky and Tasha were waiting.

❖

Tom felt that finally they had most of the picture. Caroline and Natasha, or maybe just Caroline, had been targeted for some reason. The car that Natasha said was blocking the road had gone by the time the police got there, and the men – by the sound of it the same men as this time – were hiding behind hedges. It could have been a random carjacking that had gone wrong, but Tom didn't think so.

Then Caroline had died and the gang was left with a problem. Whether it was ransom or something else they were after, once there had been a death and police were crawling all over the place, it had to be called off. And they were left with Natasha, who had seen the whole thing. She wasn't a baby – she would have been able to tell the police exactly what had happened.

It was hard to tell what David Joseph was feeling about all this. He was definitely pale and drawn and his eyes had a haunted look, as if in his head he was reliving every second of the accident, but

Tom hadn't quite decided what to make of him yet. It probably wasn't the best time to meet him, given everything that had happened in the last few days, but Tom's gut was telling him there was something going on beneath the surface – some fear that was beyond the obvious. He could see the attraction of the man – average height, slim build, boyish fair hair and fine-featured good looks – but he had yet to decide whether the charm was more than skin deep.

Is he good enough for Emma? He took a deep breath and let it out slowly. It was none of his business.

Tom sat down again and leaned forwards.

'There's another reason why Becky's coming back with you, David. She has another job to do – with you. Do you know what a tiger kidnap is?'

'Yeah, they kidnap one person to make another do something for them – something illegal. Is that right?'

'Exactly. You run a safe deposit company – Joseph & Son – yes?'

David nodded.

'That's the most likely target, and I want you to talk Becky through how they might be planning to get in and what they might be after.'

Tom was fairly certain that this wasn't the first tiger kidnap aimed at Joseph & Son, but he didn't think it was helpful to share that thought right now.

'It can't be that,' David said – in Tom's mind with more hope than conviction. 'They can't get in – at least, they can't break in. It's impossible. And even if they did, they wouldn't know what was in any of the boxes. It has to be something else they're after.'

In spite of this seeming like the most obvious target for the gang, David seemed keen to reject it as a possibility.

'We're not ruling anything out. But briefly, why do you think it's impossible?'

'It's the best security system money could buy. It's all controlled by computer – the doors are all on a time lock. Even I can't get in.'

'How long have you had the security system in place?' Tom asked.

'About nine years, but the software's regularly updated. It's your brother Jack's old company that does the work – Jack supervised it himself until he sold up. I promise you, it's absolutely state of the art. I learned that lesson long ago.' David raised his eyes as if at his own stupidity.

'What do you mean?'

'When I first took over the business from my dad, I was invited to a computer security seminar. Jack was running it. I hadn't met him before, but he was genuinely inspiring and very persuasive. I decided we couldn't afford him. More fool me!'

'Go on,' Tom prompted.

'A couple of months after I'd been to the seminar, we were hacked. I went into the office one morning, and there was a file sitting in the centre of my computer screen. Not an email – a document file as if I'd saved it there. I opened it, and inside was a list of the first twenty of our customers with their names, addresses, passport numbers – and their security box numbers. At the bottom was a message telling me I'd been hacked; my clients would be informed unless I paid up. The message told me to write down the details of the bank account that I had to make the payment to, because within five minutes of opening the message, it was going to disappear. And it did. There was no point going to the police. I had no time and no evidence once the screen had cleared.'

Tom felt his throat tighten.

'Can you remember the name of the account?'

'It wasn't a name. It was a number. Well – that's not strictly true – there were a couple of letters I think, but mainly numbers.'

'Have you still got the number?'

David blew out briefly through pursed lips. 'No. I wanted to burn it. I kept it for a while, in case the opportunity ever came to use it, but in the end I ripped it up. And then went straight to Jack and got myself the best security money could buy.'

Tom knew he should be asking more, but he couldn't. And he didn't really need to.

44

Huddled in the corner of the car, her legs hunched up onto the seat and her arms wrapped tightly around her upper body, Emma looked as if she was barely holding herself together.

Becky's voice came over the radio.

'All safe,' she said. 'David went for the car and drove it to the side of the supermarket as if Emma and Natasha were staying there to keep out of the rain. We jumped in, leaving David to load the shopping into the boot. The watchers would just have seen a flash of Emma's blue sweater, and I put the hood up so they wouldn't have had a clue it was me.'

'Thanks, Becky. Keep me up to date. I'm going to get Emma settled, then I'll give you a call – see where we're up to. Remind David of the bugs in the kitchen and bedroom, but I think it's safe to deactivate the one in the sitting room so you have somewhere to talk. According to Emma, they rarely use that room, so nobody will be expecting sound from there. You're going to have to get David to do a bit of acting when you get there. He needs to say, "Why don't you go and lie down" or something to you, so nobody will be expecting your voice. Then just move around the bedroom a bit so they can tell you're there. You okay with that?'

'No problem, boss.'

Tom ended the call and turned to Emma.

'Everything's fine, Emma. Becky knows what needs to be done, and then we'll get you back to your family. I'm going to take you to my house for now.'

Tom continued to drive in silence until he turned into his

drive. He ushered Emma quickly into the house, out of what had turned from torrential rain to a cold drizzle. Emma followed Tom into the kitchen and perched herself on a stool on the far side of the island unit, barely looking at her surroundings.

'Are you cold?' he asked. As soon as they had left the supermarket, Emma had started to shiver. She didn't seem to have stopped since. But Tom wasn't sure if she was shivering with cold, or with anxiety.

'I'm fine,' Emma looked at Tom. 'It's just that whenever I'm cold, or hot, or wet, or hungry, I just think about Ollie. Is he warm enough? Have they fed him?'

'I know. It must be dreadful. But it's important that you keep functioning too. So what can I get you to drink?' Tom asked, switching the coffee machine on. He needed a double espresso, given his lack of sleep for the last forty-eight hours.

'Would it be possible to have a gin and tonic, do you think? I really need it.'

Tom rooted around in a cupboard, certain he had gin, but not too convinced about the tonic. Finally he found a bottle hiding at the back. He heard a subdued sniff and knew that Emma was crying quietly. Her voice when she spoke was uneven, ragged.

'I've hated Natasha, you know. With every breath in my body I have wanted to kill her. But the more I learn about her past and the future she's expecting, the more I worry for her. Is that ridiculous? She took my *baby* – but now I want to fight for Tasha too. I don't want her to go back to that life. I won't let it happen.'

'We won't let it happen either. We'll get the people who took her – every last one of them. I just wish we knew a bit more, and that's why I wanted to talk to you. I want you to try to remember every single detail of your conversations with Natasha and what you heard when she was talking to Rory Slater.'

Tom handed Emma her drink and looked at her face. She

was chewing her bottom lip and wouldn't quite meet his eyes. He pulled up another stool.

'What?' he asked. 'Whatever it is, just tell me.'

Emma waited, as if she was trying to find the right words.

'I can't see how it's relevant but, according to Tasha, Caroline shouted a man's name before she crashed the car. David and I have talked about it, and as far as he's aware, Caroline only knew one man with this name. I don't understand it, and neither does David, but the name she shouted was Jack.'

Tom felt his body jolt. Jack had been so much in his mind recently with the SD card, the Swiss bank, the list of names and dates, not to mention what David had just told him. But somehow that had felt like an intellectual exercise. The fact that Caroline Joseph had called the name Jack as her car went into a spin punched a shot of adrenaline into Tom's system. It could be some other Jack – but what were the chances of Caroline knowing another Jack, one that her husband had never heard of?

He barely listened to Emma as she explained how Caroline had known his brother, but he remembered that David Joseph's name had come up when Leo was talking about Jack's clients.

'What are you thinking?' Emma asked.

He had to focus back on Natasha and Ollie.

'I'm trying to think how accurate a six-year-old's memory is likely to be. I can't remember much from when I was six – can you?'

'No, but with all due respect that's more than thirty years ago. When you're thirteen, six isn't so long ago. And it was a traumatic night for her.'

'I think her memory seems pretty accurate when she says the men looked as if they were walking on their heads. We know the car was upside down – that's how it was when the emergency services got there.'

'When Tasha was telling us the story, she said something else. She said she remembered Caroline saying, "What's going on?"

to whoever was on the phone. She may have got it wrong, of course, but if Caroline sounded scared Natasha might well have remembered accurately.'

A picture had started to form in Tom's mind when Natasha had first told him about the men, and this made the picture so much worse. He didn't like the shape of it at all.

❖

Tom had settled Emma in the sitting room with her drink so he could make some calls. He wanted to talk to her and to milk from her every drop of information that Natasha had shared, but for now Emma said she was happy with notepad and pencil. She would try to relive each moment and write it all down.

A call from the incident room had revealed that Rory Slater had been allowed home, there being no proof whatsoever that he had anything to do with the drugs being carried by one of his lads. The police had searched the Slaters' home and found nothing – not that they expected to. Anything of interest would have been whisked away the moment Rory and Rick had failed to arrive home from the train station. But it had given them a chance to bug the house, and Tom was praying that something would come up – something to give them a clue where Ollie was.

Becky had also asked DC Nic Havers to go back to Silvia Briggs's house and get a DNA sample from her. They could rush it through, but it would still be twenty-four hours before they had the result, when they would know for sure if the body in the wood belonged to Isabella aka Izzy Briggs. Twenty-four hours – if they were lucky. If it turned out to be positive, the Slaters would have to be questioned because Izzy had been living with them, and if they hadn't found Ollie by then it would all get so much more complicated.

This case was so complex and problematic that Tom wished he had Jack here to draw him a flowchart. His brother was never far from his thoughts at the moment.

When he returned to the sitting room, Emma was leaning back on the sofa, eyes closed, clutching some paper in her hand, but not paper from the notepad. She opened her eyes and looked at Tom.

'Talking about Jack reminded me. I've got something to show you. They're the two letters I received from Jack – the one when he dumped me, and the other when he was asking for forgiveness just before he died. I brought them for you.'

Tom stood still. He didn't know if he wanted to read the letters or not. He had enough on his mind without clouding it with more memories of Jack. Emma put the letters on the coffee table.

'I printed them out. I knew he'd wipe them from my computer as soon as I'd opened them and had time to read them – so it was the first thing I did.'

'You said he ended your relationship by email?'

'Well, technically not email – he hacked into my computer.'

'And did what, exactly?'

'You know Jack couldn't be bothered with things like email. And if you remember, he hated using the phone with a passion.'

Tom did indeed remember. Whenever Jack had no option but to use the telephone – mobile or landline – he would hold it in one hand and rub the top of his head with the other, as if totally perplexed. It had always been a source of amusement between Tom and Emma.

'If he wanted to send me a message,' Emma said, 'he would write something and then hack into my desktop and leave a folder or a file sitting right in the middle so I couldn't miss it. He liked me to know that he'd been there and could look at anything on my computer if he wanted to. It amused him.'

Tom was silent for a moment. 'Did you tell David any of this?'

Emma looked puzzled. 'He knew Jack had dumped me by email – sort of – but if you mean about the hacking into my computer, I don't think so. Why?'

'Doesn't matter.' Tom didn't want to voice his suspicions out loud, even to Emma.

He took the letters and glanced at the first one. He realised immediately that this was something he needed to do in private and he was trying to work out how to excuse himself without appearing rude when Emma picked up her notepad and pencil again and mouthed the word 'Go.' He didn't need telling twice.

Dear Emma

I am finding this email very difficult to write, but I don't think I could bear to have this conversation face to face.

For the last few months, I've felt that we have drifted apart. Perhaps it was because I was no longer working full time and had too much time on my hands, but being together 24/7 showed me that we have little to say to each other. It was only when you went away for a brief stay with your family that it struck me how liberated I felt by your absence. And now that I'm away from you in London, it is even more apparent.

I'm sorry if that sounds cruel. It isn't meant to be, and we have had some wonderful times together in the past. But our future is not as a couple.

I must tell you this now, as you will be certain to find out. I have met somebody else. She is a woman who has the same values as me, who enjoys the life of freedom that I now have and isn't always in search of the next worthy cause to contribute to. She wants fun just as much as I do, and with that in mind we leave tomorrow for Monaco where I plan to buy a home in the sun.

I hope you can find it in you to forgive me for the hurt that I have inevitably caused, but I think you need a man who is more serious than I am.

I have transferred ownership of our home into your name, and you can keep it with my blessing. I have also taken my name off our joint bank accounts, and you are welcome to the not inconsiderable

sums in each of them. As you know, I have funds in other places
and if you find yourself in need of anything financially, please do
not hesitate to contact me.
With affection always
Jack

Tom read the letter again. He couldn't believe Jack would have done this to Emma. It seemed so unlike him. He would have been much more likely to end things by causing a monumental row, so that somehow it wasn't his fault.

Tom opened the second folded note, and saw a much shorter message.

My darling Em
I'm sorry if the letter I sent all those months ago hurt you. You
deserved better. You are, and always have been, wonderful.

I've made many mistakes in my life, and the day of reckoning
has finally arrived. The decision I've made is going to cause pain
to many people, particularly my family, but they have Tom. It's
the only way out of an unbearable existence. I'm sorry it's come to
this, but the time for me to leave this life has arrived. This time
it's goodbye forever.

Please forgive me for all my failures, and find your own happi-
ness. If anybody deserves it, you do.
Jack

Tom felt his throat constrict. What could have happened to his brother to make him feel that life wasn't worth living?

45

Becky had managed to complete two of the tasks assigned to her, but was struggling with the third. Natasha had locked herself back in her bedroom and wouldn't speak to her. At least Becky had managed to convince Natasha to leave her phone downstairs, so she knew the girl wasn't contacting any of those bastards and sharing information. She would deal with her later. First, she needed to feedback to Tom.

He answered his radio immediately.

'Tom – we're doing okay here. I've done a risk assessment, and it's not great. There are several possible points of entry downstairs – front door, back door, French windows in the sitting room and dining room, and then there's a huge kitchen-living room at the back of the house that not only has the back door, but also some glass doors to the garden.'

'Bollocks – that makes it hard to protect them. Can we get a team in?'

Becky hated giving Tom bad news. She wanted to solve problems, not create them. But she had no ideas that would work.

'I know we checked for surveillance, but this lot seem smart and I'd hate to risk it. There's no back way in – all the paths lead down the side of the house and out the front. With a bit of time we could do something to bring more of us in, but creating a point of entry to the garden through the thick hedge and bushes would be noisy at night.'

'What's your recommendation, Becky?'

'I don't think Natasha is safe, and I think she knows it. If it all goes wrong they'll blame her – and we know what will happen to her then. If it goes right, they'll expect her back – they can't afford to leave her here. If we're going to protect Natasha, I suggest we have an armed response team standing close by. Very close by.'

With Tom's agreement to organise the team and set up liaison with her, she moved on to describing her conversations with David Joseph.

'I'll be as succinct as possible. The vault and all the offices at Joseph & Son are below ground. Access to the building is via a communal entrance – lots of people know the code, but it only gets them as far as the entrance hall. There's a coded keypad to Joseph & Son, but it's on a time lock and can't be opened outside working hours.'

'Is he sure about that, Becky?'

'He says so – we'd have to ask the people who installed it to be sure. Anyway, each safe deposit box has two keys – one kept by the owner, the other by Joseph & Son. You need both to open a box. The company's keys are stored in a room that's protected by a biometric lock and only four people's prints can open it. David, of course, is one of them. There's another biometric lock to the main area of the vault. That's it.'

Becky hoped she hadn't missed anything. David Joseph had gone on and on about how it was impossible, pacing the room, hands in pockets, repeating over and over that it couldn't be done.

'What about the contents of the boxes? Does he know what's in them?' Tom asked.

'He says they don't have a clue. The owners pull their box from its safe and take it into a private room to put whatever they want in. There are ordinary safes too, without boxes inside, in various larger sizes. According to David, a random attack would be a complete waste of time. He thinks most of the boxes hold personal documents, wills, house deeds – even love letters. But he says it's irrelevant, because nobody can get in. Whatever's going to

241

happen, he says he's convinced it's got nothing to do with the vault.'

'I can hear a 'but' there, Becky. What are you thinking?'

Becky knew she was sticking her neck out; Tom would understand, though, even if she turned out to be wrong.

'I don't believe him, Tom. He knows it's the vault – but he doesn't want us to *know* that he knows.'

❖

There was nothing from his conversation with Becky that Tom thought worth sharing with Emma. Certainly he didn't want her to know that her home was vulnerable. But as he made his way back to the sitting room he decided there was one thing he needed to ask her, because no matter how hard he tried to forget them, Jack's words kept spinning through his mind. *Unbearable existence.*

'Are you okay?' she asked when he returned to the room.

'I'm okay, but I need to ask how you would feel about me speaking to a professional about the last letter from Jack, to see if it's possible to understand his frame of mind when he wrote it.'

Emma leaned back, resting her head against the sofa. 'Do what you want, Tom. Do you mean a psychiatrist?'

'No – a forensic linguist. They study how language is used – analyse the words and the structure of sentences – to get an understanding of the underlying meaning.'

Emma shrugged her shoulders. 'It's up to you. But it's all a bit academic since he's dead anyway.'

She was right, of course. But he was finding out other things about his brother and struggling to make sense of it all.

'Thanks Emma. I appreciate that, and you'll be pleased to hear that Becky's nearly done at your house – she just wants to talk to Natasha and then we can get you back to them. How's the list going?'

'I don't know if any of it's useful. Tasha talked about the kind of jobs she had to do and the punishment she received. I'm not sure it will help, Tom, but I'll carry on until Becky's ready and see if I can think of anything else.'

'Fine,' Tom said. 'I'm going to check in with a few people. I'll go to my study, but I'll let you know the minute there's any news. Is that all right?'

Emma gave him a distracted nod of the head. He was certain she would prefer to be alone.

His study was actually a wide area off the hall at the front of the house. It had a small fireplace, and was surprisingly cosy even in the middle of winter. He sat down, the letters still in his hand, and stared at them for a moment longer, then pushed them to the back of his desk.

He wanted to call Becky back, but he knew she would call him when there was something to report. He looked at his watch.

'Bollocks,' he muttered. He knew he had to do this. He pulled the letters back towards him, grabbed his phone and stood up, walking towards the window as he dialled. He looked out at the dark and dismal night, the fine drizzle creating a shimmer around the yellow street lamps, their light reflecting back from the wet pavements. Surely Jack would have realised that no matter how depressing the outlook, there was always the hope that the next day would be brighter?

The phone was answered on the fourth ring.

'Clara? It's Tom Douglas. I wonder if you could do me a favour?' he asked.

Tom explained about Jack's suicide letter, and Clara suggested the quickest way to get it to her would be for Tom to take a photo of it with his phone.

'Do you have any other examples of his writing? Something for me to compare it to?' she asked.

'Sadly I have a letter in which he ends a long-standing relationship with his fiancé – will that do.'

'Perfect. I can give you a preliminary view very quickly,' Clara said. 'It'll be superficial – first impressions only. Anything more in depth will have to wait, I'm afraid.'

'An initial reaction would be great. If it needs more, then obviously I'll pay for your time.'

'Let's worry about that later. Send them now. I'll have a quick look and get back to you with my thoughts.'

Thanking Clara, Tom ended the call and used the side of his hand to iron out the creases in the letters a little. He quickly took a photo of each and, as he forwarded them to Clara, he felt a slight lessening of tension across his shoulders.

He looked at his watch again. Time seemed to be standing still. He walked into the kitchen and made another cup of coffee. Thinking he should see if Emma wanted anything to eat, he realised he had barely eaten for hours. It had been too late when he arrived home the night before, and anyway he had been keen to wrap himself around Leo's warm body.

'*Shit*,' he muttered, realising with a stab of guilt that he hadn't phoned Leo since abandoning her in the middle of the previous night. He grabbed his private phone.

'Hi,' he said. 'I'm sorry I've not called, but things have been hectic.'

'Where are you now? Are you at home?'

Tom paused, not quite sure what to say.

'Was that a particularly difficult question, Tom?'

'Sorry, Leo, I *am* at home, but I'm not going to be able to see you tonight. I can't explain at the moment. It's a bit tricky – but I will when everything's sorted.'

His work phone started to ring.

'Bugger. I'm really sorry, I'm going to have to go – there's another call coming in.'

He was about to tell her he loved her, and say he would call her tomorrow, but she had already hung up.

With a shrug, he accepted the incoming call.

'That was quick, Clara – I thought you would need hours.'

'I would, to do a detailed analysis. But they're short letters and there are some immediate observations I can make. This is a five-minute analysis. Are you ready for this?'

'Fire away,' Tom said, almost wishing he hadn't started this.

'The first thing to say is that while they made interesting reading for me in my professional capacity, they must have been pretty heartbreaking to receive.'

'I couldn't agree more'

'Am I right in thinking that he died right after he sent the second note?' Clara asked.

'He sent it the day before he died. That's why Emma was so upset – she felt she should have done something.'

'Well you can tell Emma from me to stop beating herself up. I'd be very surprised indeed if this were a suicide note, Tom.'

Tom frowned. What on earth could she mean? It had seemed pretty clear to him.

'We both know there are two types of suicide – those who mean to die, and those who are sending out a cry for help and then somehow it all goes wrong. Your brother was killed in an accident, wasn't he?'

'That's right. The boat was a total wreck, ripped to pieces.'

'That doesn't sound like a botched cry for help – not like taking tablets and hoping somebody gets to you in time. If he intended the accident to happen, then he intended to die.'

'I'd say so, yes,' Tom responded, wondering where this was going.

'Well, then, I'm even more convinced this isn't a suicide note.'

Clara had his full attention.

'How can you tell?'

'Generally speaking, people who've truly decided to take their own lives have usually stopped relating to the outside world. They're psychologically isolated from others. They've come to a decision, and death – in their mind – is the only option. It wouldn't be typical of a person who had genuinely decided to kill himself to show awareness of the pain it would cause to others – this is from a man who doesn't appear to be introspective enough. He is concerned for Emma, his family.'

Tom was silent. This was good news, wasn't it? Why didn't it feel that way?

'You're sure about this, are you?'

'I would say that Jack was certainly about to do something, but at the time of writing – and that's the crucial point – I don't believe he intended to kill himself. Obviously that could have changed, and he could have had a moment of irrationality a day later. But real suicides, as opposed to those who are hoping to be stopped in time, tend to kill themselves immediately after writing their note. They intend the note to be found after their death because they don't *want* to be stopped.'

'Thanks, Clara,' he said quietly. 'I owe you one.'

'Well, before you go, you might be interested to know that the other letter – the one ending the relationship with Emma – may have *come* from Jack, but I'm fairly certain he didn't write it.'

Tom's thoughts had been drifting – harsh, colourful images of Jack's last moments invading his mind. He caught the last few words.

'Sorry – what did you say?' he asked.

'I suspect that this letter was written by a woman. It could be that the new woman he mentions told him what he had to write, but I'm sure they're not his words.'

'What makes you say that?'

'All those personal pronouns and social relationships, for one thing. But there are other clues: females tend to progress information using the negative, such as "I don't think", or "our future is not as a couple". They hedge – you know, use polite forms – to soften the information – "perhaps", or "I'm sorry if…" – and they refer more to cognitive and emotional processes: think, feel, hope. I'm happy to give you a comprehensive breakdown if you want, but it would have to wait.'

'No, Clara – that's not an issue, really. I need to think about it all.'

As Tom ended the call, thanking Clara for being so prompt with her response, he couldn't drag his thoughts away from the letter that Emma had assumed was a suicide note.

He had always believed that Jack's death was an accident, but given everything he was learning or surmising about his brother, he now had to come to terms with the possibility that Jack had been murdered.

46

Becky ran across the hall, cursing under her breath. She had only popped into the kitchen for a glass of water and now, through her earpiece, she was getting a message. She couldn't respond until she was out of the kitchen – away from the bug.

'DI Robinson,' she answered breathlessly as she closed the sitting-room door.

'Ma'am, we've picked something up on one of the bugs in the Slaters' house. Donna Slater received a phone call a few minutes ago. It was from a mobile, so we only heard her side of the call on the whole – but the woman at the other end was shouting, and we've done a quick clean-up and managed to get some of her part of the conversation.'

Becky felt a renewed shot of energy. They wouldn't be contacting her if it was nothing.

'The call is from another woman, who Donna calls Julie. We'll piece the whole thing together as best we can and send it to you, but we thought you might like the headlines now.'

Becky tapped her foot impatiently.

'The woman called Julie was talking about a baby, saying something about not sleeping. She said – or rather screamed – that nobody had ever told her having a baby was so difficult. Donna replied, "Well when it's your first it's always difficult to know what to do when they cry," so we assumed this Julie had just had a baby and was asking advice from somebody who appears to have had about ten.'

'And…'

'And then Donna said, "Give him a biscuit." Now I've never had a baby myself, but even I know that you don't give a newborn a biscuit.'

The blood was suddenly pounding through Becky's body. A woman has just 'had' a baby, but this baby isn't a newborn – and they referred to him as a boy. It was too much of a coincidence. It *had* to be Ollie.

❖

It had been good of Tom to leave Emma in peace, but much as she had craved solitude in the past twenty-four hours, there was a huge difference between curling up in a chair in Ollie's room, where she could feel her son all around her, and sitting in a room she had never seen before, surrounded by somebody else's possessions. She felt lost, alone, even though Tom was just outside the door.

She angrily wiped fresh tears away. She didn't want to think of her own pain. She wanted to focus every thought on Ollie – to let him know how much she missed him and loved him.

And now all this business with Jack and his involvement with Caroline was confusing her. How could he have known something was about to happen? Why did it feel that the past and the present were somehow colliding?

It had taken Emma a long time to admit that she would never again love anybody the way she had loved Jack. That rush of excitement when he came home after a day or two away; the passion with which he had loved her; the moments of joy when he would impulsively pull her to her feet and dance with her, holding her close, or whizzing her wildly round the room, laughter finally making them collapse together in a heap on the nearest chair – they were moments never to be repeated.

He had hurt her so deeply, though, and more than anything she had wanted a calmer type of love with David. She felt they'd had that until this week. Now they had both seen a side of the other that neither had known existed. David would never have expected her to sneak out in the night to follow Natasha, and she would have expected him to be more proactive, more energised. He seemed prepared to sit back – to let everything take its course and to pretend that it was all going to be all right in the end.

Would they ever get back to the couple they had been?

She had no more time to think about it, though, as Tom burst into the room, a look of excitement lighting up his tired face.

'I've just had a call from Becky,' he said.

Emma pushed herself to her feet, knowing this was going to be good news.

'Do you remember Natasha mentioned somebody called Julie? Well, we think that Julie may be the person who has Ollie.'

Emma closed her eyes and swallowed.

'But we don't know who she is, so how the hell do we find her?' she asked.

There was only one answer.

'We ask Natasha.'

❖

Natasha lay on the bed, staring at the ceiling, its deep shadow brightened in one large circle by a single lamp on her bedside table. She didn't like the dark – never had since that night when, just for a moment, everything had gone black as her mum's car had turned over and over, her head banging on the roof of the car, her legs swinging backwards and forwards. The next thing she could remember was being dragged from the car, screaming. One of the men had shaken her until she had stopped. It seemed as if everybody was talking in urgent whispers, their voices low. The one who shook her had the deepest voice of all of them. He'd sounded as if he had a sore throat or a cough, because his words had jagged edges. She couldn't remember what he had said. Except for that one thing – the phrase that had gone round and round in her head ever since.

'Her mam's dead. She's no use to us now. Get rid of her.'

Then he had pushed her towards a man who smelled bad – the man who she now knew was Rory – and he had chucked her in the back of a car.

She had thought she was going to die, and for a long time she wished she had because when they took her out of the car they threw her in The Pit – to hide her, to keep her quiet. She could still taste the stench of the room, feel the cold and damp that left her shivering. They said she had to stay in there until it was safe – but she didn't know what that meant. She did now, though. She had had to stay in there until she believed herself to be Shelley Slater, not Natasha Joseph. She had to forget the past. It was done. Over.

Now here she was – back in that past that was supposed to all be behind her. Was she Natasha Joseph, or was she Shelley Slater? She no longer knew. And what about the future? She couldn't stay here. They wouldn't let her.

She felt alone, as if she had been dumped in the middle of a vast desert with no sign of life in any direction. It was a bit like a film she had watched with the little kids at home.

It would probably be best for everybody if she was dead. Maybe that was the answer. Maybe that's how Izzy had felt.

Her body tensed as she heard a soft knock on the door. *What did he want – again?* But it wasn't David.

'It's Becky. I need to talk to you, Tasha. Can I come in?' Becky's voice was an urgent whisper.

Natasha watched as the handle went down, secure in the knowledge that nobody could get past the chest of drawers that she had pushed behind the door.

'I can't shout – the bug in your dad's bedroom might pick me up, but it's about Ollie. We think we might know where he is and we need your help.'

Natasha pushed herself off the bed. She felt numb. She was sorry about Ollie. She didn't want anything to happen to him, but if the police found him because of her, Rory or Finn would come and get her.

She used all her strength to push the chest of drawers out of the way and let Becky in.

'What's happened?'

Becky walked over and sat on the bed, patting the cover by her side. She was pleased and more than a little surprised when Natasha sat down.

'You know how important this is, don't you?' Becky asked, turning to Natasha and clasping the girl's hands in her own. 'You mustn't tell anybody what we know – you do understand, don't you?'

Did they think she was an idiot?

'Tom says you mentioned somebody called Julie. What do you know about Julie?'

Natasha's mouth went dry. She had never met Julie, but she knew all about her – what she did and how she managed her girls.

Natasha shook her head. She really didn't want this to be happening.

'Come on, Tasha. Ollie needs your help. You need to decide whose side you're on. I know this is hard. You're terrified of Rory Slater and the rest of that lot, and so you should be. But we can't protect you unless we can trust you. You're one of them, or you're not. Which is it going to be?'

Natasha felt the last of her resistance drain away. She was tired. She had spent her life being scared – scared of doing something wrong at home; scared of being caught nicking stuff; scared of being Shelley Slater when she knew she was Tasha Joseph. Now her biggest fear was of Finn coming to get her.

They thought they understood, but they didn't. They didn't know it all, and when they did they would understand why she'd done it – but there was no place for her here, or anywhere else. She had no idea what to do, but it suddenly felt easiest if she just gave them what they wanted. She had no idea what was going to happen to her, but the one thing she did know was that since he had gone, she had missed Ollie. Missed him calling her name and trying to hug her leg; missed just knowing he was there. She wanted him to be safe. And the only way she could make sure was by helping them – the pigs – her father – all the people she had been taught to hate. But Ollie was innocent. Perhaps he was the only one who was, but it was Ollie she was fighting for now.

'I don't know where Julie lives,' she said quietly. 'If that's what you're hoping for, I really don't know. She's got two houses, though. I heard Rory saying that to Donna. She has girls working for her – some on the streets, the young ones like me at one of the houses. Not the one she lives in. I don't know nothing else.'

Becky looked disappointed, but gave her hand a squeeze.

'Okay, but if you think of anything, let me know. Do you want to come downstairs?'

Natasha shook her head and Becky turned back towards the top of the stairs.

There was something else that Natasha knew – something that might help. She was in it up to her neck now. What difference did it make?

'Becky – Julie has a burger van. It's where Rory picks the skunk up from.' She felt a tiny prick of something like pride when Becky turned and flashed her a huge smile.

'That's great, Tasha. Brilliant. Well done. Come with me. We'll speak to Tom now, and he might want to ask you another couple of things. Okay?'

At that moment David came racing upstairs brandishing Natasha's phone. It was ringing. Without a word, he thrust it into Natasha's hand and she felt instantly sick. She didn't want to speak to anybody. Not now, not ever. But she had to.

'Hello,' she whispered, looking from David to Becky as she listened. She hung up the phone without another word and turned to Becky, ignoring her father. She knew if she spoke her voice would crack and break, and she swallowed hard, trying to stop it. What Rory had asked couldn't be done, and she – Natasha – would get the blame for not telling him. She might as well be dead.

'What, Tasha?' Becky was asking, and Natasha realised it wasn't for the first time.

'It's all going down tonight after all. They want to speak to David in ten minutes – but they want Emma there too.'

❖

Tom was just debating whether to begin the reverse swap when his radio beeped.

'Becky? What's up?'

She quickly filled Tom in on everything that Natasha had told her, including the content of the call from Rory Slater.

'Good work,' Tom said. 'If Natasha's right and Julie is the woman with the burger van, I'm fairly certain Paul Green from Titan told me that one of the gang's enforcers has a wife who runs a burger van. It sounds as if it's not the only thing she does. I'll get hold of Titan and ask if they have an address for Julie's husband, Finn McGuinness. Then I'll get a covert team out there. We need to know for sure that the baby's there before we go charging in.'

Tom walked quickly back into the sitting room. Emma leaped up from her seat, clearly identifying from Tom's urgent tone that something was happening.

'We don't have time to get Emma back in the house before the call comes through. Becky – you're going to have to coach David. He's going to have to tell them that Emma is being sick. He has to insist that they tell him what has to be done and he'll write it down.'

Emma was standing right by Tom, looking as if she wanted to rip the radio from his hands and shout, 'What? Tell me!' Tom lifted his hand and grasped her shoulder.

'You need to tell him to put the phone on speaker. He can make the excuse that he needs his hands free so he can write down their instructions. You leave your radio open – mute any incoming calls, and remember not to make a sound or the bug in the kitchen will pick you up – but I want to hear what they're asking for.'

Tom ended the call and immediately consulted his contacts to get Paul Green's mobile number.

Emma's face was a mix of hope and fear, but he didn't have time to explain everything to her yet.

The Titan officer answered the phone immediately.

'Tom – are things hotting up at your end?'

'They are – and for you to know that, I can only assume the same is happening at yours. We need you to give us an address for Finn McGuinness – can you get somebody to radio it through to Inspector Robinson, please?' Tom hung on while Paul passed on the instruction. 'What's the score with you, then?'

'Our CHIS has said it's going to happen tonight, but he's still unable to tell us exactly what "it" is.'

'What's your informant's role in this, then?'

'I can't say at the moment. Sorry – you know how it is. I may be able to tell you more later, though.'

'Okay, we're waiting here hopefully with an open line to listen to their demands. I'll get back to you the minute we know more.'

Tom hung up the phone, and was about to bring an anxious Emma up to date when his radio signalled a call from Becky.

Nobody spoke, but they could hear a phone ringing in the background. Then a voice.

'This is David Joseph. What do you want, and where the hell is my son?'

47

Emma was rooted to the spot. What was going on? Tom hadn't had a moment to speak to her since he had come back into the room, but he kept giving her tense nods which she thought were probably supposed to be reassuring, but they weren't. She couldn't interrupt him, though, because he had switched up the volume on his radio and she could hear David talking.

'Tell me what I've got to do. Let's get this over with, so I can get my family back.' David's voice was thick with tension.

There was silence for a moment, then he spoke again.

'You've no right to say that to me. You want my help, don't you?'

Emma saw a puzzled frown on Tom's face.

'No, she's not here. She's being sick, if you must know. She can't keep anything down – not even water. You tell me, and I'll tell her.'

There was a pause.

'No, I will *not* get her. You'll have to tell me.' David said, somehow managing to put several days of pent-up rage into the word 'not'. 'Just tell me what I've got to do.'

Silence. Emma wondered if he had overplayed his hand. *Why hadn't he put the bloody phone on speaker?*

'Can we not do this? I've told you – I'll do as you ask. I'll do anything to get my son back.'

There was a longer silence.

'You know that's not true,' David said quietly.

Then the silence stretched and stretched. The call must have been over.

Tom switched his radio off.

'Becky will call me from the other room in a moment. I don't understand exactly what went on there, but there's some other good news. I don't want to get your hopes up yet, but we think we know where Julie lives. We need to be certain Ollie's there before we blow our cover and go charging in, but if we're right, we could have him back very soon.

❖

Tom's radio crackled. 'Yes, Becky – what the hell happened? Why didn't he put his phone on speaker?'

Tom was frustrated with David Joseph. It would have been so much better if they could have heard both sides of the conversation.

'He says he forgot, I'm afraid, Tom. I kept signalling him, but he ignored me.'

'Did you ask him what they said? Some of his answers seemed a bit off.' Tom had started to march backwards and forwards.

'He said they want both David and Emma to be by the phone again in one hour for final instructions. I tried to go through the questions word for word, but David seemed really stressed and I didn't want to push him too much.'

'Okay. Have the armed response team been in touch? They're in position?' he paused. 'Excellent. You know what to do. Take the Range Rover, as if you're going to fill it up. You know where and when. See you in about fifteen minutes. Well done, Becky.'

Emma's white face appeared ghostlike in the lamplight of the sitting room, the shadows around her eyes jet black, and Tom felt a pang of guilt. She must be desperate to know what was happening.

'They're calling back in an hour and they want you there. What you need to understand is that we've been unable to get any support into the house for you, so whatever they send David off to do, you're going to be left in the house on your own with Natasha. You'll be exposed, and I don't like it.'

'Let's just do what they're asking. Please, Tom. You said you know where Ollie is – can't you get him back now and then it won't matter who's where, will it?'

'We've got a team checking out the information about Ollie. But it might take some time. You can't barge into a house full of gang members, Emma, and if he's not there we'll have blown it. Look, this is what's going to happen.'

Tom quickly laid out the plan to get Emma back into the house.

'You can talk me through your notes on the way, and I'll tell you how to keep safe when you're on your own. But you *must* do what I suggest, Emma. These men don't play nicely.'

❖

Neither Tom nor Emma spoke for a few moments as the car sped away from his home. Emma was sitting up straight in the car, leaning slightly forwards as if she were willing him to go faster.

They were about to meet up with an officer who was bringing a radio and had arranged to meet Becky at a petrol station about ten minutes from Emma's home. They would swap jackets in the ladies again, in case Becky had been followed. It was still raining, so they had the perfect excuse to hide under hoods.

'Why do you think they want me there, Tom?'

'I don't know. It's pointless speculating. They probably want confirmation that everything's the way they're expecting it to be.'

To keep Emma's mind active and prevent her from thinking through all the possible scenarios, Tom asked her to read the notes she had written, prompting her for more information as she spoke. He only expressed an opinion once.

'*Christ*, that poor kid,' he said when Emma described how Natasha had been thrown in The Pit until she accepted that she was Shelley Slater.

Tom saw the lights of the petrol station up ahead.

'As soon as you get home, make sure your mobile is fully charged – the Australian one you've been using. Switch it to silent, vibration off, and leave it turned off completely unless you need it. Give it to David when he goes to do whatever it is that they want. We can't give him a wire – it's the first thing they would check. Same with the phone, but if he does have to meet them, tell him to switch the phone off and hide it in the car.'

He felt Emma shudder at the thought. He needed to make her understand, though.

'In the meantime, remember to put your phone on speaker if you call me. I'll be able to hear every word. I'll mute my end so they can't hear me. GPS is switched on so we can track whoever has the phone. They don't know about your Australian phone, so they can't track you, but we can. David should take it with him when he goes to do whatever they ask, but he has to be very careful about when he uses it. If he has to meet with the gang for any reason, it must be switched off. They'll have signal detectors, so make sure he understands that.'

Tom quickly gave Emma instructions how to use the radio, which she could keep with her in the house.

'This is your lifeline, Emma. Once David has left, lock yourself and Natasha in an upstairs room – put something heavy behind the door. If you hear anything that concerns you, press that red button. It will put you straight through to the support team, and they'll be less than three minutes away, so don't worry.'

Tom pulled into the petrol station forecourt and got out to walk Emma into the shop. Her movements felt jerky, and Tom casually draped his arm around her shoulders, trying to pass some of his strength through to her. At the back of the shop, Emma made her way towards the toilets and disappeared from view. Tom bought a magazine and some mints and walked back to his car, looking at his watch – for all the world like a man wishing his wife would hurry up.

There was one call he had to make.

'Philippa, it's Tom.'

'Tom – how's it going? DI Robinson has updated me on the news about Ollie. Where are you now?'

Tom told her what the gang had demanded.

'Bloody hell, Tom – the family's a bit exposed'

Tom gazed at the empty forecourt and at the fine drizzle that hadn't stopped for hours. He knew leaving them in the house was a risk, but if Emma did exactly what he had told her, they should be fine. If he pulled them all out and tried to open negotiations with the gang, he didn't think they would ever see little Ollie Joseph again.

'Keep me informed, Tom. I don't like it, but I can see you had little choice.'

48

Natasha sat on the edge of her bed, legs dangling just above the floor and hands jammed under her thighs to stop them trembling. Becky had gone and Emma was coming back – coming to discover what the gang had planned for them all. She was alone in the house with David for the first time since she had taken Ollie.

One thought had been forcing itself into her mind, however hard she had tried to keep it at bay. *What would have happened if I hadn't taken Ollie?* What if she had disobeyed them?

It was a stupid thought. They would have sent Finn to get her. The only way she could have stayed was if the whole family had gone into hiding, and Natasha didn't believe England was a big enough country to hide from the likes of Finn McGuinness.

There was somebody else who had to take some of the blame, though.

David.

This was her chance – a chance to get him to explain while they were the only two people in the house. She was scared to know the truth; maybe Rory had lied to her all these years and she had hated David for nothing, but she had to know. She pushed herself off the bed and made her way quietly down the stairs, hands gripped into fists straight by her side.

Her father was in the sitting room, standing with his back to the door, arms on the mantelpiece, leaning forwards with his head bent. Natasha silently stood behind him, struggling to find the courage to speak. She must have made a sound, because David spun round.

'Goodness, Tasha – you scared the life out of me. What are you doing just standing there? Come and sit down.'

Natasha didn't move. David frowned.

'I'm not getting the silent treatment again, am I? Surely we're past that by now?'

'I need to ask you something, David.'

'Ask me anything you like, but come and sit down.'

Natasha didn't move.

'I want to know why you did it.'

'Why I did what?'

'You know what.'

'Tasha, darling, I really don't know what you're talking about.'

She swallowed a lump in her throat, finding it hard to say the words out loud.

'Was it because you didn't love me? Or didn't you love Mummy? Which was it?'

David couldn't meet her eyes.

She didn't really need to ask anything else. His face told the story. All she wanted to know was *why*.

❖

Everything had gone to plan at the petrol station. Becky had handed over the keys and they had exchanged tops. Emma had rushed back out, wiping her face with tissues and letting her hood fall back. If they were watching, they could see her face. She had filled the car, paid the bill and was now on her way home. She had no idea what the next few hours would bring, but with every cell in her body she hoped they would bring Ollie back to her.

She felt safe on the main road, but as soon as she turned into the lanes, she was struck by how vulnerable she was. The windscreen wipers swung rhythmically backwards and forwards, and the headlights reflected back the tiny shards of silver light from the thin rain. She turned a bend and was on a straight stretch. Nothing ahead.

Suddenly a blinding light flashed into her eyes – a reflection from the rear-view mirror. There was a car behind her.

'Shit.'

Without lifting the phone to her ear, Emma pressed a button to make a call, and another to put the phone on speaker.

'Tom,' she said. 'Can you hear me?'

'Yes I can. Loud and clear. Are you okay?'

'No. There's somebody behind me on the lanes. What should I do?'

'It's okay, Emma. He's one of ours. At the next junction, he'll turn off to the left when you go right, and another car will take over from there. You're safe.'

'Why didn't you tell me?'

'Sorry – I didn't know they were going to make it on time. I didn't want to promise something and not deliver. I just want to make sure you get back safely.'

As Tom had said, the car behind her tailed off at the next junction, and a few moments later she picked up more lights in her mirror and prayed that this was another police car. She saw the gates to her home ahead and felt her muscles sag with relief.

She pulled into the drive, glad to be home, but dreading the hours ahead. She leaned back against the headrest for a moment.

The adrenaline of the last half hour had seeped from her body, and with it the last trickle of energy. She felt like an old woman as she got out of the car and quietly let herself into the house. The hall was dark. Nobody had bothered to switch on the lamps.

The door to the sitting room was half open, and Emma could see David standing there, not hurrying towards her as she would have expected. He hadn't seen her. He was staring at his daughter, a look of horror on his face.

Emma was about to burst in and demand to know what had happened when she heard Tasha speak.

'Tell me,' she said. Emma could hear the throbbing note of misery in the girl's voice.

'I don't know what you mean. *Honestly.*'

'You're a *liar.* Tell me what happened. Tell me about that night, six years ago.'

Emma stepped back slightly. She didn't know what was happening, but this was between the two of them.

'I don't know how many times I have to say how sorry I am that I didn't come with you.'

'Oh *please*,' Natasha said, 'don't start all that again. You were *never* going to come with us, were you? It wouldn't have worked then – would it?'

From the shadows of the unlit hallway, Emma watched her husband. He swallowed and she saw his Adam's apple move up and down.

'What do you know, Natasha – or what do you think you know?'

'Can you not just tell the truth – for once in your sorry life?' she said, her voice harsh with disappointment. 'What was the plan?'

'Tasha, let's stop this now. It was all six years ago, and you're back with us. Let's get Ollie back too and move forwards.'

'That would be great, wouldn't it? Forget the last six years. I will *never* forget the last six years, David. Just tell me. Why did we have to be kidnapped, me and Mum? Why was that the only way?'

'It wasn't like that, Tasha. Nothing was supposed to happen to you, I promise.'

Emma smothered a gasp. *What was he talking about?*

'So what *was* supposed to happen, then? Did Mum know?'

David turned away, and somehow Emma knew that he didn't want Tasha to see his face.

'Of course your mum didn't know. She would never have agreed to it, and she wasn't much of an actress. It had to be real so the police would believe her afterwards. It was all supposed to be over really quickly. You and your mum were going to be taken somewhere safe. Just for an hour or two. I would never have put you in danger. You wouldn't have come to any harm.'

'*What?*' There was a note of incredulity in Natasha's voice.

Oh David, what did you do? Emma didn't want to hear any more, but she couldn't drag herself away.

'I couldn't have known that your mum would crash the car. I don't know why they took you – I didn't expect that.'

'What did you think they would do? I was *six* – not a baby. I could tell the police what had happened. I might have even recognised faces.'

David was silent.

'So they were telling me the truth, then,' Natasha said quietly.

'I'm so sorry, Tasha. It seemed like the best way out at the time. I owed some money. I owed it to some…brutal people.'

'Yeah – funnily enough, I know them. I've *lived* with them for six years, remember.'

'I knew there were diamonds in one of the safe deposit boxes, and I knew which one. If they'd just broken in and stolen them, though, I would have been implicated. So the plan was that they would pretend to kidnap you – but it wouldn't be *real*.'

'It would have been real to me and Mum, though, wouldn't it?'

'Yes, but not for long. I was going to help them get into the vault so they could steal the diamonds. My debt would have been paid, and then you and your mum would have been set free. The police would know I'd only done it under duress. Nobody would have been hurt. That was the plan.'

'So when it all went wrong, if you knew who had me, why didn't you tell the police?'

'I *didn't* know. I *never* knew. I promise you. The guy I owed the money to disappeared, and I never knew his name. We used to meet – to play cards. I got in over my head – kept thinking my luck would change. He was the only link.'

Emma heard a high-pitched laugh from Natasha – a cross between that and a sob.

'You really are dumb, aren't you? They would *all* have been in on it – all the men you were playing cards with. I bet they pretended not to know each other, didn't they? They set you up from the start – another mug who doesn't know how to hang on to his money. How did you pay the bloody debt then, when the robbery went wrong?'

He closed his eyes and spoke in a voice so soft that Emma could barely hear him.

'Your mum's life insurance.'

Emma heard a sharp intake of breath that turned to a sob. She'd had enough of this.

She pushed the door fully open and walked over to Natasha, wrapping her arms around the girl, pulling her close. She felt Tasha relax against her for a moment.

'Emma,' David said, his eyes flicking backwards and forwards between her and Natasha, clearly wondering how much she had heard.

All Emma could think of was her husband's grief when she had met him; he had talked endlessly about how much he had loved his family, about how, if he had his time all over again, he would have done things differently. Maybe it was more than grief, though. Or maybe it was something else entirely.

Guilt.

49

Becky was glad to be back in what, to her, felt like a normal world, with people she knew how to handle – such as the riffraff of Manchester. At least she could usually read them – know what they were thinking. The last few hours had been difficult to say the least. She felt David was stonewalling her, even though on the face of it he was trying to be helpful.

Natasha was a different matter, of course. She was understandably very confused, but she had committed a serious offence. *And* she had been brought up to steal, cheat, ferry drugs – so was she a criminal or was she a victim? Becky could deal appropriately with either, but when both were rolled up into one person, it confused her. To her, it was a simple dichotomy. Actions were either right or they were wrong.

Tom had always told her that few things were black and white, and that sometimes good people did bad things. For Becky, life was simpler when the good behaved themselves, and the bad were the rotten bastards she expected them to be.

'You're very quiet,' Tom said as he drove through the dark, wet streets of the Manchester suburbs.

'Sorry – I thought we'd covered everything.'

'We have, but that doesn't normally shut you up.'

Becky turned her head slowly and raised her eyebrows. She saw a half smile on Tom's face.

'Come on, Becky – what's bugging you?'

She was quiet for a moment longer.

'You know when David was on the phone to whichever

scumbag called – we don't know who, because we couldn't hear. Well – he could see me signalling him to put the phone on speaker. In fact I tried to lean over to do it for him, but he moved away. Why would he do that?'

'Do you think he's involved?'

'I don't know, Tom, but I hope and pray that he's not.'

Tom drew his car up next to Becky's.

'You and me both.' He left the car running and turned to Becky. 'Okay, we've got an armed response team in place close to the Joseph family, and another in Salford at Finn McGuinness' home address. We're assuming Julie will have taken the baby there rather than to her other house, which is no doubt full of inquisitive women and punters. Can you get over there and wait for the all clear so you can go in and get the baby? With any luck we'll have Ollie Joseph safely home before anything else has a chance to happen.'

Becky looked at Tom's strained face. She knew how difficult he was finding all of this and felt like leaning over and giving him a kiss on the cheek. She paused for a second then turned her head away.

'I'm on it, boss,' she said, pushing open the door and racing through the rain to the sanctuary of her own car.

❖

Tom watched Becky's car pull away. He wanted to feel confident that by the time she got to Salford, little Ollie would have been found, but he knew he mustn't be too optimistic. The minute that Ollie was safe, Tom would want to call a halt to the job, whatever it was – but he wasn't sure where that would leave the Titan team. For them, it would be best if the gang's plan continued, so Titan could catch them red-handed – finally, after all their years of effort.

Tom hadn't had time to process the information that had been flying at him from all quarters in the last few hours, and he wished he could find the time to think about Jack – the letters, the bank account and his brother's habit of hacking into people's computers to leave them messages. Jack's life was becoming clearer, and it was a picture Tom wasn't enjoying. But his death was more confused than ever. Accident, suicide or murder?

Would he ever know?

He needed to stop thinking about Jack, but at every turn in this investigation he seemed to rear up unexpectedly, and, more than anything, he was concerned about Jack's call to Caroline. How the hell had he known what was going to happen?

Tom had suspected for some time that Natasha Joseph's abduction six years ago had been no accident. He couldn't believe that Caroline's death was planned, though – nobody could plan a road traffic accident so precisely that death was a certainty – so was the plan that Caroline was taken, or Natasha, or both of them? Was that a tiger kidnap too?

And had Jack known about it? It certainly looked that way – but how?

Becky was right about one thing. David Joseph's behaviour on the phone suggested that he was hiding something. Tom felt certain that David was the key to it all. He wanted to shake the truth out of the man, but at this moment David Joseph was off limits.

Tom slammed his car into gear. There was little he could do now but watch – and wait.

50

The Josephs' sitting room was silent. Since Emma had appeared in the room, nobody had spoken, and it was almost as if none of them dared, because when they did the floodgates would open. David was staring anxiously at his wife and she looked back, her expression blank.

Natasha was glad that Emma had come home. She couldn't help feeling a quick rush of pleasure that Emma had heard at least part of David's confession, but she hadn't finished with her father yet.

She freed herself from Emma's arms but stayed close to her. David was still gazing only at Emma, no doubt trying to work out what she was thinking.

'I've got one more question for you, *Dad*,' Natasha said – putting as much disgust into that word as she could. 'Why didn't you get me back when you had the chance?'

David's body seemed to freeze. His eyes didn't move, his hands hung at his side. He was like a statue. The only sound was the soft ticking of the huge wall clock in the hall outside. Natasha waited, half expecting Emma to interrupt and tell her she was being ridiculous. But she didn't.

Finally David spoke.

'I never had a chance of getting you back. Why would you think that?'

Natasha felt her anger force its way to the surface again. He really was pathetic. 'They played me the tape, David. You know – the one where they said you could have me back if you would do something for them? Remember? And you said, "No."'

She would never forget the moment when Rory had played the tape to her. He had been mad because David had refused to go along with their plans. 'He doesn't want you,' Rory had whispered, prowling the room, circling her body, playing the tape over and over – as if it were her fault. 'You'll disrupt his happy little home – so he says we can keep you.' Then Rory had hit her on the back of her head. 'Useless, you are. Fucking useless,' he'd said.

'For God's sake, Natasha – it wasn't *like* that.' David was pleading with her, but she felt sick. How could he think this would ever be all right?

'What *was* it like, then,' she asked, 'to be offered your child back after four years? How did it feel to say, "No thank you"?'

Emma reached for her hand again and Natasha grasped it, trying not to remember what had happened next.

'I had no way at all of knowing that they really had you. There was no time for them to prove it.'

'They sent you a fucking photo – what more did you want?'

And after the photo Natasha had once again become a liability. What if David had taken it to the police? Behaved like any normal father? The photo could have been shown around – she could have been spotted out on the street, or by one of the social workers who came to the house – more often than Rory liked. So she'd had to stay hidden – and Rory had thrown her in The Pit just because he could – because the plan had failed and he had nobody else to take it out on.

David was still trying to make excuses. His voice sounded weak, whining. He would have had that knocked out of him as well, if he'd been brought up like she had.

'It could have been a child that just looked a bit like you. I didn't know. If I'd known it was you, it would have been different.'

'They asked you to make one phone call. That was all. One pissy little phone call when some guy who had been boasting to the world about his stash of money in your vault was about to clear it all out. Was I not worth the risk?'

She really didn't want to listen to his lies any more. To think she had wondered, even for a short time, if everything she had been told was a lie – if Rory and Finn had faked the tape, if perhaps she could be happy here. What a choice, even if she had one. Live here, with David, or go back and take her punishment.

Natasha's eyes stung. *What a choice.*

❖

Emma's eyes were drawn to Natasha. How terrible for the girl to hear this, to know that her own father was prepared to let her suffer – even if only for a couple of hours – to solve his own problems. She would *die* before she would do something like that to Ollie. She had no words.

David seemed more concerned about Emma's reaction than his daughter's.

'It was a *mistake*, Emma.'

Explain that to your daughter – the thought pulsed in her head. *Tell Tasha – not me.* But she knew he wouldn't. He wanted Emma to be on his side, to support him, to understand just as she always had.

'Why didn't you try harder to contact these men – do whatever they wanted so you could get Tasha back? Or tell the police the whole sorry tale?'

She knew the answer, of course. He didn't have the guts. He was more concerned about what would happen to him if he went to the police than he was about what was happening to his daughter. He would have hoped that, somehow, it would all come right without him having to do anything at all.

Memories of the hours they had spent together talking about the loss of Caroline and Natasha painted vivid pictures in her head, and she realised that David had found Caroline's death easy to deal with. It was always part of the conversation, but it was the loss of Tasha that had troubled him the most. Was it because of grief, guilt, or could it actually have been fear? Fear that at some moment in the future – at a time he couldn't control – it would all come back to bite him? Tasha and everything that had happened to her was the one problem that would never go away, however much he ignored it, because it was always lurking at the edge of his consciousness. And then two years ago, it really did come back – and he did nothing.

David was running his fingers through his hair again, and an action she had once found endearing suddenly irritated her beyond measure.

'I had never been able to contact them,' he said. 'They always contacted me. I tried everything. I thought when things had calmed down after the accident and the police had finished crawling all over me, all over our friends, family, it would be back on and I would get Tasha back, but three weeks later the customer took his diamonds out. He had a buyer.'

'And you did *nothing*?' Emma could hear the disgust in her own voice.

'What could I have done?' David asked, looking genuinely bewildered.

'You could have told the police.'

'What, tell them what I'd done?'

Emma couldn't believe the look of horror on David's face, as if this was a totally ridiculous suggestion.

'Yes – of course you should. And what reason could you possibly have for not telling the police when you had the chance to get Tasha back two years ago?'

'You make it all sound so black and white, and it wasn't. Anybody could have made up a story to say they had Tasha. And I *would* have gone to the police, but they said they would hurt you if I did, Em. You were pregnant with Ollie. I couldn't lose a second family.'

'So you sold out your first to protect your second, did you?' Natasha asked, making it sound like a reasonable decision.

'If I'd gone to the police I'd have had to explain what had happened six years ago. They would have locked me up – surely you can understand?'

Suddenly, Emma felt as if an icy blast had swept into the room and the surface of her skin tingled with cold and fear.

'And Ollie? Is this you too, David? Have you let them take my baby to save yourself from some other stupidity?'

She heard Natasha gasp, 'No,' but her eyes were on David's face. She thought she could read the answer in his horror-struck gaze – but maybe she didn't know him at all.

The momentary silence was shattered as Natasha's mobile rang.

❖

David and Emma hurried to the kitchen at Natasha's insistence. She thought their voices should be picked up by the bug in there, and they walked in, playing their parts, although Emma wanted nothing more than to grab David by the neck and shake him until he told her everything. She wrapped her arms around her stomach, trying to control the sick feeling lodged deep inside her. Whether David had anything to do with Ollie's abduction or not, if he hadn't set this ball rolling six years ago, none of this would be happening now.

She banged a few dishes around and switched the tap on, so the listeners would know they were there. She couldn't bring herself to talk to David.

Natasha followed them into the kitchen a minute later.

'David – they're on the phone. They want to speak to you. On speaker.'

Natasha laid the phone down on the table and a distorted voice echoed around the room.

'Write this down. At 2.30 a.m. you will drive to Joseph & Son.

Inside the back porch you will find a duffle bag. Take that with you. Let yourself into the main building foyer the back way. You know the code. At 3.01 a.m. you will type the following number into the security keypad at Joseph & Son's door: 1563974. This will give you access to the vault. The time locks have been dealt with. Wedge the door open. If it closes, it will restart the timing system and you won't be able to get out.'

David scribbled frantically. Emma made her own notes – they couldn't afford any mistakes.

'Open the door to the key room and take the key to box 2909. Empty the contents of the box into the sacks you'll find in the duffle bag, and put them in your car. You have exactly 58 minutes to do this before the security system does its automatic check for breaches. You have to be out of the building with the door closed by that time. If not, the police will catch you and you'll never see your son again. Do you understand?'

David looked up at Emma and she nodded. She could remind him of the details and they could go over them together. There was time.

'We will call on this phone at 4.10 a.m. when you must be back in the car. We'll tell you where you've got to go to make the delivery. Wear black – head to toe. There will be no lighting at all in the vault.'

Emma looked at her husband and felt a moment's sympathy. The idea of going into that place alone, at night, below the streets of Manchester, in a building that had been there for years and held who knew what secrets was enough to make the strongest man blanch.

'Have you understood all this?'

'Yes,' David answered.

'And you, Emma?' the voice said.

'No. When do I get my baby back?'

'When the job's done. Natasha comes back to us and the baby

comes back to you. We'll let you know where you can find him once the girl's back with us. He'll be safe.'

Emma turned horrified eyes to Tasha. She had always said she would have to go back, but Emma had never thought it would really come to that.

The man was speaking again.

'Are you listening, Emma?'

'Yes,' she answered softly, still staring at Natasha's pale face.

'Good – because David's not the one doing this job. It's you. You're the one who's going into the vault – if you want your son back.'

The line went dead.

51

It had been easier than Becky had imagined to locate the house where they believed Ollie was being held. The Titan team had confirmed that Finn McGuinness's wife ran the burger van, and the supposedly respectable couple had a house in a surprisingly prosperous area of Salford, on a street of beautiful detached homes. That in itself was a relief, because a covert operation in a road where houses were crammed together with neighbours within two metres of each other was a nightmare.

Becky had been banished to her car, parked down the street beyond the outer cordon set up by the firearms team, and she tapped her fingers impatiently on the steering wheel. McGuinness was an organised crime group's enforcer, so there was every chance of finding a gun in the house. Unfortunately, that meant Becky couldn't just barge in and demand Ollie back. The firearms silver commander was responsible for putting the operation together and making all the decisions now, leaving Becky temporarily redundant. All she could do was wait for the all clear – the moment when she could go in and rescue Ollie.

She was too far away to check what was happening, and anyway she could barely see through the windscreen as the individual fat drops of rain joined together to create silver rivers down the glass. She couldn't draw attention to herself by putting her windscreen wipers on, so she peered out of the side window at the black silhouettes of trees lining the narrow cul-de-sac, hiding the expensive properties that were set well back from the road.

It didn't seem right that one of these lovely houses was Finn

McGuinness's home, and Becky thought about all the lives that had been ruined by drugs and God knows what else to pay for this lifestyle. She had seen pictures of McGuinness. He was not what she expected. He looked strangely like a bank manager – a man who would fit easily into this middle-class street. Apart from what appeared to be a perpetually worried frown, his face was fairly lacking in memorable features. His short, well-groomed grey hair was receding at the front, but there were no discernible signs of the life of crime he was purported to have led. He wasn't even a big man at five feet ten inches, and in each of the photos she saw he was wearing a smart overcoat and a snazzy red tie. A businessman through and through.

Even in a two-dimensional static image, though, the eyes said it all. Nothing could disguise the flat, black stare that Becky was sure – if cast upon you – would turn your legs to jelly – and not in a good way. She hoped and prayed that she wouldn't be finding out tonight.

A light in an upstairs window was on, suggesting somebody was home, but as yet nobody had seen any movement or heard a sound. She knew the team was getting into position but it was a delicate operation with too many unknown factors for Becky's liking.

A sudden downpour of rain washed the windscreen clean, for a moment forming a solid sheet of water that enhanced the image through the glass. Peering at the distorted view, Becky watched as a member of the team approached the house cautiously – little more than a dark shadow, keeping close to the wall.

The listening devices were being put in place. They needed to hear Ollie or Julie. If they got this wrong, Ollie might not get out alive.

❖

Emma locked herself in the bathroom. She couldn't let either Natasha or David know how she was feeling about carrying out the robbery, but the look of horror on Natasha's face had said it all.

She hadn't been expecting this. David's expression of relief that it wasn't going to be him sickened her.

Was this the man she had married? Images of their life together flashed through her mind – of times when she had perhaps misinterpreted her husband's actions. She had always assumed his inability to face the harsh realities of life was down to his optimistic nature. Now she was sure that it was more a case of hiding from the truth. Right now, he would be convincing himself that it was fine for Emma to do this. He would have devised a list of reasons to justify why it was better for Emma to go down into that dark, silent vault. That way, he didn't need to feel guilty about it.

Whatever he was thinking, she wasn't going to give him the satisfaction of knowing how terrified she was.

She had visited David's company in daylight hours, when the half dozen people who worked there had been around. Even then, she had found something spooky about the place. It was months since she had been there – not since the time she went to show Ollie off to David's colleagues just after he was born – and she tried to visualise the place, to fix the layout in her mind.

The customer entrance was on the main road, but she had been told to go in the back way – an entrance she didn't know. It didn't matter, because everything – the offices, the reception, the safe deposit boxes – were all in the bowels of the earth, under the streets of Manchester.

There was a long flight of narrow steps leading down to a small reception area, with just enough space for a couple of security men and a bank of CCTV monitors behind a counter. A door led from there into the key room.

Then there were more stairs down into the tile-lined spaces below. David's office was in this part of the building; he always said that he felt a bit like a mole, buried beneath the earth all day. In the winter, he never saw sunlight during the week. There were no windows – they were too far underground.

There had been one moment during her last visit when she had been left on her own while David went to answer the phone. Emma remembered having the same sensation that she'd once had on a deserted underground platform in London. The silence had a dead quality to it, and there was the sense of being watched by the hordes of people who had passed that way before.

Then David had come back and shown her the individual rooms that led off the cavernous central space, each one lined with row after row of safe deposit boxes. There was a tiny viewing room where customers could take their boxes to examine the contents – to add or remove whatever they were storing there. It sat, like a polished, wooden coffin, at the side of the room: a place to hide your secrets.

The vault was like a rabbit warren – room after room hidden round corners, opening up into unexpected spaces. She knew it had been used as an air-raid shelter during the war, and Emma pictured people huddled against the walls, listening to the blasts as the bombs of the Manchester Blitz destroyed the Palace Theatre only a few hundred metres away.

She shuddered. It wasn't a place she wanted to visit on her own, even with all the lights on. She had no idea how she would cope in the dark. But it was for Ollie. She would do anything for Ollie.

She perched on the side of the bath, knowing she was going to have to phone Tom, but she couldn't decide how much to tell him. Should she tell him about David – about the deal he had made six years ago? Would it make a difference to what happened now? She didn't think so, but it might. She didn't want to tell him – she felt such a deep sense of shame.

She couldn't regret David, though. Without him there would be no Ollie, and even if David wasn't prepared to fight to the death for his wife and take her place in the vaults he knew so well, she was damned sure she would battle to her last breath for her baby.

Using her Australian phone, she pressed the call button.

'What's happening, Em?'

❖

Tom listened as Emma repeated the instructions and told him all she had learned since she had arrived home.

Emma's revelation about David was sadly no real surprise to Tom; it certainly explained some of his actions and Natasha's attitude.

'Do you think he's got anything to do with what's going on this time, Emma?'

He had to ask, even though the thought might not even have entered Emma's head.

'I don't think so,' she answered, without a hint of shock at the suggestion. 'He genuinely looked horrified that I could think that, as if it was a totally ridiculous idea.'

He heard Emma's voice catch and wondered how much more she could take.

'You don't have to do this, Emma. We can do another swap; somebody else can go into the vault for you.'

'That's not going to happen, Tom. I'll walk over hot coals for my baby if I have to. If somebody else does this and it goes wrong, I'd never forgive myself. And besides that, they need my fingerprint on the locks.'

'Bollocks, I'd forgotten the biometric locks. Why are your prints stored?'

Emma explained that it had been a precaution when David was ill once. The gang must have hacked the system to clear the time lock so no doubt they found out about her prints at the same time.

'There's a chance you might not have to do this at all,' Tom said. 'If we get Ollie before your deadline, that'll be the end of your part in it.'

He heard a whispered plea from Emma and gave her a moment.

'Are you all right?' he asked.

'It's okay. I'm not going to mess this up,' she said quietly.

'I know. There'll be somebody with you every step of the way, Em. Just remember – we've got your back.'

52

'All set, Boss,' Finn said, looking at the younger, taller man standing warming himself in front of an open fire.

'Confident?' the man Finn called 'Boss' asked.

'Yeah, I think so. The wife's not going to blow it. Didn't trust the tit of a husband to get it right, but she's a bit more solid. Timing's an issue. If she doesn't get out the alarm will go off and we're fucked – or rather she is. But I doubt she's going to let that happen.'

'Is the hacker on standby?'

'Yeah – he's confident he can override the alarm to get her out, but he's had no way of testing it. He's probably got a window of a couple of minutes to free up the auto locking of the doors before the police arrive.'

'The buyer? You checked him out?'

The Boss moved away from the fire, briefly rubbing the back of his trousers with both hands. He reached for a glass of clear liquid on the table. A couple of ice cubes bobbed around on the surface, clinking against the side.

'As much as I could. He's given us eyes on his money – so we know he's got it. That's as much as we can be sure of.'

'It's time to get rid of Rory, Finn.'

'Yeah – he's a fucking liability. We need him for this job, but after that... He didn't manage those kids well. Rick and Shelley caught on camera, and then there's the other one – Izzy.'

'Are we sure it's her?'

The Boss drank the whole glass of liquid. Finn knew it would be water; the Boss never drank before a job.

'Ninety per cent. According to the intel, she was wearing the right clothes – the nightdress that Julie gave her. They think she was pumped full of ket, too. That sounds about right. Could have picked that up at Julie's.'

'Well – at least she's dead. That's one less to worry about.' The Boss looked pleased, and it was Finn's job to keep him that way.

'Shelley shouldn't have blabbed to her. If Izzy hadn't already been dead…' Finn didn't need to say more. 'Speaking of Shelley, we've got a couple of hours before the handover. I'm going to pull her out. She did okay with the baby, but she's made some stupid mistakes and she needs to pay for them. She nearly fucked up the whole thing, and she's not to be trusted any more.'

Shelley Slater was about to find out what happened to people who crossed Finn McGuinness. He hadn't quite decided what to do with her – how severe to make the punishment. But Julie wouldn't want her marked. She said Shelley could net them a fortune.

'Back here in one hour, then – when you've sorted her,' the Boss said.

Finn nodded, pulled on his leather gloves and made his way out of the door.

53

When Tom arrived at the control room in Salford West there was an air of restrained tension. Operators sat at computers, quietly and efficiently getting on with their jobs. In spite of the apparent calm, though, Tom knew that every person in the room would be feeling a tightening in their gut at the burden of their responsibility.

A bank of monitors along one wall was showing three simultaneous operations, and the silver commander of the firearms unit was issuing instructions to the operational team on the ground at Finn and Julie McGuinness's home. But nobody as yet had heard the sound of a baby.

Two screens were being set up to monitor activity in the vicinity of Joseph & Son. A team would be standing by in case Emma got into any kind of trouble.

Three further screens were displaying images from a location that Tom didn't recognise. Paul Green was staring at them intently, and Tom realised that these must be related to the Titan operation.

'Where are we?' Tom asked, turning to Paul Green and pointing to the screens.

'A cemetery just off the M60. They've chosen well. No CCTV and several fast exit routes. It's where we believe the goods are going to be handed over to their buyer, and the word is that the big man likes to be there. He doesn't trust a soul, it seems.'

'They haven't told Emma where she has to go after she leaves the vault, so I presume your informant has given you this location?'

'Yeah, he has. I hope to God he's not been pulling my plonker on this. But I don't think so.'

Tom suddenly felt a crushing need to know more. It wasn't just about Emma – although she and Ollie were his priority – but this was so closely related to the events of six years ago, and he desperately wanted to know what Jack's role had been back then. He'd clearly known something the night Caroline died, and Jack had installed the security system at Joseph & Son in the first place, his company chosen because the system had been hacked by somebody who left messages on people's desktops.

There was no longer any doubt in Tom's mind where the money in his brother's secret – and now empty – account had come from. The link between the sources of his funds and his clients was too strong. He had been hacking into people's computer systems and then selling them his services, and Tom knew exactly how Jack would have justified that.

'If I could do it, so could somebody else.' Tom could hear him saying it now. But Jack didn't have to cheat people. He could have done it legitimately by pointing out the weaknesses in their systems.

Jack's voice filled his head again. 'They wouldn't have trusted me after that. They would have thought I was a slimy bastard, and they'd have gone to somebody else. Don't be a moron, Tom.'

It didn't help Tom understand how Jack had known that Caroline and Natasha were going to be abducted, though. Or why, having warned Caroline, Jack had left the country the next day. A few hours later, he was dead.

Too many coincidences, and Tom didn't like coincidences. Was Jack killed? Was he murdered for his part in it all – for warning Caroline Joseph?

Paul Green interrupted his reverie.

'Tom, we've got about half an hour until Emma has to leave home. Have you got five minutes for me to fill you in on what we know about the gang?'

Tom walked across to a whiteboard displaying any and all information that might help in their investigation.

'Do we know how the gang is planning to bypass the security system to get Emma into the vault? According to David Joseph it's watertight – but that's clearly not the case. I assume it's been hacked.'

Paul Green nodded.

'I agree. Emma won't be able to get in unless at least the security on the main door has been breached, but it would be absolute foolishness to go into the vault without knowing what you're looking for, so they must also know exactly what's in the box.'

'Do you think this organised crime group have their own hacker?' Tom asked.

'No – I think they'll have advertised for one. The dark web is responsible for so much these days – a hacker's paradise with more jobs than people to fill them. But this is a really specialised job – they would have needed somebody exceptional, and I guess they found him – or her.'

'So the hacker isn't your informant, then?'

'No. He's not.'

Tom had a vague sense of unease. He knew the Titan team would handle it well, but if the informant was discovered, he wouldn't be long for this world.

'I thought you might like to know a bit more about this group. You know about one of the bottom-feeders – Rory Slater. There are plenty of others like him. We know of at least two enforcers – Finn McGuinness being the most active – and we're also aware of Julie McGuinness's various businesses. We're ready to go on those as soon as we've got the main man.'

Paul Green pointed to images of each person as he mentioned them.

'We don't often manage to get a picture of the boss. He's quite reclusive and very good indeed at disguise. But we grabbed this as he was going through security at Manchester airport.'

Paul Green pointed to an image of a tall man wearing a dark

overcoat – smart, stylish, it hung well from his broad shoulders. Tom looked at the man's face and slowly walked towards the whiteboard until he was inches from it.

'My God,' he whispered. It wasn't what he was expecting, but somehow he wasn't surprised. It felt like another piece of the puzzle, but he had no idea where it fit.

'Do you know him?' Paul Green asked. 'He's called Guy Bentley.'

'He might be called that now,' Tom said, 'but he used to be Ethan Bentley. His dad owned Bentley's Hotel.'

'He did indeed. As bent as they come too, until he died when his hotel burned down – most believe at Guy's hand, but it's never been proven. Provided girls, boys, drugs – whatever his clients wanted. But Guy's been much smarter. His profile's so low it's barely in existence. How the hell do you know somebody like Guy Bentley?'

'He knew my brother, Jack.'

Green looked at Tom sharply.

'Is this the same brother that installed the security system at Joseph and Son? He died a few years ago, didn't he?'

Tom nodded, unable to speak. Because this was adding up to something very nasty, and if his sums were correct, there was every chance that the person responsible for Jack's death was the person whose face he was now staring at on the board.

54

'I'm doing this for Ollie. I'm doing this for Ollie.' Emma said the words over and over in her head as she drove, quickly taking a drink from a bottle of water she had brought with her. Her mouth was so dry, yet her skin was clammy and cold.

She was nearly there.

Much as she had hated every second of it, she had gone over and over the plan with David, making sure she understood everything she had to do. She had given him the police radio, showing him how to use it to call in help if he needed to, telling him to make sure that he and Natasha stayed safe. She wasn't convinced he was listening, though.

She let go of the steering wheel first with one hand, and then the other, wiping her damp palms on an old pair of black cargo pants. Her phone was buried deep in one of the pockets, and switched to speaker. A head torch was on the seat beside her, fully charged with a new battery.

Emma took the Range Rover down a narrow alleyway that led to the back door of the building under which lay the Joseph & Son vault, and pulled it into the loading bay of the clothing manufacturer next door.

The streets in this part of Manchester were deathly quiet, although she knew that less than half a mile away there would be plenty of activity as the clubs emptied and people struggled home.

There were no lights down this backstreet.

'I'm here,' she said softly, reaching down to open the car door. She stepped out onto the wet tarmac, her feet in their dark trainers making no sound. She closed the door as gently as she could, but the small click seemed to echo against the dark brick walls, so close across the alley that she felt hemmed in – trapped. There was a smell of damp clothing from the piles of discarded fabric left in the loading bay, soaked by the weekend's driving rain, overlaid with the stink of rancid fat from an all-night kebab shop on the main road.

If she spoke, Tom and his team would hear her through the phone. But once she was out of the car, he wouldn't respond to her unless it was a real emergency. Anything she said out loud had to sound as if she was speaking to herself. Tom didn't know if sound was being picked up in any way by the gang.

She had been instructed by the man on the phone to take Natasha's phone with her too, and Emma knew they could switch it on remotely if they wanted to and pick up every word she uttered. And of course they could track where she was at any time through the GPS.

The building in front of her had been standing for over a hundred years and had once been at the heart of the textile industry. Now it housed a number of organisations, from insurance companies to solicitors' offices, but only Joseph & Son was below ground.

As Emma slowly approached the communal doorway she glanced around, twisting from the waist to look first in one direction, then the other. She was sure Tom had said they would have eyes on her from the moment she left the house to the minute she was inside, but somehow it didn't help. A deep, dark recess led to the door, and not a hint of light penetrated the cave-like entrance.

She pulled on her head torch over her hair and switched it on.

An opening to the right led to stairs going down into the boiler room. She forced herself not to glance in that direction, knowing that the light from her torch wouldn't penetrate the furthest reaches, and she wouldn't know if anything – or anybody – was there, watching her. She glanced down. In the corner was the duffle bag, as promised.

To get into the building's foyer she had to type a password into the keypad to the right of the door. That was the easy bit. A few clicks and she was inside, standing by the main security door to Joseph & Son.

'Okay,' she muttered, as if to herself. 'I'm in position and ready to go.'

She pulled Natasha's phone from her pocket to check the time. 03.00 it said.

The final sixty seconds dragged, each second seeming longer than the last. *Would the time ever change? Did she want it to change?* She was about to pull out her other phone to check when the minute digit clicked over.

03.01.

She slowly punched in the seven digit number she had been given and heard a reassuring click. She pushed the door open and stepped into the black passageway.

'No lights,' David had told her. 'They are on a time switch in case somebody leaves them on at the end of the day. With your torch, you're probably okay in the dark.'

It was easy for him to say that. He wasn't the one standing here with just a steel door separating him from a staircase leading down into the abyss. The beam from the head torch probed the blackness just a few metres ahead. Beyond that was an inky silence. She moved her head to one side and gasped.

What's that?

Her narrow beam had picked up a reflection from a stainless steel inner door – flashing a bright light back at her. It had looked for all the world as if somebody was standing there – shining a torch into her face. She moved towards the door, and the mirror finish of the vertical bars blinded her momentarily. Never had anything looked more like a cage to Emma – a cage that contained a threat greater than any wild animal. It was the threat of the unknown. What else might be beyond this gate? What if somebody was here, waiting for her?

She pushed the steel door open and started her descent into the dark void below.

❖

Despite the lack of any noticeable activity, the monitors for the three operations were being closely scrutinised in the dimly lit control room. The lights were low so as to give greater definition to the night-time images, but Tom couldn't draw his gaze away from the monitor at the back of Joseph & Son. He didn't believe he would look away until Emma reappeared in about 54 minutes' time.

As he watched the screen, something moved. It was difficult to see, but he was sure he saw a shadow.

'Paul, have you got a moment,' he said, his tone clipped with an urgency that was driving him closer to the screen. He spoke to the operator as he moved. 'Could you replay the last thirty seconds?'

Paul walked across the room and both men stared at the screen.

'See – there.' Tom leaned forwards and pointed at the screen.

'And again, Luke,' Paul said calmly to the operator. The section was replayed.

'You're right, Tom. What do you want to do about it?'

But both men knew there was nothing they *could* do, other than alert the team on standby.

They couldn't talk to Emma without putting the whole operation in jeopardy, but Tom was in no doubt at all that somebody had just followed her down into the vault.

55

A sharp gust of wind blew drops of rain from the overhanging tree on to Natasha's bedroom window. Their soft splatter was the only sound in an otherwise silent house. She could no longer bear to be in the same room as David. How could he believe that no harm would have been done to her and her mum, kidnapped and locked up, even if only for a few hours? For years she had hoped that Rory had been lying about the accident, but tonight she had been forced to listen to David making excuses and she'd had to accept that everything she had been told was the truth.

Natasha could remember her mother. She remembered the smell of her perfume – something soft and flowery – and she was so gentle, so timid compared to the people that Natasha had lived with since. She remembered her first day at school, when her mum had tried so hard not to cry. And then at the end of each day, she would be waiting by the school gates – not standing chatting to the others mums and dads, but anxiously watching the door until Natasha came out, at which point her she would jump up and down on the spot, madly waving at Natasha as if they hadn't seen each other in months. She said she missed her every single moment of the day and counted the hours until Natasha came home.

Somehow, she knew that if her mother hadn't died but had been abducted that night instead, she would never have recovered. Her mum would probably have ended up like a woman up the road from Rory and Donna's. She hadn't been out of the house for twenty years, all because of something that had happened to her – although nobody knew what. Some of the kids played tricks on her to get her to open the door, but she just looked out of the window with a round, sad face.

How could David not have known how much damage he would do?

Natasha glanced at herself in the mirror, the shiny tears on her face matching the droplets of rain running down the window. For a while she had hoped that Rory had told her a bunch of lies – or at least that David would give her an explanation that she could live with. She had even allowed herself to wonder what it would be like to stay here, with David, Emma and Ollie when they got him back.

But that was just a childish dream. She wasn't sure what would happen to her dad and Emma now, and it was all because of her. She had ruined their lives, as David had ruined hers.

She knew she wouldn't be allowed to stay – even if she was wanted here, which she wasn't. She couldn't think why they would want to fight for her – a girl who was the best shoplifter in the west of Manchester, expert mobile phone thief, drug mule and baby snatcher. *Really?*

She thought of what was going to happen next. The police would rescue Ollie, and then they would all know – Rory, Finn, the Boss – that she had betrayed them. They would know that either Emma or David had called the police, and she hadn't stopped them. She would get the blame. Even if she said she hadn't known, they wouldn't believe her. And anyway, they would beat the truth out of her. Then there would only be one outcome.

Natasha stood up from the bed and went to the drawers. She grabbed a carrier bag that she had liked the look of when Emma bought her some clothes and started to push things inside. She stopped. That would be thieving, and they would hate her even more.

She slowly took off all her clothes, folded them, and put them away in the drawers. At the bottom of the wardrobe was the bag of clothes she had arrived in, and she put them on, piece by piece, feeling for the first time the rough texture of cheap fabric, smelling the odour of age and seeing the dark stains where other children who had worn the clothes before her had spilled their food.

She was ready. Now she just had to wait.

56

Emma wiped her damp hands on her jeans again and reached out the forefinger of her right hand for the second time. Her print had been rejected. If it didn't work this time, she was fairly sure that she would only have one chance left before her print became invalid and she wouldn't be able to get into the key room.

She placed her finger on the screen, waiting for the beep and the green light. It took a moment, but the red light flashed again.

Shit. If she couldn't get in, she was going to fail, and she was losing too much time. But she was so hot.

As she wiped her sticky forehead with the back of her hand, she felt what seemed like a cold draught of air on her back, but it was over in a second. She spun round, the light from her headlamp illuminating the small reception room behind her. Nothing. She must have imagined it. It must have been a cold trickle of fear.

She turned back to the door, knowing she had one chance left. Wiping her finger hadn't worked. She remembered that there was a thermal indicator as well, and her hands were so hot and sweaty that they were probably unreadable. She placed her finger in her mouth to get it wet, and then waved it above her head, hoping the body heat would dissipate from her finger as the saliva dried.

Without giving the beads of sweat time to reform, she placed her finger on the screen. As she waited, she could feel dampness oozing through her skin.

Beep. The green light, a dull, thick click and the door sprang open.

'Thank God for that,' she said under her breath – loud enough for the listeners to hear.

She moved her head around to shine the light at line after line of hooks, each holding a key with its own numbered tag attached. It took her just seconds to find the right one.

'Two, nine, oh, nine,' Emma mumbled, pulling the key from the hook. She turned to leave the room.

The key room had given her a false sense of security. Standing in the centre of that confined space, spinning around, she could see all four corners of the room. But now she was at the entrance to the vault, and the thought of what lay beyond – the expanse, the myriad side rooms, the dark depths that her torch wouldn't penetrate, the corners around which she couldn't see – filled her with icy terror. Her body started to shake, although she had still gone no further than the doorway.

Once more she used her fingerprint to gain access. The door clicked open on her first attempt. She stood still, dreading the moment when she had to enter the main chamber, a vast open space.

Come on, Emma. This is for Ollie. She couldn't afford to waste time. She pushed the door gently, and it slid open on well-oiled hinges. She knew this door was left open during the day, and she pushed it as far back as she could, dreading the thought that the door would close and she would be trapped inside.

She took a step into the black space, turning her head in an attempt to light the shady reaches of the room. To the right were several individual doorless rooms with wide, thin boxes around the sides and back; two hundred down each side, a hundred along the back wall, ten deep from top to bottom.

To her left were further rooms leading from the central vault, and in one corner was the viewing room – the only room with a closed door. Emma twisted her body to shine the head torch towards it, feeling strangely drawn to the room – the compulsion to check that it was empty almost overpowering her need to get the job done.

She was wasting time. She hitched the heavy duffle bag higher on her shoulder, scared to move in case the soft sound of her footsteps masked other sounds in the yawning space. The corners of each side room seemed remote, concealing their secrets in the shadows.

She *had* to get on with it.

The room in which box 2909 was situated was the furthest from the door. It was a wide room with larger boxes. To one side were some of the last of the walk-in safes, many unused, some with their doors standing slightly ajar to reveal their gaping emptiness, each one potentially harbouring an unseen threat.

She placed the duffle bag on the floor and bent down to examine the contents. Inside were several hemp sacks, rolled neatly together around something solid: a screwdriver, and underneath that, a drill. David had warned her that the chances of the gang having the owner's key to the target box was remote. He had talked her through the process of drilling the second lock, but she had no experience of using a drill, and so little time.

She had forgotten to speak.

'I've got to sodding drill it,' she whispered, as if talking to herself.

What was that?

She was sure she had heard a noise, coming from behind her, somewhere in the vault. It was a click, as if a button had snagged against one of the metal doors.

Emma spun round, swinging her head to see into the inky shadows behind her. Nothing.

The strange stillness that she had remembered from her earlier visit descended like a blanket, flattening the silence. She looked at the gaping doors of the huge safes on the other side of the room and realised she was going to have to stand with her back to all of them, her ears assaulted by the whirring of the drill, blind and deaf to anything behind her.

Her heart thumping against her thin T-shirt, she turned back to the box and placed the drill bit against the top of the lock cylinder and started to drill. The bit slipped and clattered noisily against the front of the steel box.

'Shit.'

She put the drill back in position, and started again. Once more it slid off the metal. Emma stifled a sob. She couldn't do this. It was too hard.

Suddenly, she was still. In the unexpected silence as she had taken her finger off the drill's trigger, there was a noise again. This time she knew she wasn't mistaken.

She had her back to the room. If she turned, she would have to spin her head around in circles to reveal all the corners of the wide, black space. Her heart was pumping, but in her second of indecision she heard the rushing sound of soft shoes on the concrete floor, felt the movement of air as a body flew at her and pressed her with force against the wall of steel boxes, a gloved hand snaking round, clamping itself hard over her mouth, stifling the scream that was trying to escape.

❖

Tom was standing very still, listening to every sound Emma made. He could hear her fear, taste it even, as his own mouth dried at each hurdle she had to overcome. He had been so tempted to take his phone off mute and yell, 'Get out!' to her. Whoever was in the vault with her was already there, though, and she would have to get past him to escape.

She had stopped drilling a few seconds ago and he'd heard a sharp intake of breath, then what sounded like a stifled squeal.

The room had become silent. Paul Green turned to look at Tom. He didn't speak, knowing this was Tom's shout.

Tom turned to the silver commander of the firearms team.

'Emma's in trouble and we're going to have to send somebody in to help her. That will blow the whole operation wide open – I know it's your call, but I would urge you to get that baby out of the McGuinness house as soon as you can.'

Tom picked up his radio.

'Nic – you're going to have to follow Emma in. We've no idea what's going on down there, but there's somebody in the vault with her. I don't see any way you can do this discreetly, but do your best.'

Paul Green's hand suddenly shot up.

'Wait,' Tom said urgently to Nic.

Through the speakers there was another sound. The sound of drilling.

'Stop,' Tom said.

He waited. He would give it two minutes to hear Emma's voice. If not, Nic would have to go in.

57

David Joseph sat alone in his kitchen, his arms folded on the table, his bowed head, resting against one clenched fist. He couldn't believe that Tasha had known all this time what he had done. And now Emma knew too. The look on her face had frightened him – a combination of puzzlement and disgust. But they'd had no chance to talk about it before she had to leave – to go down into his vault and do the gang's bidding to get Ollie back.

Tasha couldn't even bear to be in the same room as David now; she was closeted upstairs in her bedroom. He understood how hurt she was, but he was going to have to make her understand – Emma too – that at the time everything he had done had seemed like the best solution. When you owed money to people like this gang, you couldn't just walk away. He would have had to sell the house or the business, and Caroline would have been miserable for months. The abduction would only have given her and Tasha a few difficult hours if everything had gone to plan.

He knew he was making excuses for himself. He had known since the day it happened that he had done something terrible – so awful that there *were* no excuses. All he could hope for was that both Tasha and Emma would understand how sorry he was.

For a moment, he thought about Emma – all alone in the depths of the earth below Manchester. He had grown to love the special silence of the vault, but he could remember going there as a child with his father and hating it. The only sound had been the gentle hum of fluorescent lights, and he had felt disconnected from the world above. Emma would hate it too, but he couldn't have gone in her place. He would have failed – made a mistake, made everything go wrong. Emma was solid, practical, reliable. Everything that he wasn't.

Now he felt a different kind of disconnection. The kitchen didn't have the same sense of suffocating silence – the rain was pattering on the roof, the wind rustling the trees outside – but he felt isolated. He wanted to make things right, but he had no idea how.

Before she left the house, Emma had said that he should barricade himself into a bedroom with Tasha and take the police radio with him – to keep safe. But that wasn't going to happen. He was perfectly safe in his own kitchen, and Tasha wouldn't let him into her room anyway. The truth was, he couldn't bear to see the hatred in her eyes, so it was better if he left her alone for a while, to give her time to understand everything he had told her.

There was no danger from this gang. Emma would do what she had to, take the contents of the safe deposit box to them, and then Ollie could come back. That was all these people were interested in.

A thought was trying to creep into David's head, and he pushed it away. But it wouldn't go. They had said that Tasha had to go back, that only then would they tell Emma where to find Ollie. But that wasn't going to happen. How could he let Tasha go now? Was he supposed to choose between his children? Would Emma expect him to choose Ollie, if it came to it?

Maybe he should try to talk to Tasha again now, convince her that he had no intention of letting her go – whatever she had done. It wasn't really a question of whether he could forgive Tasha for the agony she had put them through, though. It was more a question of whether she could forgive him for the years of pain that she had been subjected to because of him.

All this introspection was getting him nowhere, and he roused himself, lifting his head from his arms and sitting up.

The awareness of another noise, beyond the ticking of the

clock and the sounds of the weather outside, came upon him slowly. It was a rhythmic clunk every couple of seconds. David realised that it was the sound of the side gate, banging in the wind. But they had closed it, he was sure, when Becky was here.

He stood up and walked the length of the room to where the window over the sink looked out over the side garden. The light from the window spilled out onto the path and he could just make out the shadow of the tall side gate, open, swinging to and fro.

He should go out and close it, really – but despite his earlier confidence in their safety, he suddenly felt hesitant.

The decision was taken out of his hands as an explosion of sound shattered the silence of the kitchen – a huge crash as a steel-clad boot smashed through the back door.

David spun round, diving for the police radio on the worktop. But he was too late. Two men burst into his kitchen, dressed head to toe in black, balaclavas pulled down over their faces. A mountain of a man in a black T-shirt slammed what was left of the door back on its hinges and charged forwards, shouting words that David couldn't make out, his senses assaulted by sound and vision. The man's heavily tattooed biceps rippled as he tensed and relaxed fists that were wrapped around an iron bar.

Following at a slower pace was a slimmer man carrying a semi-automatic rifle.

'Mr Joseph,' the slimmer man said in a voice that rattled in the back of his throat. 'I've come for the girl. Where is she?'

David didn't answer. His tongue was glued to the roof of his mouth, and he was gasping for breath.

The man spun the gun round until it was pointing at David.

'I asked you a question.'

David swallowed. 'She's not here. We've taken her somewhere safe.'

The man laughed. 'You're lying. Don't tell me you've suddenly grown a pair, Joseph?'

He turned to the man with the muscles.

'Get her.'

The big man headed towards the door to the hall, the iron bar held tightly in his left hand.

'Wait,' the man with the gun said.

He walked across the kitchen to the worktop and David felt a rush of blood to the head, grabbing hold of the table for support as the man picked up the police radio.

'You stupid bastard,' he said, waving the radio at David, his voice barely more than a hiss. 'What part of "no police" did you fail to understand? Was it you – or your wife?'

David said nothing, and the man laughed – a deep, nasty, cackle.

'No, you wouldn't have had the bottle, would you?'

The man spoke to the guy with the muscles even though his black eyes never left David's face.

'Bring me the girl. And don't be gentle – she's let us down.' He pointed at David with the barrel of his gun. 'Then you can have this piece of shit for five minutes to get everything he knows out of him.'

Even under the balaclava David could tell the big guy was smiling.

He wasn't having Tasha, though. Whatever he'd done in the past, David couldn't leave her to these men.

He flew across the kitchen, slammed the door to the hall closed and stood in front of it. 'You're not taking her. She's my daughter, and she's staying with me.'

The man barked out a laugh. 'Isn't it a bit late to think of protecting your girl, Joseph? And she's not yours now – she's ours. One of us. She's let us down, but she'll take her punishment. Now shift out of the fucking way before you get hurt.'

The big guy watched his boss, waiting for the nod. It wasn't long coming.

David knew long before the first blow hit him square in the centre of his gut that he couldn't win this battle. But maybe when Tasha realised how hard he had fought for her, she would finally know how much he loved her.

He lashed out at the big man in front of him with his fist, but it was like hitting a wall. Then he felt the second blow to the side of his head, and he crumpled to his knees. He was hauled back to his feet and propped up against the door. The big man transferred the iron bar to his right hand, and the third strike came – up, under his chin, shattering his jaw. He felt the fourth as his cheekbone disintegrated.

David never felt the fifth.

58

Emma's heart pounded. *What was happening? Who was this? Why was this man in the vault with her?* Pinpricks of fear rose from every inch of her skin as the man's body pressed her hard against the wall of cold steel. From the strength of the arms and the wide, solid chest pressed against her back she knew it was a man. His thighs pinned hers in place, and her arms were trapped against her body. She couldn't move. She could barely breathe.

Maybe some down-and-out had followed her into the building from the street. She had left the doors open as instructed. *He's going to rape me.* She breathed in through her nose, sniffing the hand covering her mouth. There was no smell of stale body, just the smell of a clean man.

His left hand still clamped tightly over her mouth, he grabbed the drill from her with his right, and pressed the trigger.

He's going to kill me.

She couldn't see what he was doing, she could just hear the drill, so close to her head.

She heard the first pin of the lock break. *What was he doing?*

Very gently against her ear she felt, rather than heard his words – they were merely breaths with shape, and she knew no phone anywhere would pick them up.

'This would be a whole lot easier if I could let you go.' The words had so little substance or form that she couldn't be certain that was what he had said.

He gradually relaxed his weight against her so she could move back a little. She turned her head slightly, and he brought his forwards to rest next to hers on the shiny surface of the locked boxes. Her head torch had been knocked upwards as she was pushed against the wall, so it didn't shine directly at him, but there was enough reflected light to see that the man wore a mask covering his head, his face. There was no more than a gash where the mouth should be, and a slit for the eyes – eyes that were looking straight into hers, a hypnotic electric-blue.

She barely stifled a gasp as the steely expression communicated its message: *I'm here to help.*

Finally, he let her go completely, his eyes never leaving hers, waiting to see her reaction.

She shook her head slowly from side to side, returning his gaze. She wanted to shout, scream, hit this man with the last remnants of strength in her body. But she was here for Ollie.

He looked down at the drill in his hand, and he pointed to the phone in her pocket.

'Speak,' he mouthed.

'Stupid, fucking drill,' she muttered, noticing a flicker of a smile through the slit in the mask, and imagining for a second the relief Tom would feel at hearing her after the brief silence.

The drilling took mere minutes in more expert hands, and finally the last pin snapped. A twist of the screwdriver, and the lock turned. It had worked.

'Bingo,' she muttered, playing the part. Her eyes still followed the man's every move, her heart still hammered in her chest.

She inserted the other key, and the door swung open. It was one of the larger boxes with no separate container inside. Pulling her lamp back down over her eyes, she looked into the space and this time didn't try to suppress her astonishment.

'*Gold*,' she said, as her eyes took in row upon row of stacked bars, their yellow light bright in the beam of the torch. Each bar was about eight centimetres long and four wide. She reached in to pick one up. For such a small thing it was really heavy and her lamp picked out the words imprinted in the metal.

1 KILO

She had no idea how many bars there were here, but she was sure there would be over a hundred.

The pale eyes watched Emma's face as she stared in wonder into the depths of the box. Then she moved her head and returned his gaze, screwing her eyes up into a question.

His head came down to hers and she felt rather than heard the words. 'Not now.' He pointed to his watch. Only twenty minutes left to move all of this. How could they ever have believed it would be possible?

He bent down and picked up a bag, holding it open beneath the edge of the box and nodded at her. Emma put her hands in and started to pick up the gold bars one at a time. He nudged her and mimed a scooping action. It felt like sacrilege for something so beautiful, but she had no choice. She leaned into the box with both arms and swept the bars forwards, letting them fall into the bag.

One bag went down and another was picked up. It took five minutes to empty the box, then he was on the floor, moving the bags around, lifting them up, testing them. He stood up and passed two of them to Emma. They were seriously heavy, but she could see that he'd put more in the other bags.

'Get them to the door, outside the time lock,' he mouthed against her ear, his lips touching her skin.

She leaned against him for a moment, her mouth next to his ear.

'Thank you,' she whispered, pressing her head briefly against his. Then she turned and jogged as fast as she could towards the door. Running up the stairs was painful; there must have been at least twelve kilos in each bag, but she made it. She dumped heavy bags at the top and ran down for the next two, passing him coming in the opposite direction. And so it continued. The time was nearly up. She had four minutes. She raced down the stairs for the last two bags, once more passing him on the stairs as he heaved three bags, all heavier than hers, upwards. Their eyes met and she smiled – it felt like her first smile in days. There was no time to stop, though. She would thank him properly when it was over.

Emma grabbed the final two bags and staggered towards the stairs, the last of her strength almost gone.

'Nearly there,' she muttered to anybody who was listening, no longer caring whether Rory or his bosses could hear her.

She practically threw the bags out of the door, turned round and slammed it. One minute to spare.

She leaned against the door in the black corridor and looked around. Nothing.

She walked to the turn in the corridor and shone her torch into the blackness.

There was nobody there. He had gone, melted back into the night.

59

A huge sigh of relief went round the control room as they listened to Emma close the time-lock door. There seemed to be a brief moment of inactivity, and Tom imagined her leaning up against the wall to recover her breath. He guessed that she could perhaps carry ten kilos in each hand, and it sounded as if she had done three trips up the stairs. Given the market price of kilobars at the moment, that would be about one and a half million pounds worth of gold.

'Come on, Emma,' he said under his breath. She had less than ten minutes to get the bags into the back of the car, ready for the phone call.

He heard grunts as she lifted the bags, and thumps each time she threw one in the car. It seemed to be taking longer than he expected, and time was getting critical.

Tom heard the other phone ring and imagined her grabbing it out of her pocket.

He could only hear Emma's part of the conversation.

'No, I'm not in the bloody car, you're quite right. I've just shifted about ten bags of stuff for you – and it wasn't easy.'

Tom frowned. That seemed like something of an exaggeration.

A thought struck him. He had been so focused on listening to Emma as she brought the bags upstairs that he had stopped looking at the screen while she was obviously out of shot.

'Can you play back the video from about three minutes before the time-lock please?'

The operator obliged.

Tom had been right. A dark figure had slipped out of the door and around the corner, back into the night.

So intently was he watching the screen that he almost missed what Emma was saying, her tone of voice alerting him.

'What do you mean?' Emma wailed. 'I don't understand. I've done everything you asked.'

And then she started to cry. Deep, wrenching sobs, with one word choked out between each gulp of air. 'No. No.'

He didn't know what was happening, but they couldn't wait any longer.

Tom turned to the silver commander.

'Get that baby out of there *now*. I don't know what's going on, but we're out of time.'

Tom's attention was focused on the images being relayed back to the control room from the covert team at Julie McGuinness's house. They were in.

He heard sounds of running feet. Becky's radio was live, and he could hear her breath as she jogged into the house. He heard her shout a question, and then she sounded as if she was running upstairs.

'Come on, Becky,' Tom said quietly.

'What?' he heard her say. 'Are you sure? Shit! Tom – he's not here,' she said. 'Ollie's not here. And Julie's out cold.'

'Fuck!' Tom shouted, slamming the palms of his hands down on the table.

❖

'Tom – are you there?' Emma was shouting through her tears, using Tom's name. She wasn't even attempting to hide who she was speaking to, and that said it all.

He took his phone off mute. 'What's happened, Emma?'

'Have you got Ollie, Tom?'

Tom closed his eyes.

'*Tom*,' she screamed. 'Have you *got* him?'

'Emma, I'm so sorry. He wasn't where we thought he was. We're trying to find out where he's been moved to.'

'*No!*' Tom felt the agony in that single syllable and he had nothing to give her.

Suddenly he heard a car door slam, and seconds later the roar of an engine.

'Emma!' he shouted. There was no answer.

Through his radio he heard the voice of Nic Havers.

'Sir, she's driven off – she's going fast. Really fast. We're following – what do you want us to do?'

'Stick with her for now. I'll get back to you Nic.'

Tom picked up the phone again. 'Emma!' he shouted. There was no answer.

❖

How did they know? Tom said it would be safe. How did they know?

The noise of her own thoughts battered Emma's exhausted brain.

'You've got our gold, but we've got your son,' the voice had said. 'We told you no police – you lied to us, Emma. We don't like that.'

She had screamed at them down the phone, but it had made no difference.

Oh, Ollie, I'm so sorry.

'You need to lose the police – and do it now. What have they given you – a wire, a radio? A phone? Drive away and throw it out of the window. We'll be watching. Get away from them, then we'll tell you what to do next. Fuck this up, and your son's as good as dead.'

Emma didn't care about the police – whether they caught these men or not. She wanted her baby back, and this time she was going to do exactly as they said. She flattened her foot to the floor.

Calm down, Emma. She knew that if she drove too quickly she would be stopped by traffic police – and with a boot full of gold that would be the end of everything. But she had to lose her followers.

The phone, the phone. She wound down the car window and threw her Australian phone out of the window. She glanced in her rear-view mirror. There was a motorbike behind her, driving in the middle of the road so nobody could get past. She speeded up and the motorbike slowed slightly to block any pursuit. She knew who this was – and he was keeping the detectives from following her.

She waited, hoping and praying for a call on Tasha's mobile from the man with the rasping voice.

❖

'Sir, we're losing her.' It was Nic Havers again. 'There's a motorbike in the middle of the road, going slowly but we can't get past unless we switch the siren on. He must be one of theirs.'

Rory Slater, thought Tom.

'And sir – she's thrown something out of the window. Looks like a phone.'

Bugger. Somehow they had known that the police were involved. How was that possible?

'I'm going to call David Joseph,' Tom said to Paul Green. 'Maybe Natasha felt she'd made a mistake in helping us and decided to contact them. I can't see how else they could have known. I'll speak to David and see what he can get out of her.'

He asked an operator to get through on the Josephs' home number. There was no reply.

'Try the radio,' he said. He really needed to speak to David.

There was no response.

'Send the team into the Josephs' house,' he instructed. 'The gang knows we're onto them, so there's nothing to lose. I don't like this silence.'

'Tom,' Paul Green had walked over to stand beside him. 'According to my CHIS, everything's going ahead as planned. They may be aware that we know about Ollie and the robbery, but Emma was never told where the handover point was, so as long as she's not followed they've got no reason to change it. As far as the CHIS is aware, the handover point is the same. If it changes, he'll let us know.'

Tom nodded his thanks and picked up his radio again. 'Nic – you need to look as if you're trying to get past the bike – but don't try too hard. Make it look as if you're trying to tail her, but lose her. We believe we know where she's going. If they know you're still following her, they'll change to a different handover location, and she'll be very vulnerable.'

Tom's attention was back on the cameras – to the place where he hoped and prayed the exchange was still going to take place. The cemetery was dark, deserted. There was nothing to see.

A call came through on his radio.

'Mr Douglas, we're at the Josephs' place now. The back door's been kicked in. We found David Joseph on the kitchen floor. He's in a bad way, sir. We've called an ambulance, but he's been given a real going over.'

Shit. This was going from bad to worse.

'What about Natasha? Is she okay?'

'Just a moment, sir.' Tom heard the policeman speak to somebody else. 'We've searched the house and the gardens thoroughly, sir. There's no sign of the girl. They've got her.'

60

The McGuinness' house was stiflingly hot. Becky wiped her face with a scrunched-up tissue. How could they have got it so wrong? The entrance to the property had gone entirely to plan. They'd waited as long as the command team had believed sensible before going in. And now they had nothing. Bugger all.

Julie McGuinness was lying on her back in the centre of the bed, fully dressed. She was out cold. On the bedside table were a plastic bottle of Temazepam and a blue litre bottle of Bombay Sapphire.

'Bollocks,' Becky spat the word in frustration into her radio. 'She's taken sleeping pills. I've no idea how many – there's a prescription bottle half empty, but she's been drinking gin with them. Doesn't look like a suicide attempt – there's still plenty left in the bottle. At a guess, she hadn't coped well with a baby screaming for his mum. We need to get a medic – see if we can bring her round.'

From the control room, she heard agreement and knew it would be in hand.

She looked at the body lying on the bed. What must it be like to be married to a thug like Finn McGuinness? Julie herself was no angel, of course, and was running her own part of the business from a separate property – seemingly involving girls as young as thirteen. Had Julie been like this when she met McGuinness, Becky wondered. Or is that what happened when you got involved with a man like him?

The woman on the bed had shoulder-length hair, too dark to be natural, and her skin had the orange tinge of a fake tan. In repose, her mouth turned down sourly at the edges, and her heavy dark eye makeup was smudged, running into the creases at the corners of her eyes. Becky imagined that when Julie McGuinness was looking her best she would be quite stunning with her slim body and large chest. But it was all artifice. There was something depressing about her – as if this body on the bed was the real, sad person behind the glamour and riches that her chosen life had brought her.

'You got a minute, ma'am? You might want to look at this.'

Becky turned at the voice from the doorway. A young policeman, chunky in his ballistic vest, a semi-automatic disarmed and held safely across his body, was indicating a room across the landing and Becky followed him into a large bathroom with a Jacuzzi corner bath and huge walk-in shower. In the middle of the floor there was a plastic changing mat, and a pack of nappies with a picture of a toddler on the front. The policeman picked up one of the nappies and handed it to Becky.

'Don't know how much you know about nappies, ma'am, but we've got a new baby at home and these would go round her twice.'

Becky nodded and walked over to the bathroom bin. Inside were several nappy bags. Ollie had been here.

So where the hell was he now?

61

Stupid, stupid woman. Why did she always have to think that she knew best? Why hadn't she just gone along with everything like David had wanted?

The thought of David brought it all back to her. How could he have done that to Caroline and Tasha? And now – all because of his reckless actions six years ago, she had lost her baby. She lifted both hands and banged them on the steering wheel.

Where's Ollie? Why hadn't Tom found him?

'Ollie, darling, I'm coming for you I promise,' she shouted out loud, hoping that some telepathic channel of communication, as yet undiscovered, was working between her and her baby boy.

Emma tried not to think about what had happened in the vault. She parcelled up the thoughts, the questions, and pushed them to the back of her mind. There would be time to unpick everything later. For now, there was only Ollie.

The man had called her again on Tasha's phone and she had followed his directions. The exit from the motorway was ahead.

She had no idea what was going to happen. Was she about to meet the men who had taken her son? The men that had taken and kept Natasha for all these years? The men who thought it was acceptable to send a kid shoplifting, stealing, ferrying drugs and so much more? With all her heart she wished she had an automatic rifle so she could rattle off a stream of bullets and shoot the whole lot of them down. It felt for a moment that a lifetime in prison would be worth it to rid the world of scum like these men.

She took the third exit from the roundabout and drove on.

There was no light, the darkness settling like black velvet around her, the yellow beam of her headlights cutting through it, the rear lights leaving a red stain on the wet surface in her wake.

❖

The control room fell quiet as the images on the screen showed something happening in the empty cemetery. It had begun as a low hum, getting louder as the vehicle came into view. Three men got out of a van, balaclavas rolled up, their faces revealed.

'*Thank God*,' Paul Green said softly. 'He's here. The main man.'

Tom felt a moment's sympathy for Paul. This should have been the moment they prepared to move in and take Guy Bentley – everything they had been working towards. But with Ollie still missing, it was a risk they couldn't take.

Tom looked at the screen, and although it was more than twenty years since he had last seen him, he would have recognised Ethan Bentley anywhere. Maturity had improved his looks, and what had appeared a haughty face on a skinny seventeen-year-old had filled out to become distinguished. His hooked nose and thick lips gave him the appearance of a wealthy playboy, and even on a night vision camera it was easy to see the confidence with which he held himself.

Finn McGuinness was carrying a gun. His mouth was set in a grim line and his eyes were watchful. He turned a full 360 degrees around, his gaze seeming to penetrate the surrounding shrubbery.

The third man was somebody Tom didn't recognise. He had been half expecting Rory Slater, but this was probably way above his pay grade. The man had a similar demeanour to McGuinness, but he was much bigger, with the shoulders and upper body of a wrestler.

They hadn't spoken, but McGuinness looked at his watch.

'Five minutes,' was all he said, his voice being picked up by the equipment planted by the Titan team.

Paul Green spoke into his radio, quietly keeping his team informed. But there was still no sign of Ollie Joseph. Arrest Bentley now, and Ollie might never be seen again. These weren't men to cave in under interrogation.

Tom knew that Emma was coming before the audio kit in the cemetery picked up the sound of her car.

He knew, because three hands went up and pulled balaclavas down over faces.

❖

Emma rounded the final bend.

There they were. Three of them, each wearing a mask with a gap for the eyes and the mouth. Just like the one she had seen earlier.

The men were standing in a row at the back of a van, legs apart, the arms of two of them firmly by their sides, the third clutching a gun that looked like some kind of short-barrelled rifle. A new shockwave of fear tore through Emma's body. Her chest tightened and her breathing speeded up. She felt a moment of dizziness but fought it back.

Should she get out of the car, or stay there? She didn't know. Fighting the temptation to put her foot down hard on the accelerator and ram them all, squashing them flat against their van, she pulled up about four metres away. The man signalled her with the barrel of his gun to get out of the car.

Not entirely sure that her legs would support her, Emma opened the door and got out. The tallest of the men approached her, signalling to one of his sidekicks – a man with huge shoulders – to get into the Range Rover and pull it around closer to their van.

'Mrs Joseph, or may I call you Emma?' he said in a voice practically free from any trace of an accent. He spoke as if they had just met at a party.

'Call me what you like,' she answered. 'I've done what you

asked. Now give me back my son.' The last two words came out as a sob.

'Of course. We're men of our word, Emma. You shouldn't have told the police, though. We know that was you.'

Emma didn't like the sound of that. How could they have known it was her?

The man with the gun approached and pulled a device that Emma didn't recognise out of his pocket. He switched it on and read the screen. He held up one hand.

'Where's the phone?' he asked, the thick, harsh tones instantly recognisable as belonging to the man she had spoken to on the phone.

Emma hadn't thought it possible to be more frightened, but a chill of terror ran through her body.

'What phone?' she asked. She had thrown the damned thing away – what could they mean?

'Don't piss me about, lady. Where's the fucking phone?'

Emma stood stock still. He lifted the gun so it was pointing upwards, slung the strap over his shoulder and approached Emma, reaching his hands out and sliding them over her body, lingering on her buttocks. She shuddered. He laughed.

He ran one hand unnecessarily up the inside of her thighs, as far as it could go, lingering there, stroking her with his thumb. Emma stood as still as she could, her skin crawling with disgust.

'Stop arsing around, Finn,' the boss man said without rancour. 'Save it for later.'

The hand moved to the outside of her thighs and stopped at a pocket.

'This phone,' he said, removing Tasha's mobile. Why hadn't she realised they meant that one? She was too terrified to think straight.

'You won't be needing this again,' he said, sticking it into his own pocket.

The man by the Range Rover nodded, and Emma assumed he had checked her car for phones or bugs too. He jumped in and drove it closer to the van and opened the rear doors.

'Shit,' she heard.

Had she done something wrong? Panic swept through her. What?

'Watch her,' the boss man said to the man called Finn as he walked over to the Range Rover.

He peered into the back, where the bags of gold were stacked, and then he looked at her.

'Bring her over here,' he instructed.

She didn't want to be touched by Finn again, so she went of her own accord.

'How the fuck did you get all this up the stairs on your own, little lady?' the boss man asked, the enquiring note in his voice barely masking his suspicion.

'Wasn't that what I was supposed to do?' Emma could hear the quiver in her voice.

'Don't be smart with me, Emma. We thought you'd only get half this. How did you do it?'

Finn grabbed her ponytail and pulled it down her back so that her throat was exposed. She was going to die if she didn't give them the right answer.

'Bloody hard work, that's how,' she answered. 'Adrenaline can do miraculous things to the body, you know.'

The boss indicated with his head that the gold should be moved into the van, and her hair was released.

She watched as the huge man hurled the bags into the back of the van as if they weighed little more than a sack of potatoes.

The last one was transferred.

'What about Ollie? Where's my son?'

She saw a nod pass between the man who was obviously the boss and Finn – the weasel with the gun.

'Get in the car,' Finn said, walking round to the passenger side of the Range Rover. He threw his gun to the man with the shoulders, then pulled a handgun out of his pocket, pointing it at her head.

'Drive. I'll take you to your son. Do anything stupid, and he'll be dead before we get there.'

62

Once again, the control room was silent. The only sounds came from the radios and the monitors. The audio equipment had picked up every dreadful word.

Tom couldn't believe what he was seeing. McGuinness was getting into the car with Emma. She would be thinking of Ollie – trusting that Finn would be taking her to her son.

The silver commander of the armed response team was issuing orders, telling his team that McGuinness was on the move and possibly on his way home. He turned to Tom and Paul Green.

'I think we all know how this is going to end for Emma Joseph. We're going to have to take McGuinness. Anybody disagree?'

Nobody did.

There were unmarked police cars covering all the exits to the cemetery, and Tom listened as Titan reassigned some of the detectives to follow McGuinness, who probably believed Ollie was still with Julie. Just in case he had other plans for Emma, though, they couldn't let him out of sight.

Tom radioed Becky. 'You've got at the most ten minutes to find out where Ollie is, then get out, Becky. McGuinness could be heading there. Make Julie talk. Finn's got Emma with him, and he's armed.'

He heard a muffled expletive from Becky, who would understand perfectly what that meant.

There was an edginess to the atmosphere in the room now, as plans were put in place to covertly tail Finn McGuinness. Any indication that he was being followed could be catastrophic for Emma.

Tom wanted to be there – to make sure that Emma was safe. He forced himself to be rational. If this wasn't Emma, what would he do? He'd be here – in the control room – managing the situation.

Tom's attention was diverted to one of the monitors. In the cemetery, the two remaining men were standing by the van.

'What now?' he asked Paul Green. 'Why are they still there?'

'They're waiting for our informant. He's the buyer.'

'You knew it was gold, then?'

Green shook his head. 'Not for certain. Our informant wouldn't tell us what he's buying – too nervous of a bent copper leaking it to Bentley. But our cyber team came across some guy on the dark web who had exchanged a load of his illegally acquired bitcoin for stolen gold – it's regularly traded there. He'd been talking on a forum about where best to store it, and safe deposits were mentioned.'

'And your informant?'

'Another frequenter of the dark web. I am fairly sure this is a personal vendetta against Guy – or Ethan – Bentley. He said Bentley was setting up a heist, and that he – the informant – was going to buy the goods.'

'So how did Bentley know the name of the bloke who was stashing the gold? He'd have needed that for the hacker to find his box number.'

'Given who your brother was, I expect you know that a half-decent hacker can find out every small detail about a person from next to no starting information – he would have tracked back through his comment trail, sites visited, that kind of stuff, and worked out who he was.'

'What's your buyer doing now?'

Green tilted his head. 'Check out the third monitor. He's there – waiting.'

Tom followed the finger that Paul Green was pointing at the

screen. A tall man in a black bomber jacket stood in the shadows invisible to Bentley and his minder. Tom could just make out a shaved head and what looked like a goatee beard.

'He's at the far end of the cemetery. Hang on – he's getting his phone out.'

As the man on the monitor lifted the phone to his ear, he lifted his other hand and rubbed the top of his head.

Tom listened to Paul talking to him, asking him questions. The man lifted his hand and rubbed his head again.

Tom stared at the monitor for a moment longer.

'Paul, can I speak to your informant please?'

Paul Green frowned. 'What for?'

'Will you ask him if he'll speak to me please?'

Green shrugged.

'Blake, I have another policeman – a Detective Chief Inspector Tom Douglas – who would like a word with you if possible.'

Tom would have laughed at the pseudonym Blake, had he not felt so ill, so cheated, so deceived and at the same time, so elated.

Green handed the phone across, and for a moment Tom couldn't speak.

'I guess I've stunned you into silence, little brother,' came a voice Tom knew so well and had never expected to hear again in his life. 'Still the white hat, I see – still putting the world to rights.'

Tom finally found the words.

'What the fuck's going on, Jack? What have you done?'

63

Feelings of fury, relief, joy all mingled together as Tom listened to his brother's voice. More than anything he wanted to be in that cemetery – he wanted to punch Jack in the face, knock him to the floor, then pick him up and hold him as close as he could.

'Why are you involved in this, Jack?'

'I've always been involved. I thought you might have worked that out by now.'

Tom had indeed worked it out, even if he hadn't wanted to admit it to himself. What he hadn't realised was that Jack hadn't been working alone. It was obvious now, though. Guy was in it with him. All those days and nights together in Jack's room, with Tom banished. Probably they set Guy's father up together. Either that or Jack did it and Guy figured it out. It didn't much matter now. After that, Guy probably picked the targets and Jack hacked them.

'Hacking's one thing, but abduction is another.'

'Don't be stupid, Tom. I had nothing to do with Natasha Joseph's abduction six years ago. My role was to hack the system, and when I found out what Guy was up to, I tried to stop it.'

'Maybe you weren't involved in Natasha's kidnap – but you were still involved in planning a major robbery. That was okay, was it? When did you hit the big time, then?' Tom asked, sarcasm dripping from his tongue to hide his distress.

'When Guy decided I was indispensable and set his band of warriors on me to make sure I did what I was told. I was in way above my head. What had started as a bit of a lark suddenly turned serious, and Guy wasn't prepared to cut me loose.'

'You're a shit, Jack. You caused so much pain to so many people.' The carousel of emotions took another turn and stopped in a different position.

For a moment, there was silence. When Jack spoke, his voice was quiet, controlled.

'I thought Caroline and Natasha were both dead. I could cope with the scams – just about – but people were getting hurt and I couldn't be part of that. I had to find a way out. If I hadn't died, Guy would have set Finn McGuinness on me, and if I'd just disappeared he'd have hit on you or Emma, or maybe even Lucy, to flush me out. I've been waiting for the opportunity to screw him, and finally it's payback time. Why else would I risk everything to be here now?'

Tom couldn't think of anything to say, but he didn't want Jack to go – to lose connection with him.

'Anyway,' Jack said, 'much as I'd love to debate my choices with you, it seems we have a different problem. Green says Guy's got Emma's baby. I never thought he'd try that trick again.'

'Ollie was the only card he had left to play. He'd offered to return Natasha to David some time ago in return for his help. He refused to play ball.'

'He always was a twat.'

'Twat or not, he's been badly beaten up and Natasha's missing. They must have pulled her out when they were beating the crap out of David. And they've found out Emma's been helping us. She's in a car with McGuinness now.'

'*Shit.*' One word, but to Tom it conveyed a wealth of emotion.

Tom wanted to hang up. He wanted to tell his brother to go to hell. He wanted to sit here and listen to his voice. He didn't really know what he wanted or how he felt. The one thing he knew for certain, though, was that Jack knew this gang better than anybody else, and Emma needed help.

'How did you know this was going to happen, Jack – what Guy was planning?'

'Because I've been watching him. I've followed Guy's every move on the dark web for six years, waiting for a chance to bring him down. I guessed who his target was, and when he was looking for a buyer, I put in a bid.'

A vivid image of Jack, sitting in a lonely dark room in some remote part of the world, glued to computer monitor, waiting to exact his revenge, flashed into Tom's mind. He pushed it forcefully away.

'You know these bastards – you were one of them,' Tom said.

'Uncalled for, little brother, but you are – of course – correct.'

'So what do we do now?'

'I'm going to buy you some time. And you, Tom, have to keep Emma safe.'

The line went dead.

❖

Tom put the phone down and closed his eyes for a second. What had just happened? He could scarcely believe it himself.

'Do you want to tell me what that was all about?' Paul Green was looking at Tom very carefully.

'No, not really. Obviously at some point I'll have to, but for now let's just get this child found, Emma safe and Guy Bentley arrested. Your guy Blake…'

'You mean your so-called dead brother Jack?"

'…is going to buy us some time.'

'Did you know he was alive?' Green asked.

'Of course not. Did you?'

Tom knew what a stupid question that was. As if Tom would have been allowed to run the operation if they'd had any idea. Fortunately, they were interrupted as one of the sound devices picked up a ringing phone in the cemetery.

'Hang on,' Green said. 'We need to listen to this.'

It was Guy Bentley's phone. He answered without grace.

'Yeah,' he said. There was a pause while the caller spoke.

'What do you mean, you've delayed the payment? On what basis?'

They couldn't hear what Jack said.

'Listen, wanker, we agreed a time and a place. We're here. Where the fuck are you?'

Another moment of silence from Guy.

'That's bollocks. She was just the courier. Of course she wasn't followed – they'd have taken us down by now, wouldn't they?'

Guy was striding up and down the path, and his words came in highs and lows of volume depending on which way he was facing.

'I know you could walk away from this deal. But you're not going to, are you – and yes, if you insist, my gorilla with the gun will put it on the floor and stand on it, if you think that's entirely necessary. I'll see you in an hour.'

Guy hung up the phone and stood, hands on hips, gazing around him.

He turned to the other man.

'I'm not standing out here freezing my balls off for another hour. Besides, that's too late for this place. We need to find somewhere else. We'll give him the location when he calls back. He's not having it all his own way.'

Green turned to Tom and pulled a face that signified a silent groan. Wherever they chose to go now, there would be no chance to set up any surveillance. They had gained time, but lost all other advantages.

64

Tom was striving to force the image of Jack with his shaved head and goatee beard from his mind, but it was a struggle. Had it not been for his brother's stance and the characteristic stroking of his head when he answered the phone, Tom believed he might well have passed Jack in the street without recognising him. Gone was the long, scruffy ponytail, the unshaven, stubbly cheeks. Only the dazzling light-blue eyes would have given him away.

Jack had bought them an hour to find Ollie and rescue Emma, and they needed to use every second of it.

He called Becky on the radio.

'We're moving Julie out of the house now,' Becky said, her breathing laboured. 'I'm trying to get her to walk, to bring her round. We need to get clear before McGuinness gets here. But I think we're making progress. She's muttering something.'

Tom could hear groans in the background. He heard Becky's voice.

'Come on, Julie. Where's that lovely baby you were looking after?'

Tom heard some slurred speech and then a gasp from Becky.

'Say that again, Julie,' she said, her voice harsh and demanding. 'Shit and bloody more shit.'

Tom waited.

'Tom, she says she gave Ollie a pill because he wouldn't stop crying. The pills are Temazepam. I've asked her how many and she just shakes her head. Hang on, she's saying something else.' There was a pause and he could tell from the ambient sound that they were outside the house, clearly trying to drag, or carry, Julie away in the remaining minutes before her husband returned.

'She says Mel's taken the baby. We asked who Mel is and where she's taken him but we've got nothing. She's being sick now, but she keeps passing out. I don't remember anybody called Mel in the list Titan gave us, so I'm clueless. We're bundling her in the back of one of the vans and getting her out of here. The firearms team are getting into position, melting into the shadows. They've told me to wait in my car well out of the way until McGuinness is back and Emma's safe.'

'Okay, Becky. Stick with it. We'll follow Mel up from this end and keep you informed. As soon as you're finished there I need you to get over to the Josephs' house. Something has happened to Natasha. I don't know what, but we need to find the poor kid. Nobody knows where she is, and we don't want another dead girl on our hands.'

He heard a groan from Becky, but didn't have time to say more because Paul Green was back on the phone and Tom heard the name Blake again. They must be agreeing the handover point for the money. Tom signalled to him that he wanted to talk to Jack, and when Paul had finished he handed over the phone.

'Jack – are you actually going to hand over the money to buy this gold?'

'Not unless I absolutely have to. I can't risk Guy recognising me. If he knows I'm alive, he won't rest – even from prison. He believes I'm dead, and it needs to stay that way.'

'Have you *got* the money?'

'I had a hidden account, which I cleared out a few months ago. So yes, I've got it.'

Tom could scarcely believe what he was hearing.

'*You* emptied the account? The one in Switzerland? I thought *they'd* found it.'

'Ah – you found the SD card then. I was hoping you wouldn't.'

Like the lock that had been drilled in the vault, the pins were one by one dropping into place in Tom's head and soon he knew he would be able to turn the key to understanding everything. So close.

'Forget that for now. I want you to think hard, Jack. I need you to think if you have ever heard the name Mel before.'

Tom heard the intake of breath down the line.

'Keep Mel out of this, Tom. None of this was her fault.' His voice was harsh, protective.

'Who is she? Don't mess with me, brother – she's got Ollie.'

'*Jesus*,' Jack muttered. 'What the *fuck* did she do that for?'

'Who is she? Just bloody tell me because Julie's given Ollie a sleeping tablet to stop him crying.'

'This just gets worse. Julie always was stupid, but you know who Mel is. You met her twice, and hated her. Mel – you know – Melissa.'

'Bloody hell – your *lover*? The woman you dumped Emma for is part of this gang? Words fail me, Jack.' Had he ever known this man, he wondered.

'You really haven't got it yet, have you, little brother? Never mind. I can track Mel down. Get me somebody here now with a laptop and a mobile wireless signal – Green knows where I am. The faster you get it to me, the faster I can find Ollie for you.'

Without further explanation, Jack hung up.

❖

It had only taken five minutes to get a laptop to Jack, and just a couple of minutes later Tom's mobile indicated he had a message. An address for Melissa had been sent to his personal email. Jack hadn't lost his touch, it seemed.

Tom pulled his open laptop towards him. The usual crap was littering his email inbox, but as soon as he saw the name BLAKE he knew which one to open. And there was the address, and a message.

Mel is Guy's mistress, always has been, so be careful. She's not dangerous, but Guy's thugs are, if they're around. Your best bet is to take Emma. Mel probably won't hand the baby over to somebody she doesn't recognise – and she'll know who Emma is.

Mel's seen Guy do some horrific things, but she would draw the line at him killing a baby. My guess is that's why she took Ollie. But it's only a guess. She must have a plan, because Guy will kill her when he finds out. Good luck, little brother.

Tom looked across at the silver commander of the firearms team. He was staring at the monitor showing the McGuinness house in Salford, all quiet, waiting, not a person in sight. But they were there, hiding in the shadows, watching, anticipating the moment when they could take McGuinness down. He could just make out Becky's car, parked down the street, out of the range of any gunfire.

The minute Emma got into McGuinness's car the team in the control room had accepted that the planned return of Ollie was never going to happen. They gang hadn't tried to hide Finn's identity. They had even used his name, and now – according to the team following the Range Rover – he was taking her to his home. Tom knew that Emma's fate had been decided long before she arrived at the cemetery.

❖

The inside of the Range Rover felt claustrophobic. The air was dead, and Emma thought she could smell her own fear. She had no idea where they were, but all she could think about was Ollie – getting him back, holding him tight.

Finn had spoken to her just once on the journey.

'The boss tells me you used to be Jack Douglas's girl.' He gave a dirty laugh. 'What goes around comes around, eh? Pity he died.'

332

Emma frowned. He smiled at her expression and leaned towards her. She could smell stale cigarette smoke on his breath.

'I was denied the pleasure of killing him myself,' he said, his face inches from hers.

She turned away in disgust, and he laughed again. What did he mean? How did he know Jack? She couldn't afford to give Jack any head space now, though. She was going to get Ollie. Her breathing became fast and shallow as her excitement grew. It wouldn't be long now.

They had left the motorway behind; on Finn's instructions Emma turned down a wide avenue with houses set well back from the road.

'Turn left ahead, then third drive on the right. Let's see if Julie has kept your baby safe. You'd better hope she hasn't got herself pissed and dropped the little bugger on his head.' He cackled, but Emma was no longer listening.

Julie? That was the name of the woman Tom thought had Ollie – but he'd said they hadn't found him. What would Finn do if he got home and Ollie wasn't there? Emma had no idea, but she felt her thrill of anticipation at getting Ollie back disintegrate, shattering into tiny fragments.

All of this – everything she had done – was for nothing. She wanted to howl, to scream her misery into the night. Should she warn him – tell him that the police had already checked out Julie and they knew Ollie wasn't there?

And then from nowhere came the realisation of how it was all going to end. She had heard Finn's name. She was about to pull into the drive of his home. The boss man had told Finn to 'save it for later'.

He wasn't going to let her go.

How had she been so *stupid*? Was this her punishment for involving the police?

It was too late to think of what else she could do, so she turned the wheel of the car, drew up on a narrow drive and switched off the engine.

She needed to get him on her side – make him realise that she was no longer working with the police – do something that would make him trust her.

'Finn,' she began.

'Shut up and get out of the car.' He dug the tip of his gun into her thigh as if to remind her of its presence then stuffed it into his pocket. Before she could protest, he opened his door and started to get out.

Emma knew she had to say something to him before he made it into the house. She felt she would be safer outside. She pulled on the handle to open the door, ready to chase him up the drive.

'Finn,' she shouted. 'There's something I need to tell you.'

Her only hope was that she could reason with him – make him give Ollie back in exchange for her co-operation with the police.

He turned round towards her, his hand flying to the pocket of his jacket.

Suddenly the quiet night was ripped apart. Sound erupted from all around, and Emma felt strong arms reach out and grab her as two black figures emerged from behind a hedge and dragged her to the floor.

It was over in seconds. By the time Emma was helped back to her feet, four men were surrounding McGuinness, his hands already cuffed behind his back.

His black eyes looked into hers, and she swallowed – the knowledge of what had been about to happen to her shining from Finn's inky stare.

She turned away and saw Becky Robinson sprinting across the road towards her.

'Are you okay, Emma?' she asked, putting an arm gently round Emma's waist.

Emma felt her legs weaken. Too much had happened and for one dreadful moment, she didn't think she could take any more. She felt Becky's grip tighten.

'Listen, Emma – Tom thinks he knows where Ollie is. I need you to go with this policeman,' Becky indicated a middle-aged man that Emma hadn't even noticed. 'Tom will meet you there. I've got to be somewhere else, but are you sure you're okay?'

Emma had hardly registered anything past Becky's first sentence, and she nodded vaguely, only one thought in her head.

Ollie.

She forced some strength into her legs, stood up straight and took a deep breath.

I'm coming, baby.

❖

Tom ran from the control room. He needed to get to Melissa's home, right on the border of his jurisdiction. His journey would be longer than Emma's, but at this time in the morning he could risk going through the centre of town.

They didn't have much time left. Jack had bought them an hour, but nearly half of that had already gone.

65

Melissa's house was at the top of a hill, standing alone, isolated, surrounded by bleak, empty moorland. It appeared to be a converted barn, with huge sheets of glass replacing the original arched barn doors. Light spilled out from the uncurtained window, but Tom was still too far away to see into the depths of the room.

He turned his car onto a farm track that was partially hidden from the road by a thicket of rowan trees. He walked back to the lane and could see instantly why Guy Bentley's mistress lived here. The view stretched for miles, back to the nearest town. No car would be able to approach at night without its headlights being seen, and when Guy was visiting he no doubt put one of his henchmen on lookout duty. The lane ended at Melissa's house, a narrow, stony track continuing on to the moor beyond, and Tom had to hope that nobody had been watching the road tonight.

A call came through on Tom's radio.

'Tom – Paul Green here. A problem, I'm afraid. Bentley's playing hardball. He's told Blake – Jack – he doesn't like the new meeting place. He's got a better one. It's a disused cow shed about five hundred metres from Melissa's house.'

'Bugger,' Tom muttered. It would be reckless for Guy to invite his buyer to Melissa's home, but if he had chosen a location so close by, the chances were he would be planning on visiting his mistress too.

'How long?' Tom asked, his calm demeanour belying his true feelings.

'We don't know, but I suspect he's in his own car. The gold will be in the van. He could have been halfway there before he called Jack. You need to hang on until we get there.'

'Thanks, Paul. How far out are you?'

'About twenty minutes, but we're going to have to approach with caution. We've seen the satellite image of the area, and we can't just come charging in; they'll have done a runner before we get there. There's a chopper on its way, and an ambulance. The locals will get to you before us, but wait for firearms, Tom.'

Tom ended the call. He could see headlights approaching, and he darted back across the road to stand behind the trees.

Thirty seconds later a car turned onto the track and pulled up behind Tom's. Emma leaped out of the unmarked police car almost before it had stopped.

'Is this it, Tom?' she called as she ran towards him.

'Quiet, Emma. I know you want to race in there, but let's be sensible. Let me check it out first.'

Tom knew he wasn't going to wait for the armed response team. If Ollie had been given drugs, every second counted. But he needed to be sure Melissa was alone.

'I'm sorry about before, Tom. I had to do what they asked, but I know it was stupid,' Emma said.

'You've nothing to apologise for, I'm just glad you're safe. We'll talk about it later. There are a couple of things you need to know, though, and something I need to ask.'

Emma looked at him, her expression wary.

'What happened in the vault, Emma?'

Her eyes slid away from his, and he knew he was right.

'Who was in there with you?'

'It doesn't matter. Let's just get Ollie.'

'It was Jack, wasn't it?'

He watched as Emma's eyes screwed tight shut, as if she was barely holding herself together.

'Not now, Tom. I can't let myself think about it. Let me get Ollie. *Please.*'

Tom knew she was right. It could wait. He debated whether to tell her about David's injuries, or that Natasha was missing, but he decided against it for now. He'd had an update on the way here, and there was still no sign of the girl.

There was one thing he had to tell Emma, though. 'You need to know that Mel – the woman who has Ollie – she's Melissa.' He didn't have to say any more.

'I don't care who she is, as long as she gives me back my baby. What are we *waiting* for?'

'Get back in the car, Emma. I'm going to check it out.' Tom leaned across to the driver. He needed the man to keep watch over Emma. 'Stay out of sight for now, and look after Mrs Joseph. I'll radio when it's safe for you to bring her in.' He turned to Emma, willing her to understand. 'Just *do* it, Em.'

Emma opened the door and sat sideways on the seat, her feet out of the car – ready to move at a second's notice. The driver reached up and switched off the interior light.

Tom made his way across the road. He had no idea whether Guy knew that Ollie was with Melissa. He was going to have to get the baby out before Guy arrived, though.

He made his way around the side of the house, keeping off the cobbled drive. There were no cars visible, but he skirted round the back to check for ways in and out, not knowing if he would need an escape route. He could hear nothing from inside the house, and he moved deeper into the undergrowth, beyond the reach of the light flooding from the huge arched window, hoping to see in without being spotted.

He was too late. While he had been round the back of the house he hadn't been able to watch the road, and suddenly a pair of powerful headlights swept into the drive. Tom ducked down behind a holly bush as a dark red Aston Martin Vanquish pulled up on the cobbles.

A man got out, one hand deep in his overcoat pocket, the other holding a phone to his ear.

Guy Bentley.

'Wait there,' Tom heard Guy say. 'The buyer should be with you in thirty minutes, but I'll be back by then. I'm at Mel's picking some gear up. And where the fuck's Finn – have you heard from him?'

There was a pause.

'Stupid bastard. He'd better not be shagging the Joseph woman. I told him to lock her and the kid up – save playtime for later. Keep trying him.'

Guy punched the screen of his mobile angrily and turned towards the house. At that moment Tom sensed movement to his right and a pale face was caught in the lamplight from the drive.

Emma.

What the hell was she doing? How did she get away from her driver?

Tom had no time to think. He couldn't let Guy see her. He moved out from behind his shrub, banging against the leaves to make them rustle. Guy turned towards him, his hand automatically going to his right pocket.

Gun.

Then Guy's face changed. He knew – knew that they had him, but had no idea how or why. And Tom was certain he wouldn't go down without a fight. He would have an escape route from here – a plan. And at the moment, all that stood between Guy and freedom was Tom.

'Well, if it isn't Tom Douglas. What a pleasant surprise, Tom. How are you keeping?'

'Ethan,' Tom responded, seeing nothing more than a grown-up version of the kid who used to hang out in his brother's bedroom. He didn't for one second doubt that this man was far more dangerous, though, and thoroughly lacking in morality.

'Ethan?' Guy responded, laughing. 'Nobody's called me that for years. Your brother christened me Posh Guy all those years ago, and I liked it so much that I kept it. Dropped the Posh, of course. Nasty connotations. Would you like to come in? This is my girlfriend's house – but then I expect you know that, don't you, a smart policeman like you. You've met her, of course, when she was pretending to be Jack's lover.'

Tom could see Emma over Guy's shoulder, but he could do nothing to pass any signal to her, and hoped that she had the sense to keep out of sight.

Guy indicated the way into the house with his left hand, his right still in his pocket. They made it as far as the porch.

'Stop there, Tom,' Guy's voice had hardened from the previous friendly tones. 'Turn round.'

Tom turned slowly.

Guy was smiling at him, but his eyes were hard. 'Radio, please, and mobile phones. I'd be surprised if you only had one, so unless you produce them both, I'm going to have to search you. I'd rather not, if it's all the same.'

Tom took his time. Any delay right now would be good.

'Now, Jack's little brother. What *am* I going to do with you?' Guy said, his tone conversational as he pulled a gun from his pocket and pointed it at Tom.

66

Guy indicated with the gun that Tom should lead the way. There was a door to the left off the hall, with light seeping out from its edges, and Tom pushed it open.

Seated in a comfortable armchair facing a roaring fire was a young woman holding a sleeping baby boy. *Ollie.*

The woman turned her head slightly, showing Tom her profile. She gasped as Guy entered the room, his gun pointed at Tom's head.

'Guy,' she said, visibly swallowing her fear. 'I wasn't expecting you.'

'Clearly,' he replied. 'What the fuck are you doing with the baby, Mel?'

Tom could hear the surprise and anger in Guy's voice, and Mel turned back to the fire so Guy couldn't see the panic that Tom had glimpsed in her eyes.

She spoke without looking at Guy, her tone of defiance made less convincing by her shaking voice.

'Julie told me you weren't going to give the baby back. She was pissed, so I took him. I wasn't leaving him to Finn. He's an evil bastard.'

'You left the *house*?'

Tom could hear the incredulity in Guy's voice.

'It was dark. Nobody saw me. Only Julie, and she's seen her husband's handiwork before.'

Tom had no idea what any of this was about, but he kept quiet.

'You're a stupid bitch, Mel.' Guy's casual tone was somehow more threatening than if he had shouted. 'I thought you might have learned your lesson six years ago. This is Tom – Jack's brother – and he's filth. But I guess you knew all that, didn't you? How far behind are the cavalry, Tom?'

Tom shrugged. He wasn't giving anything away, but this still had the potential to go horribly wrong.

'Never mind, my men will tell me when they're close. Why did you contact Tom, Mel?'

Guy was now pointing the gun at Mel, who was still holding Ollie close to her chest, but Mel was looking past Guy, at the door. Tom followed her gaze, and closed his eyes briefly in horror.

'Leave her alone, Guy. I told Tom where to find her.'

Guy swung round at the sound of the voice, pointing his gun at the man in the doorway.

'Hello, little brother,' Jack said, looking at Tom with a sad smile.

'Jack Douglas,' Guy whispered, his eyes narrowing to slits. He waved his gun to indicate that Jack should move next to Tom, but Jack stood his ground. 'Who'd have thought it. Come back to see Mel, have you? I guess you owe her one.'

Guy sneered at his mistress.

'None of it was Mel's fault,' Jack said. 'I tricked her too.'

'That's crap, Jack. After screwing up that job for us you'd never have got away without Mel's help. But she suffered for it, didn't you, darling?'

Tom looked at Mel, who was still staring at the fire. Much as he wanted to grab Ollie from her and run for the door, he knew it wouldn't work. Not with Guy waving that gun around.

'She never leaves the house now, did you know that Jack?' Guy said. 'Not since the day she helped you run away. Show Jack what he did to you.' Guy was maintaining his pleasant tone. Mel didn't turn her head.

'I don't want to have to make you, Mel. Show Jack.'

Slowly Mel turned her head so that the left side of her face was visible. From just below her left eye down to her chin was a jagged scar, brownish pink in colour, pulling her eye down and exposing her inner eyelid, wet and pink.

'You bastard,' Jack said.

'It was only a punch or two. Finn stitched it for her.'

Tom knew without asking that any stitching would have been without the benefit of anaesthetic and for a moment he felt Mel's pain as the needle pierced her flesh. She hadn't been blameless, but this was sheer savagery.

'I'll deal with Mel later. For now, it's just you two.' Guy's tone had changed. 'On your knees, both of you.'

'Why not get out while you can, Guy?' Jack asked, not moving from the spot.

Guy ignored him, lifted his gun and pointed it at Tom.

To Tom's dismay, Jack stepped in front of him and started to move towards Guy, stopping only when they were face to face.

Guy smiled and pushed the barrel of the gun against Jack's head.

'You forget, I'm already dead,' Jack said, his eyes locked onto Guy's. 'You can't kill a dead man.'

❖

The sound of the gunshot cutting through the silent early-morning air sent the first birds of the day, waiting to sing out their tuneful dawn chorus, fluttering into the bare trees. And Emma felt as if a pointed blade had pierced her heart.

She pushed herself out from behind the bushes where she had been hiding since Tom had gone into the house, and sprinted up the drive. Her mind was focused on one thing – Ollie.

Her legs pounded, strange pains running through them as the tension in her limbs fought and lost the battle to cramp up. Head down, she cried out in agony, but kept running, limping, dragging

343

one leg with its rock-solid knotted calf muscle to the black front door of the secluded barn. She pushed the door open and forced herself onwards, towards the silent room on her left – the only room showing light.

One hand pressing against a stitch in her left side, she flung herself over the threshold.

To Emma, it was as if the whole room had faded to darkness, the only bright light glowing from Ollie who had started to cry, no doubt woken by the gunshot. She barely noticed two men lying on the floor in a pool of blood. She had eyes only for her baby, and for the woman holding Ollie tightly in one arm, and brandishing a gun in the other, its barrel waving around the room in the woman's shaking hand.

'Don't hurt my baby,' she screamed. 'Shoot me, but don't hurt my baby, *please.*'

She looked directly at the woman and gasped. What had happened to her poor face? But the woman had Ollie, and at that moment it was all that mattered.

'Give me the gun, Melissa.'

Tom. Thank goodness.

Without a word of protest, Melissa turned the gun around, and handed it to Tom. With both hands free, she clasped Ollie tightly one last time and stood up to hand him over to Emma.

'He's lovely, Emma. I'm so sorry for everything.' She sat down again as if her legs had given way, a dazed expression on her face.

But Emma barely heard her. Ollie had stopped crying when he heard his mummy's voice, and Emma pulled him tightly to her. So tightly that he gave a small 'ay' of protest, and then she was laughing and crying at the same time. She lifted him away from her so she could look at his soft skin, his pudgy little cheeks and his fine hair. Ollie lifted one hand towards Emma's tears and stroked them with his fingers. 'Mumumum' he said softly, a big smile spreading across his face.

She pulled Ollie close again and looked at where Tom was lifting a body from the floor, rolling him onto his back. Underneath the body, covered in blood, lay Jack. Without his wild hair and unshaven cheeks he looked so different, but at the same time, so familiar.

Emma couldn't breathe, certain that he had sacrificed himself for Ollie.

Then Tom reached out a hand and Jack's eyes opened – looking first at his brother and then over at Emma and Ollie, his eyes searching hers, making sure she was all right.

He took the outstretched hand and Tom hauled him to his feet.

'Christ, Guy's heavier than he looks,' he muttered.

'Never, ever, do anything as fucking stupid as that again, Jack. If it hadn't been for Mel, you'd be dead now. What were you trying to do, for God's sake?'

'You forget, Tom – as I said to Guy, I'm already dead. He would have killed us both. He nearly killed me by falling on top of me. But at least if he'd shot me you'd have had a second or two to take him down.'

Tom exhaled a breath of air and shook his head.

'Later, Jack. We need to sort Ollie out. Melissa – Julie said she'd given him a sleeping tablet. Do you know anything about it?'

Emma spun her head round to stare back at Melissa, her body rigid with tension. Melissa seemed dazed, staring at Guy's dead body, a hint of a smile on her lips. She spoke without lifting her head.

'It's fine. She'd given it to him just before I got there. He was probably crying because he was thirsty – she won't have thought to give him a drink. His little mouth was dry, and the tablet was stuck under his tongue where she'd shoved it. I peeled it off, and wiped away any residue with a tissue. Then gave him loads of water. He's been asleep, but he's fine now.'

Mel was still staring, trance-like, at Guy's body.

'Thank you,' was all Emma could think of to say.

'I still think we need to get Ollie to a doctor,' Tom said. 'I'm going to take Emma outside and hand her over to an officer who can look after both of them until the ambulance gets here.' They could hear sirens close by, and the steady throb of a helicopter overhead.

Tom turned to Jack and Melissa.

'I don't want to leave you two, but my first priority is Ollie. I'll be two minutes. Stay here – both of you.'

Emma walked towards the door, holding Ollie tightly. But her eyes were on Jack, boring into him, trying to read what was in his mind, trying to show him what was in hers, and in her heart.

'Jack,' she said quietly.

His eyes softened as he gave an almost imperceptible shake of the head and lifted his chin as if to tell her to go. She had to, for Ollie, but there was so much still to say.

As Tom closed the door behind her, Emma felt certain she had lost Jack for the third time in her life, and this time was the saddest.

67

Tom wasn't happy to be leaving a murder scene, but Ollie had to come first, and Tom needed time to think. He put an arm round Emma's shoulders and steered her towards the front door, collecting his radio and phones on the way. An out-of-breath policeman was standing doubled over halfway up the drive.

'I'm sorry, sir,' the policeman said. 'She said she needed a pee, so I could hardly follow her. I've been looking everywhere for her.'

Tom gave Emma a look, but he couldn't really blame her. He hurried her towards the gate, looking anxiously for the promised ambulance.

'You've been amazing, Emma,' he said as his eyes searched the lane. 'Are you okay?'

'I am now. What happened?'

'Jack played the hero, the stupid bastard. Guy had a gun against his head, but Melissa was hiding another gun down the side of the chair. She shot Guy. He fell on top of Jack, and for a moment I thought they'd fired at the same time. I thought Jack was dead too.'

And that had been a strange feeling. A brother who he already thought of as dead, dying again. How could he feel such pain twice over one person?

'Melissa was never Jack's lover, was she?' Emma asked.

'I don't think so. She was always Guy's – and his watchdog – living with Jack to make sure he complied with Guy's ever-increasing demands. I guess she became fond of Jack and helped him escape.'

Tom looked at Emma's face, wondering if that made everything that had happened better, or worse. She was staring at Ollie, almost in wonder. He had snuggled up close to her, and she was trying to wrap her arms more tightly round him. Tom slipped his coat off and put it round both of them, relieved to see a flashing blue light approaching.

'Did you know what Jack was doing, Em?' he asked. 'I'm not accusing you of anything, but I just wonder how he got himself in so deep.'

Emma was quiet for a second, as if deciding what she should say.

'I knew about the hacking. But in the months before we split he seemed to be battling with something – I didn't know what. He was angry all the time – with himself, not with me. I guess it was because of the things that Guy was forcing him to do. He's not a bad person, Tom. He made some mistakes as a kid and got in too deep.'

At that moment, Tom wished he could be somewhere else. Jack had just tried to save Tom's life, probably saved Ollie's, and had put his own life at risk to get Guy Bentley locked up.

But he was a criminal. And Tom was a policeman.

'Well, when all this is put to bed we'll have to see what happens, but Jack's committed crimes and I can't pretend he hasn't.'

Talk of past crimes reminded Tom that Emma still didn't know what had happened to David. He pushed thoughts of Jack to the back of his mind.

'I'm really sorry, Em, but I've got some bad news. After you left home earlier, your house was broken into and David was badly injured. He's been taken to hospital.'

He looked at Emma's bewildered face.

'How bad?' she asked.

'Bad,' Tom answered.

'Oh God. Poor David. They didn't hurt Tasha, did they?'

'When our men got there, they searched the house, but there was no sign of her. I'm so sorry, Emma. They must have taken her.'

After everything Natasha had done, Tom would have thought there might be a sense of relief that she had gone, but one look at Emma's stricken face, and he knew she didn't feel that way.

'She's in trouble, Tom. They must realise that Tasha knew I'd involved the police. I've no idea what they'll do to her. Find her for me – please? I don't want anything to happen to her.'

'We're looking for her. We're not giving up on her.'

Tom signalled the officer to take Emma and Ollie as the ambulance pulled onto the drive.

'I need to get back inside. Is that okay?'

Emma nuzzled her nose against the top of Ollie's head and nodded vacantly, shrugging off Tom's coat – clearly concerned only with holding her little boy close, driving all the other horrors out of her mind.

Tom turned back towards the house. He should be euphoric. They had saved Ollie, Guy Bentley was dead and Finn McGuinness was in custody – soon to be followed by the rest of the gang. But he had two people to arrest, and he wasn't looking forward to it.

❖

Tom stood in the open doorway of Melissa's house and watched the ambulance leave. He knew he was putting off the inevitable – procrastinating, as Leo would say – but he did need to call Becky.

'Ollie's safe, Becky' – he heard a whoop from his inspector – 'and Guy Bentley's dead. That's my good news. Now tell me we've found Natasha.'

Becky's voice changed from delight to sadness as she answered his question.

'Not a sign, Tom. I'm sorry.'

Tom felt a cold fury at the thought of what this child might now be suffering. He should have protected her better than he had.

'Arrange for somebody to arrest that bastard Rory Slater, and his wife for that matter. Make sure the house is searched thoroughly. Emma told me about a place under the cellar that they called The Pit. If Natasha's been taken, that's where she'll be, poor kid.'

'I'm on it,' was all she said.

Tom ended the call and decided there was one other person he should speak to.

'Paul – how far out are you? There are a couple of arrests to be made, and I don't particularly have the heart for either of them.'

'Understood. Just keep them there. The firearms team should be with you any time now. I'll be about ten minutes.'

Tom added the news about Guy and heard a cheer go up from the car that Paul Green was travelling in. It was a good night for Titan.

With a heavy heart Tom pushed open the door to the sitting room and stepped round Guy's inert body.

Mel had turned her face back to the fire.

'Mel – where's Jack?'

'Bathroom,' Mel answered, without turning round. 'Washing some blood off, I think.'

Tom walked across the room and took a seat opposite the woman who had saved Jack's life.

'Thank you for what you did tonight. I feel uncomfortable saying this, but other officers are on their way, and they will have to arrest you for shooting Guy. I don't understand why you did it, though.'

Tom could see a sad little smile on the unscarred side of Mel's face.

'You've seen what Guy did to me for helping Jack. What do you think he would have done if I'd handed the baby over to you?' Tom couldn't find any words that wouldn't sound like platitudes. 'I hadn't planned to kill Guy; the gun was for Finn. I couldn't let him kill a baby. Finn wouldn't have turned a hair, but I knew he'd come for Ollie as soon as he'd spoken to Julie – and I was ready for him.'

'How did you know I was coming?' Tom asked, aware that Mel had shown no surprise at his appearance – only at Guy's.

'After Jack tracked me down and told you where I live, he called me. He took a huge risk, you know. He couldn't be sure whether I'd tell Guy. But Jack said all he cared about was getting Emma's baby back to her. I didn't know who'd get here first – you or Finn. I wasn't expecting Guy, though.'

'You saved the baby, you saved me, and you saved Jack. I'm sure the courts will understand that and be lenient.'

Mel laughed.

'I *want* to go to prison, Tom – can you believe that? In a women's prison I'll feel relatively safe. Out here, Finn will see to it that I suffer, even if he's locked up in Strangeways for life – which he should be. But I'm not blameless.'

Tom listened as Mel talked about her life with Guy and the mistakes she had made. But she was talking too much, and Tom knew why. He glanced behind him at the door.

'Jack's not in the bathroom, is he, Mel?'

She turned her ruined face towards him, affecting a look of innocence that would have fooled nobody.

'Who are you talking about, Tom? There's only you and me here. There's only *ever* been you and me here.'

68

Natasha plodded along the narrow track, head down to hide her tears. There was nobody to hide them from, but she had been taught not to cry and was ashamed of the sobs that threatened to choke her. She had no idea where she was going, but all paths led somewhere, didn't they?

It hadn't been hard to sneak out of the house. She'd just had to wait for the right moment. David had been feeling sorry for himself in the kitchen, wondering whether the police would ever find out what he'd done. His last words to her had been 'We don't need to tell anybody about this, do we, Natasha? It was a mistake, that's all. A stupid mistake.'

She trudged down the ruts where tractors had been, her trainers soaked and covered in mud. The rain had seeped through her old duffle coat and she could feel icy droplets running down her back, but she still had a lot of walking to do. She knew where she was going, but she wouldn't make it before it was light. She was going to have to find somewhere to hide during the day. They'd be looking for her – Finn and Rory. Not because they wanted her, though.

That was the thing, really. Nobody wanted her. David hadn't wanted her back when he'd had the chance, and although Rory's lot would insist she came home – at least, what had passed for home for the last six years – it wasn't that they wanted *her*. They just wanted to show her there was no escape, and they wanted the good money she could bring in. She knew too much – all the scams, the routes on the trains, the dealers for the stolen phones.

This had seemed like an easy job. All she'd had to do was refuse to speak to anybody, tell nobody anything, then find the right time to walk out of the house with the baby, phone Rory, and then go back to the house and watch her father suffer for a few hours until the job was done, then leave again.

She'd known David and Emma would be mad at her and thought they might slap her around a bit when she told them that Ollie was gone – just to make her talk. But she was used to that. What she hadn't expected was to feel the way she did when she had seen how much Emma loved Ollie. For a while she had even thought that maybe, just maybe, she could have some of that for herself.

She *hated* David, of course, but Emma had been kind to her. And what had she done in return? She'd stolen her baby. That's what.

Natasha let out a wail of grief that had been building in her for days, which faded unheard into the night.

And now she had done something else that they would hate her for. She might have left all the nice clothes that Emma had bought for her, but there was one thing she had needed, that she'd had to take.

Money.

She didn't need much because she could nick stuff to eat. But she might need a bit of cash, and she was a rubbish pickpocket. She had tried when she was little, but the bloke had grabbed her by the scruff of the neck and shaken her, so she'd stuck to nicking things from shops. The trouble was, Emma had taken her purse with her, and David's wallet was in his jacket pocket – with him in the kitchen.

It had left her with only one option – one that she had hated to take. She pushed the thought of what she had done to the back of her mind. They hated her anyway, so it wouldn't make any difference.

The place she was heading to was full of kids like her – kids that nobody wanted, or who had been forced to escape from something even more dreadful than living rough. She was heading for the tunnels that ran under Manchester, a huge network of spaces built over a century ago. She thought she might be safe there, but she was going to have to walk for miles, all at night along the back roads and alleyways. Natasha didn't even know where she was, but she had seen some signs when they were out shopping, so had an idea that Stockport was the closest big town. If she could find her way there, she could probably get somebody to help her for a few days until she made it to Manchester.

Her mind kept going over things. Had she made the right choice? Should she have stayed?

The thing was, if she was still there – living with her dad and Emma – she didn't think Finn and his boss would let Ollie go until they got her back. David and Emma would have had to make a choice. Her, or Ollie. And there was no contest, was there? Better to leave now than to listen to their excuses as they told her she wasn't wanted. But if she'd gone – disappeared for good – Finn had no reason to keep Ollie.

Maybe she should have stayed, though – stayed so that Emma had some bargaining power – stayed and sacrificed herself so Emma could get Ollie back. She kicked a clod of wet earth in front of her. She couldn't even do that right.

She scrubbed at her tears with the heel of her hand and lifted her face to the rain, her body shuddering with the force of her unhappiness and the sense of loss.

❖

Becky Robinson was keeping out of the Joseph's kitchen. It was crawling with crime scene technicians, and there was nothing to see – except blood, of course. Emma was at the hospital with Ollie, where he was being checked over, and the news was good. There didn't seem to be any lasting effects from any grains of the sleeping tablet that he might have swallowed.

Becky didn't know if Emma had been to see her husband or not. She wouldn't really blame her if she hadn't, having learned what David did all those years ago. Everything that had happened since, to Natasha, to Caroline, and now to Ollie and Emma was a direct result of his actions six years ago.

Jumbo and his team had finished in all the rooms except the kitchen, so Becky was free to look around the house. She went into Natasha's bedroom. The bed was made, and the room was tidy – the kind of tidiness that you don't normally associate with thirteen-year-old girls – at least, not if they're anything like Becky had been.

She opened the drawers. Inside were good clothes – perfect for a girl like Natasha – all folded neatly as if somebody really cared about them. She thought back to what Natasha had been wearing when she had first met her. She remembered the red jumper with the loose thread and searched the room. It wasn't there.

Where are you, Tasha?

She wasn't at Rory Slater's house. It was empty. All the children had been taken into care and both Slaters were locked up.

The team had searched the house and found nothing. Nothing, that is, other than a terrible chamber below the cellar. Little more than a hole in the ground with bare earth for the walls. Cold and damp, it reeked of fear.

Becky shuddered and made her way into Ollie's bedroom. She could see evidence that the fingerprint team had been in here, but they hadn't moved a thing, and her eye was drawn towards a toy, sitting in the middle of the rug. She bent down to pick it up, but it wasn't a toy, it was a ladybird moneybox. She shook it, but there was no sound. It was empty.

As she went to put it on the chest of drawers, she noticed a tiny slip of paper, sticking out of the slot. Becky carefully drew it out. Unfolding it, she moved to the light to read it.

'Oh God,' she muttered, tears flooding her eyes. She knew she was going to have to call Tom, but for a moment she had to pause. She didn't think she could say the words out loud.

To Ollie Joseph
IOU £7.36
Signed: Natasha (your sister)
Sorry x

69

Day Six

It was midday before Tom was able to get home. He couldn't remember how long it had been since he had last slept, or eaten anything other than the odd chocolate bar or packet of crisps.

Mel had tried to stick to her story that there had been nobody else in her home, but Tom couldn't go along with that. Jack hadn't been involved directly in Guy's death, but there was no point in lying. Paul Green knew who Jack was, and although he had committed no offence – merely acting as an informant and never actually buying the stolen gold – his past crimes were bound to come out. The fact that he had helped the Titan team to catch Guy would go in his favour, and Tom had a feeling that Jack would have happily come back to face the music. But it wasn't the police Jack was hiding from.

Mel's words, just before she was driven away, came back to him.

'Jack loves you, Tom. He always called you White Hat – said you had more honour in your little finger than he had in his whole body. Everything he did six years ago he did for the people he loved, and now that Guy's dead the only people who know Jack's alive are a few policemen, you, me and Emma. That's the way it has to stay. Whatever Finn has in store for me, even from his prison cell, it would be ten times worse for Jack – and possibly anybody close to him. He has to stay dead.'

Tom hadn't been able to find any words. His throat had closed completely, and it hadn't been the time to lose control.

He pushed open his front door, for once, the pleasure of his home eluding him. He knew he should make something to eat and then go straight to bed, but he couldn't. He was restless, and more than anything he wished Leo was here. She must have wondered what was going on, but although it felt like weeks to him since he had seen her, to Leo there would just have been a couple of days' silence.

He walked into the kitchen and switched on the kettle.

While it was boiling, he plugged his laptop in to charge and turned back to the worktop.

There was a ping. He stood, motionless, his back to the computer. Only one person he knew could do that. He held his breath, not knowing what he was waiting for, then slowly turned round.

In the middle of his screen was a folder – the title was 'White Hat.'

Tom pulled up a chair, sat down and clicked. The folder contained a single file.

Sorry to have left so abruptly. I'm sure I don't need to explain.

I've let you down – I know that. I let Emma down too, and now she has to deal not only with what I was, but what David is too.

I loved her. Still do.

Don't ever change, Tom. You're the hero of the family. I'll be watching you from afar, but you won't know I'm there.

The money I left you was all earned legally – so don't panic. I know you will use it wisely. I hadn't wanted you to discover the SD card though. I tried to get it back, but I couldn't find it. Sorry about the mess, little brother – but I had to make it look real. Your cottage in Cheshire is wonderful by the way – especially the kitchen.

My ill-gotten gains will now be distributed appropriately – you don't need to know the details.

Forget you saw me. My death was my choice.

Black Hat

Tom read the note and reread it until his eyes were blurred, whether with tears or fatigue it was difficult to say. He knew as soon as he touched the keyboard the note would disappear from the screen and from his computer, just as he knew Jack would never contact him again this way. It was his last link to his brother – perhaps the last ever – and he couldn't let it go.

Did he really have to remain dead? Was there no other choice?

He had found and lost his brother today, and his emotions were too tangled to unravel.

Finally, he sat back, lifted his finger and pressed the space bar. The image disappeared, as he had known it would. He stared at the blank screen for a few moments, then pushed himself up from the chair and moved back to the worktop to reboil the kettle. As he poured the hot water into a mug, he glanced across to the phone. The message light was flashing. He should ring Leo, let her know what was going on, he thought, as he pressed the replay button. He needed her now more than ever. She was the only person who could bring him the comfort and love that he suddenly craved.

As if answering his thoughts, it was Leo's voice that he heard on the answerphone.

'Tom, it's Leo.' That almost made him smile – as if he wouldn't recognise her voice. 'I'm ringing to say that I'm going away for a few days. You're obviously very busy, so I thought I'd take the opportunity to have some time to myself. I'll ring you when I'm back.'

Tom leaned against the wall and gazed at the ceiling. Leo's instinct to withdraw was nothing new to him, but for the first time in months he had to ask himself what he was doing with somebody who couldn't promise to be there for him when he needed her support.

He remembered the passion, the fun, but most of all the unmistakeable love within Emma and Jack's relationship, before his brother had been forced to end it. Even today he had seen it flash into Emma's eyes when she thought Jack had been shot – after everything she had been through.

Had he ever had that with any woman?

Right now, he wanted somebody to hold him tight to ease the pain of his loss. But that wasn't going to happen.

70

One month later

Looking out of the kitchen window, Emma noticed all the new growth on the plants and trees. So much had been happening that she had failed to realise that spring was now well and truly with them. It was a bright, clear day outside, but she found herself wishing that the sky was dark, and that she would see a pair of eyes reflected in the window from a young girl standing behind her. Each time she turned round, she expected to see a child with straggly blonde hair wearing an oversized duffle coat. She would have welcomed her with open arms.

She should really sell this house and move; she knew that. But she was staying for Natasha. It was the only place that the girl knew, and to leave here would give her stepdaughter nowhere to return to, if ever she wanted to. She couldn't bear the thought of Natasha's life ending the way her friend Izzy's had. Tom had confirmed that the girl found in the woods was Izzy. It seemed fairly certain that she had tried to kill herself with a massive dose of ketamine, stolen from Julie's house. Apparently the girls regularly used ketamine to anaesthetise themselves a little before the men arrived. Even though Julie's had been shut down, other places would no doubt open to fill the gap in the market, and the thought of Natasha ending up there sickened Emma to her stomach.

In the first few days after Ollie's safe return Emma's emotions had swung between irrepressible joy that her baby was safe and concern – for Tasha and for David. She sat by her husband's hospital bed for three days, holding his hand, thinking of the happy times they had spent together over the last few years, wondering what the future would bring for them both. But he never spoke to her again. His injuries were too severe, and he died at the end of the third day. She hoped he had known that Ollie was safe; she had whispered it over and over in his ear, praying that David could hear her. She had lied about Tasha too, telling him that she was well and at home.

Emma was a realist, though, and she knew that – had David lived – she would never have spent another night in his bed. The fact that he had even contemplated putting his wife and daughter through a few hours of terrifying hell to get himself out of a hole kept hitting her, like a punch to the head. She would never have felt safe with him and would never have allowed Ollie to be left in his care. She was sorry he was dead, but her life with him had been over the minute she learned what he had done.

Emma was finding it really difficult to let Ollie out of her sight. She sat with him while he slept and had to stop herself from moving his cot into her bedroom. Just because fear ran through her each time she heard footsteps on the gravel path, she didn't have to make her little boy feel like that.

Tom had been a source of strength, although she knew he was struggling with the knowledge that Jack was alive and out there somewhere. Just as she was.

'I feel I should pack in my job and go and find him, Em,' he'd said one day, sitting at her kitchen table. 'But it's not what he wants – I know that.'

He had seemed so sad since those dreadful few days. She knew he had a girlfriend; he had mentioned her briefly when she visited his house. But when she asked Tom if he would like to bring her round some time, he said, 'Not at the moment,' and she hadn't been able to get anything more out of him.

Every night Emma went to sleep thinking of Jack and of what might have been. She relived the moment when he'd touched her, the feel of his body as it pressed against hers in the vault. She had been terrified, and yet there was a heat coming from him that communicated with her at some level. Even before she realised who he was, she had felt electricity fire through her. Then she had seen his eyes, and she was lost again.

Her nights were taken care of, checking on Ollie and dreaming of Jack. But there was something else that she and Ollie did, and would continue to do for as long as it took.

Each morning as they came downstairs, Emma had a quiet word with the portrait, still hanging in the hall.

'I'm not giving up, Caroline,' she said.

Then, most days of the week, Emma and Ollie took the car and drove into Manchester or Stockport – changing the times and the venues as often as they could.

Emma then found the most crowded place and put an upturned plastic box on the ground next to Ollie's pushchair and climbed up on it. People always turned to stare, and that's when she started shouting.

'Tasha! Natasha Joseph! Come home, Tasha.' Ollie joined in. 'Tassa,' he shouted.

She chose places that were busy with shoppers, thinking that small-time crooks – the kind of people that Tasha might know – would be out and about picking pockets, stealing mobiles. She stopped every child that was on the street when they should have been in school and showed them Natasha's photograph. She took fresh sandwiches and cakes to give to the homeless – all they had to do in return was take the picture of Natasha and show it to as many people as possible. She printed thousands of posters, and gave handfuls to anybody who looked as if they might be living the same life as Natasha – or whatever she was calling herself now – asking them to find the girl in the photo and give her the poster.

More often than not, the posters would be dumped as soon as Emma had walked on – sometimes in a bin, but usually dropped indifferently onto the pavement. That was okay, because on the poster was more than just a photo of Natasha. There was a picture of a smiling Ollie with a message in a speech bubble, and the more posters floating around the windy alleyways, settling against greasy walls, lying in the dusty streets, the more chance that somehow it would reach its target and she would read the message.

Natasha Joseph – please come home to your family
Your baby brother misses you

Acknowledgements

As with every book I have written, the help and advice so willingly given by so many people has made a huge difference, and I can't thank them all enough.

I had a new advisor on the police procedural aspects of this book, Mark Gray, who steered me through some very tricky sections, only holding back when I strayed into confidential areas. His response to each query was so detailed that my mind frequently strayed onto new paths and I genuinely couldn't have written *Stranger Child* without him. Of course, there were times when I had to dispense with the real-life efficiency that the police would have employed and allow some personal creativity to sneak into the procedures in the interests of increased tension. So any and all mistakes are entirely mine. But thank you Mark – you have been truly inspirational.

Stranger Child introduces a new kind of specialist – the forensic linguist. I would like to thank my good friend Dr Isabel Picornell for inspiring me with the types of enquiries that might call on her unique form of expertise. She has filled me with ideas for future stories, and was rigorous with her checking of my words in the appropriate sections of *Stranger Child*. Who knew that a woman's style of writing was so different from a man's?

As always, there were many people who offered small nuggets of information on everything from Swiss bank accounts to how container storage bases work. I didn't necessarily use all this information, but my thanks go to Nick, Patrick, Alan and Sheila for offering their help.

My early readers have – as always – been fantastic, providing excellent feedback and suggestions – in some cases throughout the whole writing process. Thank you Kath, Judith, Ann, John, Ruth, Barry, and Andria.

I would struggle to keep my head above water without my two excellent virtual assistants – Ceri Chaudhry and Alexandra Amor. Who would have thought that VAs in Hertfordshire and Canada could work so well? But both, with their own unique style, have solved so many of the day-to-day problems of being an independently published author, and I don't know what I would do without them.

Alan Carpenter, my long-suffering designer, has produced yet another wonderful cover and this time there was no need to change the design numerous times. Thanks to great photography from Rick, and a fantastic model in Alicia (a really happy, smiley girl – and a good actress), we knew we had the cover we wanted almost immediately, and Alan turned it into something that we really hope will stand out.

Some new members of the team have been helping with *Stranger Child* and my particular thanks go to Lucy Ramsay for being so enthusiastic about helping to publicise the book. Helen Hart and her team at SilverWood Books also did an amazing job preparing the paperback advance review copies in such a very short time.

Finally, as always, I cannot say thank you enough to my agent, Lizzy Kremer – the best there is. She has been a wonderful source of support and guidance, as have the rest of the team at David Higham Associates – especially Laura and Harriet. I don't know how many times Lizzy and Harriet read the manuscript for *Stranger Child*, but their help and direction, together with input from editors, Clare Bowron, Lizzie Dipple, and David Watson have made this a far better book than it might otherwise have been.

It really has been a terrific team effort, and I count myself lucky to be surrounded by the best group of professionals, friends and family there is.

Also by Rachel Abbott

ONLY THE INNOCENT

A man is dead. The killer is a woman. But what secrets lie beneath the surface - so dark that a man has to die?

"This is an absolutely stunning debut novel from a writer with a gift for telling a tale. I can't wait for more!"
– Amazon Top 500 reviewer

THE BACK ROAD

A girl lies close to death in a dark, deserted lane. A driver drags her body to the side of the road. A shadowy figure hides in the trees, watching and waiting.

"A clever psychological crime and mystery novel."
– Little Reader Library

SLEEP TIGHT

How far would you go to hold on to the people you love?… Sleep Tight – if you can. You never know who's watching.

"Just when you think you've got it sussed, you'll find yourself screeching in frustration at your foolishness."
– Crime Fiction Lover